Praise for Ja

EVERY SIGH, THE END.

(A novel about zombies.)

"Jason Hornsby's *Every Sigh, The End* may be the best zombie novel I have read. It feels like a grand truth is peeking through the enigmatic and conspiratorial fog that suffuses the novel. It all seems to mean something... Every Sigh is a fine novel, period."

—Devon Kappa, *None May Say* blog

"[Hornsby's] writing is angry, nihilistic, and sad. But it might also be brilliant, and may prove to be the future of angry, nihilistic, and sad literature as we know it."

—Tom Abrams, author of *A Bad Piece of Luck*

"[T]his is the most unusual zombie novel I have ever read... creative, imaginative, and intriguing."

—Steven W. Woeste, author of *To Wake the Dead*

EVERY SIGH, THE END.

(A novel about zombies.)

by

Jason S. Hornsby

Editing and Interior Design
by Travis Adkins

Cover Design by
Christian Dovel

Permuted Press
The formula has been changed... Shifted... Altered... *Twisted.*™
www.permutedpress.com

A Permuted Press book
published by arrangement with the author

Every Sigh, The End.
(A novel about zombies.)

ISBN-10: 0-9789707-8-0
ISBN-13: 978-0-9789707-8-9
Library of Congress Control Number: 2007930630

Preface

TO THOSE WHO HAVE HAD THE UNFORTUNATE EXPERIENCE of being a part of my circle of friends and loved ones, my decision to write a novel about zombies was not a surprise. I have been talking about writing one for years, usually while inebriated or wishing death on disingenuous party junkies. So, when I announced last fall that "I think I'm going to write a book about zombies," there were no exploding heads, dizzy spells, or even nods or grunts from my small but loyal group of companions. This served as an indication to me that, a) no one cared, and that b) perhaps my zombie novel was truly overdue.

But there were problems.

One was that I was afflicted, for years it seems, with the notion that a zombie novel could not speak the way a pretentious coming-of-age novel or interrelated short story collection might. Another was that, until New Year's Eve of 2004, I had no idea what exactly I would write about other than particularly gratuitous gore scenes and the fact that these acts of carnage would be inflicted upon young people like myself.

Then, ironically enough, it hit me on the very night that would become so integral in this little book of the undead. Sitting on the porch of my good friend John Windsor's ramshackle house in the deep woods of Polk County, Florida, the novel finally came together. As the minutes trickled down to midnight and all the people around me decided who they would sleep with to celebrate, every aspect of my entire terrifying universe came together: the cameras, the paranoia, the conspiracies and Montauk mumbo-jumbo and blunt symbolism—I realized that there was an entire world out there that just seemed to get *lost* in the wake of faux-reality television and apathetic pseudo-Americans—and I suddenly had to exploit it *all.* I wanted to scream my outrage on paper, and now had a flimsy plot outline in which to do it.

So the next morning, after wading through a living room littered with unconscious strangers and tainted ex-girlfriends, I sat down and began writing. And now, almost a year later, the zombie novel is complete, and I have no shortage of people who have *literally* made this work possible.

First of all, I feel it necessary to shine the shoes of some of my forefathers: Bret Ellis, Mark Z. Danielewski, Chris Carter, Russ Kick, Preston Nichols and Al Bielek (you are *not* crazy), Max Brooks, and especially George Romero all share the distinction of setting the bar too high for a novice like me to ever reach. For that, sirs, I both admire and detest you.

I would also like to thank two very talented and inspirational professors, whose knowledge, wisdom, and foresight have aided in this novel's fruition. The first, Tom Abrams, my three-time writing instructor, has played one of the most important of roles in my career as a would-be writer. His experience, natural talent and accomplishments in the wake of adversity have made me work twice as hard and write twice as carefully, in fear of being humiliated by him and competing writer kids at the next workshop. Tom, I never forgot about the beer we shared in your office several years ago.

On the other side of Cooper Hall, I want to extend heartfelt gratitude to Professor Nigel Malcolm. He is the reason I decided that English was not the right major for me (granted, it *was* two months before I graduated, but nonetheless), and that American Studies was indeed the study of everything that made this nation so unique and tragic. Professor Malcolm's lectures on personalism in particular proved that there might still be some of the fire in us that made the 60s counterculture so interminable and beautiful. It gave me a bit of hope for the future in a time when the future looked as grim as ever.

To my gang, whose genuine adoration for the art of horror filmmaking and faith in my writing guaranteed that this novel would be finished and put into print, I want to thank you personally. Shawn, Kyle, Adam, J.P., and Damon—you guys are the best. I am truly lucky to have found friends and fellow zombie junkies like you. The perimeter has been deactivated, gentlemen.

Jessica Dawson, as wicked as she may be, deserves perhaps more accolades than anyone in regards to this book. Quite simply, if it were not for Jessica's constant prodding, cajoling, support, and love, I would still be waiting on tables, putting hexes on customers, and whispering about writing that zombie novel. She is the reason this book was finished, and for that, I offer these words: "Good night, and good luck."

Lastly, I would like to give my sincerest thanks to John Windsor. He has played the role of long-term confrere, shoulder to cry on, debate partner, band-mate, roommate, and favorite critic. Now he plays the role of Muse.

This book was written with only two people in mind, and one of them was me. Rocky, you have always been, and will continue to be, my ideal audience.

And on a side note, those ex-friends, sex partners and unsupportive family members (all *not* zombie fans, I might add) who worked diligently to make 2005 the worst year in my collective memory, I can only assure you that suicide has not been contemplated, that God does not love you, and that neither do my cats. I hope one of your resolutions for 2008 is to die.

—Jason S. Hornsby
OCTOBER 5, 2007

PART I

"Dystopia through a Telephoto Lens."

1999

"I write only for myself, and I wish to declare once and for all that if I write as though I were addressing readers, that is simply because it is easier for me to write in that form. It is form, an empty form—I shall never have readers."

—Fyodor Dostoevsky

"A paranoid is a man who knows a little of what's going on."

—William S. Burroughs

"If you ask a member of this generation two simple questions: 'How do you want the world to be in 50 years?' and 'What do you want your life to be like five years from now?' the answers are often preceded by 'Provided there is still a world' and 'Provided I am still alive.'"

—Hannah Arendt

13

"THE END OF SOMETHING WAS ALL I COULD RELATE TO. When I entered a room, the need for a new beginning, catastrophic upheaval, slash and burn method, was overwhelming, stifling even. In every new place, at every party or restaurant or video or music store that no one really bought anything in but hung out at nonetheless, all I could see were the faces of people whose lives were made up of perpetual worst days.

"Everything needed reorganization; to fall apart and be rebuilt from scratch. All I wanted was the entire world to drown, to choke on the blood of its own sigh. It was late December, 1999, and I'll tell you everything. It's just—"

12

It's just
It's just
It's just
It's just
It's just

11

It's just that tonight is weird.

I park in a vacant lot fifty yards away from the party on a cold Wednesday night in late December, glancing in my rearview mirror as a car that I could have sworn followed us here all the way from the south side of town slowly passes me and veers around a corner. Lydia smiles in the seat next to me and says, quite stoned, "Someone asked me at the bookstore today if I could draw a sound." Preston says nothing in the back seat and lights a cigarette. I notice for the first time how cold it is outside tonight and sigh, a terribly unoriginal gesture.

Walking into someone's front yard, we pass an old black man who smiles at me as he hobbles along. I shiver, wonder why he would be here, and turn back to look at him slouch away down the street, humming softly to himself.

At the party, there are people milling around, telling secrets behind the bushes, coughing into the fire in the back yard while catching up on who is pregnant or dead or the two or three girls who are both, and inside the house, funnels are being drained in the dining room and a few feet away someone has pulled a popsicle out of the freezer that wasn't theirs and they eat it in an empty den while making a call to their ex-girlfriend on a crimson cell phone. A guy that I went to high school with for six months, a guy whose neck doesn't turn to the right is worried about an influx of cannibalism in the next millennium, even though he pretends to be totally enthralled in a conversation on bands that sound like Nirvana that come from Australia. Preston, who thinks the world is coming to an **end** and is stocking canned goods in preparation, is leading Lydia and I into the back yard but not paying attention to me. Instead he is speaking in a fake British accent to someone else, a

Californian art major girl that I tried to talk into committing suicide while she was drunk at another party three months ago. Meanwhile, around back, a half-drained pool is being stared at by a brunette girl that I do not know, but who is thinking that she never wants to live in a trailer. I don't want to either, I realize, and contemplate staring into the algae-infested water with her, but I can't, because this guy Adam that I barely know shuffles over, hugs me, introduces himself to my girlfriend, and then starts talking about his new haircut, which is kind of long but not and wavy and brown but in the light it shines purple, or so he says while pointing to it.

After a considerable amount of valuable time is wasted trying not to listen to this moron go on and on about his hair and all the girls he has had the chance to sex because of it, I finally just walk away and leave Lydia behind with him, making my way to a nearby beer keg, which is already on the edge of emptiness even at a little after eleven. I saw another one up front on the way in, but it seemed that the only way it was being drank from was by people hanging upside down.

Preston jots the California twit's number on the back of a movie stub and says, "Blimey!" Then he approaches me.

"Pres, remind me when we get back to my place to dub *Toolbox Murders* for that British guy."

"I love the British," Preston says.

"Is that what inspired the accent this evening?" I ask, holding a red plastic cup to the keg.

"No, that's me wanting to get laid," he says. "And by the way, the girl over there—you see her?"

"My girlfriend?"

"No, a real girl. By the bonfire."

I scan over the crowd throughout the back yard and spot the girl Preston is motioning toward. She's short, thin but not anorexic, medium-sized tits, and she is wearing a rainbow-striped sweater and gaudy star earrings, which she cannot stop fingering with her free hand as she chats with two guys that I wish were dead next to a fire that I hope gets out of control.

"Who? Princess Star Bright?" I ask.

"Yeah, that girl. Her name's Mindy and I heard her say a few minutes ago that she thinks the other people at her high school are just too nave."

"What is this 'nave' she's talking about?" I ask, drinking. It tastes like MGD. I'm not sure though.

"I think she's going for 'naïve.' But you know what this means?"

"That seventh grade vocabulary fails her?"

"No, Ross," he says, elbowing me lightly in the chest. "It means you have a pretty good chance of talking her into something dirty."

"As great as that sounds, I'll think I'll pass. Lydia's like ten feet away. Let's just do our rounds and split."

"I thought we came here to get laid," Preston says.

"*You* might have," I say, lighting a cigarette and finishing the cup of beer. I start pouring another.

"Then why did you come? To discuss Sartre with the varsity cheerleaders?"

"It's a keg party. I wanted the free beer so I'll be hung over tomorrow morning."

"Why?" Preston asks me.

"Because I don't like paying for beer."

"No, why do you want to be hung over tomorrow morning?"

"Because my sister's getting her Master's," I mutter as I scan the crowd, which has started to thicken and surge and swell into an unstoppable mass of people who either like Three Doors Down or the Backstreet Boys, sometimes both.

"A little jealousy residue there, Ross?"

"No, just a lot of potential for her in a very shallow grave." I pause. "Preston, why are we here?"

"You're here to get drunk, Lydia's here to buy pot from the guy who owns this place, and me, I'm here—"

"No," I interrupt. "I mean, why are we still doing this? We're older than everyone at this thing except maybe that girl over there hitting on the stereo speaker."

"Where do you see that?" he asks, his eyes skimming over the crowd.

"We need a change, Preston."

"No, *you* need to stop giving me this speech at every party we go to. *You* need to chill out, take yoga, break it off with Lydia and start listening to Enigma, *something*, but you definitely need to calm down and just *go* with it."

I finish the beer.

"Oh, I've got to show you this thing I bought," Preston says at one point.

"What is it?" I ask.

"I was thinking about having a party maybe for New Year's Eve."

"Really?"

"Yeah, and yesterday while I was in this gift shop at the mall I saw this thing that counts down to the millennium. It was kind of neat, so I bought it. I put it in my living room."

"Okay," I say, confused by now.

"I don't know what happens when it gets done counting down," he says to himself. "What if it explodes?"

"Tonight is weird," I say, but am drowned out by a fat bald guy with a cowboy hat hollering from the porch to the girl hitting on the speakers.

"What?" Preston asks.

"I said tonight is weird. This party is weird."

"How so?"

I do not answer, and begin pouring another beer.

"How so?" he repeats.

"It just is," I say.

Later, Preston explains to Princess Star Bright how incredibly profound and important the zombie genre is to the entire world, both in terms of influence in film and universal popular culture, and also for its philosophical ramifications. She giggles but listens to his rehearsed speech. I giggle and have another three beers. Then fifteen or so leave after all the kegs are tapped, but then twenty-eight more people show up and cases of Bud Light are presented for a five dollar donation from everyone who wants to drink, and then the most popular guy from a high school in Georgia arrives but no one cares and then Preston winks at Lydia and Lydia turns away quickly and makes conversation with a Greek girl named Aimee. I see Preston twenty minutes later making out with the girl I called Princess Star Bright on a wicker bench underneath a palm tree on the side of the house. I don't pay for any beer but say I did and point one of the three beer-holders in the direction of some random person on the other side of the party, and drink plenty more and then someone hands me a joint, a short guy who whispers in my ear that he is a direct descendent of a Viking named Buliwyf, and then I keep drinking and Preston is laughing with Princess Star Bright at me, but I can't figure out why, and then I am seeing a field burning in Brazil, a child drawing the sound of a woman being raped by a cold murky lake. I am seeing a clam shell dancing to a reggae tune, maybe Marley but I'm not sure, and then the half-rotted corpse of my mother is asking me for a bite of the mango I am holding but I won't let her have it ("But I'm not dead yet," I keep hearing her say, this cadaver).

And in the car ride home Lydia is driving and has put on Orgy and Preston and my girlfriend exchange a suspicious glance just before he asks her why she calls me Holden and cackles that I'm a mess and when I look out the window of my own car into an empty parking lot, I see a fox the size of a man with the head of a wolf. Preston tells us that he found a tiny surveillance camera inside the living room smoke detector at his house and Lydia doesn't believe him but I do.

10

PEOPLE ARE ALWAYS TRYING TO CONVINCE ME that "of" is not a word. That the world is really flat. That putting tiny strips of tin foil in my shoes will squelch not only static electricity, but any attempt by a dark government agency to bug me. I am told lots of things, advice and tidbits of useless information and cacophony that I never asked for and yet receive and process anyway, as if any of it may prove useful someday.

My younger sister is—was—an English graduate student and was constantly telling me things like this. So was Stacey. I'm not sure why. After reading *Macbeth* her freshman year of college, Cordelia commented at Sunday dinner that if the world was indeed a stage, then she wanted better lighting. The family laughed and asked me if I was going to graduate on time. Another time, she told me that in non-English speaking countries, most people cannot pronounce the–*Th* sound in words, and that, in fact, it hurts their ears to even hear it. Actors imitating a Scottish accent often quickly develop abrasions and painful wounds on their vocal chords. She told me that everyone is categorized and packaged as a product of whatever town, dialect, tradition, culture, religion, customs, transportation system, or history that they happen to be born into. Escape was all but impossible. She told me this the day I got my Bachelor's, four-and-a-half years ago.

I watch her approach the stage as she graduates a second time from college.

"Ross, are you filming her?" my father asks, concentrating on zooming in with his Kodak. "Don't screw this up."

"I think I can handle it," I say, looking through the lens of the camcorder as I veer away from Cordelia and onto some random already-walked graduate with "vampire killer" written on the top of his blood-red cap.

When Cordelia told me that most Americans can't pronounce the name Ricardo correctly, and that a Spanish name without the roll of the letter *R* was an insult, I told her that we lived in a decade without meaning. She reminded me that I dropped out of society forty years too late.

"Ross, how many more names are there?" Preston whispers in my ear. "I've started imagining everyone in this auditorium as a zombie, and that's usually a pretty clear sign that I'm bored."

My mom and dad got here after the ceremony had already begun, and we were saving them seats. My father is wearing an alumni sweater for this college, and my mother is wearing the same crimson dress that she wore to Cordelia's first graduation. Dad looks good. The bleach he has been using on his teeth really worked, and I see that his hair has gone from smoky gray to brown again. But he still looks like a total stranger.

Mom looks thin and draped in shadows. When she sees me filming this event, a confused look comes over her face and her eyes well with tears. She looks like a stranger, too, but a benevolent one.

Through the zoom lens of my father's camera, I watch my blond-haired sister take her first step up toward the stage. She waits, says something to another obvious English twit in front of her, and then another step. The school president shakes the hands of a black guy that dances with his Master's in Business afterward. The crowd goes wild.

"Would your parents think it was rude if I went outside to smoke a cigarette?" Preston asks me.

"Yes," I tell him.

Cordelia reaches the top step, and then waits for her name to be called by one of her college's deans. I hear the name Morris Fletcher. Cordelia shifts from one foot to another.

"Cordelia Leanne Orringer, Master's in Literature," someone announces.

I veer the camera away from her sharply, focusing on her boyfriend Brad as he whispers something in one of Cordelia's friends' ears on the opposite side of the auditorium. I believe that it's Monica Number 1, judging by her perfect sort-of wavy brown hair and complete lack of realization that there are ten of her at every campus party. Through the lens, Monica 1 is clapping. Then she giggles at whatever Brad coos into her ear.

I turn the black-and-white option on and videotape their silent conversation. She mouths something. Brad delicately picks at his brunette hair, careful not to ruin the pseudo-artsy, pseudo-clubber spike that he surely toyed with this morning for an hour. She turns away from something he says, at which point Brad relents and claps for his absent girlfriend. On stage, Cordelia stoops low enough so that a gangly man can lower some kind of garb down over her shoulders. She stands up, smiles, and receives her diploma. She shakes people's hands. She walks off stage. Her moment is over. I turn the video camera off.

I glance over at my mother, whose eyes are tearing up even though she is not looking anywhere near her daughter. I think she is looking at the floor. She is not clapping, but four hundred other people are. My sister's apparent popularity surprises me for a moment, but then I realize who my sister is and what she stands for at this tiny campus (the pretentious English major who sleeps with everyone), and I smile and whistle.

"Ross, you got all that, right?" my father asks.

"Perfectly," I say, unable to take my eyes off the maroon tassel hanging from the graduation cap of a moon-faced girl below my sister's boyfriend. The tassels' colors vary according to the students' major. My sister's is white. The psychology department's is blue. American Studies graduates: maroon.

"Okay," my father announces, "let's go before it gets too crowded outside." He looks at his wife standing next to him. "Clarissa, stop it."

Cordelia poses with my father. A flash. With my mother. A flash. With my grandparents and her boyfriend and her group of friends, who obviously stayed up all night. Flashes.

"Ross, now you and your sister together."

I suddenly realize that I am awake before noon, and that this is all because of my sister. A grimace.

"Dad, you don't have to," Cordelia is saying. "You can spare Ross the pain."

"No," I interject. "I want to help commemorate this moment."

I march up the hill in front of the auditorium next to Cordelia, glancing over at Preston, who is standing underneath a palm tree with a half-smoked cigarette and snickering. My sister smells stale and her crimson gown feels rented against my arm.

"Your breath stinks," I whisper to her, smiling. "What kind of a bullshit college has their graduation ceremony on a Thursday?"

"They can't do it any other time. Tomorrow is Christmas Eve, you idiot. And besides, regardless of what day it is, Ross, how does it feel to actually attend a graduation?" she asks, also smiling, her words half drowned-out by an ambulance siren in the distance.

"It's not like I didn't do it, too," I mutter. "And mine was on a Saturday afternoon."

"Oh, touché," she says. "And if I recall, I just did it for the second time, and I'm twenty-four years old. How old are you now?"

"Okay, kids, smile," my mother says, her make-up ruined, a camera gripped so tightly in her hands that I expect it to shatter.

"I hope you get into a car accident and suffer brain damage that wrecks your ability to read," I mutter, smiling for the camera. "And have a holly jolly Christmas."

"I hope you always stay the same," Cordelia says. A flash. "That in itself is punishment enough."

"Congratulations, Sis," I mutter, fingering the cigarettes in my shirt pocket as I walk away.

I have to pull off to the side of the road twice on the way back from Cordelia's graduation ceremony. Both times police squad cars race by in groups of two or three at a time.

"So I was thinking today," Preston says as I drive towards his house.

"I like trying new things too."

"You are quite the quick wit," he says with a jerk-off motion of his hand.

"What were you thinking about, Pres?"

"If you have sex with a zombie, would you turn into one of them from the exchange of sexual fluids? Or does it have to be blood only?"

"You don't already know this?"

"I'll have to check through the literature when I get home, but I don't think it would turn you into one of them."

"Lucky for me if Lydia ever turns," I say. "There's literature on zombies?"

"Not literature. Movies. I hope someone writes a zombie survival guide one day. But, um, how *are* you and Lydia, by the way?"

"Don't ask."

"Already moved on," he says. "Isn't your sister having some kind of party or something for her graduation?"

"Perhaps, but I will not be attending that event."

"I don't get you, Ross."

"It's not that hard, Pres. I don't like Cordelia. She's a pretentious cunt."

"No, not that. I know that part. I don't get how you do what you do for a living and yet know nothing about any of it. Furthermore, I don't know how you can surround yourself with something that you hate."

"It's not that hard to figure out. You have the supplies. I have the talent."

"No, you mean that you have the VCRs, some blank tapes, and a vision of how to take advantage of a bunch of poor guys' obsessions. Beyond that it doesn't require much."

"Well whatever," I say. "You get your cut."

Silence.

"Hey Ross," Preston finally says quietly, "did you notice anything weird about your mom today?"

Through town. Past the shopping mall, two Taco Bells, a franchise coffee house, grocers, a Denny's, houses, salons and porn shops, a bar, a sandwich shop named Ernie's run by a man named Carl, and a doctor's office that recently shut down because the doctor was giving out meds without a prescription.

On Main, between the 89 and Pittsburgh intersections and cluttered between several small businesses and near a hotel that's haunted, Preston's house is a decrepit white two-story across the street from a Cuban deli and an elementary school. Two-and-a-half bathrooms, four bedrooms, and one acre of land amidst a city that long ago forgot it existed. Preston's parents once told me that there are no other residences within two hundred yards in any direction. Then they died when Preston was nineteen years old.

"Do you want to come inside for a little bit?" Preston asks me as I pull into his driveway.

"I don't know. I maybe have to go."

"What could you possibly have to do on a Thursday morning at eleven—?" He glances down at his watch. "At twelve-fourteen on a Thursday afternoon?"

I shrug.

"A nap maybe." I yawn. "I need to stop by Lydia's too. She's cooking some kind of…something or other. Then I have some dubbing to do. I didn't do *The Toolbox Murders* last night like I planned."

"One bowl?"

"Not today, Pres."

"Ross, I woke up this morning before the sun was up to go to your pretentious cunt of a sister's second graduation. Which, I might add, lasted over two hours in another town? And now, after you've thoroughly taken advantage of me, you refuse to come inside and smoke one bowl with your best friend?"

I put my Corolla in Park. I look up at the house. I breathe carefully, measuring each inhale, trying to think of a song to turn on in my head. Nothing comes to mind. I nod and get out of my car, following Preston up some steps and onto his large screened-in front porch. A beer bottle that I distinctly remember wedging underneath an old black shoe three weeks ago is still underneath the same old black shoe. A sketch of a cannibal-looking tribesman that Preston was working on out here last week is yellowing on a rusted metal table at one corner of the porch. On the table next to it is a half-elliptical black digital clock with the wrong time displayed. It is only after a long moment that I realize that the red digits counting backwards are part of the New Year's clock Preston recently acquired.

203:44:06. Two hundred and three hours, forty-four minutes, six seconds and counting downward.

Preston fumbles with his keys.

"Did I tell you what I bought the other day?" he says, finding the right one.

"No. What did you buy?"

He unlocks the door and goes inside.

"I found a mini-poster online for *The Blood on Satan's Claw* and ordered one. It will be here in like two weeks. Oh, and some guy from Indiana placed an order for three copies of the unedited second *Friday the 13th*. I don't know why he would need three. Nobody's ever done that before. It's not like the stuff we sell makes a good stocking stuffer on Christmas. And even if it did, what kind of moron orders them only a few days before Christmas morning? God, everyone is so stupid."

Preston Nichols likes horror movies. What ample amounts of money he once had are now for the most part in the pockets of a thousand video collectors and entrepreneurs. However, a couple of years ago, to make up for some of the vast sums of money he had spent of his dwindling inheritance, and since I myself was working the third shift in a ramshackle hotel downtown, staring mindlessly at my useless college transcripts, Preston and I decided to take out ads in *Fangoria*, *Rue Morgue*, *Heavy Metal*, and a couple of low-rent film magazines. My "company," which consists of a small guest room in my apartment lined with dubbing equipment, a couple of TVs, a stack of magazines to pass the time, a closet full of glossy film covers, and hundreds of blank videocassettes and fresh white plastic cases, offers uncut quality sleaze, underground horror, adult Anime, both the American and Japanese derivatives of *Faces of Death*, Hammer films, and Italian schlock. We also make t-shirts. And actually, we do well. Something Wicked Inc., a name Preston penned while trying to articulate the brilliance of Ray Bradbury if Ray Bradbury were on mushrooms, brings in between five and seven thousand dollars a month, about a thousand going to expenses.

Where most young men who inherit a three bedroom house and half an acre from his dead parents sell the property, fix it up, rent out rooms, do something, *anything*, Preston has instead turned his home into a vault of zombie island massacres and cheap excuses for voluptuous female serial killer victims to run around naked and fuck before being impaled or having splintered wood go through an eyeball.

Where most young men who graduate at the top of their class from a major university go out, find a job, take up teaching, master Microsoft Excel and Power Point, and work on achieving a mortgage and 401K plan, I have dedicated my time to selling box sets of *Guinea Pig* and unedited copies of *Army of Darkness* to single guys who live with their mothers and rant incessantly on how terrible the *Scream* films are and yet are first in line to see them.

"How many movies do you own now, man?" I ask Preston.

"Two days ago I had eleven hundred and forty-eight," he says. "But it's been a couple of days. Oh, that reminds me: this guy left a message asking if we were interested in four Dario Argento cuts of *Dawn of the Dead* and two different versions of *Night of the Demons*. Did you hear it?"

"Yeah, I heard it," I say, following him into a living room full of old furniture and new posters. "Pass on the *Demons*. I've never had anyone ask for it and doubt that I ever will. Yes to one of the Argento *Dawn*s, provided that you can watch them first and make sure at least one of them is decent-looking. The last copy of *Zombi* I saw looked like someone's last known photograph."

We head up a flight of rickety wooden stairs, down a hallway full of framed mini-posters not unlike the one he just mentioned ordering, and into what Preston refers to as Monroeville. An entire wall has been covered with a makeshift series of shelves consisting of wood planks on cinder blocks. On the shelves is Preston's huge collection of movies.

He pulls out a VHS copy of *Titanic*.

"What do you have tonight?" he asks, retrieving a plastic bag full of mediocre pot from behind the movie.

"I don't know. The *Toolbox* thing, another three orders for *Cannibal Holocaust* and one *Women of the SS*."

"Those weirdo Nazi buffs creep me out."

"I need a new job," I mutter.

Preston sighs melodramatically.

"What?" I ask.

"Yeah, Ross, you *should* get a new job. You should be teaching English to the brilliant youth out there. You should be giving lectures on Dostoevsky to the ten derelicts at the local library. You should be discussing Corso with a customer at Geico. Come on, Ross. You could be doing a lot worse and you could be doing it a lot more pathetically. So, like, spare me the regret and melancholy. It's getting tiresome."

"This just isn't where I pictured myself when I graduated from college," I say. "I mean, I didn't picture myself up at four on a Sunday morning drinking a Rolling Rock while taping eleven episodes of *Blue Girl* for a fifty-year-old who lives with his mother. That's not exactly what I wanted with an American Studies degree."

"Hey," Preston says, "you make pirate copies of *Last House on the Left* and in your spare time print t-shirts that say 'Fuck *I Know What You Did Last Summer*.'"

"Your point?"

"My point," he says, "is what could be more American than that?"

We get high and Preston turns on a taped episode of *The X-Files*.

The room becomes murky and elongated. Preston giggles maniacally at something an alien says on the show and has to pause the tape and use the bathroom. The room is silent and stale in his absence.

There was a time when things were different. When Preston and I being high would be called a revolutionary act. When a handful of college kids could get together with a common purpose and change history. When a man with an acoustic guitar and an opinion on the disintegration of America could influence millions into action with nothing more than some simple chords and a nauseating voice of authenticity. The youth were divided, but at least there was something important enough to divide them so clearly and distinctly. At least there was something to write about.

There was no loud silence then. Now, its cacophony is so much that my ears bleed. The silence is overwhelming, and worse, has lasted my entire life.

My father told me once that you never hear the gunshot with your name on it. My worst fear is that my death will be as silent and forgettable as my life.

Preston comes back from the bathroom.

"I was thinking about throwing a big New Year's party here. What do you think?"

"I think there's already two thousand to go to anyway?" I say-ask.

"Actually, there isn't," he says, heading into the kitchen. He comes back with a bag of chips. "The only one I heard about that was even mildly interesting was on the other **end** of town at Scott Rhinebeck's apartment. The situation looks grim."

"Then throw one yourself," I say dismissively.

"Do you plan on going back to school?" he asks. "I was just curious, seeing your younger sister getting her Master's and all. I don't care one way or the other."

"I don't either I guess."

He plops himself back down on the couch while lighting a cigarette, picks up his bass guitar, and begins picking at the low string.

"If you don't care about going back to school anymore, Ross, then why do you still make faces like that?"

"Faces like what?" I ask, lighting a cigarette of my own.

"That face that you're still trying to think something brilliant. You were making it when I came out of the bathroom."

"Just because I'm not in school anymore doesn't mean that I can't have a random thought now and again, Pres."

"It doesn't?" he asks, looking back at me.

"I don't know," I admit. "Maybe."

"Ross."

"What?" I ask, getting up.

"Next time you come over, I've got to show you this thing I just bought online. It's this surveillance camera footage of this guy in Saudi Arabia getting his arms sawed off. You need to see it. I think it will be a big seller."

9

I PASS A MAN ON THE SIDE OF THE ROAD selling flowers for no particular reason, and consider stopping and buying a bouquet for Lydia. Instead, I pull over for an ambulance and a sheriff's car and turn the stereo up louder on the way home to my apartment. It begins raining as I cross 89 and I pass a man in front of the overpass holding a sign that reads REPENT, FOR THE KINGDOM OF HEAVEN IS AT HAND. THEY'RE TAKING PICTURES. I park in front of my building and head up a flight of narrow concrete stairs. The apartment is unlocked for some reason, the third time in a little over a week. I never used to leave it unlocked, and don't remember doing it now.

Inside everything is stale and freezing. Back issues of *Bizarre* litter the glass coffee table, and *The Spirit of the Sixties* lies half-read and open on a white couch with a tiny red wine stain on the left cushion. The computer in the place of a dining room set has gone into standby, but turns on for some reason as I walk into the kitchen to grab a Snapple. I hear a noise in my bedroom, a clicking sound, but when I check to see what it is, everything is *still*: the bed is still unmade; the TV is still off; the fish tank light still needs to be turned on; the eight cichlids swimming around inside it still need to be fed.

I check the messages on both of my voicemails: Lydia asking if I'm going to be at her place by six, my mother on her cell phone asking if I'm going to Cordelia's graduation luncheon and mentioning in a low tone that she needs to speak to me, Preston giving me the correct Visa number on an order for *Cannibal Holocaust*, my friend Michael inviting me to a party downtown near the First Baptist church, someone canceling their order for *House by the Edge of the Park* since Bizarro Video has it for less, and then one of my t-shirt distributors telling me that my three dozen shirts are ready for pickup downtown.

In the bathroom, I try to read this book on the American Indian Movement and the Jewish Defense League that Lydia borrowed from her store, but can not concentrate and I have a headache from the lack of sleep and from the hangover that, around one this morning, seemed like a marvelous idea.

The phone rings. I let voicemail answer and check the message immediately afterward. My father asks if I'm going to be attending dinner with them tonight. He sounds pissed off. I'm not sure why, but I'm sure he has his reasons. Maybe he took a look at Cordelia's graduation footage. Maybe he's mad that I didn't meet them at the Country Club for the luncheon. Then, he coughs and tells me that he needs to talk to me about my mother. He hangs up.

I immediately erase the message and climb into my bed. On the TV, a news anchor is reporting live from in front of a tall glass building somewhere. He is talking about the New Year only a little over a week away and, inevitably, goes into the mounting fear of the Y2K virus. An expert, someone in a brown sports coat and bow tie, tells us to be prepared for massive power outages and ensuing hysteria. Then someone else comes on and I turn the television off. I think I fall asleep.

In my dream, I am standing in front of an empty apartment building. The clouds overhead look ominous and a swing set in a green yard nearby has been turned over and a Tonka truck floats in a kiddy pool. Thunder rumbles in the distance. From the top of a nearby building, a flash. When I look over, I see a man taking pictures of me on a camera with a long lens. I hear someone whispering, but can not understand what they are saying. A little girl in a blue Sunday dress comes out onto the balcony of one of the apartments. She looks at the man taking pictures. Then she turns to face me. She holds a finger to her lips, urging me to keep quiet. And I am screaming.

I awake and for some reason have to call Stacy.

After.

Stacey is looking down at my penis, now shriveled and reticent, and smiles.

The wind was howling on my way to her house. It was freezing outside, and a breeze was turning into a wind. A used bookstore that I bought a copy of *Slaughterhouse Five* from when I was nineteen had burnt down and a team of fire fighters were spraying water into the charred black shell. A man disguised as a bum on the side of the road inconspicuously mumbled into a microphone hidden under his jacket lapel as my car passed. A Santa Claus on Griffin was handing out flyers for the seafood restaurant behind him. The sun was hidden behind a cloud and I was still sweating from the dream.

"What?" I ask, lighting a cigarette and staring out the window of her bedroom.

"Have you ever heard of Koro Syndrome?" she asks, lighting a badly wrapped joint and inhaling thoughtfully.

"Is that the one where you don't believe the left side of your body exists?"

"No, that's Sensory Neglect Syndrome," Stacey says, passing the joint to me. I accept it, take a small hit, and cough before passing it back to her.

"Well what is Koro Syndrome? Your weed is kind of haggard."

"It's a psychosis first diagnosed by the Japanese, and when you find out what it is, you won't be surprised. Koro Syndrome is when you believe that your penis is shrinking, getting smaller and smaller, and that when it finally disappears, you'll die. Isn't that weird?"

"Yeah, but what's worse is that you thought of bringing it up while staring at my dick."

"No, sweetie, I don't think you're shrinking. It just reminded me of it, that's all. I read about it in the *DSM IV* and wanted to mention it to you."

When I knocked on the door to Stacey Shimmerly's parents' huge two-story house, she answered wearing Umbro soccer shorts, a sweater with her—our—university's seal on the breast, and bedroom slippers. She was holding a lit Parliament menthol in one hand and a TV remote in the other. When I came inside, incense was burning in the living room, covering up the pot that I was sure she was smoking, and strewn about were unwrapped Christmas gifts, two days early, and old issues of *Cosmopolitan* and videos and bits of tinsel that their Yorkshire terrier had managed to finagle off of a seven foot tall tree in one corner of the room. Stacey led me to her bedroom, slipping off the sweater on the way, exposing a pair of perfect breasts encased in a Pepto Bismol-pink bra.

"When did you get the *DSM*?" I ask.

"Oh, it was an early Christmas present," she says, her eyes scanning the room. "By Christmas Eve I'll have every one of them opened."

"Where's the fun in that?" I wonder aloud, realizing how much she and Lydia truly have in common. "What are you looking for?"

"My panties."

Stacey tosses the black covers off of our naked bodies and begins fishing around the floor for her underwear. There is a small blue-black bruise on the back of a tan, smooth thigh, and I cannot stop staring at it. She picks up a teal

Radiohead t-shirt and throws it on over her bare tits first, and then gets up and begins rummaging through books, magazines, clothes and CDs until she finds her zebra-print panties. Then she turns on the TV and flips from Sci-Fi Channel to MTV2. A Spineshank video flashes across the screen and Stacey lies back down in bed with me.

"I have a weird bald spot in my pubic hair," she says, gesturing down. "Look at it."

"Um."

"Just look at it," she groans.

I inspect her pubic hair, which is sand-colored and trimmed into a Christmas tree formation. Indeed, there is a quarter-inch circular area just above her labia that is completely bare, her pale white flesh exposed.

"That's pretty odd," I admit.

"I know, right?" she says. "So what are you doing today?"

"I think I have to meet my parents for dinner," I tell her, not daring to mention the other dinner I was supposed to be having with Lydia. "Cordelia got her Master's this morning."

"Good for her. Now, when is her older brother going to get his?"

"You couldn't resist, could you?" I ask her, sitting up and snatching my boxers from off the top of a pink, purple, and tan candle on the bedside table.

"I'm just trying to get you out of your funk, sweetie."

"I didn't know I was in one."

"Yes you did," she almost whispers.

She turned the television in her room off and grabbed the remote to her stereo. She pressed buttons, and a moment later, "Sour Times" by Portishead began playing at Volume Level 6. Stacey grabbed a book by Aldous Huxley and an album by Queens of the Stone Age from off of the bed and tossed both into the pile on the floor. She sat at the edge of the mattress and unbuckled my belt. Then she unfastened her bra and motioned for me to remove my shirt. She smiled, waiting, her legs spread in anticipation. I could not stop staring at a wall clock hanging above dozens of clothes. I nodded and waited for her to do the same. Her shorts ended up in a heap on the other side of the photographs of Stacey with a menagerie of people. It was no longer functioning, and the hands were resting at 11:11.

"When does school start again?" I ask, making small talk while putting my cigarette out in a Coke can.

"January tenth, but I move back into the dorms on the sixth. And I can't *wait* to get the hell out of here. These parental figures of mine are driving me insane. I swear to god, if they don't go to the beach house for New Year's, I'm going to kill them *and* the little adopted kid they keep trying to make me call 'Bubby' for some unknown reason."

It occurs to me that I have never met Stacey's family, and I ask, "Where are they this afternoon?"

"Malik, my new African brother, is rehearsing for his school Christmas play tonight. He's playing the second palm tree behind the three wise men. The parents are at the new mall doing last minute shopping. As if a smaller mall than either of the two we have here in town already is going to solve all of their consumerist dilemmas."

"I've been meaning to shop there," I mutter, smiling.

"God, you're hopeless," she moans, rolling around in bed and grabbing her pack of cigarettes from off the floor. "Just leave, Ross. Shouldn't you be recording *Evil Death II* or something for some kid in an ICP shirt? Or is it Practice Counting to Twenty Day with your brilliant girlfriend?"

"First of all, Stacey, it's *Evil Dead*, not *Evil Death*. Second of all, a kid wouldn't be ordering anything from me. You have to be eighteen and up."

"I see that you run your company with morals."

"No," I say. "I run my company by law. If I didn't, I might actually make some real money."

"And your defense of Lydia?" she asks, raising her eyebrows.

"I just don't understand you. That's all." I shrug. "I mean, considering your history with her and everything."

"I know. I'm like the wind, aren't I?" she says, and leaves the room. She pauses in the long white hallway for a moment to inspect herself in a hanging mirror. She straightens her blond hair back into place, adjusts the t-shirt she has on, and disappears around a corner. When she returns, she is wearing a red Santa's cap and carrying an orange Popsicle in one hand and an unlit cigarette in the other.

"Did you want a popsicle?" she asks, but I do not answer her, as MTV News is reporting on a teenager who shot himself while listening to Blink 182, and Kurt Loder mentions that, in the young man's suicide note, the troubled adolescent swore that the world would be **end**ing before New Year's Eve. Then there is a story about Korn, and Stacey changes the channel to Fuse.

"Stacey," I say.

"Let me guess: you blame Blink 182's terrible music for that young man's demise?"

"No."

"You *do* want a popsicle? A red one?"

"Shut up for a second," I say. "For real, do you like, worry?"

"About what?" she asks, putting the wrapped Popsicle down on the bedside table and lighting her cigarette.

"About this whole year 2000 thing. I mean, does it make you nervous?"

"No," she says, starting to laugh. "God, I thought for a second that you were going to ask me if I worried about Lydia finding out about us or if I believe in karma or infinite being."

"I know you don't believe in karma," I say, looking around the room for the sweater I had on. "But *do* you worry about Lyd finding out?"

"No, not really. But it would suck if she *did*, her being my best friend and all. Are you *sure* you don't want a Popsicle? They're really good. Malik pretty much lives on them, my mom said. I'm not sure if they have them in Africa."

"So what about the world **end**ing?" I say casually, shrugging. "Do you think it's retarded or what?"

"No, I don't think it's retarded. I just think that we have nothing to worry about?"

"Are you asking me or telling me?"

"Telling you?" she manages, trying to suppress laughter.

"Stop it," I say, pointing out my sweater to her on the floor behind the bedroom door. She brings it along, giggling now. "So you don't think the year changing to a new millennium is going to upset any of the computer systems or anything?"

"*Upset* any of the computer systems?" she repeats, grinning. "No, I don't think it will upset them. Maybe slightly *offend* them, but we can talk it out afterward, maybe buy them some flowers to smooth things over."

"You're stoned," I sigh, a terribly unoriginal gesture, and stand up to retrieve my pants, which somehow made it during foreplay into a half-empty laundry basket on the other **end** of the bedroom.

"Ross, do you hear what these people are saying?" Stacey asks. "They're saying the machines are going to become self-aware. They're saying the machines are going to revolt and destroy us all. They're saying that the machines are going to start their own Utopian society. And that's not even the Christians."

"Well, what are the Christians saying?"

"The same thing they were saying in 1899, 1599 and especially *999*, sweetie. They're saying this is the beginning of the Apocalypse."

"That doesn't scare you?" I ask, shivering.

"Babe, what is it with you? Is this like a guilt thing about Lydia? Because if it is, then just remember what I said—"

"No, this isn't a guilt thing," I interrupt. "Although I do feel *extremely* guilty for that and need to talk about it with you in the very near future, I'm not talking about that right *now*. I'm just—it's like—you haven't felt weird lately?"

"Not really. Weird about what?"

"I don't know," I mutter, slipping my khaki pants back on. "Forget it. I'm just paranoid and creeped out. My best friend in middle school was the son of a Baptist minister, so…"

"You know what Blechman said about Armageddon, sweetie?"

"Who?"

"He said that it's only frightening to those who fear progress."

8

Back at my apartment, I begin folding the inserts for some of the videos, noticing that the printers made the *Zombie* covers too red again. Glancing out the window, I see someone on the roof of the apartment building across from me, a guy in a black suit and sunglasses writing in a spiral notebook. He glances up at me, frowns, and moves out of view.

I shut the blinds and move back into the living room, exhausted, a headache building, memories flooding over and pounding at the backs of my eyes.

Stacey Shimmerly just sort of happened, much the same way my almost three-year relationship with Lydia Lawton did. The business just sort of happened as well. A three-by-four inch ad wedged between Bizarro Video and a promo for a book by Tom Savini just sort of appeared, and to this day I am not sure whether it was Preston or me who arranged its placement in the magazines.

It was pure inertia that everything I saw myself doing, every great statement I saw myself making, every obstacle I would ever overcome to succeed in the **end**, somehow dissolved into a stack of grainy photographs lost in a random tin can.

Lydia calls and asks me to pick her up at seven. Before I can question why I would be picking her up, she says she has to go and I think that I hear laughter in the background. I sigh, a terribly unoriginal gesture, just as she says something about loving me and hanging up. Feeling disgusting and sexed, I take another shower and brush my teeth. While I am shaving, the phone rings again. I answer it.

"Does any of this *go* anywhere?" Martin interrupts, fuming.

"Yes," I say.

"Well, it needs to get there *very* soon, Mister Orringer. I need not remind you that we don't have much time."

"Look, you wanted the whole story; I'm giving it to you. It's December 23, and what you're asking me about happens on New Year's Eve, eight days later. It's all interconnected. So calm down."

He lights a cigarette and walks behind me. Words are exchanged with the man I am not allowed to see, the man whose voice has been altered.

"Mister Orringer, if the events in question did not occur until December 31, then why do you continue to give us inane details on seemingly random and meaningless events and your own personal feelings on these events, all of which are entirely inconsequential not only to what is happening to us *now*, but to what happened that night five years ago?"

"And furthermore," the man behind me says nervously, "why do you insist on recounting it in the present tense?"

"Have you looked out the window?" I ask, trying to look up at them, but someone's gloved hand grabs my head and props it downward. I **end** up staring at the surface of the pale blue table I am sitting at, and then up into the lens of the video camera mounted on the other side of the room. "It's *all* present tense," I mutter, speaking to the camera.

"What?" one of them asks.

"I said that it's *all* present tense, you fucking *morons*."

"Mister Orringer—"

"I'm on to what's really going on," I say.

"Mister Orringer, we are in a crisis here," the first man, Martin, continues, coming back into my frame of vision. "Do you know how low our supplies are?"

"I don't care," I say, shaking my head while lighting a cigarette. "And you know what? You are not in a position to rush me. So I will take however the fuck *long* I *want*—"

"Do you not understand what's going *on*?" he suddenly shrieks, slamming a newspaper on the table and storming away.

I roll my eyes and inhale hatefully on my cigarette. At some point I casually glance down at yesterday's local paper and read the front page headline: MILLIONS FEAR **END** SOON.

"So are you coming tonight or not?" my father immediately asks.

"I don't think so," I say.

"Look, if this is because of Cordelia and you not getting along—"

"It's not that," I interrupt. "It's just that I have a lot of work to get caught up on here tonight, and Lydia is cooking dinner at her place and she's sort of mad at me, and it's just like—I'm totally booked, Dad."

There is a silence between us that lasts twenty-three seconds. I keep count.

"Well all right then," he finally says. "But your mother wants to see you. Soon. Can you come by tomorrow?"

"Tomorrow?" I repeat, pretending to think out loud while mulling over a calendar that I do not own. "Tomorrow..."

"Ross, it's important, damn it. Just be here before two. The party is at 7:30 but I know you won't be attending anyway so I won't even bother. Is that okay, though, son? Will you still be in a drunken stupor at *two* tomorrow after*noon*? Is it asking too much of you to come by and visit your god-damned *mother*, Ross?"

"No," I say. "No drunken stupor. I'll be there. Bye, Dad."

I finish getting ready, answer a call about the party tonight downtown, feed my fish, begin making the bed but stop because everything is just so heavy, and leave the apartment, making sure to lock the door behind me. I do it twice, checking the knob each time. I grab the newspaper that I forgot to pick up this morning before Cordelia's satanic ceremony. On the front page is a huge spread about the Y2K virus, with the headline MILLIONS FEAR **END** SOON.

7

INSIDE LYDIA'S APARTMENT, everything is warm and stoic, not elevated by steam or made cozy by the smells of asparagus frying in a pan or breaded pork loin baking in the oven. Instead, I smell whorish perfume and see Lydia standing in the bathroom applying mascara.

"I take it you didn't cook?" I say, making eye contact with her evil white cat Spiral, which is propped up on the head rest of a recliner in the living room.

"Good guess, Holden," she says, not looking at me. "Guess what else."

"We're going out instead?"

"Bingo."

"Why didn't you cook?" I ask, sitting down on the couch and thumbing through her copy of *On the Road.* The bookmark is still on page 14, the same page it was on a week ago. A disgrace.

"I didn't have time to cook," she says, finishing up in the bathroom and turning off a light.

"You didn't have *time*? What the hell were you doing all day?"

"I didn't feel like it, all right?" she snaps, coming out into the living room in black pants, a blue button up shirt, and non-prescription glasses. She grabs her Prada jacket from off of the foodless kitchen table and turns to me. "I feel like Chinese. And are you still going to the Christmas party tomorrow night? My mom needs to know whether or not to get you a gift card. Oh, and by the way, how was your sister's graduation this morning?"

She lightly touches her long auburn hair immediately after I compliment her on it, as if to make sure it really exists. When I order two glasses of wine, she asks for a glass of water also. Her red lipstick leaves a stain on the glasses. Before our meal comes, I tell her about my sister's graduation this morning, and as I tell her this, her fingers graze the bottom of her fork and she smiles at all the wrong points in the story, and when a waiter passes by, she always glances at his back.

I picture myself dead and buried, Lydia getting away with murder, her head tilted back while she laughs hysterically before driving away in a cherry red Porsche.

Our food comes. I stir a plate of chow mei fun about while Lydia attempts to pick at a piece of lobster with a pair of chop sticks. She gives up and grabs the fork. We eat. No one speaks for almost three minutes. Lydia smiles as she finishes her second glass of wine. I have to say something.

"Lyd, have you ever thought about how truly ridiculous the notion is that our nation has actually landed men on the moon? I was on the Internet the other day, and the counter-evidence against it is...pretty overwhelming. One minute, we're twenty years behind the Russians in the space race, and the next, we're sending men through impossible radiation belts and landing them on the surface of a planetary body that has not been touched upon by a single other nation before or since? I mean, do you see my point here? And the photos are just *ludicrous*—"

"I'm not interested in this conversation," she says. "How is your pasta?"

"Fulfilling," I answer, disappointed. "But it's not pasta, sweetie. It's chow mei fun. Slight differ—"

"Holden, will you do me a favor?" Lydia interrupts. "Could you not call me sweetie? Stacy calls everyone that and it is extremely irritating to have to hear it from you too."

"Sure thing," I say.

"How's work?" she asks, impaling the pod of a snow pea with her fork and holding it up for me. "What is this?"

"Snow peas," I say. "Did you just ask me about work?"

She nods and eats the green pod gingerly. She smiles.

"I don't know why, but everyone seems to want to get their hands on *Cannibal Holocaust*. It just serves as a testament in the **end** of how sick a society we are."

"What is *Cannibal Holocaust*?"

"Nothing," I say. "Well, it's just this terrible, sick movie that everyone seems to be obsessed with. It was the first one Preston showed me of his collection. It was the first thing Something Wicked sold. I don't like it at all, but I suppose it has its place in any twisted person's vault."

"What is it about?"

"Well, you know that movie I took you to see this summer, *Blair Witch Project*? Well, it's actually a little like that, except it was made in the early 80s and the wops don't believe in the 'less is more' philosophy like the *Blair Witch* makers did. *Holocaust* is an Italian movie, if that tells you anything, where this professor guy goes to track down a documentary team that was lost in the Amazon. Well, he makes friends with the natives, and baby, these people look the shit. The whole thing looks like it has real Indians, real rape, real everything. I really hated it. But anyway, the natives give the professor all the documentary team's film cans right after he sees their nasty skeletons. He takes them back to New York, which is weird since it's an Italian flick, and when he watches the tapes with some television people, the movie gets very upsetting. The music alone gave me nightmares for weeks."

"What's so upsetting about it?" she asks, totally interested now. They always are.

"Actually, once I got into the business, I found out that *Holocaust* is not really very unique. Just about all the shit I sell has rape, torture, animals dying, cannibalism…the whole gamut of disgusting, perverse shit. It's just that *Cannibal Holocaust* got to it early and went all the way, I guess. But to the uninitiated, it will make you wretch. It has real animals dying, abortions, a girl getting raped with mud and a rock dildo, and then—what else?—oh, it has this guy getting his penis sliced off, but it's weird because you actually want him to get his by the time the whole thing is over. Basically, Lydia, it's just like every other thing I have for sale. I hate it, and yet it's one of Preston's favorite movies. *And* it's our biggest seller."

She looks down at her half-eaten pile of Seafood Delight, then across the room at a pimply Asian girl folding napkins at a table near the corner. I myself become mesmerized by a painting on the wall of a Chinese mountain range. I feel so far away, so quiet in this almost totally empty dining room that everything around me falls away, and I am plunged into that mountain range. It is real.

Lydia says something. I lose my mountains and return to Great Wall the night before Christmas Eve.

"What?" I ask, fishing a cigarette from the pack in my jacket pocket.

"I asked why people would make movies like that. Like the movies you sell."

"I used to wonder that too," I say. "But you know what I realized?"

"No, what?"

"This shit, and I do mean that: most of the things I sell are *shit*—these films wouldn't be made unless there was a market for them. In other words, people make the kind of movies that I sell because a whole lot of other people will pay to watch them. Jesus, did you know that *Cannibal Holocaust* was the second most popular film of all time in Japan after *E.T.*? Until *Titanic*, anyway."

"That's disturbing."

I nod, and we become quiet for a moment. I finish my plate of chow mei fun.

"I want to see it," she says.

"See what?"

"The cannibal movie. Let's watch it after the party."

"Oh, Lydia, I don't want to watch that. It will make me sick to my stomach and I won't be able—wait. Wait a second. Lydia, how did you know there was a party tonight? I haven't mentioned it yet."

"Preston told me," she says, looking away. Our check comes.

"When did you talk to Preston?"

"I don't know, Ross. But I want to watch it. Tonight. Can we? Please?"

I do not say anything, stare into the painting, into the future, shivering and clenching my—

"*Holden*."

"What?" I chirp, returning to the scene.

"I asked if we can please, please, *please* watch it tonight. Please, Holden?"

"Sure," I say, deep in thought, something flashing behind me.

I began seeing Lydia Lawton when I was twenty-three. Oddly enough, we met in the same bookstore that a few months later, she would begin working at. I was about to go into the hotel for third shift and stopped by for coffee and maybe a Boyle novel to read at the hotel when she caught my eye. She was in the café, reading *Catcher in the Rye* while munching on brioche and sipping from a tall latte. I was taken aback. She was gorgeous, despite the fact that she was obviously a college student reading a book that I read in tenth grade. Her hair was blond then, straight, radiating with static electricity, and her nails were painted midnight, which only sort of matched the black sweater she was wearing. Underneath that sweater, beautiful full breasts bowed and bucked as she inhaled, exhaled, inhaled, exhaled. When she finished the brioche she did not wipe her mouth with a napkin.

Once I had grabbed the nearest intellectually stimulating novel I could find from a nearby rack, *The Satanic Verses* for some odd reason, I ordered a coffee and walked towards her.

"Let me guess: this is the umpteenth time you've read that, right?" I asked, standing over her.

"Not quite," she said, looking up, her eyes rolling over the pants, the forest green turtleneck, the earrings, and the short black hair. A grimace, not a good sign. "Can I help you?"

"It's just a pretty good book," I said sheepishly. "That's all."

"Yeah, that's what I've heard, so I decided to read it over Spring Break. Is he like in a mental asylum or something at the beginning?"

"Who?" I asked, confused.

"Holden. The guy in the book."

"Oh, the guy in the book. Yeah," I said, cracking a smile. "He is, actually."

"Good," she says, closing the paperback and laying it on the table. "It was kind of confusing. So what are you buying?"

"Oh, this?" I say, looking down at the Rushdie book I was holding. "It's called *The Satanic Verses*. It was really controversial, so I wanted to read it. It's really good so far."

"Controversial?" she asks. "Why? What's it about?"

My throat closed. My head swooned and the sweat began to materialize on my forehead and underarms.

"Well, it's about…these people from India…and it's a religious book sort of…" I nonchalantly peeked at the synopsis on the back of the book. "These two guys die in a plane crash—"

"You haven't been reading it at all, have you?" she said, laughing.

"Not a sentence," I admitted. "I haven't read any of it. I was…trying to flirt with you?"

"I see," she said, smiling.

Two nights later we were in the next town over on the beach, walking on an empty boardwalk in front of a subdued ocean. Then we were at the top of a ten story parking garage looking down on the festival grounds at a Toadies concert. When they played "Tyler" Lydia told me how much she loved that song. I nodded in agreement. She told me about her first year of college so far, commented that Liberal Arts math "is *so* gay," told me that Descartes irritated her because "he is *so* fake," and then I told her how she had missed my graduation by almost a year, how we had gone to the same university and that I had the same Intro to Philosophy professor. She told me that she was a Sociology major and I pretended to be impressed. When I tried to explain what American Studies was and why I dedicated my college career to it, she pointed to a homeless man in a random alley, asking me if I felt sorry for him.

We stayed out 'til the tide changed. I stole a kiss while we were cuddling near the pier, which I told her was haunted. I'm pretty sure that we had covered eight miles by the time we trudged back to my old car and I drove her home, four hours late she announced with a nervous chuckle. When she got out of the car she called me Holden and kissed my forehead before darting for her door to face her insane father's wrath.

I loved Lydia right away. She was so energetic and funny and fresh.

So was her friend Stacy, whose lips first touched mine two New Years ago while Lydia was having sex for the second time with a guy from Dartmouth named Tony ("I couldn't find where the god-damned party was," was her explanation, though I knew better because Lydia is a terrible liar and I'm not).

"Remember our first date?" I ask as we walk along the beachfront. "It was right here. I think I kissed you over there in front of that pier."

"No, Holden," she says, "It was in the parking lot right before you drove me home."

"Oh, right," I agree, trying to remember. "That's much less romantic."

She shrugs. "It's more romantic than the first time we had sex. My mom walked in."

"Yeah, but she was cool about it," I interject, laughing. "Thank god it wasn't your father. Jesus, he reminds me of the dad in *Say Anything*."

I stop walking and rest my hands on the railing. She stops too.

"What is it?"

"I love you, Lydia," I whisper, staring her down.

"I wish we had some pot before the party," she says wistfully. "And I love you too."

"Let's go," I sigh, a terribly unoriginal gesture, and then I glance down at my watch.

We leave the boardwalk and cross the street, taking the sidewalk about a block, passing closed beach shops, a Baskin Robbins, two tattoo parlors, and an art gallery, where Lydia pauses uncertainly and glances over her shoulder. We reach the same empty parking lot that I kissed her at almost three years ago. I unlock Lydia's car door and open it for her, but she does not get in. She looks nervous.

"What?" I ask, smiling.

"Ross," Lydia whispers, her eyes wide. "Why is that man following us?"

6

THEY SHADOW ME ALL THE WAY up Beachfront across the drawbridge, and then down 89 back to our own town and into the city. I run a red light, sure that I lost them, but on careful examination through my rearview mirror, I see that the sedan has kept up but has fallen back to about fifty yards behind me. All I can think about is the unread copy of *On the Road* decaying on Lydia's coffee table, and the bookmark wedged between pages 29 and 30 of *A Conversation on Belladonna*, a book that has been lying on Lydia's washing machine for two months. It is as I am wondering if my significant other ever finished one of my books on the JFK conspiracy, *High Treason*, when I suddenly become aware that the sedan is now in the lane to the right of mine, ten feet back and gaining. There is the flash of a camera, but not from the car following me. It's coming from somewhere else.

"Did you piss somebody off?" Lydia is asking me.

The sedan keeps pace next to mine. It is a black BMW 320i with illegally tinted windows and an antenna on the roof for what I can only guess is some kind of powerful phone.

"Ross, this is totally freaking me out," Lydia says. "What should we do?"

"I don't know," I say. "I have no idea who that is and I have no idea what our options are at this point. The party is just up the road. We'll be there in like three minutes."

I keep glancing at the BMW next to us. When I slow down, it slows down. When I run a red light, it does too, swerving ever so slightly to avoid being side-swiped by an Econoline. I speed up. It stays with us.

"I'm scared," Lydia says, and that's when I make the unprecedented left turn onto Havenbrook, the followers soaring down 89 and losing us.

I exhale.

"Lyd," I say, smiling, "I have no idea what that was all about, but one thing is clear: I am a bad-ass—"

"Oh my *god,*" Lydia shrieks, pointing straight ahead.

"Déjà vu," I whisper upon seeing him, remembering a night at the hotel.

The gangly wreck of what was once an old man is lurching up the middle of the two-lane street in front of us, toward my car, which is barreling down on him at forty-miles an hour.

We're about to hit him.

I am slamming both feet down on the brakes. My headlights turn his eyes a translucent cave-fish blue, and for a moment all I can see is the blood pouring down his neck, onto the lapel of his black jacket. It is when my car's tires begin making terrible noises, when the rubber begins to churn up a terrible burning smell, after Lydia braces herself for the impact by lowering her head between her legs and screaming, that the reel slows down, and everything happens in slow motion.

The female figure lurking in the darkness underneath the weeping willow, the woman wearing latex gloves and a black turtleneck who is standing on the sidewalk to my left, carefully documents the moment with a small camcorder. She seems terribly familiar, despite her shadowy presence in the scene.

The squat man in the white radiation suit, gas mask and all, the one poised on the sidewalk to Lydia's right, records the sounds of the imminent wreck with a boom mike.

I am seeing these things as my Corolla barrels toward the old man.

My eyes meet his just as the car comes to a halt, my front bumper three feet away from his torso.

He shuffles to my side of the car without a word, ignoring us as if we had not just come within inches of running him over. Then he turns toward me and attacks, hobbling over and slapping his gray hands against my window.

"Jesus Christ, what the fuck *is* this?" Lydia bursts, but I do not answer her and hit the gas hard, panicked, speaking to myself in tongues, as I leave everything shrinking into nothingness on the way to the party.

5

"I JUST DON'T UNDERSTAND why people can't buy the movies un-pirated from like Amazon or Best Buy or something, that's all. It would be a lot cheaper, wouldn't it, dude?"

"Shannon, listen," I begin, about to explain this for the third time. "The stuff I sell—you *can't* buy it from those places. Do you *understand*? Do you get it? Tu comprendes? If you want to buy *The Sound of Music* or *The Crying Game*, yeah, go to Best Buy, log on to Amazon, Video Vault, whatever. But if you're trying to get a hold of *Traces of Death Part III,* or *2000 Maniacs*, or if you want to see a guy on a surveillance camera as he leaps over a fence into an impound yard only to be devoured by two Dobermans that rip his larynx out, then you come to me and Preston. If you want to see the unedited news helicopter footage of a guy in LA who sets his truck on fire in the middle of the freeway just before blowing his brains out the back of his head with a double-barreled shotgun, then you come to me and Preston.

"The point is that, Shannon, you are an *idiot*, first of all. Second of all, the movies we distribute are not Hollywood products. They aren't produced in bulk, and they don't usually have a fancy synopsis on the back of the box loaded with exclamation points and reviews by Peter Travers, either. The footage we sell is made by guys who have extensive backgrounds in the porn market, by guys who never stopped jacking off to naked women getting hot candle wax poured on their tits. I sell shit that was made by Italian men who do not share our American views of sex, or violence, or the value we put on life. The things we copy and sell at pretty ridiculous prices are expensive because they are scarce, because they were never meant for mass consumption, because a lot of them dance on the line between what is legal and what is not. Now, before I lose my voice and freeze my ass off out here trying to explain the intricacies of the underground gore, schlock and porn scene to you, please acknowledge that something, *anything*, has gotten through. Nod, smile, grunt, *whatever*. Just tell me that if you're ever looking to pay $39.95 for *Twitch of the Death Nerve* that you'll give me a call."

Shannon, who threw this little shindig, is silent for a moment, twisting his long frizzy hair with the tips of two fingers. He finishes the rest of his beer, glances at a trio of newly-arrived community college students, and then stares at me.

"Well...why would people want to see stuff like that?" he asks as I head inside the house.

Alone, I am trying to locate Preston or Lydia or Michael or even Cordelia, who I was told by a girl who is slightly famous for her controversial paintings of mounds was at this party tonight.

Instead of finding any of them, I try to maintain calm while mucking my way through a large colonial-style home seething with sexually active college band geeks; fire swallowers; cum swallowers; people who like to stick their tongues on batteries during a bizarre drinking game going on in the billiard room next to a depressing match of pool; a few people I went to college with who now work at Boston Market or Pier 1 Imports; and twenty or so whores with Chlamydia being chatted up by twenty-three guys with genital warts. This is all done to the beat of some band Preston turned me on to, Heroin for Nine-Year-Olds, the song "Pretending My Thumb is a Dick."

Everywhere you go, you find out what trendy stench is popular this month: Truth, CK One, Drakkar Noir, Brownies Left on the Kitchen Table, Unwashed Soccer Shirt Covered in Dog Hair, Sex. Everywhere you turn is the smell of hormones, the total apathy of the room, all these boys' loss of ambition, all these girls' loss of a family member that was important to them. Everywhere I turn is another young person's imminent death.

I don't find any of my people on the stairs, which is littered with girls who have leukemia, boys who have blond dreadlocks and listen to Dave Matthews, and this girl who one will find by the dart board of a local bar called City Limits every Friday night between 9:52 and 11:48 before she goes home with a man twice her age. When I go back into the kitchen for another drink, a hot blond is guzzling beer through a funnel that is being held by a guy who personally bought a copy of *Caged Heat II* from me. As I finagle a cup from behind two girls fingering each other on top of the counter next to the sink, a hand grips me by the shoulder and whirls me around.

Stacey is slouching in front of me, her fingers nestled around a large Pepsi cup with a clear half-consumed drink sloshing around inside. Her hair is down, she smells like strawberries dipped in chocolate and tobacco smoke, and the tattoo she has on her right side just above the beltline, a little dancing Grateful Dead bear, is exposed and turning me on.

"Your sister is looking for you," she says. "So am I."

"I was looking for you guys, um, too," I say, heading for the keg.

"I'd kiss you or unzip your pants, but I spoke to your little Sally when I first got here and I know she must be lurking about somewhere in the skating rink."

"My little who? In the what?"

"Sally," she says, waiting. Nothing. "Like, Sally who goes with Holden to the skating rink. In the book. God, Ross, you idiot, I was making a fucking *Catcher in the Rye* joke. In your defense though, it *was* kind of obscure."

She pushes me and I try to chuckle but it comes out like I'm simply unable to breathe.

"I thought maybe you were likening us to Jack and Sally from *Nightmare before Christmas*," I say.

"You're not *that* cool, Ross."

"So why is my sister looking for me?" I ask, walking with Stacey through a huge living room full of dancing partiers and terrible hip hop music.

"Beats me," she says. "Last time we spoke, Cordelia asked me why you hadn't killed yourself or overdosed from depression and anhedonia yet."

"Well where is she?"

"In the neighbors' backyard. She told me that she wanted to see the moon and to not have the obligatory cache of broke losers asking if they can get in on the pot she has."

"Is Brad with her?" I ask, trying not to make the face I make every time I ask anything regarding Cordelia.

"No. He won't be here 'til later, I don't think. Don't ask me any more questions about your sister, Ross."

"Um…okay."

I follow her down a hallway and through a set of French doors onto a pool deck and then into a backyard, where Shannon is still standing where I left him, looking into the swimming pool now, watching steam rise from the lit blue water. We pass one of Stacey's ex-boyfriends, a guy that I didn't get to cuckold because it was two years ago that they went out. I try to remember why they broke up as Stacey steers clear of him and gives him the finger when he tries to speak to her, and then it comes to me, the threesome story…someone's best friend, someone else passed out in someone named Jaeger's band practice room…a frantic punch, a jittery social life. Another tragedy.

Stacey points to a latched gate, which I help her climb over, and then I follow behind into the neighbors' open back yard. There is a covered pool, and a little further back a car port, where I see an old Mustang and three shadowy figures. I glance up, looking for the moon. I don't see it.

I smell the sweet pungent odor of marijuana as I approach, only now that I spot Cordelia lying on the hood of the car while inhaling on a joint, also detect the light stench of cheap cinnamon gum and White Rain hairspray as well.

Flanking Cordelia this evening is Monica Number 2 and Monica Number 2's boyfriend Quentin.

Monica 2 paints Mark Rothko-like images on similarly huge canvasses and then calls them statements of modern femininity. She made the cover of her art institute's newspaper when she churned wet concrete in a blender until the blender shot smoke out, as this was a very artistic blow to modern America's stoic views on the role of woman. In her spare time Monica 2 reads her own terrible brand of poetry at coffee houses that always shut down within three months of opening, and even argues Nietzsche in Barnes & Noble with the Christian intellectuals. Cordelia has mentioned on more than one occasion how much she really does not care for Monica 2, but Monica 2 is Cordelia's gateway to this city's lame art scene and things like that are important to Cordelia. This evening, Monica is wearing a black sweater from Wet Seal and a pair of blue jeans stained with paint that she probably swore "I just didn't have time to change because I was painting right before I came here."

Quentin wears intense black t-shirts he bought from either Rotten Cotton or Unamerican.com everywhere he goes. He is always wearing the same pair of Old Navy cargo pants and dyes his hair black before shaving it bald. His old band opened for Will Haven and Hatebreed just before breaking up because of artistic differences…in their *hardcore* music. When he is handed the joint, he inhales on it thoughtfully before picking at a brand new tattoo of the Aphex Twin logo on his neck.

I arrive with Stacey just in time. Cordelia is holding Mass with her disciples:

"—and what's amazing is that we make jokes about how these films play off of our favorite sitcoms, movies, our pop cultural icons, while all the while they are laughing at us. They are *laughing* at us, people. Pornography comes out with fuck versions of *Seinfeld, Clockwork Orange*, whatever, because the only thing missing from all of this is the one thing we can't stop hoping to see the entire time we're watching them."

"Sex," Monica says, nodding in moronic agreement.

"Another brilliant Cordelia rip-off of something I bellowed while drunk and stupid four years ago," I say, approaching the group ready to attack. "I only came here for the pot, so let's cut the formalities, ladies and gentleman."

"You were missed at dinner tonight," Cordelia says, sitting up on the hood and backing herself against the windshield. "Not by me, of course, but Mom and Dad were hoping that you could regale us with your tales of sleeping 'til the sun has safely set and the guys who refuse to pay shipping and handling on soundtracks to *Maniac Cop*."

"Can one blond girl be this funny?" I inquire, reaching out for the joint, which Quentin reluctantly hands over.

"God," Monica 2 sighs, disgusted.

"Are you throwing in?" Quentin asks me suspiciously. "Because this is mine and it was expensive."

"I don't understand the question," I say.

"Are. You. Throwing. In. *Ross*."

"Does Monica do your laundry?" I ask back slowly, inhaling. Stacey holds her mouth to keep from laughing.

"Fuck you," Monica spits. Then she turns to Stacey. "How you can think this asshole is funny is beyond me. You are *so* shamefully twentieth century."

"Hey, we still have eight more days," Stacey says. "Then I'll wear more tank tops and rant on and on about Lillith Fair and make a point not to shave my armpits and buy that new Paula Cole album."

"Where *have* all the cowboys gone?" I ask and pass the joint to her. "Well, Sis, what can I do for you? This is fun, but I need to go and track down Lydia at some point before she starts telling the frat guys how she's never had anal."

"Are you going to see Mom tomorrow?" she asks.

"Maybe."

"You need to."

"Why?"

"You just do, Ross. It's important."

"Did she eat tonight?" I ask.

"Not really. Look, Dad said he called you and told you to be there by two. Just once, don't be a total jack-off and do something for someone else."

"Well what's going on?" I ask, trying to suppress the mounting rage towards this succubus standing before me.

"I'm not sure, honestly. But it's not good, I don't think. Mom's been upset lately."

"You mean more so than usual?"

"Um...yeah," she murmurs, finishing what has now become a tiny roach. "You just need to talk to her and find out what's going on. And Dad made me promise to ride your ass about it tonight. So here I am, riding your ass about it. This is cashed."

"I have more," Quentin immediately chimes in, saving the day.

"I'm not kidding. Almost every time The Scottish Play has been professionally performed, a fourth witch shows up in Act IV."

"Dude, I've heard about that," Quentin gasps. "And when my high school did it, this kid Bryce said *Macbeth* out loud, and after that, all kinds of creepy shit started happening. A light fell on the black kid who played Banquo, our drama teacher caught the flu, and we couldn't find the knife that Macbeth sees on his way to kill Duncan."

"Where did you hear all this, Cordelia?" I ask, trying to get comfortable on the hood of the Mustang, but instead being cold, high, and fidgety.

"My Late Shake professor told us."

"No *way*," I mutter, rolling my eyes. "So what's next for the girl with the Master's in Literature? Are you going to take that managerial position at Borders you always wanted?"

"No, I thought I would make copies of videos for the rest of my life, go to parties I'm too old to attend and attack whatever knowledge I actually gained when I was in school four years ago with a healthy regiment of moronic movies, keg beer, and pot."

"I'm pretty high," Stacey says on cue. "Cordelia, when I was in Hawaii for Fall Break I was on the Road to Hana and I thought of you for some reason. Do you know what the Road to Hana is?"

"Is it Christmas Eve yet?" someone asks, looking at their watch.

When I was sixteen and my little sister was fourteen and it was summer and excruciatingly hot and sweltering everywhere you went...there was no school and I spent most of my days sleeping until two in the afternoon before working every night on a story called "Stranger" about a young man who finds himself in a totally ransacked and deserted city combating monsters who look like people, not to mention the other last human survivors and a creature who hides in the shadows and calls himself Cameron...Cordelia awoke at nine as my mom left for work and wrote rhyming poetry for her first boyfriend, a kid who lived in the subdivision behind ours named Eliot Bremond and Eliot liked to skateboard and make movies with his dad's video camera...Cordelia sometimes wrote "I love Eliot" on both sides of college ruled notebook paper for hours and when she wasn't sneaking over to Eliot's house to make out, watch home movies, play Scrabble, eat microwave meals and drink Tab, Cordelia was reading Lord Byron and Doris Lessing and Margaret Atwood and Hemingway's shorter works...

I was sixteen and Cordelia didn't know I was sneaking out of the house twice weekly that summer to meet Jennifer Jennings at this church on Dwight...and Jennifer would use her mom's custodial keys to unlock the door to the youth group room where Jennifer met on Sunday and Wednesday evenings to sing and praise Jesus...then she would be naked and droopy and sweating above her lip as we tried to figure out how to take each other's virginities (but what you would find out a year later was that Jennifer Jennings was not a virgin at all, and had slept with someone else in that church on Dwight that same summer, a guy named *Dwight* of all things—you were always being tricked and laughed at behind your back) and be romantic and talk about moving to Australia together...Cordelia would sometimes be awake as I climbed back in through my window...I could always see the blue light streaming out from her bedroom, the flashes of a TV that she only watched as she fell asleep...but I didn't get caught, because if she had seen me, she would have told the parents—Cordelia was always like that and I'm not sure exactly why we never got along, but we didn't and then it was the nineties and I was finishing up high school and moving onto campus for college and Cordelia graduated higher in her class than me but it didn't matter because there was an orgy in one of the dorms and I started smoking Camel cigarettes and sympathizing with Communism outside of Cooper Hall with my philosophy friends, one of whom really liked horror movies and wore a shirt every Thursday with the cover of *I Eat Your Skin* on the front (Cordelia never liked horror movies, did she?)...

It's getting late and when I get back to the party, stoned, teary-eyed, alone, everything is turning blurry, lost in smoke. Inside, the cacophony is overwhelming and a vase lies in shards on the hardwood floor. Outside, far away, Stacey is on the dented hood of a '63 Mustang talking to Cordelia and her goon squad friends about the aesthetics of the ellipses in long fiction and I can not find Preston or Lydia or any of my other friends here, only strangers and people who I used to call my best friend on the beachfront or while drunk on someone's front porch, but who now I don't want to speak to at all.

"Have you been initiated?" some random guy asks me as I pour myself another beer, which is mostly foam in my plastic cup.

There are sex noises coming from all of the bedrooms I wander past, and I think of the possibilities before asking myself if it even matters.

It is not until I steal a copy of *100 Years of Solitude* from the bookcase in the den and wander back outside for the last time that I see everyone: Preston, Lydia, Stacey, Cordelia, Princess Star Bright even, all standing next to a Honda Civic drinking beer and smoking menthols.

"Ross, where have you been?" Preston shouts, grabbing me by the shoulder and reeling me into the circle. "I've been looking for you everywhere, man."

"I was telling Preston what happened earlier," Lydia says to me, her eyes lustrous in the glare of the floodlights.

"About what?" I ask, confused.

"About the old man who was coming towards the car, Holden. What else would I be telling him?"

"Oh," I say, nodding. "Did you tell them about the weird people filming it?"

"What?" she asks.

"Nothing."

"Cordelia and I have really been hitting it off," Stacey says without missing a beat, putting her arm around my sister. "Why didn't you ever tell me that Cordelia was so cool?"

"Yeah, Ross," Cordelia says, staring at me, seething. "Stacey is an absolute *gem*. Why didn't you tell me that not everyone you hang out with is as totally hopeless as you are?"

"I'm standing right here, you know," Preston points out.

"Be nice, Cordelia," Lydia giggles. "That's my boyfriend." She glances towards me with a smile as if these two sentences make up for whatever she has gotten away with in my absence.

"Where were you two?" I ask, pointing at Preston and Lydia.

"Right here at the party, man," Preston says. "Well, we walked out to my car to listen to CDs for a little bit, but we've been here most of the time. I burned an **End** of the World Tribute mix. You should hear it."

"I was with them," Princess Star Bright says. "I really like that Sunny Day song you put on there, Pres."

"Holden, don't forget I still want to see that movie tonight."

"So everyone is innocent after all," I say.

4

I SLIP THE TAPE INTO THE VCR and drink a glass of water in the early morning hours of Christmas Eve, 1999. The room is bathed in blue light. On screen, shots from a helicopter: a brown river, a lush green jungle, terrifying music playing over the proceedings.

Lydia sits next to me, wearing a pair of 3-D glasses that she found on the floor of my car. I have no idea where they came from, but Lydia wearing them is very unnerving for some reason.

In the recliner, Preston fidgets with a Magic 8 Ball while occasionally taking tokes from a thin joint in his hand.

We watch a native take several bullets to his face. We see a skull covered in maggots and disgust, young brown girls fascinated with a professor's penis, someone eating a human heart, bad things. I finish glass after glass of water from the kitchen sink, staring at the front door, which was unlocked when I got home. Preston glances toward me again and again. He murmurs something about the chances of Sam Raimi making another *Evil Dead* film extremely good, pointing to the Eight Ball. Lydia takes the glasses off but does not put them down.

I wish to myself that this was the fifties. We would be asleep by now and tomorrow would be Christmas.

Instead it's dark and Lydia's trying to figure out how to light a cigarette with a Citronella candle. We're watching a professor watching a native rape a woman with a phallic rock and some mud, and Preston points to the Eight Ball and whispers that something is definitely happening.

3

SHE REALLY IS NORMAL. It's just that the holidays have always upset her.

A couple of years ago, after hearing me casually mention that I hated cooking and ate fast food most every night, my mother bought me a George Foreman grill and I opened it on Christmas morning. When Cordelia mentioned how much she also wanted one of those for her dorm room, my mother excused herself and watched taped episodes of *Melrose Place* in the bedroom for over a week. During my senior year of high school when I was trying to decide on a college while writing my senior thesis on Hunter S. Thompson, someone I admired and hoped to emulate one day, there was a laptop computer wrapped up underneath the tree. I remember it was the ugliest tree my father had ever bought. It died a week before Christmas and shed needles by the hundreds. My mother broke down over this and stayed in the bedroom all night during our annual party. She was missed, and when my father mentioned this to her a week later, she locked herself in the bathroom and sat in a tub full of cold water for hours.

Her sadness culminates and almost spills over every winter until around the New Year, and then it slowly dissipates and she is back to her old self again by February. It has been this way for the past five years, at least. After her spell is over, my mother goes right back to normal and does not mention the events previous. When questioned on why she behaved as she did, she always replies that "something was just off" and the conversation is over.

She's never been to a doctor. My dad has not insisted upon it, either. He calls her depressions merely a product of Seasonal Affective Disorder, and ascertains that the symptoms will fade like clockwork every year around early January or so. I'm not sure how he knows this, since he's a director of programming at DigiCom and does not deal with very much abnormal psychology.

I pull up to my parents' two-story house outside of town on the lake. I park on the street and notice that they did not put up lights this year as I stop at the front door and try to decide whether to knock.

I knock, taking stock of myself. I look like shit. When I woke up this afternoon, I was hung over and Lydia was in the kitchen at the bar drinking strong French coffee while reading her horoscope in the paper. My back hurt and the sun came streaming through the windows, piercing holes in my brain. A shower didn't help, and when I came out of the bathroom and glanced through the blinds of my apartment, I saw a man in the parking lot down below speaking in codes into a walkie-talkie while looking up at my floor, at my apartment, at me staring at him through a window not nearly thick enough to keep what was happening all around me out.

My father answers the door and immediately looks me up and down. This afternoon, he is wearing a pair of khaki Dockers, a forest-green sweater and a pair of Oliver Peoples prescription glasses with tinted frames. His teeth are white but deceiving, and his hair is looking healthy, but also illusory. The strong scent of Drakkar Noir hangs in the cold air, stale and nauseating.

"So," my father begins, "hung over? Haven't showered in three days? What's the story? Why did you *knock*, son? Is your home *that* unfamiliar?"

"I'm just tired," I say. "I know I look like shit. I didn't want to come at a bad time, so I rushed right over here."

"But you did," he says. "You *did* come at a bad time. You came at almost four in the afternoon. What the hell happened to you being here at two? Didn't Cordelia talk to you at that party last night?"

"She did," I tell him, walking into the house, straight through the living room and into a newly remodeled kitchen where I open a stainless steel fridge and pull out a bottle of Aquafina.

"You're hung over," my father declares behind me.

"Yes, Richard, a little."

"Well, get your act together. Take off your sunglasses; you're inside the house. Your mother is in the den."

"Doing what?" I ask, taking huge gulps of water.

"Watching home movies," he sighs.

"Terrific," I say, finishing the water and throwing the bottle into one of the three recycling containers in the garage. I come back inside the house, where my dad is sitting at the bar drinking a mug full of potent egg-nog. "So Dad, what do you want me to do?"

"I don't know, Ross. She already told me that she didn't want to have the party this year, but I told her that it was too late and everyone was already coming. I don't know what the hell to do with her. This is ridiculous, though."

"Poor Mom," I mutter to myself.

"Poor *Mom*?" my father repeats, shaking his head. "You mean poor *Dad*. I've had to do everything for this party tonight. I've been at it since six this morning. Your mother wouldn't even get her act together and make a batch of Divinity for tonight. I ended up ordering all the pies and hors d'oerves. I hope she's happy."

"Well why was it so important for me to show up?" I ask. "She's like this every year. Usually all I **end** up doing is making her worse."

"Because she asked for you. Right after she started watching the videos yesterday immediately after Cordelia's graduation. You need to talk to her, though, son. She won't even let me in the room without breaking into hysterics. She started crying not long after your sister's luncheon and told me that she wanted to speak to you as soon as possible. When we got home she planted herself in the recliner in the den and started watching, I think, every god damned home movie we ever shot."

"This is weird."

"Tell me about it. Well, if she wants to sit in there all day long and act stupid, that's fine. I just don't want her stumbling out here tonight in front of your aunts and the Clarks from across the street and going *Exorcist* on me. I have a lot going on right now."

"Of course you do, Dad," I sigh, a terribly unoriginal gesture. "You don't want your crazy wife embarrassing you in front of the Clarks. God, you are such an asshole, aren't you?"

"Watch it," he snaps. "Watch it, Ross."

"Or what, Richard?" I ask, glaring at him.

He does not take his eyes off of mine, and his hand is gripping the mug so tightly that I brace myself and wait for it to shatter. After a long moment, he seems to realize something. His lips curl up and what I think is the beginnings of a smile crease his face.

"Just go and talk to her and then get the hell out of my house," he says through gritted teeth. "Take her and Cordelia with you, for all I care. I'm tired of all three of you and decisions have been made."

She's thin. I couldn't tell yesterday at the graduation, but now, planted tautly on Dad's brown leather recliner wearing a t-shirt with a cat on it and gray sweat pants, I can see how much weight she has lost. Her wrists are like twigs, the gold bracelets my father bought for her in Christmases past hanging limply on each wrist. The shirt that Cordelia bought for her birthday four years ago is like a huge queenly shroud.

All around my mother are used Kleenex and open tins of photos from many years back. In front of the television are dozens of disorganized HG tapes, the small rectangular ones that fit inside a VCR adaptor. There are enough of them to document our entire lives.

I look in fear at my mother. Her neck is inflamed and covered in tiny scratch marks. Her face is tear-streaked and swollen. Her eyes are glassy and focused on the 52-inch screen on the other side of the room. I glance at the television. Cordelia is six or so and splashing saltwater up into the air on a beach in St. Augustine. She laughs in silence; the sound has been muted.

My mother smiles weakly at the image, then looks up at me standing over her.

"Merry Christmas, Mom," I say.

"Merry Christmas, baby."

"So I just came by to see you and Dad. I wanted to see you before the party tonight."

"The party…" She looks down, confused.

"Yeah, the party. The one here? Tonight?"

"Oh," she finally murmurs quietly to herself. "Yes. The party. I don't think I want to do all that this year."

"Well, I think it's too late, Mom." A pause. "May I sit down?"

"Yes," she says, picking up the VCR remote and pausing the image, which is now of my father in Polo shorts and a pink golf shirt cooking swordfish on a grill in front of the beach house. "I'm glad you came, Ross. I really need to talk to you."

"Yeah, that's what I heard," I say, sitting down on the love seat across from her. "What's going on, Mom? Are you okay?"

She does not say anything; instead, she focuses on the image on the TV of my father grilling fish in the sun.

"Mom? Mom."

She comes to, looks back at me. Her eyes well up with tears.

"Ross, I have to show you something," she whispers. "Where is your father?"

"I don't know—he was—I think he's in the kitchen or maybe in the living room."

"He can't hear this," she whispers furiously. "I think that he's a part of it, maybe."

"Mom, I—"

"I've suspected it for years. I always thought it was just during the winter, but now—oh my god—"

She begins sobbing quietly to herself. I rub my hand on her back, trying to calm her down. My father peers around the doorway, and I silently wave him away before giving him the finger. Several minutes later, my mother coughs, takes several deep breaths, and looks up at me with an intensity that sends me into a cold sweat.

"Watch this tape and tell me what's wrong with it," she says, rewinding the home video back to the opening image of a sunset casting our beach into shadows.

I am watching the tape, my head starting to throb again, dying for a cigarette or at the very least another bottle of water. On the television screen, the camera pans right and we see a spacious balcony and then a pair of open sliding glass doors. The camera moves forward into a messy condominium, where I see my mother, much more youthful and ginger-haired, holding a sullen Cordelia. Cordelia pouts in silence, yawns, and rests her head on my mother's shoulder. My mother smiles at the camera and her eyes point down at her daughter, who I now realize has always been a cunt.

"I liked your hair that color," I say.

"*Shh*," my mother whispers harshly. "Just keep watching."

The screen goes black, then blue, and then I am seeing an image of a windy day on the shores of St. Augustine. Fifty yards away is a boy with the beginnings of sunburn fumbling with a mask and snorkel before plodding out into the surf. I remember how red I was by the time that week was up.

"That was you," my mother says, fast-forwarding the tape through an extended scene of me gadding about in the waves before disappearing underwater.

We pan left, and for a moment there is the long shadow of the cameraman in the sand. My mom noticeably shudders. Then we see a hazy figure far down the beach, towards the lighthouse. My father. He and my mother were fighting. I remember that they were, but cannot recall what it was over. It was almost twenty years ago.

"Your father was down the beach," she says, animated now as she fast-forwards to Cordelia purposelessly digging up sand from underneath a big craggy rock on the shore. "Do you see Cordelia? Do you *see* her, Ross?"

"Yeah, Mom, what's the—"

"Watch what happens next."

The camera stays trained on Cordelia as she uses her green plastic shovel to kick up a wad of sand into her face. She glances up at the condominium and tears up, on the verge of childish panic, rubbing furiously at her eyes—

"*Here!* Here it is," my mother hisses.

On the home movie, Cordelia is bawling. She is blinded and twists in clumsy circles for help. On cue, my mother walks into frame wearing Capri pants and a sleeveless blue Polo shirt. She picks her daughter up and begins to gently wipe the sand from her face. They move off-screen just as everything turns to static.

My mother stops the tape, waiting.

"You were always really nice to Cordelia," I say, confused and obviously not picking up on whatever it is my mother has lost her good sense over. "Um, what time do you want me here tomorrow—"

"Don't you *understand*, Ross?"

"Understand? Understand what, Mom?"

"Don't you realize what you were seeing?"

"Yeah," I say, nodding. "It was our trip to St. Augustine. I think I was eight, so Cordelia was like five or six, right? We took a ghost tour of the town and I started crying when they told the story about Osceola in the fort. Why have you been watching all these tapes, Mom? Is it nostalgia or are you going through one of your—?"

"Shut up, Ross."

"Okay."

"I just want to know one thing, all right, son?"

"All right, Mom. What?"

"Who filmed this tape, Ross?"

I am eight years old and running furiously to where the waves break. I see a sting ray cruising through the surf, though, and slow down. I stop and fool with my mask and snorkel, which I bought at Kash & Karry the day before when the parents were buying groceries. The sun is out and I forgot to put on lotion, but I am not worried. I look back to the beach. I wave to the man videotaping me just before I cautiously make my way out into the water, which is cold around my ankles.

The man who was videotaping me. The man who documented our vacation. His shadow on the sand. The man I waved to. He existed.

I don't know what's happening.

Meanwhile, my mother ejects the adaptor, opens it, and flings our beach trip tape across the den before quickly snatching up another one. After she slips another video in, there is a pause, a blue screen, and then I see my mother associating with friends, with her husband, who she kisses on the lips, and then it cuts to everyone singing her "Happy Birthday" on mute. My mother blows out a thick arrangement of candles on a chocolate birthday cake and everyone claps in silence, including Cordelia, who was fourteen or so at the time. I am not present, since I was at Preston's that day playing *Legend of Zelda*, lost in the gray cemetery trying to find a magic sword.

"Who was filming *that*, Ross?" she asks me just before ejecting the tape and putting another in.

Play. Cordelia and I swim around in a clear spring somewhere just north of Ocala. This was during our trip to Dublin, Georgia to see Grandma when I was thirteen. I watch my mother and father smile at us from the shore just before they smile at the camera. All in silence.

The Orringer family in rerun. The Orringer family as silent reality show.

"I remember *all* of this," my mother says at one point. "I remember Ocala and I remember my thirty-ninth birthday. I remember when Cordelia started crying about a bunch of sand in her eye when she was six. But no one filmed it. I don't remember anyone being there. And yet there we are waving into the lens. There we are smiling and nodding hello to whomever that is taping it. But it wasn't one of us, Ross. *It wasn't one of us.*"

"A family friend? One of Dad's coworkers?"

She shakes her head furiously, pauses, considers something, and then says quietly, "Not any coworkers that should have been there."

A trip to Yellowstone. A normal weekend afternoon when Cordelia and I rode our bikes up and down the street. Hot dogs and hamburgers when we went camping near Silver Springs. All filmed, usually by my father or mother. But sometimes...

"But sometimes it's being filmed and it's not one of us filming it," my mother is saying. "Usually, almost always, it's your father and I, and I can remember that. I remember your father filming the three of us at the Fourth of July party at your Aunt Melanie's. I remember me being the one to have to do it when your father jumped off that bridge into the river in Tennessee when he was trying to impress those teenagers. But I don't know where some of these other scenes come from."

I look at the TV screen. The four of us take turns opening Christmas gifts, three years ago. I bought my father *The James Bond Collection* that year. The four of us are on screen and the camera pans back and forth between us as we unwrap gift after gift during a particularly shaky winter (the parents' discovery of an abortion Cordelia had performed a year previous, Mom's Seasonal Affective Whatever, Dad's suspicious liaisons in Tampa with a woman from his company, my inexplicable and not yet altogether cured bout of total hatred towards all three of them).

"How did you figure this out?" I ask my mother, who is on the hardwood floor rummaging through a stack of tapes.

"I can't talk about it right now," she says, not looking up at me. Then suddenly, she lunges up holding another small cassette and whispers in my ear, "Don't trust him. Don't trust your father. I have something to show you. But not now. Take it home with you. And you'll see. He's not him."

"What?" I whisper back, shaking.

"We aren't ourselves, either."

My father follows me through the house. I grab another bottle of Aquafina from the fridge and make my way towards the front door.

"So what time are you going to be here tomorrow morning?" he asks.

"By eleven? Is that okay?"

"That's fine," he nods. He rests his hand on my shoulder. "So what's going on with your mother? Do I need to call Charter?"

"No," I say, a sideways glance as I open the door to leave. "It's just her winter depression or whatever. I guess she just wanted to be around me. She's been watching all the family trips and everything and I guess she just got nostalgic."

"Is she okay now?" he asks in a low tone. "I mean, I don't need to cancel the party, do I?"

I turn to face him, my father, a man who I once quietly despised and ignored but who I am now suddenly terrified of. I step outside onto the patio. He looms over me in the doorway.

"She should be fine. The party will be fine. Merry Christmas, Dad. I'll see you tomorrow morning."

"Yeah. Lydia still coming?"

"Ostensibly."

"Are you going to her thing tonight?"

"Yeah," I say, glancing up the street. A blue BMW turns into a driveway six houses down. It rolls into a garage. "Her family does their gifts on Christmas Eve."

"Look," he begins, looking down. I notice that I am shaking. "I'm sorry that I got all pissed off at you when you first got here. It wasn't right. And I'm glad your mother is okay. Son?"

"Fine. It's fine."

"I'm sorry."

"It's all right, Dad. I'll see you tomorrow. Merry Christmas."

As I open my car door and reach into my jacket pocket to finger the tape my mother slipped me back in the den, a white van pulls up in the driveway.

I am turgid with fear.

The side door opens. A man with black pants and a white jacket climbs out of the van. There is a detailed nautical star tattoo on his neck. He gives me an icy stare. I stare back, unable to move, unable to speak, unable to comprehend the temperature that is dropping all around us.

"This is the Orringer residence, right?" he finally asks me.

"Yes," I say, nodding dumbly.

"Okay, good," he says, reaching back into the van and pulling out a plastic bag full of whole pies.

I sigh, a terribly unoriginal gesture, and climb into my car. The delivery man knocks on the door and my father answers it, then fingers through his money clip. It occurs to me that my mother and I are both losing our minds, a *folie à deux* of sorts, until I see the glare radiating from him in my direction, and the look of recognition and familiarity between him and my father. Dad eyes me nervously and the delivery man speaks into his jacket lapel as I drive away, and then I think someone in an Escape follows me to Lydia's but I'm not sure.

2

A FAMILY POSES IN FRONT OF A FOUNTAIN. What was once a passerby with no significance to the family now asks which button to press. A moment later, what was once a passerby awkwardly asks everyone to smile, and snaps a picture of a family posing together in front of a fountain. The camera is returned, gratitude is expressed, and the family moves on. The photographer returns to his original role of passerby and disappears from the family's life.

The passerby may never be seen again, but he has captured not only a mother, a father, and a number of variously aged children in his work of art, but a glimpse of the entire world around them in that one moment. There is the teenager's back as he sat on a bench on the other side of that fountain counting cigarettes; a man with a beard hurrying down the steps of a random building in the background; the blue high heel and attached right leg of a lady walking towards an office up the street.

It never stops. Everyone is being watched.

How many backgrounds do I help compose? How many times has my arm, my foot, the edge of my head, become entangled in the drama of a stranger's photo album? How many times was I pondered over, forgotten, ignored, either despite or because of someone else's moment? When was the last time I was filmed and not even aware of it?

Sweat pours down my forehead, drips from my armpits, and collects on my neck and sides. Everything feels hot-cold as I drive Lydia towards her parents' home for Christmas. I light cigarettes and take constant short drags until they are gone. Lydia asks me what is going on, tries to mention the party last night, the cannibal movie, zombies, anything to rouse my attention, but her sound is turned off like a home movie that shouldn't exist.

Rum cake, fruit cake, chocolate-covered pretzels, chips and dip, celery sticks, cups full of soda or egg-nog or tea, matchboxes from Lydia's uncle's car detailing business. I take each, try to nod, offer a ghastly smile, make comments, gesture, wave stupidly, shake hands, and then wipe my hand off on my jeans after every exchange. Lydia's mother gives me a hug and offers a Merry Christmas three times before Lydia's father comes along and explains that she has had too much egg-nog and should eat something. Lydia shrugs when I look at her in disgust.

Our first Christmas together, Lydia and I spent the twenty-fourth with her small family and their close circle of friends. I was handed a gift certificate to Barnes & Noble by her drunken mother and disappointed father and later Lydia and I had sex in the laundry room while her uncle read from Matthew and then Luke in the living room to all the guests.

The next morning, she accompanied me to my parents' house, where my teary-eyed mother and grumbling father presented her with a gift basket from Bath and Body Works and a set of pajamas covered in moons and stars and little boys riding the moons and stars. She watched Cordelia and I exchange terrible comments before looking down at the floor while Cordelia and my father swapped sentiments of mutual loathing and denouncements just before Cordelia gathered her gifts and peeled out of the driveway.

Around nine-thirty or so, Lydia whispers in my ear that perhaps we should sneak off to the laundry room or maybe even her old bedroom before her uncle can break out the Bible and talk about frankincense and myrrh. I am terrified of the tiny square window in the laundry room that looks out on a foreboding backyard and on into nothingness, but I follow her anyway and she is on top of the dryer humping at my jeans and kissing my face while trying to hike up her long maroon skirt. My pants are unbuckled and pushed down around my ankles, and Lydia frees my cock from the red and green boxers I am wearing and tries to jam it inside her, but I have to finger her first and every time I glance beyond her shoulder out the window, where there are old men and latex gloves and shadowy pony-tailed women filming my father making deals with the devil, I begin to lose it. I fuck her though, and afterward, Lydia adjusts her skirt and opens the dryer and peers inside for what seems like no reason at all before leading me back into the house, where her father eyes me contemptuously and where her born-again Christian uncle is asking the three children under ten if they know what a manger is. I finger the unwatched tape my mother gave me that is burning a hole in my pocket, realizing this third Christmas that Lydia and I have spent together will probably be our last.

"This is our second Christmas together," she said to me in bed on our second Christmas Eve together. I was twenty-five and in a month would turn twenty-six and find out that Lydia's father did not want me back at his house for a while. "I'm happy."

"I am too," I said, looking over her naked body to the night stand and pack of cigarettes next to her.

"Do you think Cordelia will like that Bush CD I got her?"

"I'm sure she will. She has *Sixteen Stone*."

"I hope she does. I hope she likes it more than that Ani DiFranco album I bought her last year. She's an English major. I thought she would love it."

"I wouldn't worry about Cordelia too much," I assured her. "Cordelia is a useless smudge of banality seething with an unpredictable series of meaningless actions and whorish affairs."

"Why does your family fight so much all the time?" she asked me finally, lighting a cigarette. "Especially you and your sister."

"Why *doesn't* yours?" I asked back.

She didn't answer and rolled on top of me again. I stared at the tattoo of a cherry with a small bite taken from it on her hip. She got it before we met.

After the sex, she asked, "What did you get Preston this year for Christmas?"

"A *Re-Animator* poster."

"What is *Re-Animator*?"

"Just some zombie movie. I can't believe *this* is Christmas."

On the way home from this year's Lawton Christmas Eve party, I am drinking a can of Pepsi while visualizing a red wall; a lit white candle in a house full of pentacles; eyes staring at me from beneath the ice of a frozen lake; aromatic red wine sauce boiling in a dingy kitchen in a random trailer somewhere; the first zombie in *Night of the Living Dead;* teenagers dancing in a café in 1959 while someone drums maniacally on a bongo; warning labels on big canisters of cleaning products; a traffic light with legs running amok; the

end of the world. I finger the $50 gift card to Best Buy and try to smile at Lydia when she smiles at me, but it's late and there's not much time and the computers are going to turn on us in six days and I will turn twenty-seven nine days after that, but it doesn't matter because I have a tape to watch and the drops of rain that have begun cascading down around my car look threatening. My father is the fountain in the photo and we are not who we are.

A fountain in a photo.

The **end** of the world.

A fountain in a photo.

The **end** of

1

On Christmas morning, the first thing I hear when I enter my parents' house twenty-seven minutes late, is Cordelia explaining to my Aunt Melanie, "To me, self expression is not an outward gesture, but merely a reflection of the inner things we can no longer keep secret. That's why I want to write a book about my life."

Aunt Melanie nods thoughtfully and sips from a cup of coffee as Lydia and I enter the threshold. Cordelia immediately glances down at her watch as I stumble into the living room with a large shopping bag full of badly wrapped gifts.

"Merry Christmas," I tell everyone, immediately mouthing "Fuck you" to my sister. Hugs are exchanged, followed by the standard holiday catch-up queries.

Cordelia smirks when my Dad, who is wearing a terrible green sweater that he was probably given at the party last night, asks what took us so long. Then he offers coffee and orange juice, which I refuse. Lydia asks for some water, leaving with him as I scan the room for my mother. My father eyes me for what seems too long a time while handing Lydia a bottle of water. Then he hugs her and wishes a Merry Christmas into her ear while glancing in my direction. I shiver, disgusted and afraid.

The remnants of the party are all around us: bits of wrapping paper at the corners of the room and wedged halfway under the sofas, tinsel hanging limply from the banisters, the kitchen counter covered in half-eaten pies, dishes of chocolate and peanut brittle, and my father, not hung over enough, staring at me gravely while hugging Lydia, his "future daughter-in-law," yet again.

My mother is not in the living room.

"Where's Mom?" I ask casually, settling down on the couch and smiling at my aunt, who has already begun organizing the pile of gifts she brought last night.

"Right here, honey," my mother says, entering the room from the hall wearing a festive sweater and new blue jeans.

"Oh," I stammer, actually surprised to see her. "Hey, Mom. Merry Christmas."

We embrace. She smells like cigarettes and White Diamonds, which is odd since she doesn't smoke and claims that she sneezes incessantly around perfume. Aunt Melanie pats her sister's hand and sits down on the couch next to her. She asks me how business is going.

"All right guys, are you ready to get on with it?" Dad asks, hunching down over the tree and handing us all our first gifts to open.

Cold winds sweep through the room when he glances over at me. When he delegates a gift to unwrap, his hand lingers on the paper too long, and he is hesitant to speak to me, to play the role of a young man's father on Christmas. But he does. He arouses excitement from the family, who smile and make friendly jokes and roll their eyes and poke fun and drink coffee—even my mother, who is doing quite well at disguising the fear and mania she was surging with less than twenty-four hours ago.

I am not doing as well. My flesh ripples over the surging blood in my body; sweat beads on my neck; I smile when I hold up a pair of board shorts from Old Navy that Aunt Melanie bought me, but inside I am wondering if I have ever been afraid on Christmas before now.

When I look to my mother for something—a tiny nod, widened eyes, a whisper—anything to assure me that things will be okay and that I am not alone, nothing ever comes. She laughs at his jokes, questions Lydia about whether the pajama bottoms they bought her will fit, nibbles on just-opened Godiva chocolate that Cordelia gave her, and when I unwrap the copy of *The Nitpicker's Guide for X-Philes*, asks if she bought the right book.

She should be alone in a bedroom. She should be crying in a bathtub or whispering paranoid rhetoric into my ear every time the man posing as my father leaves the room. Instead she giggles when Cordelia regales Aunt Melanie and Lydia with some story about a Christmas several years ago, a story that never happened and **end**s with Dad covered in pancake syrup.

Four movies, two CDs (I will return the one Aunt Melanie bought me), a new watch, five shirts, boxers, two pairs of pants and new shorts, a calendar with paintings by Pollock, a video game that I won't play, a photo program I needed for business, a *Creature Features* film and video guide, another year's subscription to *Bizarre Magazine*, and three books, one being *The Bell Jar* from Cordelia, a book she assures me I will be able to relate to. I tell her that if she wants to return the brief case I purchased her for something she will actually use, then I kept the receipt and she can exchange it for toilet paper, aromatic candles, and nail polish the color of cockroaches.

Lydia re-reads the Christmas poem she presented me last night to my mother, who exalts its greatness immediately afterward. I grinned and began to tear up last night when she read it, but it is actually quite wretched. It rhymes, too.

The sweats begin again and I get away from my father, who is on the love seat playing with a new digital camera my mother got him, by going into the kitchen and reading the tabloids while eating celery. A headline on the second page points out that this is the last Christmas of the earthbound twentieth century. Next year we will be celebrating on Mars.

"Dear Lord, we thank you for all that you have given us, and on this day we gather to be with one another and to pledge our devotion to you. Please bless this food and this family, and grace them with your presence in the days ahead. In God's name we pray. Amen."

"Amen," everyone repeats.

"Amen," I whisper again, keeping my eyes clenched shut.

Ham and mashed potatoes and green beans and sweet potato casserole is passed around. Tea, water and wine are poured. Talk revolves around how good the ham is at Piccadilly, the so-so pies Dad ordered from a trendy bakery for the party, the resounding success of the party, Cordelia's new diet involving someone named Atkins, Lydia's cousin who broke her arm while jumping on a trampoline, whether we have anything to worry about in a few days. In response to the latter topic, there is a resounding no while I excuse myself and hide in the bathroom.

When I come back, Cordelia has her chin resting on her hand while speaking sweetly to Lydia.

"So you wrote it for Ross?" she is asking. "Wow. It was really, really good, Lydia. Really."

Lydia, whose back is turned to me, nods and thanks Cordelia for the compliment. Cordelia waits until the conversation has died before making eye contact with me, squinting, and mouthing "What a joke." I nod, unable to defend what Lydia wrote.

"So, son, any big plans for New Year's?" my father asks me.

"I think Pres is throwing a party of some kind," I mention cautiously, vaguely remembering a conversation I had with him a few days ago which I am certain he has totally forgotten about by now.

"I know," my father mutters, hiding a smile and looking down at his lap.

"What?" I say to him.

"Really?" Lydia asks me, surprised. "Preston is?"

"Really," I say.

"How *is* Preston these days?" my aunt asks. "Does he still have that house his parents left him?"

"Yes, ma'am, he does," I tell her. "Dad, what did you say?"

"It's the only house in that part of town, actually," my father points out oddly, ignoring my question. "Isn't that right, son?"

"I think so. It's older than the stuff they built up around it, and Preston never complains about any neighbors."

"Brad wants to go to Wauchula for New Year's," Cordelia mentions.

"What?" Lydia and my aunt ask in unison.

"He's a ghost nut, and he says there's an old house in Wauchula that caught on fire during New Year's Eve a long time ago and the people partying inside were killed. Now the ghosts supposedly come every December 31."

"So you're going to drive all the way to Wauchula to see this?" my father asks incredulously.

"I guess so," she sighs. "I don't even know where it is."

"It's in Polk County."

"Hardee," I interject, making eye contact with my father.

He misses a beat before adding, "Well, it's *near* Polk County. Near Fort Myers."

"So I guess you'll have to miss the party then," I say casually to Cordelia, finishing my glass of water.

"No, we'll just be a little late. Preston already insisted that I go the other night at Shannon's. So I promised him we'd stop by."

"Great," I say through gritted teeth.

My mother is in the kitchen retrieving an apple pie from the fridge when I approach her. The rest of the group is in the living room telling stories and congratulating one another on how well they did in gift-selecting this year.

"Mom," I whisper, standing over her as she rummages through a drawer for a pie cutter.

"Yes, honey?" she says in her normal speaking voice.

"Mom—is everything okay?"

"It's fine, honey. Why?"

"I don't know," I whisper. "I haven't watched the tape yet, but I've been really cautious and tried to act natural."

"Oh, you don't have to watch that, Ross. I was just flipping out yesterday. That tape is nothing special. Don't worry about it. In fact, it would almost be a waste of time to even watch it, don't you think?"

"No I don't think."

"Okay then, honey. Whatever you want to do."

She smiles.

"Well I'm glad you're feeling better today," I tell her, confused. "You're acting very natural around him. I'm impressed."

"Ross," she says, cutting the pie. "Your father is fine. I am too, now. I'm sorry I freaked you out yesterday, but I think we both need to come off it. Okay?"

"What?" I stammer, raising my voice now. "Mom, what are you saying to me? That you figured out who filmed all that stuff in there? Is that it?"

"Ross, nothing is happening. Everything is fine. There is nothing to worry about. Not anymore. Okay, son? Do you understand me?"

"Whatever," I sigh, a terribly unoriginal gesture.

I storm out of the kitchen back into the living room, where my father is pretending to be grinning at something Cordelia is saying.

After dessert Lydia and I pack up and head out to the car. Pulling out of the driveway and down the street, I vow not to return as Cordelia passes us in her Tiburon, her middle finger barely visible through the tinted windows.

0

In the days leading up to this millennium's last stand, the paranoia becomes rampant and all-encompassing. I bury myself in work to avoid the "neighbors" across the parking lot with the telescope and azaleas, and the men who never stop taking pictures via telephoto lens from a McDonald's two hundred yards away or recording everything I say with a microphone dangling inconspicuously as a loose cable wire from the roof of my apartment building.

At work, freshly dubbed schlock pictures are sent out by the dozen. Christmas money is collected from the college kids with a predilection towards bondage, cannibal corpses, and machetes. Herschel Gordon Lewis and Ray Dennis Steckler become household names. I cut and slip covers into boxes. Preston refuses to take any of his movies home once we are finished dubbing them ("We're just going to need them again anyway," he explains each time I create a fuss). *Cannibal Holocaust* causes a few more stoned youths out there to deny the existence of a higher power.

Everything in the apartment is bugged, as far as I am concerned, and the computer is watching me, taking notes.

I go on a date with Lydia. We see *Magnolia*, eat fudge brownies in the Starbucks café at Barnes & Noble, and I read an article in a magazine about thousands of animals across the globe acting very strangely as the New Year approaches. Afterward I take Lydia back to her place, have sex with her on the couch, and drive away into the night.

Stacey meets me on a bridge overlooking the river that same evening, and as we walk she tells me that she enjoys the cold, and that there is no such thing as global warming any more. She points to what she proclaims is a ghost down on the waterfront, but what looks to me more like a transparent tree branch with arms reaching out at me. It seems like she wants to tell me something, mentions the future a lot, but almost stops short and I do not pursue the matter further. I take her back to my place, where she stays the night and slips on one of the old Polo shirts I used to wear to work, the ones with the outline of the hotel logo on the breast. When I come inside her, I realize that it is the first time I have slept with both Stacey and Lydia in the same day, and something inside me is whittled down to nothingness.

With Stacey asleep in the other room, I go into the kitchen to pour another glass of water, my fourth since I returned home. I glance into my still-lit fish tank, where a yellow cichlid eyes me menacingly. It is December 29, around two in the morning, and I have mustered up the courage to watch the tape my mother handed me.

I put it in the adaptor and slip it in the VCR.

There is a blue screen, the word PLAY at the top right hand corner, and then *I* appear, twenty-one years old, behind a wall of glass in a scummy hotel.

I put my hand to my mouth, wondering if I will scream.

The sound is missing, but in the tape I am leaning back in an uncomfortable chair munching on a Baby Ruth while reading *To Kill a Mockingbird.* Behind me, a wall clock reads 9:14, and I actually remember the night quite well.

The man behind me confers with Martin, who is shakily bringing a cigarette to his lips.

"Look, Martin," he says. "It's clear—to *me*, anyway—that they were watching this kid from the very beginning. We need to find out what he knows."

"It doesn't matter how long they were watching him," the one in front of me argues. "We have him now. We know who was in on it. We have enough. Let's just see how much they actually documented. Let's find out what happened, how this kid and the other survivors managed to walk away from it. We don't need the *genesis* of any of this; we need answers. We need solutions."

"And you think *what*, Martin? That this *pawn* is going to have the vaccine on him? That he's going to know the identity of any of the cameramen? Wake up. This kid was the pilot episode. Nothing more. We're wasting our time trying to find secrets and survival strategies. The *only* reason he survived is that they wanted him to. Face it: our only hope is in finding out as much as we can about the reasons behind all of this. If we can understand how and why it happened, then maybe we can ascertain how we **end**ed up in this deep shit we are in now."

"This is a waste of *time*," Martin roars, spittle landing on the table and my wrist.

I wipe my hand off on my pant leg and notice the rusty brown blood stains on the fabric before lighting a cigarette, waiting.

After some time, Martin stubs his cigarette out and the man behind me says, softly, "Okay, Ross, tell us about the night at the hotel."

All I could think was that, in forty-five minutes, I would be off and it would be someone else's problem.

I re-read the word "Atticus" fourteen times, trying to concentrate, but I couldn't. The bum outside was just too nerve-racking. He appeared at first to be drunk, but his movements were not erratic; instead of randomly bursting with rage or clumsy energy, he shuffled to and fro from one **end** of the parking lot to the other, over and over and over again. At one point, he grabbed for a gray cat that scuttled by, but it escaped from his grip and disappeared behind a shrub. In the hotel office, I put the novel down and picked up my notes for a paper on the Shakers that I was writing for my Utopia course. I stared at the paper, reading each word carefully. But I couldn't focus; he was still out there.

The man first appeared around a quarter after nine. He stumbled into view from a random apartment complex behind the hotel and slouched towards me at a gait of about ten feet a minute. As he got closer, I could discern his features. The man was wearing a black sweat shirt covered with something wet and shiny, but I couldn't tell what. Maybe it was spilled beer that had run down his chin; his face was slathered in drool. He was young, though, not the typically middle-aged toothless bum I often gave loose change or cigarettes to in passing.

I thought he might actually want a room in the hotel, and prepared for the ordeal by grabbing the key to the room farthest from the office and laying it on the desk. This guy scared me and I didn't want to deal with him.

The man was only a few feet away from the bulletproof glass when he suddenly stopped, as if something forced him to. Then he turned away and began hobbling back towards the large, mostly empty parking lot.

I watched him move around on the asphalt for over an hour before considering calling the police. Then, just before eleven, there were several flashes and a helicopter flew overhead, and the man walked slowly back into the apartment complex from which he originally appeared. A black guy named Bruce clocked in at eleven and relieved me. I didn't tell him about the man, even when he asked me why I had the key to Room 237 on the desk.

The Shaker paper **end**ed up getting a B+, but I never did finish *To Kill a Mockingbird.*

From a Suicide Note I Wrote for the World:

As the century draws to a close, there is no turmoil, no fuel, no rage, to propel us into the next millennium. We are left with no new accomplishments, and nothing to develop in the future but DVD players that fit snugly inside our TVs.

We aren't dying like we used to. We have no violent revolution, no war to send our men off to in droves. Now, instead of dying in glory, we simply sit in our recliners wishing we were dead.

There are no symphonies to indulge on as if they were a delicate aged wine, no great artists to admire and mull over in a quiet museum. The nation is not divided on issues covered in Time or 60 Minutes; it is subdued on Friends and prescription drugs. Books are left screaming in the libraries and bookstores, overlooked in favor of latte in the attached coffee shop.

Cancer or a broken hip are the only answers to a generation of elderly people rotting away in a nursing home, brimming with wisdom that will never be inherited by grandchildren who would rather watch TRL and discuss the genius of Eminem.

In the end, it's all just blah. Everything is so passé: homelessness, Communism, mocumentaries, hunger, breast cancer, AIDS, rollerblades, grunge, genocide in Africa, Star Wars, the plight of Jews, rock music, tongue-in-cheek teen slasher films, illegal drugs, exercise, violence in the media, education, culture, technology, manners, self-expression, The South, controversy, history, even the present — it's all just a drag getting in the way of a huge celebration none of us should be having.

It just seems that the only relevant topic left in these final days is the future, but what future will that be in a world without a past, totally ignorant even of the terror of the present?

On screen, I chuckle at something in the book before glancing to my left, out into the city at night. My eyes widen before squinting at what is approaching. The camera zooms out, and I can see that the cameraman is standing under the canopy of a bus stop about fifty yards away. To the extreme right of the frame is the debilitated man making his way slowly toward me in the hotel office. The camera pans right, and then in on him, into a close head shot that makes me squirm.

This was filmed with my father's video camera, over five years ago. Whatever it is happening has been not just for quite some time, but to me in particular.

Suddenly, the camera rushes in a blur back to the left, where it zooms out and I struggle to figure out what I am seeing.

Steps. A railing slanted upward into some kind of cabin—

A bus has stopped in front of the cameraman, who was filming all of this from a bus stop. It would almost be comical, if not for the dark pretense of doom hanging over all of the proceedings.

Camera pointed slightly upward, a bushy gray-haired bus driver says something on Mute. He is probably asking if the man with the camera is taking the bus or not. The driver waits. He says something else, all in silence. He curses, shutting the door.

Then it happens.

In the two seconds before the bus pulls away, I spot it, rewinding and hitting the Pause button. I stare at the image, tears welling up at the base of my eyes.

He's not him.

On screen, caught on tape, is the image of my father.

His reflection was caught on the door of the bus standing next to a strange man, lanky with black hair, who never stopped filming.

I play the footage again, rewind back to the moment when the bus pulls away, and view the footage two, three, seven more times. My stomach curls over and the room feels as if it is collapsing.

My father, his head turned slightly to the right, muttering something to the guy shooting a twenty-one year-old college student and a slobbering dolt with an outdated video camera.

I watch it repeatedly, whispering to myself, making connections, stifling the screams, until Stacey wakes up and asks me from my doorway what I am doing. We go to bed, where Stacey promptly falls asleep again.

I lie awake as everything outside this room falls apart.

"This goes back too far," Martin immediately laments. "How are we going to stop what's happening from this prison?"

"I don't know," the man behind me, the man I am not allowed to see, says while inhaling on his cigarette. "I really don't know."

"Ross," Martin begins in a low tone.

"Yeah?"

There is silence. He says nothing.

"*Yes?*" I repeat.

Martin says nothing.

"I have a question, Ross," the man behind me says.

"Fire away," I mutter.

"With all that is going on around us now, with everything in whatever new perspective you have assigned it, I continue to wonder about something..."

"Go ahead," I tell him.

"Ross, what was your reaction to the tape with your father? What was your immediate thought that night when you watched it, that night in 1999?"

"Well, I thought that it was all falling apart, that we—all of us—were on our way towards something terrible, but another part of me..."

I look down at the floor, my eyesight blurry with tears.

"What did the other part of you think, son?"

I swallow.

"Another part of me couldn't help but think that this had already happened."

The room is silent. No one moves or breathes for what feels like hours.

Then, the man that I am not allowed to see says, "You can tell us the rest of your story now, son. We won't interrupt you again. Tell us the part where they attacked."

It's all falling apart.
It's all falling apart.

Between
our essence
and our descent
falls the Shadow.

Goodbye, cruel universe.

There's no turning back.

Don't try to stop us.

This is the way we ***end.***
This is the way we ***end.***
This is the way we ***end.***

Not with a bang but a whimper.

This is so pretentious of us.

Part II

"Letters from the Undead."

1999, + 6 Minutes

"Fourmillante cité, cité pleine de rêves,
Où le spectre en plein jour raccroche le passant"
—Charles Baudelaire

"What scientists have in their briefcases is terrifying."
—Nikita Khrushchev

"Hold tight, it's New Year's Eve
And it's a cold night, we killed the heat
And turned out all the lights.
And cut the phone lines too."
—Scott Lucas

13

I LIGHT A CIGARETTE. Martin leaves the makeshift interrogation room, locking it behind him. I am left alone with the man who I am not allowed to see, the man whose voice has been altered. He smells like Drakkar Noir, an odor that, like a ghostly pendulum, swings before me, echoing my father, who wore it every day of his life.

The man behind me coughs. He asks me what happened to Lydia. To Stacey. To Preston, who he calls a son of a bitch. I give him the same answer for all three of them, which is: "You should know." Then he asks if I am hungry, which I shake my head no to.

Across the room, the red camera light is still blinking. Wires emitting from the back run down to the gray linoleum below, then into several holes very recently drilled into the wall. Images of this interrogation are being sent upstairs, where superiors are surely listening intently to my every word. I stare into the lens for a moment before looking away, suddenly nauseous with flashbacks to events that may not have happened yet.

By now it must be mid-November, since I haven't left here in over three weeks. I think.

It's been a tumultuous three weeks, though. The first eight days were spent on building up ramifications and defense: stairwells were destroyed; ladders were constructed using rope, broken broom and mop handles, and four-by-twos from the wood shop; guns were checked, cleaned and loaded; the roof was stocked with gasoline cans, first aid, emergency food and water rations, and weapons; and rooms were gutted, refurnished, sealed, re-assigned as bunkers or Alamo equivalents.

It was a little over two weeks ago when we first saw them. They approached from both the south and east, tiny shadows creeping along clogged and congested highways and back roads, all underneath a setting sun half-obscured with rising smoke from the last towns they descended upon, probably Waldo and Lake Geneva, but perhaps as far away as Gainesville and Palatka. The reaction was immediate. The soldiers estimated that it would be between two to five days before the figures would reach the compound, assuming they did not run until they were within close range and the director cued them.

The mine fields would retard their approach by an hour or so, maybe, just enough time to finalize preparations, aim the rifles, and pray for a quick—and permanent—death.

The sweating began. We moved awkwardly back into what was once the state prison to finish preparations and wait.

Just before I was hurriedly ushered back to my cell, I could see the sharpshooters already heading towards the watch towers carrying their sniper rifles, boxes of ammunition, and ear guards to block out not only the impending gunshots, but the terrible din of the moans that would certainly ensue.

That was before. Now, when I sleep here at night in my second floor room, there is no longer the jittery silence, the questions moving from cell to cell and down the hallways. There are the sounds of helicopters flying overhead, the constant cackle of gunfire, and the scraping of metal as fence after fence gives way to their growing numbers.

When Martin returns, he is carrying an unopened pack of Marlboros and a Coke, both of which he hands to me.

"Your lips are chapped," he points out, sitting in the chair opposite mine.

12

I HAVE ANOTHER DREAM. This one is not so much a dream, however, as a skewed memory. It is of me, sitting in yet another class that examines the American Dream. My infamous four-time professor Dr. Nigel Malcolm wanders up and down the rows of desks, gently stroking the beginnings of a beard and scratching at the flesh of his ear lobe as he listens to his Tuesday/ Thursday class debate.

"The spirit of the Sixties is dead," I say emphatically. "In fact, it died *during* the Sixties."

"The Yippies would certainly agree with you," Dr. Malcolm quips. "What do the rest of you think?"

"I disagree," some girl, another American Studies major that I always hated, says. "How do you discount everything that's happening right now, in the Nineties? How do you discount the re-awakening of Sixties fashion, of its influence on music and on the attitudes of our society? It's all around us. The Nineties has experienced a revitalization of the hippie ideals and the experimental attitudes that made the late Sixties so awesome. Don't you think?"

"No, I *don't* think," I say, my voice not matching the movement of my lips in the dream. "Just because as a culture we have run out of ideas does not mean that this great spirit of some long-past and forgotten era is alive and well. It just means that, yet again, we are retro-ing *ourselves*. It's not rebirth. It's *pathetic*."

"But what about the new Woodstock?" a guy that I used to respect before this moment asks, his face blurry.

"What this PC culture is doing is simply running out of ideas. And we've *been* running out of them, frankly. In the Eighties, there was a short but sweet interval when America was all about bringing the greaser spirit of the Fifties back into existence. Rockabilly music and fashion was an homage to that era's barroom swing music. Years pass. And now, we're retro-ing what happened in the next decade: tie-dyed shirts; peace, love, and harmony; and crappy party music masquerading around like it has a message. Pretty soon we'll be looking into bringing back this romantic notion of the Seventies, completely ignoring the fact that it was, wholly, a shitty decade."

"That's an interesting take, Ross," Dr. Malcolm says. "But aren't you ignoring what Farrell said in *The Spirit of the Sixties*? That as long as the era is remembered at all, whether it's with nostalgia or with melancholy, what's important is that it *is* remembered and that the essence of the Sixties lives on?"

"I don't agree with Farrell, sir," I reply, looking down at my notes, at a doodle of me dreaming in my bed on New Year's of 1999. "That book hasn't been written yet. I won't read it for another five years or so. This is a *dream*."

"Okay, fair enough," he says, grinning, returning to his seat at the front of the class. "But why do you disagree with Farrell?"

"Well, reading the text after I took your class, I became disturbed. There's a whole tangent this guy goes on in the **end** of the book about how the past has been remembered, and lists countless examples. What he doesn't take into account, and which bothered me, is that there is a difference between remembering the past and wallowing in it. Yes, it *is* important to keep what has already happened in mind when paving the way for the future. But as far as trying to rekindle some kind of spiritual entity from that other time period for nothing more than another evil American marketing scheme, it's very dangerous. Even if you're trying to revamp the *positive* aspects of that other period."

"How so?"

"Right now it's the Nineties and we're retro-ing the hippie segment of the Sixties. And that's a terrible thing, because we're essentially focusing on the one part of the decade that was more commercially diluted by disingenuous youth and consumerism than any other. What's worse, America is taking the spirit of an already questionable era and beating it down to a neatly wrapped flower-pattern shirt and $80 bell bottoms. We're turning it into a Happy Meal. Get it?"

"You never said this the first time," one of the other students points out.

"It's a dream," Malcolm interjects. "Ross, go on."

"So, even if we're trying to bring the good parts from the dead back to life, inevitably, you **end** up with everything that made that corpse rotten, and nothing more. It gets old fast. People are faced with possibly having to start a *new* era as opposed to reliving an old one, and they don't like the idea of that *one bit.* America gets desperate. They retro something else. Time moves quickly. If we beat the dead horse of the Sixties now, in a couple of years, we'll be doing the same to the Seventies. And then the Eighties, as terrible as that decade was…"

The girl I dislike shakes her head, furrows her eyebrows.

"And soon enough, we're retro-ing ourselves. What is happening at this exact *moment* will already be marketed into a nostalgic money-making package. So what happens then? What happens after we already retro the *present*?"

"I don't know, Ross," Dr. Malcolm shrugs. "Guys? What do you think?"

There is a long silence. I am given terrible glances and an overweight girl in the back shuts her book and puts her head down, glancing at the wall clock. When I look up at it as well, I cannot read the time. I begin sweating.

Finally, a guy named Jordan clears his throat.

"Um…we have to become original again?" he guesses. "We have to…evolve?"

"Impossible," I say shaking my head. "We're incapable of doing that, I think."

"So *what*, then?" the girl who I hate and who obviously hates me asks contemptuously. "What happens, Ross?"

"The world…**ends**," I sigh, a terribly unoriginal gesture.

And that is when everything falls apart. That is when the walls gush blood, when the girl from all of my dreams appears in the doorway of the room and holds her finger to her lip. That is when everyone screams and Dr. Malcolm turns into the Devil, and I awake.

Japan is celebrating when I do.

I left the television on when I fell asleep sometime around four this morning. It is past ten when the nightmare I've been having finally relents and I come to. The news is on and in Japan, a country on the other side of the world, it is Saturday, January 1. The New Year has already come and gone.

The electricity is not out. Computers are not shutting down. Machines are not becoming self aware and vying for power amid human chaos. Instead, fireworks are ignited. Sentiments of oriental brotherhood and high hopes flash across huge screens all over Tokyo. Japanese people celebrate in the streets.

On the other side of the world, a new millennium has begun, and everything is all right. Here though, I am lying in bed, turgid with fear as this century begins its last stand.

11

AT A VERY LATE BREAKFAST WITH PRESTON, I am reading a magazine article while Preston stares creepily at the grizzled female waitresses.

> The Y2K Virus has been a disaster waiting to happen since the 1950s and 60s, when computers were just beginning to emerge. In these days, data storage space was expensive and in relatively short supply. In an effort to save space, computer programmers adopted a habit of using two digits, such as 58, 59, 60, and so on, in their programming codes to indicate the year. This is called COBOL.
>
> Programmers knew this practice might cause problems when the data rolled over to 2000 at the **end** of the century, but they decided to save thousands of bytes of hard disc storage space by utilizing the COBOL method. This was especially popular in the computer systems for banking and government software packages.
>
> At the time, the two-digit system was looked at as a creative and necessary method of stretching the limited data storage space on early electronic machines. Pioneering computer programmers believed the computers they installed the two-digit date coding in would be completely obsolete and replaced by the 1970s or 80s, long before the turn of the millennium.
>
> They were not entirely correct, because today, as the year 2000 quickly approaches, thousands of those early mainframe computers using COBOL are still in use, and still incorporate a two-digit year scheme that does not have the capability to adapt to a new millennium—

"I used to work in a place like this," Preston says, interrupting my reading.

"What?" I ask irritably.

"I used to work in a coffee shop like this one," he repeats, motioning with his hand at the restaurant we are in.

"Yeah, I remember."

"And I hated it. Whoring for tips. Pretending to be someone's best friend, taking it up the ass for two bucks at the **end** of their meal. Running back and forth, back and forth, trying to satiate people, trying to satisfy them when all you really want to do is gouge out their eyes and slit their throat."

I look around at the waitresses pouring coffee and bringing out cheese sticks in brown bowls for customers.

"They don't look to me like they want to gouge out my eyes," I say. "*Or* slit my throat."

"Trust me on this, Ross: they do."

"As long as they bring me an extra syrup for my French toast, I don't give a shit what they secretly want."

"I'm happy we do what we do for a living," he says, pretending to pick at his eggs with a fork but glancing up at me for my reaction. "I just worry about the new DVD craze. If the trades are right, by 2005, we'll be out of business and the poseurs will all own *I Spit on Your Grave*."

"Why?" I ask.

"All these dubbed versions of movies that we sell now underground will eventually be snatched up by low-grade DVD distributors and sold officially, in bulk. Anchor Bay has already started. They've already bought *Evil Dead* and *Repo Man* and a lot of others. I'll bet someone will even re-release *Cannibal Holocaust*."

"Yeah, right," I say. "But it doesn't matter, really."

"Why not?" he asks, suddenly alert.

"To be honest with you, Pres, I don't know how much longer I *want* to be doing this. *Let* Anchor Bay or Full Moon attain the rights to all of this crap. They can have it all. I don't want to do this anymore."

"Do what?" he says, startled, dropping his fork. "Sell movies?"

"Yeah, if you want to call it that. I call it dubbing wastes of film and selling it to losers who, for some perverse reason, love them."

"Ross, I know how you feel about the movies we deal with. And you know, I don't think you're considering their intrinsic value for society. You never have."

"Preston, I've heard your theory on how great zombie movies are, so just spare me," I sigh, a terribly unoriginal gesture, as I put a cigarette out in the ashtray.

"Sure," he says. "You've heard it. But I doubt that you've ever really listened. And I mean to any of it, not just the zombie movies."

"Enlighten me, you fool."

"The woman-gets-raped, gets-revenge flicks, they are a call for a reversal of archaic views on how women have always been regarded in a male-dominated society. They are a warning to the Biblical viewpoint that women are both inferior to men and subject to their every wanton and innately violent desire. These movies show us the grim reality of hurting the opposite sex, and inevitably, either the victim herself, or in a Craven flick, the *family* of the victim gets revenge, every time. The penis, which along with the brain is where all of these sick sexual bloodlusts originate, is always hacked or bitten off of at least one of the offenders. Others are tricked, trapped, and faced with mortal reparations by women who become *empowered,* not overpowered, by their ordeals. These movies are ahead of their time in that they speak a message to us: either we respect and admire women as equals with the same potential for harm and nefarious deeds as we have, or we will face strict, dire consequences by a sex that is, truth be told, far more cunning, vigilant, and resourceful than us."

"It's just violent, sick trash," I say dismissively. "The only reason the woman gets revenge in the **end** is so the perverts watching are absolved of guilt for enjoying these girls being tortured twenty minutes earlier. Next."

"Then you have your slasher film," Preston says, undaunted. "The inherent danger of youthful audiences ever being deprived of the lone-killer-stalking-horny-and-drugged-up-teenagers is staggering. Young people need these films for *two* reasons. One is that slasher movies keep American folklore, urban legends, and myths alive for future generations of people who don't want to hear it from their grandparents. Almost every one of these movies has hints of either the story about the babysitter getting strange calls from inside her own house-slash-apartment building, or the old hook on the door handle scenario."

"Okay, I'll give you that. Go on."

"The second important factor of a slasher movie is that it, while offering up money-making attributes like unnecessary nudity and inventively gruesome death sequences, also stands as a warning against unsavory behavior in young people. And, might I add, the slasher film is one of the only audio-visual warnings that teenagers will actually watch and follow, whether they realize it or not. Instead of parenting down to teens and giving long-winded speeches on the dangers of marijuana and pre-marital sex, slasher films slap viewers in the face with the message that sin equals death. Ross, look who gets killed in the masked killer flick: kids smoking grass, kids trespassing, kids who let their curiosity get the better of them, kids who question their parents' authority, kids who want to get laid, and especially the kids who do.

"Oh, and to top it all off, the only bona fide adults who die in your typical Jason or Freddy sequel are the ones who denigrate young people, ignore young people's plights and fears, or abuse the young people they have been assigned to protect."

"That's...interesting," I finally concede, rubbing my chin. "That's an interesting theory, Preston."

"Ross, just look at any typical teen horror movie and you'll see: nine times out of ten, the next guy who gets it didn't pay attention during youth group at church. In a way, according to Bible Belt standards, everyone who dies in a slasher film had it coming. These young people do not repent for their sins, so what happens? They pay for them by attrition; through blood, tears, crippling regret, and more than likely, death. It's harsh, but effective."

"Yeah, but people in the real world still go out and do all the things they weren't supposed to," I say. "They're still out there breaking onto private property, fucking in cars, lighting joints, and laughing in the face of the old guy who told them not to go to Crystal Lake in the first place. So the masked killer movies aren't effective at all."

"Not effective?" Preston says incredulously. "Let me ask you something. Have you ever gotten creeped out when you were doing something you shouldn't be? Have you ever been having sex in your parents' bedroom while they were at Ponderosa and thought that you were being watched? Have you ever been alone somewhere when you'd recently done something wrong and had a bad feeling that someone or something was going to jump out of the bushes or from behind a dumpster and kill you?"

"*All* kids have those kinds of moments, Preston."

"And therein lies the beauty of a slasher movie," he says, folding his arms. "They have become engrained into our American culture of teenagers so much that, more often than being afraid of facing our reverend's—or our parents'—wrath, we're afraid we're going to have to face a guy in a Halloween mask wielding a butcher knife. Jesus. I mean, do you think Depression-era kids worried about a masked psycho killing them if they cut through an alleyway? No way. They were more worried about...whatever it is kids were worried about. Gangsters? Elliot Ness? Union thugs? I don't know."

I start to chuckle.

"But the point is there, Ross. The idea of someone jumping out and harming you is not an original idea that every overly imaginative teenager invents. It is an idea perpetrated by exploitation filmmakers trying to make money, and it did not exist before the 1970s. It's the latent function of the slasher film."

We finish eating and Preston orders coffee. I drink iced tea and smoke cigarettes as I move through each genre of horror film.

"The creature on a rampage movie," I say.

"Two kinds: either they serve as a warning that some things are better left undiscovered and that some jungles are better left unexplored. Or, they might take the classic route of 'science is evil' and must be stopped before this creature is created and runs amok, killing sexy lab assistants."

"Jungle cannibals," I say.

"Leave other cultures alone. Don't try to assimilate people who are different than us into our society, because we are no better or moral than they are. In fact, they may have the right idea all along and *we* might be the ones who are backwards. Don't accuse people with a different ethical tradition of being barbarians or uncivilized heathens before turning the mirror on the everyday atrocities we commit with foolish abandon. By the denouement of *Cannibal Holocaust*, one inevitably asks the same sort of question the professor did: who are the real monsters? Basically, every jungle cannibal movie carries the same cultural relativism message. It's really beautiful."

"This is so lame. Your answers are evasive and dishonest."

"How so?" he asks.

"Because the movies you're referencing are *shit*, by any standards. Ask any serious film critic who doesn't write for *Fangoria* or *Rue Morgue* and they'll tell you that most of these are all one-star movies. They're cheap ways for Hollywood and Italy to make a buck."

"Ross, the reason why some—and I do mean *some*—critics don't appreciate these movies is because they are book-trained to think that all of these stodgy musicals and dramas and politically-correct exercises in predictable Hollywood tripe are works of art when they are anything but. They see the kind of movies we pander the same way *you* do anymore: they regard the exploitation, the crude editing, and the gratuitous violence and nudity as an indication that there is nothing for the film to offer. They don't watch it repeatedly like they do Hitchcock or Orson Welles, but they *should*. They see them once, if at all, and feel quite justified with their film school pompousness in disregarding the movie as low-budget trash, and don't ever even *attempt* to see the true messages and values just under the surface."

"That's one possibility," I say. "Then again, maybe the lower echelons of people who love these movies simply try to fill in the holes, try to create a philosophy out of nothing more than greed and mediocrity in filmmaking, in an effort to justify their terrible taste and sick urges. If the majority of horror movies were actually the brilliant masterworks you claim they are, then they wouldn't *need* a second viewing."

"There are indisputably great movies that were shunned in their own time," Preston says. "*Citizen Kane, Clockwork Orange, Peeping Tom, Freaks*...The list goes on and on. But if you really watched *Dawn of the Dead*, you would know that these movies are symbolic, and that they all *do* carry a message, whether they were intended to or not."

"I've seen every movie we sell, Preston, and some of them are good. Romero's trilogy is great, and I love Bruce Campbell, but even the best stuff we sell is a long ways from brilliant filmmaking. And the rest of it...Look, I just don't see the underlying value. I don't even see the *point*, Preston. I just see women being forced to piss their pants and guys being sucked down a drain by the Blob. It's...well, it's stupid, Preston. The movies are stupid."

"You'll see it someday. If you copy them long enough, eventually you'll crack, and next thing you know, you'll be calling John Carpenter a genius, Lucio Fulci a living prophet, and George Romero God."

"If you were a road sign, what would you be?" I ask Preston on the drive back to his house. "And don't say 'Dead **End**.'"

"'Watch for Falling Rocks.' You?"

"'One-Lane Bridge Ahead.'"

"If you had any musical ability and formed a band, what would you name it?" Preston asks.

I consider the question for a moment.

"The Pretentious Dingoes," I finally answer. "I came up with it in college. Remember that?"

"Yeah, I remember. It was the night you kept quoting *Ghostbusters*."

"There are a few things I look back on now in embarrassment," I admit. "What would you name *your* band?"

"Oh, that reminds me," he says, ignoring the question. "I talked my friend Jaime into getting his band Volatile Empty to play at the party tonight."

"That's cool," I say. "Volatile Empty? Um, wouldn't it be more grammatically stable if the band were called Volatile Empti*ness*?"

"Give them a break, man. Jaime dropped out of school when he was sixteen. He doesn't know any better. I think a grammatically correct band name is the least of those guys' worries."

"Fair enough," I say. "So, Preston, answer the question. What would you name your band?"

"Heroin for Nine-Year-Olds," he says.

"Good name," I admit, shaking my head. "It would definitely be punk rock, but you'd have instant notoriety, like Black Sabbath."

"Or G.G. Allin and the Murder Junkies or Anal Cunt."

"Who?"

"They're just some bands I know," he says dismissively. "You were talking about notorious band names, right?"

"They're not *that* notorious," I say. "I've never heard of either of them."

"They're famous in certain circles."

"Which ones?" I ask.

"I don't know," he says irritably. "Circles, man."

I shrug, move on to "What time should I be at the party tonight?"

"It's going to start earlier than usual since the climax is at midnight instead of around three when everyone starts talking about how much they miss high school and the creepy guy with the burn scars and long frizzy hair plays Seven Mary Three on the acoustic."

"So what time then?" I repeat.

"I don't know," he says. "Seven or so? I told everyone else to be there around eight."

"Sounds good. I'll call Lydia and tell her."

"I think she's coming on her own," he says casually, rubbing at fledgling goatee hair while staring into the side mirror of the car. "I mean, that's what she told me. She said she might leave if you get drunk and pass out there. Is she mad at you about anything?"

I say nothing.

We turn off the highway and head through town toward Preston's deteriorating house. As we pass Ernie's Sandwich Shop to our left, I slow down to get a better look at the two unmarked vans parked out front. They are both equipped with extending antennae for live television broadcasts. There is no one in or around the vehicles as we pass. When I turn to Preston to mention it, I find him staring out his window as he smokes a cigarette, deep in thought over something.

"Everyone keeps talking about the **end** of the world," he mutters.

"I know," I say, staring at the two vans diminishing in my rearview mirror. "Are you worried about the computers going down?"

"Not really. They didn't in Japan."

"I saw that, too."

I light a cigarette and half-wave to the uniformed police officer in the plaza to our left, who is in the middle of unloading several orange-striped road blocks from a parked utility van.

"Hey Preston," I say, nearing his house now, "do you worry about other things?" I pause, wait. "Besides the computers shutting down, I mean."

"Like what? The **end** of the world and stuff?"

"I suppose so."

"I'm not too concerned. I've got canned goods stocked and several gallons of drinking water. I'm pretty much taken care of, I'd say."

"Uh-huh. That's all you need, Pres."

"Besides," he says, "what is the Apocalypse really but just another opportunity for adaptation?"

I pick something up from the kitchen counter at Preston's house and, surging with rage, call Lydia. She does not answer. Then, I call home and check my messages. Dad called twice. My mother has not, and when I spoke—briefly—to her a couple of days ago and mentioned the videotape she gave me, she told me that she never wanted to be diagnosed with cancer. There was forty seconds of silence before I told her I had to go and hung up.

When I put the phone back on the cradle in the kitchen, Preston immediately comes in and asks me if I finished the order from the guy in Des Moines. I sigh, a terribly unoriginal gesture, and promise to get it done today before the party.

"Be here at seven," he says, not waving to me as I leave.

The black countdown device is still on the white table on the porch.

010:38:21. Ten hours, thirty-eight minutes, twenty-one seconds and counting downward.

I pass the officer again on the way home, but this time he is accompanied by two more cops. They continue to unload road blocks, and I glance down in the passenger seat at one of Lydia's maroon hair ties. I wonder why it was on Preston's kitchen counter, and pray, *Not this one, too.*

10

I AM STILL SHAKING AT THE IMPLICATIONS as she whispers, "I pray that a nuclear device wielded by a madman detonates and kills us all."

"Why?" I whisper back.

"The irony is just too much."

Stacey props herself up on her elbow and fingers absently through a magazine. Then she tosses the periodical aside and lies back down on her back, looking up at the ceiling fan.

I light a cigarette.

"Where are your parents?"

"Party at the uncle's in Largo. They'll be gone until tomorrow."

"I see."

"This house is always empty," she laments.

"How is the irony too much?" I immediately ask. "We don't know for certain that they've done anything."

"*Don't* we, you idiot?"

"It was just one of her hair ties. It might not even have been hers."

"It smells like Coconut Mango and Estée Lauder. It's *Lydia's*, Ross. Who else sprays that much perfume just to go to the mailbox?"

"So you think what, exactly?"

"Do I have to draw you a diagram, sweetie? Ross, your best friend is fucking your girlfriend. Plain and simple. It's Preston Nichols who, despite being your best friend, has slept with how many of your girlfriends now?"

"If you include Lydia Lawton, four. He already fucked Lydia Tammany when we were seventeen."

"*Four* of your girlfriends and two Lydias later and you *still* haven't told this guy to go to hell? Sweetie, there are issues there, and that's not just the psychology major in me talking; it's your friend."

"They may not be doing it," I protest quietly. "And you're biased. For multiple reasons."

"Ross, you told me yourself that you've been catching hints for months now. And let me tell you something: by the time you suspect her, she's already been guilty for quite some time."

I see her hiding the beginnings of a grin as she fumbles with a half-assembled joint on a dinner plate.

"Why are you enjoying this so much?" I ask her irritably.

"Because, sweetie, this is actually a great opportunity for you and me. It's a great thing that you found out that she's been screwing around on you."

"I don't want you to finish this thought," I say, standing up and pacing around her bedroom. There is a Smashing Pumpkins poster on the back of her door that I never noticed.

"I'm hungry," she says. "Have you eaten?"

"I had a late breakfast downtown with my best friend, who was eating pancakes. Then I found out that he's been going downtown and eating my *girlfriend* in between meals with *me*."

"I just said they were fucking," she sighs dismissively. "He's not necessarily doing all that. But it *was* a clever use of puns."

"Trust me, Stacey: if he wants to get anywhere with Lydia, he's been down there."

"So we have ourselves quite a situation here," she says, finishing the joint and standing up with me. "Lydia's best friend and Ross's best friend."

"If you just sleep with Preston now we'll have come full circle," I mutter.

"Me and Preston?" she says to herself. "Doubtful. Preston reminds me of a kid who used to draw pictures of Vikings and pick at pimples on his back. He just happened to grow up to be a handsome spaz, that's all."

"Well, whatever he has, Lydia went for it. Maybe it's the dead parents routine, I don't know."

Stacey sees me light another cigarette with the cherry of the one I am holding before looking down.

"Look," she sighs, "like you said, we don't know for sure yet. This whole thing could just be a bunch of circumstantial evidence. They may be totally innocent."

I shake my head. "*No one* is innocent, Stacey."

It has occurred to me several times that Stacey would probably be a much better choice than Lydia. It just can't happen. Boyfriend leaves girlfriend, dates best friend immediately afterward was always just too typically American for me, too cliché, too talk show. I decided a long time ago, probably in college, that I would always start anew with my life once any one project was completed. I never wanted my life on a continuum; I wanted leaps and bounds.

If the switch were to take place, a number of events would most likely transpire, up to and including the social repercussions for myself and Stacey. She would be shunned by her small menagerie of friends, though I doubt she would care much, as her nickname for Lydia and the others is The Dunces. None of my emissaries would care. As far as static from our circle of mutual friends, Stacey and I have always had little to worry over.

The real problem with my inability to leave Lydia for Stacey is that something about Lydia is just too impossible to ignore, too addicting, too terrible to turn away from. Like a car wreck, but with bigger breasts and a vagina. And whatever it is that Lydia possesses, Stacey certainly does not. Stacey is just too in love with me, too willing to do anything I ask of her.

Too pathetic.

"You've never thought, Ross, that maybe we were just meant to be together, that we should get rid of all of these assholes and just be together, you and me?"

"It had occurred briefly to me."

"And I'm finishing school," she says dreamily. "We could get an apartment, hang paintings, maybe even have a kid…"

"Okay, this is starting to get disturbing," I say flatly.

"You don't want to have kids?" she asks, sounding more hurt than she should.

"I don't know, Stacey. Um, not now?"

She turns away, wipes something from her eye.

"Who's filming you?" she asks off-handedly, still looking away.

"What?" I say, startled. "Where?"

"Over there. Outside."

I glance out the window of the same Chinese restaurant that Lydia and I dined in a week ago. The afternoon sun has disappeared behind a cloud and everything is cast in gray. A gray-looking man with a small gray camera is videotaping me from the sidewalk on the other side of the street. Cars flash by as he does this, on the way to parties and churches and funerals.

Noticing my unperturbed reaction, Stacey says, "Yeah, I'm used to being filmed by strangers too."

"It's been a weird week," I sigh, a terribly unoriginal gesture.

"And your behavior has reflected it."

"What do you mean?"

"What's going on, Ross?" she asks back.

"I'll talk to you about it later."

"Why later?"

"Because one, the walls have ears, and two, I'm not sure at the moment what it is exactly that's going on, Stacey. That's why. But I know this: something is rotten in Denmark and my mother and father have something to do with that guy out there filming me."

"I *would* say that you're a schizophrenic," she says. "Except in this case, there really is a guy outside taping you. So maybe you're just schizoid. It's not as bad."

"Thanks a lot," I say, running my hand through my short, poorly situated hair. The gel is gone.

"So are you still going to go to the party?" she asks.

"I feel there is safety in numbers," I reply.

"So is that a yes, weirdo?"

"I'm going. I'll have to give Lydia and Preston the benefit of the doubt until I actually catch them in the act."

"What a moment that will be," Stacey says, smiling slightly at the thought. "When are you going to get there?"

"Around seven or so. I need to go home and finish some work beforehand."

"Satisfying dorks' cravings for gore and full frontal nudity is a full-time job, huh, sweetie?"

"Whatever." A pause. "Stacey, listen. Look, I—I really need you to go to the party tonight. I can't, like, do this alone."

I am immediately aware of how desperate and pathetic I sound.

"It will be fun," I retort quickly.

"I'm going," she says. "Of *course* I'm going, sweetheart. But what is it that you're so bothered by?"

"Stacey—"

I lose my voice and look sharply about the restaurant: Chinese waiters scurrying about, one kneeling over next to a table where an old portly man complains about his cashew chicken being cold; a young attractive gay couple enters the lobby, scan the take-out menu; a kid drops a noodle on the floor from his high chair; someone stands in the street outside videotaping a young man with an uneaten plate of sushi.

"Are you going to eat your sushi?" Stacey asks, snatching up a California roll from my plate.

"This is New Year's Eve, 1999," I find myself saying carefully.

"You've noticed?"

"Something's been happening, Stacey."

"Okay."

"Something strange."

"Ross—"

"Something bad."

"Are you *crying*?"

"And somehow, I just know that it's all been leading up to this moment, Stacey. We're on the edge. It's just that—everything is—"

9

Everything is wrong when I enter my apartment.

The door isn't unlocked this time, but the TV is on inside and static hisses silently across the screen. It's too warm in the house, and there is the faint smell of food left out. The bedroom door at the **end** of the hall is shut. I stand motionless in the living room, sure that I did not shut it when I left, and absolutely *certain* that I did not even *touch* the television in the main room.

Then I hear it.

Something banging against the wall on the other side of the house.

I take a step forward and then stop. Someone else is in this apartment with me.

They are breathing so loudly from within my bedroom that I can distinguish it through a closed door and down a hallway.

"Hello?" I call, gripping the side of the bar by the kitchen.

No answer. The breathing continues, interrupted by several dull thumps against the wall.

Instinctively, I move toward the phone on the other side of the living room, next to the balcony door.

If someone was breaking into my apartment to steal anything, why would they shut the bedroom door behind them? Why would they lock the front—?

"Don't be an idiot," I whisper to myself. "You know better than that."

When I get to the side table where I keep the cordless phone, I find the cradle empty.

After desperately scanning the room, trying to spot the black telephone on a counter or on the coffee table, I finally stop, take a deep breath, and consider my options. I am too terrified to use the page mechanism on the charger to track it down, so instead stand motionless and try to think back, to this morning, to whatever activities I pursued that led up to me displacing the phone I would later need to dial 911.

Where the *fuck* did I leave it? Okay, think back…There was the news, a shower where I saw a spider on the ceiling above me and shrieked, and then there was some scavenging through the fridge for something to eat other than the graham crackers I left lying on the counter last night. There was a quick call to Preston to see if he wanted to have breakfast with me—

Where did I call him from? Oh god, the *bedroom*? No. It wasn't the bedroom. Where was it?

I wipe the sweat from my forehead just as a low protracted moan makes its way from the bedroom. It is then that I remember where the cordless is. When I called Preston, it was in the middle of packaging *Guinea Pig I* and *II* for the frat guy in California.

In the office.

The bedroom-turned-work-center is on the right side of the hallway, less than six feet from my room, where the moans are coming from now incessantly. Instead of doing something stupid, I could just leave. There is no one lurking about outside the front door. I could simply turn around and leave the apartment, call the police, my mother, whatever, from a neighbor's.

But I realize that this is not going to happen when I hear the handle on the front door slowly turn.

Someone is trying to get in.

I run down the carpeted hallway, towards the office. The moaning stops as I approach and slide into the room, immediately grabbing the black cordless phone from off the computer desk. I snatch it up and turn to leave, practically running from the room back out into the hallway.

When I get there, everyone has already taken position.

In the living room before me is the crewman, waiting.

In my bedroom is something terrible about to attack.

I find myself staring directly into the lens of the television camera just as the bedroom door swings open behind me and someone snarls and lurches forward.

There is screaming, possibly from me.

It topples over reaching for my arm, but grabs the edge of the sweater I have on, and wrenches me down to the floor with it. The smell immediately overwhelms me, making me nauseous with the odors of decay, rotting meat, and a record-holding case of halitosis. It is growling, trying to pull itself up, but I am kicking and yelping in fright, slapping it in the head and grimacing at the blood that is spattering off its scalp with each strike.

I squirm free of its grip, finding balance and struggling to my feet. The camera man, who is wearing a white radiation suit and a gas mask, is still filming all of this when I begin toward the living room, and silently backs away when I charge past him toward the front door. He seems uncertain for a moment whether to focus the camera's attention on me fidgeting with the locks that have somehow become fastened or what was once a middle-aged man in a suit rising from off the hallway carpet.

He decides to stay with me, running out onto the balcony as I descend the stairs and scamper toward my car. The other man is ignored, even as he stumbles out onto the balcony next to him and moans in the late afternoon sun.

8

BIKERS AND FAT COUPLES eating late night at a Denny's near Preston's. A gay man taking his Yorkshire for a walk in front of his apartment building. Three teenagers beating a thin British indigent near the train station.

Cordelia running from the deteriorating framework of a haunted house in Wauchula, screaming as Brad chases after her. Preston lighting a cigarette and talking to Lydia about a puppet show on cable, music by Radiohead coming from somewhere off-screen. Stacey standing alone next to a river, waving to ghosts. Ross getting a terrible sinking feeling.

These people and a billion more dying, over and over again.

Forever.

I stand next to a pay phone at a gas station.

Officer, I'm telling you the truth. There was a man in a radiation suit videotaping me being attacked. They've been filming me for weeks.

A black man tells some young trashy people entering the convenience store that "They tricked us; they tricked us into believing we still here."

The idea of reporting what just happened at my apartment sounds more and more farfetched each time I pick up the phone and begin to dial 911.

Someone has written KEEP YOUR HEAD LOW WHILE LIVING LIFE WITHOUT BLINKING in red lipstick on the yellow wall of the store. Just above that, in pencil, IN SOVIET RUSSIA, DICK SUCKS YOU. I grab the phone book from the **end** of a metal cord and look up the police department's non-emergency number. I dial it, describe the break-in with as few details as possible (no radiation suit, no smell of rotting meat, no doomsday paranoia) and a woman assures me that a police officer will be at the gas station soon.

I wait.

He stares at me from across the parking lot. His box of popcorn is almost gone. The kid grabs another handful of it and shoves it into his mouth, watching me while scratching the side of his leg with his free hand. He runs his fingers through greasy blond hair, never taking his eyes off of me. I sip from the fountain drink I bought, and then take a bite of the Payday. I watch him.

The kid has been watching me now since I got off the phone with the police. He came walking up from across the street, from the direction of my place, with a red and white box of popcorn. He stopped next to one of the Car Vacuums and immediately began staring in my direction. At first I thought that maybe he was waiting for someone, but after I went inside, bought a drink, snacks, and a pack of cigarettes for the party that I am not sure I'll be attending, and came back out, he was still standing there.

"Boy, what you doin'?"

I turn toward the store, where the same black man from before has just emerged holding a Styrofoam cup full of coffee.

"Me?" I ask as he approaches.

"You need to get outta here," he says, hobbling over towards me and grabbing onto my shoulder for support.

He's old, in his sixties maybe, and is wearing oversized geriatric sunglasses and a moth-ridden brown suit. His gray beard whispers dreadful things. He bundles up in the cold and stares at me through hidden eyes.

"Do I know you?" I ask, glancing over my shoulder at the kid, who is still there, watching me.

"I know you in trouble, boy," he says close to my face, his breath reeking of onions, Georgia dirt, and gallons of stale coffee.

"I'm in trouble?" I say, raising my eyebrows. "How so?"

"You really think you be standing here, boy?"

"Look, Mister," I begin, gathering breath, suddenly finding myself overwhelmed with anger, "I don't have time for your weird Christian bullshit. Preach to someone else, okay?"

I try to shift around so that his hand slides off of my shoulder, but as I do this, he just tightens his grip. The kid watches from the edge of the parking lot.

"Boy, you in real bad trouble. You know that? I don't need to preach to you; you already gone. You dead."

"Like Captain Kurtz?" I ask. The boy across the parking lot smiles in delight. What the hell is going on?

"You all so worried about the **end,** about Jesus coming back," he says, shaking his head. "You don't got to worry none about that."

"Why is that, Mister?"

"Cause we were all dead a long time ago. The world already done **end**ed, young man, and we all just trickin' ourselves. Don't you realize we already in Purgatory, waitin' for the Lord to forgive us?"

"You're saying the world already **end**ed and we're actually all in Purgatory, waiting for our own personal judgment from God. Did I get that?"

"Everybody but *you*, boy," he says, grinning widely now, exposing straight white teeth, save one dead molar long turned brown.

"So I still exist?" I ask incredulously, glancing at that fucking boy once more.

"No, you dead too."

"Then if *you're* all waiting to be judged, where am *I*, Mister?"

"You already *been* judged, boy."

He starts laughing.

"I don't—"

"They's in Purgatory, but *you*, boy, *you* in *hell.* You ain't even here but you is, too."

"That doesn't even make any sense," I sneer, and wrench myself free of his grip, backing away. I throw the candy bar on the ground, open my car door carefully, and slide into the seat, watching the old man laugh hysterically. The boy laughs as well, throwing his empty popcorn box on the ground.

Starting my car, I hear it:

"Have fun at yo' party tonight, Ross. Just remember: you can't be awakenin' somebody if they only *pretending* to be asleep. Isn't that right, boy?" And he chuckles to himself.

I floor it out of the parking lot, passing the police officer just now arriving in his cruiser to assist me. Back there, the soothsayer black man continues to laugh as the boy runs and jumps in his arms.

7

Art Pour L'Art
Support Your Local Artists, People

Lydia's bumper sticker from this town's small art museum/theatre is the first thing I see as I pull into Preston's driveway at sunset. In front of her dark red Escort ZX2 is another car, a lime green Chevy sedan with several band stickers on the back windshield. I do not recognize it, but am certain that this will all **end** badly.

I put the car into Park, turn off the engine, and wait. My stomach acids crest and topple over in a nauseous wave. The clock on my car's dash reads 5:28. I'm early, but there are two bad people in my apartment and another two waiting for me at the gas station nearby. Glancing out the top of my windshield, Preston's old white house looms over me. A headache begins as I realize there are two more bad people waiting for me here.

The door is unlocked as always, and instead of loudly announcing my arrival as usual, I glide through the dusty living room full of old furniture and new posters. On the television set, *Lost Highway* plays at very loud or very low volumes, I can't tell which.

The old office on the ground floor that Preston uses for clambakes, impressing girls with his father's old gun collection, and jogging on an ancient treadmill is empty, but the stereo is playing Suicidal Tendencies, "I Saw Your Mommy." The downstairs toilet is also vacant, as is the kitchen. I open the fridge, quickly slurp down three of the two hundred or so Jell-O shots Preston has prepared in tiny paper cups. I glance at the freshly-mixed pink Hunch Punch in an empty Gatorade cooler on the floor before leaving the kitchen and heading up the stairs.

The hallway is dark. One **end** of the hall, Monroeville, where Preston keeps his movies, is dark. His parents' old bedroom at the other **end**, now his, is only illuminated by the soft yellow glow of a night light. The door to the other bedroom, which Preston uses to store all of his parents' belongings that could not be sold or left in front of Goodwill, is shut, but Preston never goes in there anymore.

I turn to go back downstairs. Maybe there were more people here but Preston, Lydia, and everyone else went out for food, more liquor, to surprise me at the apartment and bring me here—

A soft giggle. Coming from the direction of the master bedroom.

I turn around and back toward Preston's chamber. I quickly realize that the light is coming from the crack underneath the closed door of the bathroom, and then I am approaching it, swallowing, stifling murderous rage, recognizing a young woman's raucous laughter.

And then I am opening the door to the bathroom. All movement, all evil, all everything, stops.

I am standing before a purple shower curtain, water spraying down on the other side, creating massive amounts of steam which swirl up and stick to my arms and fists, which I notice are clenched.

My hand reaches out involuntarily and jerks the curtain open.

"Dude," Preston says quietly, "you're…early."

Lydia has nothing to say, merely covers her breasts in disgrace, waiting for it.

"Ross, just listen—" Preston goes quiet upon seeing my facial expression change at the sound of his voice.

Lydia begins crying, turning her head toward the yellow tile floor, avoiding the sight of Preston's erect cock, which is quickly dissipating with each terrible second.

Princess Star Bright, to the right of Lydia, remains frozen.

"What. The. *Fuck*!"

The first punch I throw goes somewhere near Preston's face, but it is unfocused and nicks his nose before slamming brutally against the tile wall. Bloody prints of my knuckles run down in the shower water as I shriek, animal-like, and punch Preston against the temple. He falls backward against the showerhead, tumbles over, lands on his ass on the tub basin.

I do not stop.

Wailing, unleashed, unstoppable, I begin slamming into Lydia's forehead, her shoulders, the top of her skull—anything exposed as she collapses to her knees in fear and ignominy.

"Stop it, stop it, you fucking psycho," Star Bright is pleading angrily.

I punch Lydia's face the best I can through her outstretched hands serving as a shield before turning my attention to Star Bright.

"You *cunt*!" I roar. "You fucking *cunts*!"

I take a step into the shower stall with them, the hot water soaking me. I grab Star Bright with my left hand and begin punching her pale sagging tits, her arms, her left temple, then begin wrenching at her red moss-like hair, tearing out a clump of it.

Everyone is screaming.

Preston lurches at me from behind as I move back to Lydia, who has begun wailing how sorry she is. He gets a hold of my sweater, pulls me back toward him, and I lose my balance. I fall on the side of the tub, then tumble down onto the bathroom floor. Preston clumsily tries to throw a swing down at me, but I grab his advancing arm and jerk him to the floor beside me. Flailing around naked next to me, I punch his side, regain my footing, and stand up. I kick him in the ribs and stomach. Preston moans in pain, falling flat on the floor. I grab at his short wet hair, jerk his head up to face me, and then punch him in the side of the face. A small amount of blood squirts from his nose.

"Holden, stop it, baby," Lydia pleads, trying to grab me by the shoulders from behind.

I whirl around and kick at her pubic hair, which causes her to cough violently and fall down in the tub.

"Stop it, dude, just stop it," Preston manages beneath me. "Fucking stop it, asshole."

"You motherfucker," I snarl, kicking him as hard as I can in the chest. He flips upward into the air, landing on his ass and grabbing at his ribs.

I breathe carefully.

Star Bright is trying to suppress her angry, violent tears behind me. Lydia is sitting in a fetal position on the tub floor, licking at her bleeding lower lip. Preston is trying to suppress vomit, his back against the toilet.

I clench my eyes shut, inhale deeply, then re-open them. For some reason, I find myself reaching for a knob. I turn the shower off, mutter something terrible, and leave the bathroom, shutting the door behind me. For some reason, the line from the closing of *Cannibal Holocaust*, "Who are the real monsters here?" echoes in my head.

Out of the driveway, I frantically tear down Main leading toward Pittsburgh Street. My hands are still clenched tight, and when I open them and actually grip the steering wheel of my car, the flesh of my palms is bleeding from my fingernails digging in. I wince in pain and floor it, ranting like a sharp-tongued madman.

The world is truly a terrible place. Every one of my generation is lost, filling the holes which are their lives with seditious and yet passionless acts of unnecessary drama. It is a world of hypocrisy and whispers, a dark mine shaft of overfed, spoiled and thankless slaves too stupid to realize that, despite their steady stream of shallow luxuries, they are still *slaves*. Worst of all, we are far too subdued, far too encouraged by an equally vapid youth-oriented prime time television society, to revolt in favor of a return to a more self-aware time in history.

I run onto the curb, quickly grab the wheel, and thud back onto the road.

And this is when I scream at the top of my lungs. My throat burns and my vocal chords convulse and my vision blurs and for a moment I have a perfect visual image of myself on this same stretch of pavement, screaming with the same anguish, facing the same uncertain road ahead as everything changes. I see myself being betrayed by different people with the same face, again and again and again and—

The first tears form at the basins of my eyes when I see it.

At the flashing red light about a hundred yards ahead is a road block. Wooden posts painted orange and white, mounted with flashing orange construction lights, have been positioned across both lanes heading this way at the four-way stop. Accompanying the road blocks are dozens of black objects scattered along the concrete which, as I approach, I recognize as police spikes. I slow down, watch the gauge drop from a terrifying 59 to 38, then 25, and when the first cameraman emerges from behind a bush at the side of the road, down to ten.

I stop a few feet away from the spikes.

"All right, what the hell is going on?" I demand, throwing my car door open and lunging out toward the radiation-suited man before me.

He backs away as I approach him. I wipe the shower water from my face.

"Who *are* you people?" I roar. "What do you want from me? Can't you tell by now that I am in no mood to be *fucked* with?"

He continues backing away, never shifting the camera's sights from me.

"Stop filming me and tell me what the hell is happening. Who are you? What's going on?"

He does not respond and, catching myself, I turn away and approach the spike-covered steel balls scattered all over the ground. I kick them away onto the sidewalk one at a time. They are surprisingly heavy, and clang loudly as they skitter off of the road into the grass and bushes.

"I'm out of here," I say. "I'm leaving town. This is all bullshit."

My foot begins to ache from the effort, and one of the spikes jabs through my shoe when I go to kick it. It punctures the base of one of my toes, and I wail out in pain.

"I hope this *is* Armageddon," I mutter, limping toward one of the road blocks to push it aside.

The attack comes.

It's not the same man from my apartment, but the stench is all too familiar. He comes stumbling quickly out from the hedge in front of the podiatrist's office. I stand, stupid, watching him approach. His black shoe trips on one of the spiked balls, catching the razor-sharp tip and dragging it several feet before finally jerking it underneath his heel. I watch the spike slide right through the bottom of his foot, bringing bits of gray flesh and thick black blood out with it when it emerges on the upper side through the tongue of his shoe. I turn to the cameraman, who is zooming in on the impaled foot.

He does not stop his advance toward me, even with his foot a bloody heap.

I back up, sputtering blankly, "Do something, man, *do* something," to the camera guy.

There is the shuffling sound of someone else, and when I turn around, I see another man approaching me from behind the cameraman. His face is gray and missing most of the left cheek.

They're both fifteen feet away and advancing steadily, their moans more insistent and ferocious with each step. I panic, turning from one to the other repeatedly, reaching absently into my pocket for my car keys. Grabbing them from my pocket, I limp toward the driver side door and clench the door handle.

There is a pop sound from somewhere behind me. A second later, my windshield explodes. I whirl around and duck out of instinct just as another bullet shatters the driver door window. Glass rains down onto my scalp and I am screaming when the first man reaches me and tries to grab hold of my arm.

I panic when his fingers wrap tautly around my wrist. His grip is like leathery ice on my flesh.

"*Help* me!" I scream to what is now three different men filming me. "Are you people *insane*?"

A series of flashes as they photograph the creature bite into the thick sleeve of my sweater.

I yelp, panicking, flailing around and trying to stand up. Its teeth are clenched tight around the fabric of my shirt, and I begin yanking frantically to escape. Meanwhile, the second one is a few feet away, snarling and slobbering all over himself and bleeding from the cheek as he edges his way closer. I begin kicking at the one biting at my arm in its chest until finally he falls backward, taking a long stretch of my sweater with him.

Another bullet sails through my shattered driver window when I attempt to climb back into my car.

I scream, having no idea what is going on, certain only of the fact that I will die in the middle of this street, and that Lydia is sexing Preston and that trendy ugly girl two blocks away—

They both come down on me, and I collapse to the ground and crawl underneath my car. They follow, falling onto their stomachs and grabbing at my ankles as I slither away out the back side, slamming my head on the edge of the muffler during my escape. I feel blood trickle down my scalp, which somehow excites the two creatures even more. They growl and moan deafeningly as I clamber to my feet and run away, back towards Preston's house.

The technicians are mounting camera stands and setting up shots on the tops of buildings as I run back up Main Street. They work out lighting problems and uncoil wiring for the halogen lamps standing by on the sidewalk. Makeup is applied to dozens of already graying men in front of an investment banking office, in the parking lot of the small plaza with the podiatrist's office, and in the schoolyard across the street from Preston's house.

"They're gray, but not gray *enough*," I hear one of the makeup artists complain.

Up the steps, my breath gone, my wits shredded, I throw open the front door, yelling for help. It is as I am rounding the corner into the kitchen, where a light is on—when I enter the room—that I realize what is about to happen.

Lydia shrieks as she swings the baseball bat at my forehead.

The blackness descends like a curtain at the tail **end** of the second act. But even in the throes of a deep unconsciousness enveloping me, I know what is happening.

I was attacked by zombies.

And they'll be here soon.

6

THE ROOM WAS CLOUDY WITH SMOKE. *The Sentinel* was on the television, but Preston had brought out a small stereo and was playing the Pixies, "Where is My Mind?" over it. I lit another cigarette and glanced into the kitchen, which seemed suddenly very far away.

"You know how many people graduated with an American Studies degree with me?"

"How many?" Preston asked, glancing at the TV. "I like this part."

"Three."

"That's not many," he said dumbly.

"No, Preston. It's not many."

"So?"

"There were two hundred twenty-two business majors that walked that day. Fifty-eight English. One-hundred sixty-nine psychology majors. Christ, there were six quantum physics majors, Preston. I don't even know what the hell quantum physics majors *do*."

"Well, what do American Studies majors do?" he asked, searching the floor around the couch for his bong.

"I don't know," I said, my eyes filling with tears.

Preston noticed what was happening to me and turned away quickly, getting up from the couch and heading into the kitchen. He returned with two Rolling Rocks.

"I have to go to work in twenty minutes," I said absently.

"Um, did you, uh, like *Day of the Dead*?" he asked.

I looked to the rug in front of the TV/VCR combo. It was littered with videos, two of which we had watched that day together.

"It was kind of talky in the middle," I said, staring at the movies.

"Yeah, it was, but you have to think deeper about what Romero was really trying to say. Imagine: you're trapped in an underground bunker with people that, in normal life, you would not find yourself associating with. In fact, these are men that, as Sarah in the film, you would probably detest if you were stuck with them for five minutes in any kind of social situation. And here you are, on a planet where humans are no longer the dominant species, and your only prospect for survival is to lock yourself up in this dank, poorly constructed bunker, hoping against hope that you and these assholes can work together to somehow stop this plague, if for no other reason than just to finally be able to get away from these animals you have to sleep next to.

"And what happens as time passes, Ross? Things fall apart, as they always do. Tensions flare. Minds snap. Suddenly, you're trapped in a bunker not only with people you can't stand, but they have guns and they're ready to explode. Imagine it, dude. Just imagine it. That's why I always liked *Day* the best, actually."

"Preston," I said vacantly, still staring at the floor, "where do you get your movies from?"

"I buy them."

"From like video stores? Amazon? Best Buy? Where?"

"Well, some of them I buy from video stores, if I'm lucky enough to find them. But most of my movies I have to buy from online catalogues. I shop at Something Weird and Bizarro too. Those are small distributors that specialize in hard-to-find ones, like that one I showed you, *Lemora: A Young Girl's Tale of the Supernatural*."

"How much do they cost?"

"It depends. On average though, about thirty or forty bucks."

"I see."

"Why?" he asked.

I did not answer, inhaling thoughtfully on my cigarette. As Preston repeated his question, I stood up and walked upstairs. The light in his movie room was left on from earlier, and I walked into Monroeville and stubbed my cigarette out in a cereal bowl sitting on one of the side tables.

"Ross, what the hell are you doing?" Preston was asking behind me. "Do you want to watch something else?"

I scanned the shelves, staring at all the titles.

Zombies, slashers, vampires, demons, cannibals, critters, aliens, sharks, crocodiles, dentists, ice cream men, mad doctors, possessed schoolgirls, jungle islands, science experiments gone awry, ghosts, Santa Claus, piranhas, evil nuns, evil counts, Satan himself, God, nothing and nothingness…

Horror movies encapsulated everything society could and would pervert, exploit, and dumb down in an effort to denigrate its audiences.

"I have an idea," I said, smiling. "I have an idea to make us some money."

"Does it have anything to do with *Day of the Dead*?" he asked.

"Something like that," I replied, sitting down at the desk and scribbling out figures on the back of a receipt for a book called *The Phoenix Project.*

Preston and Lydia were staring out at the city one night. It was raining. An SUV sloshed by, churning up muddy water into Preston's tiny front yard. The red and white and occasionally orange and yellow lights from town looked swollen and hazy in the torrent. Somewhere, a kid was listening to Tool. Somewhere else, a black man in a stolen car was being pursued by two highway patrolmen.

"Lydia, I'm going to test you," Preston said.

"On what?" she said, sipping from her bottle of hard lemonade.

"How do you kill a zombie?"

"Don't," she sighed. I rested my hand on hers and smiled, lighting a cigarette.

"No, seriously," he said. "This could be important. Like remember that time that the girl at the party didn't want to listen to me about my idea of honorable suicide in the face of a murderer climbing the staircase? When she was killed by that guy from Gainesville last year, I heard she was tortured and raped for six *hours* before he did her in. She should have offed herself while she had a chance. Now...how do you kill a zombie, Lydia?"

Lydia strains to think, then sighs melodramatically and rolls her eyes.

"Kick it in the balls?" she says.

"God *damn it*," he moaned, standing up from his rocking chair. "This is not funny. Seriously, if there ever was a plague of undead marching towards you, what would you do, guys? Ross, this question applies to you too. Do you flee, do you shoot it, do you go at it with a sturdy ammo-less weapon like a crowbar? What do you do?"

"Pres, none of this shit matters," I said, looking up at him with bemusement. "There's no such thing as zombies."

"We don't know that," he quickly retorted, shaking his head. It occurred to me that Preston was drunk as he stepped out into the rain and stared pretentiously out at the city, which apparently was *full* of undead cannibals. "We've just never seen one."

"Not just *we*, buddy," Lydia said, throwing her empty bottle into the trash can. "Pres, *no one* has ever seen a zombie."

"You insolent unread fools," Preston scoffed. "You're both college people, and yet wholly stupid and uneducated." He smoothed his soaking wet hair and held his mouth open to catch drops of rain. Then he continued, "There are references to living carnivorous dead in every culture and holy text ever written. The Bible discusses the dead rising from the graves all the time, the *coup de grace* when it's foretelling the Apocalypse; there are accounts of undead monsters written in Hieroglyphics in Egypt; there were accounts by European explorers of natives abandoning their criminals and undesirables on islands inhabited solely by the living dead."

"No there weren't," I said, wedging my empty beer bottle underneath a shoe on the porch.

"Ross, just think about it," he said.

"No, Preston, I don't think I will. The idea is stupid. It is scientifically impossible and I would rather discuss reality television and the triumphant return of the game show. Talking, realistically anyway, about zombies makes me feel like a pimply teen wearing a Nine Inch Nails shirt."

Preston walked onto the porch from the rain. He sat down across from me and Lydia, soaked.

"If there was a virus from outer space (thank you, Romero), and it operated in a totally different manner than any virus as we know it—if an organism, if life as humans do *not* know it, were to make its way by dimensional warp, time intrusion, self-aware meteorite, intergalactic space ship full of aliens with nefarious agendas, *whatever*...if that happened, who could contest that one of its abilities might be to somehow re-animate and stabilize recently dead people? What if this virus, or whatever it is, could enable the human body to function without blood flow, without oxygen? What if it could activate and reprogram the human brain to not only raise the dead body that it's attached to, but instill in it new instinctual behavior pertaining to ingesting living human flesh? *Further*, what if one of the facets of this alien disease was *quite* earthly, in that it spread through the exchange of bodily fluids, namely blood? Hundreds of our own sicknesses spread from person to person right *now*. So, what if the living caught this life-altering disease by being bitten by one of these creatures? They become sick as well. It's really not so far-fetched.

"Look, it's only a totally dismissible premise if you continue to examine the situation from the point of view of a human problem, a human virus, an earthbound epidemic with earthly restrictions such as we've seen with every other epidemic in earth history. If you only looked at the big picture, and could admit that not only *may* there be things in the universe that the three of us cannot comprehend or fathom, but that there most *certainly* and *undoubtedly* are, then the idea of your dead neighbor coming back to eat you alive is actually not quite so preposterous anymore, is it?"

"Oh, but *yes*," I said. "It *is* preposterous, Preston. Your entire premise is giving scientific credence to a plot originally hatched by a man looking to cash in on the drive-in movie market. Nothing more. It…is…preposterous."

"I'm just saying that sometimes art imitates life," he said quietly, looking down at the floor boards of the porch. "It's just that we're used to it being the other way around, where art is so much more interesting than this…*situation* that we strain to call life while keeping a straight face."

"No, *you're* just saying that life as we don't know it, life as impossible *fantasy*, inspires art. You're basically tap-dancing around the idea of art imitating other art, which is really not a new concept. And, keep in mind, this is only if you call *Return of the Living Dead* art—"

"I do," he said sharply.

"*And* all this zombie nonsense exists only in *your* head, Preston; I don't know anyone else who shares your delusion."

"Have you ever heard of voodoo?" Preston asked. "They believe in it."

"No, they don't," I said. "Voodoo zombies are totally different than what you're talking about. Now look, it's been a while since I took my course on the occult in America, but if I remember correctly, the voodoo zombie is created by a *houngan*, or Kimbundu priest that is, Lydia. You looked confused."

"I'm following all right so far," she insisted. "Go on."

"All right. People who practice voodoo have an entirely different conception of their zombie. Their zombie is a normal person who has been cursed by a priest and then coated with a white zombification powder. It causes the body's functions to go into a hibernating state. They're often mistaken for dead and buried alive but, point in fact, they have brain damage caused by these mystics' own brand of herbal science and superstition. They're basically rendered *retarded*, and then used for the priests' deeds."

"It's still a form of zombie," Preston argued.

"Not really. What I'm talking about is still a human being. It doesn't eat people; it still breathes and pumps blood through active arteries and veins; it still has emotion and experiences pain; you can shoot it in the chest and it dies. But Pres, what you've been rambling on about forever now is nothing but classic black and white cinema conjured up by the same people who made *Creepshow*. It's impossible. Period."

"Whatever. What about that one—?"

"*Period*," I interrupted.

We drank in silence. The rain tapered off to a trickle and the same SUV from earlier passed by the front of the house again.

"Well *I* think it's reasonable," Lydia suddenly announced.

"You would," I said.

"No, seriously, it's not totally ridiculous, if you have an open mind."

"And I'll guarantee you one more thing," Preston added without missing a beat. "If this event ever does take place, I am one person who will be totally prepared for it. I'll never be walking around like *that*."

"I will," I said.

"And I'll be the one to put a bullet in your head." A pause, in which time he opened another beer. "Oh, by the way, Lydia, that's the answer to my question earlier on how to kill them. Don't say anymore dumb things on my porch, please. Man, it's not bad enough that your boyfriend is only in this business for the money. To top it all off, if the undead uprising ever did happen, both of you'd be dead for sure."

There was a long silence before Lydia cleared her throat and spoke.

"To understand the living, you have to commune with the dead," she said, the most insightful comment ever uttered from those lips.

5

"'Of' is not a word," I mumble, slowly opening my eyes. "It never was."

Through the tiny slits I am receiving images from, I see orange and white streaks of light, and a shadowy figure standing what seems like miles above me. Somewhere there are voices, muffled and oozing through the wall.

"So the shit's hit the fan," the figure above me says in a girl's voice. "And furthermore, 'of' is, apparently, not a word. They had us fooled all this time, sweetie."

"Stacey?" I ask, straining to see through hazy vision and the doldrums of a migraine.

"None other," she says, leaning over and taking my right arm.

She hoists me up, and I slowly struggle to my feet, using her arm and a treadmill railing for support. When my vision sharpens, I look around. I am in what was once Preston's office. There is light and the shadows of people coming from underneath the crack of the shut door.

"What's going on?" I ask, confused.

"You're bleeding, first of all."

Stacey holds a moist orange hand towel up to my forehead. When the cloth touches my skin, there is a sharp pain, and I recoil.

"What the hell?" I ask, touching my skin. It stings and aches violently.

"Lydia swung a baseball bat and knocked you unconscious."

"Why?" I ask, my back aching as I strain to stand straight, searching my pockets for a cigarette.

"I hope these aren't signs of amnesia or a concussion, Ross. Do you not remember what happened at all?"

I think back.

"I remember…when it bit into my sweater," I say slowly, raising my arm up to show Stacey the spot on my sleeve where, indeed, there is a large piece missing. "It didn't bite into my flesh, did it?"

After close inspection of my exposed arm, it appears that whatever it was that bit me did not break my skin. I sigh in relief, a terribly unoriginal gesture.

"Those guys are insane," Stacey says, laughing slightly. "Who bit you? I'll bet it was that little rat girl Mindy. She looks like a biter. Jesus, Ross, they're all really pissed at you. You broke Preston's nose."

"Wait," I say, nauseous, leaning over and shaking my head. "What are you talking about? That thing that bit me had a name? Mindy? That can't be right. It was an old man, Stacey."

"Preston told me that Mindy is only seventeen, sweetie. Maybe you shouldn't have hit her like you did."

"Who the hell is *Mindy*?" I stammer, finding both a half-crumpled pack of cigarettes in one of my cargo pockets and a full box. I retrieve one and light it. "What are you morons talking about?"

"I believe you call her Princess Star Bright."

It all comes back to me: pulling up into the driveway, walking into the house, catching my girlfriend of three years showering, naked of course, with my best friend. To top it off, there was a droopy slut in the shower with them, as if there were not enough debauchery already. Then there was me beating the hell from all three of them, leaving in a torrent, and then two undead men attacking me and it being filmed by a Cold War television crew.

"They're still out there?"

"Who? Preston? Of course he is; it's his party tonight—"

I shake my head violently and head for the door. Stacey blocks my path.

"Don't start any more shit, Ross. It won't do any good. Lydia already knows about you and me. She was *un-thrilled*, to put it mildly. When I found out what happened, I thought it in our best interest to tell her. Besides, I wanted to stick it to her when she started really digging into you after I got here."

"Stacey, that's all trivial," I say, trying to maneuver around her and open the door. "We're all in a lot of trouble."

"No, *you* are, Ross. Preston told me that after you woke up, he was going to call the cops unless you evacuate immediately."

"Evacuate?"

"He wants you to *leave*, Ross," she explains, frustrated. "So why don't we oblige him? We can go back to my house and watch the ball drop. It will be fun. Let's go, okay? Where'd you leave your car?"

"Evacuate?" I ask again, confused.

"Where's your car, sweetie?"

"Stacey, my car's gone," I say carefully, closing my eyes. "Has the party started?"

"Sort of."

"*Sort of?* What the hell does that mean? How many people are here?"

"Um."

"How many?" I ask irritably.

"A few."

Prophetic lines from Local H blast out from a stereo in the living room, and I prepare to venture into what was once a house, but what has now become a living, breathing organism. Upon opening the door and emerging into the downstairs living room, I am surrounded by an army of failed youth, all about to die.

Monica 1 stands at her boyfriend Chris's side by the keg while discussing with Monica 2 tonight's other parties to attend. Monica 2 is, of course, wearing a black sweater and has dyed her hair black with crimson streaks in it, and this is artistic. Monica 2's boyfriend Quentin brings both Monicas hunch punch in red plastic cups. He has a new tattoo of a directionless compass on his elbow, and this is hardcore.

From the doorway leading into the kitchen, a bruised and swollen Preston catches sight of me as I meander through the living room. He turns and slinks off into the void of people, gingerly holding his ribs.

Smoke has already begun collecting at the upper echelons of the room, twisting up the stairs and swirling about in the wind let off from a fan twelve feet above my head. On the wooden floor, cigarettes are lit, cigars are puffed, and someone spits some kind of liquid out of their mouth. It bursts into flame and people cheer. My eyes water.

"I can walk through walls," someone whispers in my ear, but when I recoil, there is no one next to me.

Two guys hold up an underage girl's legs and she does a fifteen-second keg stand. Behind them someone discreetly rips a poster from Araki's *Totally Fucked Up* off the wall and scampers off. A girl named Cody and a guy named Robin both approach me but I dismiss them by ranting and raving.

In the kitchen, the hunch punch is already half-drained. On the microwave, the time is 9:27, and Preston once told me that this clock was twenty minutes slow. Shannon is chatting with his girlfriend Camilla and someone else that I don't know. A moment later, he opens the fridge and removes four Jell-O shots. He and the other guy slurp down the red gelatin, laughing raucously.

"Hey, Ross," Shannon exasperates upon spotting me. "This is my friend Gary. Gary, this is Ross. This is the guy I was telling you about, the movie guy."

Ignoring Gary's outstretched hand, I turn around and head out of the kitchen back into the living room. More keg stands, more red plastic cups being filled, a clambake about to take place in the room I was just in. "Whoa, he has a treadmill too," someone raves, heading into the office with a green and yellow bong.

Past the couple making out on the couch, another girl named Camilla and a guy named David, and onto the front porch. It has been stocked with large metal garbage cans on either side. The old wooden planks squeak and sigh as a dozen or so people mill around, flirt, try to fuck, try to get drunk, try to forget that the world is **end**ing. A small purple stereo on top of a rickety white table plays "Rock and Roll Nigger" by Marilyn Manson. Someone in a green sweater and black leather pants stumbles backward with a bottle of Heineken, ripping a portion of the brown screen from the railing.

I head outside.

Down three concrete steps and past a small granite gargoyle that Preston stole from a haunted cemetery in Milledgeville, Georgia, I run into huge circles of friends discussing Argentina, cannibalistic settlers in 1609, a girl named Amanda who might have tertiary Syphilis. The crowd out in the cold night is devastating: a clique of spooky kids who like Thrill Kill Kult's earlier stuff *only*; alternative people who sometimes catch football games in November if *Real World* isn't on; guys dressed up as Peter Weller; Preston making a call on someone's pink cell phone; Lydia and Princess Star Bright or Mindy or whatever the hell her name is standing in front of a large amp while some kind of band sets up in the driveway. No one seems to mind the gaffer and lone cameraman in a white radiation suit documenting all of this from the street.

Lydia spots me, one of her eyes purple and swollen. I smirk at her good eye glaring at me.

A car pulls up into the driveway. "No, no parking here," Preston yells, still holding the cell phone. "Park at the church two buildings over. Thanks, Matt."

Matt and the three people in the car are soon gone. A moment later, another car attempts to pull into the driveway, followed by another shortly after. Preston redirects all of them to the church.

Someone's hand rests on my shoulder. I whirl around to face Stacey, who is eyeing me suspiciously.

"Have you had enough?" she asks. "Are you ready to go?"

"I'm not sure what happened to them. I don't know how these people—"

The drummer for what looks like a four piece punk-slash-new-metal band tests his base drum. Mounted on top of the vocalist's PA is Preston's black timer ticking away the dwindling hours and minutes until the New Year.

002:07:30. Two hours, seven minutes, thirty seconds and counting downward.

"Ross—"

Someone launches three bottle rockets from the front yard. They screech up fifty feet or so before exploding. The din is met with several other fireworks going off from somewhere else in the city.

"Ross!"

Stacey has her arms crossed in front of me, still waiting for a complete sentence.

"Stacey, we have to get out of here," I say, grabbing her by the arm and heading down the driveway. Out of the corner of my eye I see Lydia, arms folded, her eyes trained on Stacey being pulled along behind me onto Main. I decide I never want to see her again.

I tug Stacey along the sidewalk running parallel to the street leading past Preston's house. Instead of attempting to leave the same way I did before in my Corolla, toward Pittsburgh, this time I head in the opposite direction toward Highway 89, past the schoolhouse and church-slash-party-parking-lot, and then toward the Planned Parenthood, a pawn shop, a Tropical Smoothie shop, and a café that serves only breakfast. We head toward a four-way intersection a hundred yards away, which appears to be empty.

"Ross, my car's in there," Stacey protests, pointing back to the Episcopal Church. The parking lot is half-full of cars obviously owned by young people: Civics, Escorts, Cavaliers, Corollas, Rangers and the occasional van with stickers on the back windshield.

"Stacey, I'm afraid they'll shoot us if we try to leave in your car," I tell her.

She snatches her arm away and stops in her tracks.

"Ross—" She pauses, looks around, gathers a breath. "Ross, what the *fuck* is going *on*?"

I look all around us, not seeing them. There are no cameramen on the balcony of the chiropractor's office, no lights set up to capture the action, no walking corpses stumbling out from behind green dumpsters. I clench my eyes shut and attempt to put something together.

"Stacey," I say, turning to her. "Listen to me. Something terrible is happening right now, tonight. Someone stole my car, two guys attacked me, and I'm afraid that we're all in, like, danger. So you and I need to get away from here immediately. Okay?"

"Um, well, okay," she replies uncertainly. We begin to walk, but Stacey slows down and finally stops again. "You know, we should really take my car now if we're going to leave."

"I told you, Stacey. I'm afraid someone will attack us if we do that."

"Yeah, but if we don't take it out soon it will be stuck here for hours."

"What are you talking about?" I ask, lighting a cigarette.

"The police," she says casually.

"What?" I say, squinting. My cigarette falls from my trembling fingers and I bend down to retrieve it.

"They had roadblocks up at the Pittsburgh and Main intersection. They moved them to let me pass, but one of the cops told me that there was going to be some kind of downtown celebration and that my car would be trapped after ten. I told him that was fine, that I was going to a New Year's Eve party."

"Oh shit," I mutter, continuing on.

"What?" she says.

"Nothing. It doesn't matter now."

We approach 89, still over fifty yards away. A green light turns yellow, turns red at the empty intersection. No vehicles pass. Everything is dead quiet. I swallow.

"Can I have a cigarette?" Stacey asks, holding out her hand. I give her one.

There is a single flash from somewhere, but I cannot discern its origin and continue on, holding Stacey's hand now. My heart races in response to the dread emanating from the silent town all around us.

"Ross?" she says, then pauses, as if deliberating on how to broach the topic. "Ross, sweetie...are you all right?"

"I'll be better when we're back on the highway," I answer. "Around people."

"Are you sure you're okay? I mean, you're kind of freaking me—"

She does not finish her sentence. We reach the intersection, and her hand goes limp in mine and I let it go. I freeze.

"Do you hear that?" she whispers.

"Hear what?" I ask back, breathing heavily.

"It sounds like..."

But I hear it too. It's a distant, low sound, layered and cacophonous, very faint. It crescendos as we stand motionless in the middle of the street.

"Ross, what is that?" she whimpers.

It's coming from in front of us, from Highway 89. Stacey strains her eyes to see up the road into the darkness ahead. I swallow what tastes like bile.

"Ross, what is that noise?"

"It's moaning," I tell her. "We need to go back now."

Just as we are about to turn and run back to Preston's house, we see them. All of them.

They come spilling around the buildings, from across the highway, and lurch towards us. They moan, as if in agony, with each step they take.

"Ross, what is that? Who are those people?"

"Stacey, um."

"*Ross*," she yelps. "Who is that?"

"Stacey, we need to go back to Preston's house."

When we turn to flee, cameramen are waiting on both sides of the street ahead, videotaping our every movement. They scramble to keep up as we run back toward the house.

4

001:48:58

One hour, forty-eight minutes and fifty-eight seconds and counting downward.

Zombies are approaching the house from both sides of Main Street, each horde consisting of roughly fifty corpses. They're not advancing quickly, and I estimate from the edge of Preston's driveway that we have about twenty minutes before they'll actually reach us.

"Ross, you need to leave," Preston says when he sees us in his front yard again. "I'm calling the cops."

"Go ahead," I say. "Call them. Tell them to get up here quick."

"What?" he asks.

"Call. The. Cops."

"Um, I did. I really did," he says, seeing the look of terror etched across my face. "For some reason 911 isn't working on the cell phone I was using."

"Well try it again on someone else's."

"Why? What's going on?"

"You need to get everyone here inside the house."

"What?" he stammers. "Ross, you've fucking lost it."

"*Have I?*" I roar, grabbing Preston by the shoulders and pointing him in the direction of the crew setting up at the edge of the driveway.

"Dude…who is that?" he asks. "Why are they getting ready to film us?"

"Go look what's down the street," I tell him, storming away.

Doing a quick head count, there looks to be no less than sixty people here. I am about to stand on a chair and start rustling them inside when the band starts playing.

"We're Volatile Empty," the singer, Jaime, says, wearing black leather pants, no shirt, and a chain necklace with an oversized upside down wooden cross dangling from its **end**. "Happy New Millennium, faggots."

A crowd gathers in front of the band, and on the porch, loud announcements are made that they're starting. People begin pouring out of the house and collecting on the sidewalk all around me. I am surrounded by doomed teenagers, college kids, and other overage losers just like me, all of them cheering and drinking and putting their arms around girls and guys they just met tonight.

An overweight bass player begins strumming the low string of his guitar, and a moment later, the front-man jumps off of an amp while growling into the microphone. Drums kick in and suddenly I am caught in the torrent of a terrible rock song blasting across the property and drowning out the faint sounds of the moans as the creatures approach. A heavy opening riff transforms into a creepy guitar effect and light tom work on the drums.

Jaime half-sings, half-moans the line: *Black holes, PCs, self-aware traffic lights/ In this overcrowded, schizophrenic, whiskey-hipped exodus.*

Something about the music momentarily hypnotizes me. I am not sure whether I have become totally crippled by fear and a feeling of total helplessness, or if I am very surprised and impressed by Jaime's lyrics, but I stand frozen, anonymous in a throng of partiers, and I feel—

Preston whirls me around. His face is stricken with panic.

"It can't be that" is the first thing he says, having to yell over the music. "Not *again*."

"I think it is," I respond. "…Again?"

He holds both my shoulders, looking down. His mouth hangs open and he shakes his head, clenching his eyes shut.

"What do we do?" I ask. "*Again?*"

Preston doesn't answer me.

"Preston!"

He vomits.

It spills all around my shoes, a thin greenish liquid spattering on the concrete. The people around us gag and protest, backing away. I stand still, supporting Preston as he remains hunched over staring at his own throw up.

"Look," I say as calmly as possible. "I know I said it's impossible, but right before you assholes knocked me out, I was attacked by two of those things and now there's a hundred more on their way here. Preston, you need to get it the fuck together and tell me what we should do."

"Um," he says, wiping the trail of throw up from his chin with the sleeve of his jacket. "Um, we need to—we um—"

"We have to get everyone inside, right?" I ask, frantic. I can actually hear the moans now over the music.

"Ross, we can't get all these people in there!"

Jaime screams and the band launches into a menacing build-up.

"Well, we gotta do *something*, damn it."

Stacey punches her way through the crowd and grabs me by the arm.

"Ross, what are you two doing?" she stammers. "We have to get inside."

"We're working on it," I tell her.

"They're only about two hundred yards away—"

"Stacey, I said we're *working* on it! Piss off!"

She shakes her head in disbelief and leaves us. A moment later, I hear a terrible sound coming from one of the amps and then the guitar is unplugged. Jaime stops singing and asks Stacey what she thinks she's doing.

"The stairs," Preston says, the music halted now and his voice abnormally loud.

"The stairs?" I ask. "What—?"

"We need to get everyone upstairs, and then we need to destroy the staircase."

"Preston, I don't know if we have enough time," I say, wiping sweat from my brow.

"What is that moaning sound?" someone in the crowd asks.

"I have stuff in the tool shed out back—an axe and a hatchet," he says, already running away from me into the back yard.

People are milling around and asking lots of questions as Preston and I throw the door to the shed open and scramble into the darkness, emerging with tools to destroy the staircase. Stacey catches up, Lydia laughing behind her. I tell her to grab the baseball bat and crowbar mounted on the wall, and on my way out I grab the red half-full gas can and scurry back into the house.

"Get off the stairs," I shout at the people conversing above us in the living room. "Stacey, go outside and make everyone come back in here. Tell them to get to the second floor now."

She hurries off.

"How high up?" I ask Preston, looking up at the wooden steps above us.

"At least eight feet," he says, tears streaming down his face. "If you don't get it high enough, they may be able to, um, climb up."

We make it to about the seventh or eighth step and begin hacking at the wood. The first thing I attack is the old railing, chopping with the small hatchet at the posts, and when that proves too time-consuming, I begin violently kicking at it. The wood cracks and splinters and pops with each blow.

"What are you guys doing?" Shannon asks below us.

"Shannon," I bark, "Get your ass up here and help us, man."

Moments later, Shannon and I are kicking maddeningly at the wooden railing. Soon, large pieces of it begin sailing down into the living room below. People ask us what we're doing, all ignored. I can barely hear Stacey screaming at the top of her lungs outside under the groans from the approaching hordes. Soon, other caterwauls and, oddly, raucous laughter, are audible as the party attendees spot the army of undead descending on the house.

People begin scrambling up the staircase around us, slipping into the chunks of missing stairway that Preston has hacked away with his axe.

"We're not going to be able to finish in time," I say, looking at the macerated wooden planks that Preston is trying to demolish.

"We just have to create enough of a gap in the steps that they won't be able to step over," he says. "They can't jump"

"We don't know that," I whimper. "This isn't a fucking *movie*, Preston."

"Just *help* me, god damn it."

After the railing has been kicked free of the stairs by me and Shannon, we begin trying to rip out planks of wood, but it is almost a fruitless task as people incessantly tumble by, jumping over the two foot gap between steps. As Jaime, the singer for Volatile Empty begins up the steps, asking who those people are down the street, I grab him by the arm.

"Jaime, help them," I say, heading down the stairs.

"Why?" he says. "What is this shit?"

"Help us!" Preston roars, handing him the hatchet.

I run onto the porch, taking in the sight.

In the yard, people are only mildly freaking out, almost indifferent to whatever it is coming toward us at a little over a mile an hour. Stacey is at the edge of the driveway, bobbing up and down in panic. Lydia is standing next to Princess Star Bright in front of the porch, smoking a cigarette, seeming rather unworried.

"Get upstairs," I say to them, coming outside.

"Whatever, you prick," Star Bright says.

"This is some stunt you've pulled," Lydia laughs. "How'd you do it?"

I ignore her and meet up with Stacey.

"They're slow," she says, looking back and forth at both directions of Main. "But they're still coming. Oh my god, what the fuck, Ross? What the *fuck* are we going to do? What's happening?"

"They're destroying the staircase," I say absently. "Give them about another five minutes."

"We don't have that," she says.

Looking to the left, toward Pittsburgh Avenue, I can distinguish individual features now. Heading up Main Street is what appears to be a troupe of zombies of every size and shape. From Pittsburgh, the horde is led by what was once a young man in a White Zombie shirt, now a grayed corpse with his arm chewed up. From 89, they're following a bus driver with a mole on his right cheek that lurches along just ahead of the others. Pale intestines hang limply from a seven-inch gash in his stomach.

I turn my head to the right, at the other crowd. Just ahead of the rest is what looks like the first old man, the one who stepped in front of my car last week. His face is peeling away now, though, and when he sees me, his mouth hangs open and thick saliva oozes down his chin. Just behind him, with the others, is a young woman with long stringy blond hair, totally nude, her only jewelry a toe tag.

"As long as they move this slowly we'll have everyone upstairs," I say vacantly.

I look behind us at the party attachés. A few have attempted to scale the white wall of the glass factory behind Preston's yard, on the other side of a six foot chain link fence. Only a couple, though, have successfully made it onto the fire escape several feet above the ground. Others try to use a drain pipe to scale the wall, but fall back to the ground.

Devastatingly, there are still dozens of people milling around outside. I sigh heavily, a terribly unoriginal gesture.

"Let's get them inside," I say, grabbing Stacey's shirt sleeve. "Let's help finish the staircase."

"Ross," she says, pointing out to the street.

A man—a living, breathing man—has stepped out into the street from the schoolhouse parking lot. He is not in a radiation suit, but rather a pair of blue jeans and a white button up shirt. Hanging around his neck are Sony head phones attached to a device clipped to his belt. There is a sloppy goatee clinging to his otherwise clean-shaven face. I immediately recognize his role in all of this.

Another guy, wearing black pants and a tight black sweater, follows closely behind, carrying a wooden film marker.

"What is that?" Stacey asks. "What is he doing? He'll be killed, won't he?"

"I, uh, I don't think so," I say, watching him. "It's the director."

"What?" Stacey says.

He raises his arm high into the air. The crew standing about on the other side of the street, from the roofs of buildings and from behind the schoolyard fence, ready their cameras and microphones and lights and fog machines.

"Let's go," I say, pulling Stacey along. "Let's get upst—"

"Action!" the director yells, throwing his arm down. The black-clad assistant clicks the time marker.

And just like that, the zombies are running after us.

It occurs to me that this is not real, that the man was right, that the world has already long ago **end**ed, and that we are in the middle of some bizarre episode of Purgatory. It seems possible that this is all part of an elaborate set-up, that the people filming us are actually making a television show, an MTV special, a reality program to air on Sci-Fi Channel. None of this is real. It's supposed to measure our fear, our preparedness, our gut reactions as human beings raised and brainwashed on a never-**end**ing barrage of horror films and various degrees of terrible pop fiction and survival shows on TLC and Discovery Channel. I almost breathe a sigh of relief, no longer so frantic and certain of the doom I was once sure was about to befall us all.

That is, until the first person is eaten alive.

As Stacey and I run onto the porch, I turn and see Geoff Croix, a friend, slightly younger and better looking than me, a senior at the same college I attended, standing near one of the band's guitar amps. One of the creatures, a female wearing a nurse's uniform, tackles him from behind and bites into his cheek. The skin peels away, Geoff baying and convulsing as black-looking blood pumps from his missing face. Another one of them immediately grabs his arm, biting into his wrist. Two more crouch down beside his body, chomping into his neck and leg. Red liquid pours out of each wound, spilling onto the concrete. One of the crew rushes up to his body and pans into a close-up of his torn open belly.

There is screaming all around me.

The partiers left milling around out in the yard are converged upon by dozens of running corpses. They come spilling around both sides of the street, up the driveway, and into the crowd, who scream and try to run, but to no avail.

Volatile Empty's bassist, who was grabbing his guitar to take back upstairs, is grabbed at both arms. They are quickly bitten off, and the rest of him disappears into the hordes of undead.

One of Preston's ex-girlfriends, a girl named Clara, is attempting to scale the fence in the back yard when her leg is bitten into and she is jerked down onto the ground by six or seven of them. Her vociferations become wet and trickle off into a gurgle a moment later.

I remain still, two or three people making it onto the porch and inside the house, before Stacey grabs me by the arm and tries to tell me something.

"Ross, look out—"

One of them, a brown and gray cadaver in Dickies shorts and no shirt, who is missing a nipple and half the flesh of his chest, dives through the screen, collapsing over the wooden rail onto the deck. He clambers to his feet, snarling and erratic, and when his eyes meet mine I see nothing but a dull gray where his pupils should be shining, and he comes stumbling at us, tripping on an overturned plastic chair.

There is screaming all around me.

Another comes running up the steps onto the porch, followed by one of the cameramen, who zooms out of close-up to capture the entire scene. The zombie attempts to tackle me, but when he comes down on me, my strength gives way and I fall to my knees. His heavy body topples over my back and runs into the other zombie.

Stacey drops the bat and begins swinging the crowbar at their faces. The hooked **end** slashes across one of their skulls, pummeling out thick red blood and chunks of rotting flesh. She raises the bar to strike again, but two more of the creatures rip through the screen at the other **end** of the porch and her mouth falls open and the weapon falls to the floor. I snatch it back up just in time to strike one of them in the face. Its nose is broken and its left eye is punctured at the blow.

Preston is shouting for us somewhere behind me, and I grab Stacey by the hand to pull her into the house. The cameraman tries to follow us inside, but I stick my palm against the camera lens and shove him backward. He falls, not saying a word. I slam the door behind me and lock it, but one of the ghouls immediately punches through the glass and reaches out for me. We move deeper into the living room.

Inside, people are running around in all directions, one or two at a time trying to make the three or four foot jump from one section of the destroyed staircase to another several feet above it. Two different crewmen stand on the other side of the room, filming each jump from two different angles.

Monica 1 tries to make the leap, but when her foot lands on the hacked wooden step above her, the plank snaps and she falls between the two sections of staircase to the floor. Her leg breaks at the femur and she wails out in agony. As Stacey and I approach the steps, I see that the bone has actually pierced through the skin. Blood oozes out and Monica begins crying at the sight.

I hear one of the windows shatter in a back room, and a moment later, one of the party attendees gagging and choking in his death throes.

"We need to get up to the second floor," I tell Stacey next to me, but my voice is drowned out by the chaos. There is screaming all around me.

I ascend the two bottom steps and look up at the gap between us and see Shannon and Preston waving their arms about wildly and assuring us we can make it.

"You go first and help me up," Stacey says behind me. "Hurry."

A zombie enters the living room from the office, fresh blood smeared across his face, yellow bits of flesh hanging from his lips. The closer of the video crew moves in for a close-up. Stacey shrieks and asks who those people are.

Its arms outstretched, the creature marches toward us, moaning and twitching. For some reason, it is not running, as the others have, and I have ample time to ready myself for the attack. I kick at its hands and swing the crowbar back and forth clumsily. One of the blows breaks the creature's arm, but it is not even remotely stunned and advances toward me again and again.

"Jump," I order Stacey, and amazingly, she does this without a second thought, leaping up and grabbing for what is left of the railing above her. Her feet hang from the edge of the staircase and Shannon grabs her sweater sleeve and hoists her up the rest of the way.

When Preston wails, "Dude, help him," to the two crewmen documenting the battle, he is ignored.

Between the monsters' advances, I glance up at her on the second floor of the house. Her eyes meet mine for only a split second before everything goes wrong.

The zombie attacks again, and I kick it square in the chest, bringing it to the ground. It occurs to me to deliver a heavy blow to the head, possibly killing it. But, as I raise the bloody crowbar to strike, two of the living room windows shatter simultaneously and two more of them climb into the room. Instead of attacking me, however, they come down upon Monica 1, who is still tending to her injured leg in a pile of wooden debris between the sections of staircase. She tries to cry out, but the first thing they bite into is her throat. Blood spurts out in every direction, actually streaking across the wall on the opposite side of the room. The zombie I was about to finish off ignores me standing over it and instead joins the other two in devouring Monica's corpse.

I sigh, a terribly unoriginal gesture, and pause, trying to decide what to do. If I do not make the leap onto the second floor, I will fall to certain death at the hands of the three corpses who are now devouring Monica's intestines, breasts, and heart. I decide I need to make the jump—at all costs—and head for the stairs.

"Ross, look out!" Shannon yells, pointing at something behind me.

I turn just in time to see the front door knocked from its hinges. The naked woman and an obese man wearing a blood-stained jersey come slouching inside, only a few feet away from me. The camera crew follows.

"Oh, he's *fucked*," Preston says, panicked.

I have no time to react. I bolt into the kitchen to my right, the only direction available. By this time three of them are coming after me.

The fridge door, when opened, blocks the doorway into the room. Dropping the crowbar, I grab the handle and swing it open harshly. It slams into the woman's torso. She sneers, grabbing at me. I duck below the fridge door, putting all my weight against it as they try to force their way into the room.

"Ross, are you okay?!" Stacey is screeching from the other room. "Please, *answer* me!"

I ignore her request, pushing the fridge door backward as hard as I can. Jars of pickles and catsup bottles and grape jelly tumble off the racks onto the floor. Above me, the lady reaches down and grabs my hair, tugging at me painfully and I groan, reaching for anything I can find. My hand touches something—a jar of jelly. I snatch it up and swing it as hard as I can upward. The glass container shatters on the top of her head, and she loses her grip on my wet black hair. I jerk my head away from her outstretched fingers and am covered in thick purple jam and bits of glass.

I leap to my feet and pick the crow bar back up. Taking a single strike out against the zombie's forehead, the steel rod caves the roof of her skull in, and blood splatters out of her ears and eye sockets. She falls backward silently and does not revive.

A child-like voice inside me laughs.

You have to get them in the head.

More of them are right behind the female, and they quickly come for me. The kitchen is too small. There's no way of making a stand against them. Instead of taking on the two new adversaries, I quickly scan the room for an exit. There is a square window above the sink, and outside, one of the cameramen films my desperation. I pitch the crow bar through the glass, sending splintered shards everywhere. The bar crashes against the large TV camera and the crewman stumbles backward.

One of the re-animated corpses grips my sweater, but I wrench it free and leap up onto the counter. My foot slips though, and I slam my knee onto the edge of the sink. The pain is excruciating, but I do not have time even to scream, as they are pawing for me. I am left with no alternative but to jump, head first, out through the broken window, into the darkness below…

The wind is knocked out of me. My arm twists upward when I hit the grass and I wail out. The two zombies are reaching out of the shattered kitchen window six feet above me, trying to find their prey.

Outside, there is screaming all around me.

There are three packs of the ghouls, all feasting on different friends of mine. As I get to my feet, several of them that had been trying to reach the people wedged between the chain link fence and the building behind Preston's property spot me, and they head my way, arms outstretched.

"Ross, get up here," a familiar female voice shouts.

Lydia, Mindy, and someone I do not recognize, a guy with wavy brown hair, are perched on the flat metal roof of the tool shed. Without thinking, unarmed now, I head for the small building. I grab for the edge of the roof, seven feet from the ground, and Lydia and the guy try to pull me up by my arms. At that same instant, the two undead both grab me by the legs. I kick furiously as they try to bite into my pants, momentarily knocking them off. They come back quickly though, and one of them reaches for an exposed area of my heel.

"Ross, look out," Mindy says, pointing at my left foot.

I jerk my leg away as Lydia and the guy hoist me up onto the flat roof of the shed with them. The creatures surround the shed, moaning and waving their arms about in an attempt to reach us. They can't. I fall to the sheet metal serving as a roof. I pant and try to gather my wits, but succeed only in collapsing into an hysterical bout of sobbing. Someone, maybe Lydia, begs me not to pass out.

3

"LOOK OUT!" someone wails, but it is too late.

The five or six people trapped between the fence and the back of the glass factory are converged upon from both sides by zombies that have somehow managed to find their way onto the property. We watch helplessly as each one of the youths is devoured in gruesome fashion. The carnage is documented from four different angles by different radiation-suited crew members.

The monsters go for the more vulnerable extremities first: legs, arms, necks and faces. Then, as each one of the victims ceases to struggle and their eyes roll back (if they have not already been gouged out of the sockets) and they go into their final spasms, the ghouls rip their chests and stomachs open, exposing glistening insides and thick red blood that comes spilling out all over the ground. More corpses soon join the feeding frenzy.

All around us, zombies stalk. Slowing back down to their original deliberate gait, they devour what's left of the fifteen or so carcasses littering the ground which, after the first fifteen minutes or so, consist of mostly blood-stained half-denuded bones and stringy bits of meat that could not be bitten away. After that, they wander down the street, into the house, and surround the tiny shed. The door to the enclosure was swung shut, and none of them have made it inside. For some inexplicable reason, this relieves me.

Ghouls wander in and out of the house. They stumble out of the shattered windows onto the crowd and slowly rise to their feet to continue gadding about aimlessly. They reach out for us, give up, leave, come back, reach out again, and then meander back inside the house. When they leave the yard, they are quickly grabbed on the arm by one of the film crew and escorted back.

The moans die down after the first few minutes to a low constant din, but never totally stop.

"Are you three all right?" I ask my companions.

Lydia and Mindy do not respond, both tending in quiet little whimpers to one another. The guy across from me, wearing a black hooded Deftones shirt smeared with blood, nods. He takes in deep breaths and begins to almost laugh but stops. He does this three more times.

"Who are you?" I ask him, reaching into my pocket for cigarettes. The pack is smashed, and when I pull it out and examine the contents, I see only three smokes that are not bent or broken. I pull one out, offer him one, which he shakes his head no to, and light it. I ask, "Are you one of Preston's friends?"

He nods. "Pres and Lydia come into my restaurant a lot."

I snicker at this and glance at Lydia hatefully. She meets my glare and offers one of her own, followed by the finger.

"What's your name?" I ask.

"Mark."

"Mark, I'm Ross," I say, about to extend my hand, but it is covered in grime and congealed blood. I retract it. "You don't have a cell phone, do you, Mark?"

"Actually," he says thoughtfully, reaching into his pants pocket. His hand emerges holding a small black device. "I'll call 911."

Mark presses buttons, holds the cell phone to his ear and waits. A moment later he curses and presses buttons again.

"It didn't work?" I ask.

He shakes his head. "The call doesn't go through, like I'm low on battery. But I'm not so I don't get it."

"We aren't going to be making any phone calls out of here," I say. "I think they anticipated that."

"Who?" he asks, slipping the phone back into his pocket.

"Them," I respond, pointing at the crew.

"Who are they?

"I don't really know, Mark."

He looks out at the creatures all around us. "Um, like, do you have *any* idea what's going on?"

I am staring at the camera crew approaching the shed, standing just behind the throng of zombies surrounding our tiny island. Across the street, several others film us from the rooftops of the school.

"Mark, I am clueless," I mutter indifferently, sitting back and leaning on my elbows.

A moment later, one of the upstairs windows across from us slides open. Preston sticks his head out.

"Oh man, thank Christ," he sighs, seeing us. "Are you guys okay?"

"I think so," I say, having to almost shout over the dead people's groans. "Are you?"

"Are you okay, Lyd?" he asks, ignoring me. "Mindy?"

Lydia nods, wiping away tears. Mindy does not respond. She flicks a spot of dried blood off of her cheek.

"How many of you are there?" I ask. "Is Stacey all right?"

"Um, I'm not sure. Hold on." He disappears inside the house. Several minutes later, he re-emerges. "Stacey's not hurt, but she's kind of freaking out. She won't come near the window. I think you guys need to get over here."

"Yeah, we'll be right over," I say, rolling my eyes. "Um, in case you haven't noticed, Pres, just a couple of feet below me, denizens of the morgue are *seething*. Get it?"

"Well, we've got to figure *something* out," Preston says. "There are four of you and there are eleven of us, including me. I think you guys would be better off over here with us."

"Holy shit," I say, stunned. "There are only fifteen of us left? I thought more made it upstairs before the attack."

"More did," Preston says. "Only that was before four of those fuckers climbed in through my bedroom window."

"How is that possible?" I stammer.

"I don't know," Preston says. "But they got up here. I got the door shut and tied a rope to the door handle that leads to one of the stairway banisters. It's pretty taut. I don't think they can get out, since only one can pull on the door at a time."

"How many of us did they get?" I ask.

"Five are dead, and one more alive but bitten before we were able to get them locked in the bedroom. You know, I think I killed one of them actually. I broke a stool over its head and it fell down and never got back up. Ross, you know what that means? I think you have to—"

"Yeah, I know," I say. "You have to get them in the head, right?"

"Ross, what's going on, man? This is impossible, right?"

"Apparently it's not," I say, lying flat on the metal roof.

Through the throng of dead people, I can still see Preston's black box that tells us how much of the millennium there is left. The bass drum it was planted on has been knocked sideways, and I can read the digital numbers.

000:44:58. Forty-four minutes, fifty-eight seconds and counting downward.

"Ross, Jaime and Gary are throwing the dead bodies out the window into the side yard," Preston says from the movie room window. The ghouls below moan at his presence. "Oh, shut *up*," he says, glaring down at them.

"That's maybe a good idea," I agree. "You never know."

"But now we have to deal with the others."

"What others?" Mark suddenly asks. "What are you guys talking about?"

"He's talking about the one who was bitten," I explain, staring at the seconds counting backward on the timer.

"What about them?" Mark says, suddenly very agitated.

"Won't they…turn?" Preston says.

"Dude, for you two having no idea what's going on," Mark says, "You both seem to have it all figured out."

"I know," I say. "That's because these are, from all appearances, zombies."

"Wait!" someone shouts from ground level. "Hold on a moment, please."

The director, who speaks in a slightly non-distinguishable European accent, comes walking up from the street smoking a cigarette. He pushes his eyeglasses up on the bridge of his nose and rubs his face, looking exhausted. As he approaches, he begins pushing his way through the crowd of corpses. They pay no attention at all to his presence, and within moments, he has stopped just underneath the edge of the roof. He looks up at me. All of us, Preston included, stare at him dumbfounded.

"If you could, Ross, I need you to start that speech for me again," he says soothingly. "You see, the angle—I did not—the angle was not good, no? Further, I am afraid that the mikes may not have picked everything up adequately. Could you begin again, please? This is important. I just want to get it perfect, no?"

I do not say anything. The director does not wait for my response; he walks back through the horde of zombies that just devoured most of the people I know. He joins several crew members, all waiting at the **end** of the driveway with cameras and microphones and halogen lights.

"Mark," I say, my head suddenly spinning. "Um, these are, from all appearances, the same kind of zombies you would see in a—"

"Hold on," Lydia says now, standing up and looking at me with disgust. "Wait just a minute."

"—movie," I finish.

"Why are you cooperating with *him*?" she asks. "These assholes aren't here to help us. They're just filming it. They're just as bad as those…*things* down there. Ross, you idiot, I watched them stand right there in the front yard and tape your friend Geoff get eaten. So why the fuck would you do what they ask of you?"

I have no response to her inquiries, and decide to begin where I left off. "Mark, if these creatures go down when you destroy the brain or sever the head from the rest of the body, and if they're dead people who have come back to life to eat us, then it's reasonable to believe that if they bite one of us, then we will eventually become one of them."

"But that's in a movie," he argues. "You don't *know*."

"No we don't," I say. "But I think I'm right, regardless."

I explain to Mark that, according to the popular theory of zombies, if a normal human being is bitten then, without fail, they too will eventually become one of the undead themselves. Times vary according to different films and the number and severity of bites. For instance, Flyboy, who was bitten savagely in the neck and right leg, turned within minutes; in the same film, Roger took what seemed like days from two small bites in the arm and leg. All zombie films, however, reach the general consensus that once a human being is bitten, they too will join the ranks of carnivorous walking dead.

As Lydia listens to my spiel, she groans loudly and slams back down into a sitting position on the metal roof of the shed. The zombies below grow agitated and moan loudly.

"They go down with a blow to the head," I am saying to myself, nodding. "They're eating us. They're dead and they're walking around like *that*. Hey, Preston!"

"What?" he says from across the yard.

"Who was bitten?"

"Robin, in the arm when we were trying to get them back into the bedroom."

"Where is he now?"

"In the spare room with the others, tearing up the wooden furniture to board up the windows."

"How does the wound look?"

"Infected," he admits.

"Shit," I mutter, turning away from him. I think for a minute, and then turn back to Preston. Mark waits anxiously next to me for my response. "Put him in the spare bedroom and barricade him in. And I'd do it soon."

"Right," he says. "That's what I thought. But they're not going to like it."

"They?"

"His girlfriend Melanie will freak out."

"Do you care?"

"She might not want him to be locked up in there by himself," he says, more quiet now as not to be overheard. "They'll fight it. I can't really blame them."

"Look," I say. "First things first. This shed's going to collapse under us. We need to get over there with you guys."

"I agree," Lydia says.

"But how?" Preston asks.

I look down all around me at the cannibalistic ghouls, knowing that, eventually, either this roof will cave in or the entire shed will topple over. Next to me, Mindy mutters something about the stench just before vomiting over the side. The corpses eat her throw up.

Preston takes an inventory of the upstairs area of the house. He comes back five minutes later.

"There's nothing," he laments. "We don't even have rope to string across the two roofs. The one tied to my door handle isn't long enough anyway, but even if it were, those things would get out and we'd be screwed."

"That's right," I nod.

"I don't know how you're going to get over here."

"What about the shed?" I ask, remembering that they have not ventured inside. "Is there rope in the shed?"

"I'm not—no, I don't think so."

"Damn."

"You might be stuck," he says. There is the sound of glass shattering from inside the house. Preston looks behind him. He ducks back inside and disappears.

A moment later we hear the screams.

The four of us stare silently at the house. There is loud crashing and different voices all yelling and cursing simultaneously. This agitates the undead around us, which push against the sides of our shed. The thin metal creaks and bends at their dead weight.

For almost ten minutes we stare across the yard, waiting. Then there is another crash, and I see the shadow of a body falling to the ground from the side of the house.

Preston re-appears at the window five minutes later, sweating and spattered with blood.

"One of them tried climbing in through the window in the bathroom," he pants.

"Are you guys all right?" I ask.

"Shannon's not. It tore his arm off just below the elbow."

"Jesus," Mark says next to me.

"What are you going to do with him?" I ask, wiping away tears that come to my eyes when I hear this news.

"I don't know, man," Preston says, shaking his head. "He's going into shock, but I think he's done. He's going to die."

"You need to get rid of the bodies," I say. "Throw them out the window."

"What the hell are you talking about?" Mark asks me. "You're going to feed them to those things down there?"

"No," I explain. "We're going to get rid of future zombies. Besides, they only eat warm flesh. Our friends' carcasses will be safe, as trivial as that point is."

Mark says nothing, stares at me, then Preston, in disgust.

"Never mind," I say. "Just take our word for it. This is necessary."

"I'm going to go and check on him," Preston says. "I'll be back. Try to figure out a way over here."

"Oh yeah," I say. "The geniuses and I will get right on it."

"Fuck you, Ross," Lydia croaks.

"I'm on to you," Mark says after a moment.

"What?" I ask, confused.

"I'm on to you," he repeats quietly. "Both of you."

"On to us?" I repeat. "On to us about what?"

On to you.

On to you?

On to you. Something dark comes over me. Whatever Mark is saying about me and Preston knowing more about this mess than we let on becomes garbled noise. I rub my temples and close my eyes. I have a memory, a memory of me saying these two words, of me accusing someone of knowing more than they let on. A memory of me saying that I was on to what they were really up to. Only it seems less like a memory of something I already said and more like something I will say. But that makes no sense.

Has this already happened?

"Mark," I pick up, snapping out of it. "I assure you, again, that we have no clue what's going on. We just know what we see."

"And what is that?" he asks, glaring.

"Preston and that slut right there," I say, pointing at Lydia, "We've been discussing a situation like this since I started selling horror movies three years ago, several times on the front porch of this very house. Now listen to me, Mark: I didn't believe in the idea of a dead body getting up and eating people ever in my life until about forty-five minutes ago. But, there it is, right now, happening all around us. There are indeed dead bodies getting up and eating people. So if we are, in fact, in this situation now, Mark, whether you like it or not, Preston and I are going to deal with it the only way we know how. So if you have any better suggestions, I for one am all ears, since I never really wanted this responsibility to begin with."

"I guess we need to get over to the house," he says, looking away from me.

"I think it's a good idea," I agree, looking all around the shed. "I just don't know how we're going to get across this yard."

2

It's the only time in my entire life that I have ever been happy to see Cordelia. I fear that it will also be the last.

Brad's green Tundra pulls into the driveway from Main Street, having taken 89 to get here. It creeps up into the yard about fifteen feet before Brad hits the brakes. Three dozen zombies or so stop their aimless wandering and immediately begin slouching towards the truck. I hear Cordelia curse.

By the time I realize the opportunity presented it is almost too late.

As Cordelia's boyfriend begins to back up, corpses pile out of the house from the unseen front door. They block his retreat, and Brad stops. He pulls forward at an odd angle, running into Volatile Empty's drum kit and knocking the New Year's timer onto the ground. Then the truck slams into the side of the tiny back porch. The entire house shudders. The truck cuts off. A zombie topples over the porch railing and onto the hood, and Brad responds by punching the horn.

"We gotta go *now*," I say, already jumping from the side of the shed into the newly vacated back yard.

Most of the creatures responded to Brad and Cordelia's arrival by giving chase, leaving the area between the house and shed relatively open. Only three, near the back fence, spot my movement, and they begin their approach. On the trampled grass, I look up and try to coax the girls down. Mark immediately sits on the edge of the roof and then pushes himself off to the ground next to me. Lydia begins to follow, but cannot get Mindy, who is all but catatonic, from off her perch.

Meanwhile, Cordelia has slid the back window of the truck open and climbed onto the bed. She is surrounded by ghouls reaching out for her, one slowly climbing up onto the tire.

"Mindy, we have to get inside," Lydia says.

"Leave her," I bark, already being attacked from my left.

I push the cannibal down onto its back, and as it struggles to its feet, I pick up the crow bar from the ground, since it was left behind after I threw it through the kitchen window. I smash the ghoul's skull, and there is a loud crack as its head caves in, spattering me with congealed blood.

A teenage girl's corpse comes at me from the side of the house, snarling and grabbing for my shoulder. I kick her in the stomach and grab her by the arm, jerking her to the ground. Mark, holding his lower left arm, follows behind me, butting another zombie down with his shoulder.

Cordelia makes a quick sprint from one side of the bed to the other, using a portion of the truck's railing not covered by zombies as a spring point. She leaps over the heads of two rows of ghouls onto the back porch balustrade. Then, screaming the entire time, she kicks one of the undead in the face, sending it backward. Mark and I are close behind, dashing up the steps after her.

Once on the porch, I look behind me. Mindy finally jumps down from the roof of the shed, but falls to her side, wailing in agony and holding her heel. Lydia stands by, bobbing up and down as some of the monsters have become disinterested in Brad and have turned towards the girls.

"Come on!" I cry.

Brad slides through the back transom into the bed of his truck just as one of the zombies picks up a large rock from Preston's parents' unkempt flower bed and smashes the driver side window.

"*Brad*," I squeal from the porch, "Jump! Come on!"

Lydia picks Mindy up from the ground just as two of the corpses round the shed and follow after them.

Brad makes the same short sprint as Cordelia did, but when he jumps from the bed to the porch railing, one of the creatures reaches up and grabs at his leg. Brad falls short of clearing the banister and his legs slam against the wood. He somersaults awkwardly down onto the deck. I grab his arm and hoist him up. Lydia and Mindy run inside behind me.

"I can't believe that bitch left me," he groans, hobbling inside the house. "By the way, what's going on?"

"I'll tell you later."

In the living room, Mark has already leapt over the broken section of stair case, and is now helping Preston and Mark hold onto a knotted white sheet that Cordelia uses to scale the eight foot vertical ascent.

Zombies begin pouring back into the house. They come in through the front and back doors, moaning deafeningly.

Lydia helps Mindy up the sheet rope, and then climbs up herself. As Brad is lifted up, I make a run for it just as one of the ghouls grabs for my arm from the front entranceway. I make the jump, slamming into Preston and knocking him over. One of my legs dangles from the last dismantled step. Brad, next to me, is still climbing up, the lower portion of his body exposed to the ghouls that clamber over.

"Get him up!" Preston yells. "Hurry!"

In one final pull, the rest of Brad's body is lifted onto the safe ledge. Only his right foot dangles from the edge.

"Welcome to the party, Brad," I say, offering my hand to help him to his feet. "Watch out for your—"

Brad suddenly jerks around in horror and lets out a terrible squeal. When he pulls his right leg the rest of the way up onto the staircase, his heel is missing.

Preston downplayed the dire straits the people inside the house were enduring.

The upper half of the stairs is smothered in crimson liquid. The upstairs hallway is worse. An arm, probably Shannon's, rests in a pool of red, two large chunks of flesh missing just below the place where one of the creatures gnawed it off. As Preston and Cordelia help Brad, who is bleeding profusely from where the back of his foot used to be, into the spare room with most of the others, I stay behind to try to figure out what to do next.

Stacey is lying in a fetal position next to the movie room door, crying silently to herself. When she sees me enter the corridor, she immediately smiles, sits up and holds out her arms for me to come to her, and so I do.

I get down on my haunches and give Stacey a hug. She squeezes so hard I cough.

"Are you all right?" I ask. "Have you been bitten?"

"No," she whispers. "But I am definitely *not* all right, Ross. What's happening?"

"I'm going to try to figure that out, sweetie. But I need to go for a minute and check out the situation. Okay?"

She nods, relents her tight grip around my shoulders, and I move on.

The first thing I do is take in who has survived thus far. I decide to grab a sheet of scrap paper from Monroeville and write down who is left, who is who, who has been bitten, and who will be a problem. It takes longer than I thought it would, and in that time, Shannon, who has been lying next to the boarded-up window in a pool of blood so thick it looks black, dies. When his girlfriend, one of the Camillas, tries to stop Preston and Jaime from snatching up the body to chuck out the window, Preston kicks her in the shoulder. They leave her sobbing hysterically in the closet of the spare room.

After five minutes, I compile a sloppy list on yellow notebook paper. I look it over, adding notes. Just before the New Year, the Armageddon, the **end** of the world, the list reads as thus:

Zombie Survivor List

1. *Ross—Potentially a leader. Has this already happened?*

2. *Preston—Another potential leader, although I will kill him if he survives.*

3. *Princess Star Bright (a.k.a. Mindy)—Unbitten, but will die. She weighs us down, and in the event that someone must be sacrificed for the greater good of us all, she goes.*

4. *Lydia—Dies after Mindy.*

5. *Mark—Useful if reasoned with, but could be trouble. May also be bitten in the arm and hiding it. Interrogate later. If bitten, knock unconscious (he will not go quietly) and isolate immediately. If not, utilize his strengths and keep him close.*

6. *Stacey—Unbitten, strong if provoked.*

7. *Cordelia—Probably not bitten, but a cutthroat who left her own boyfriend to die. Do not trust her.*

8. *Brad—Bitten and already dead. Isolate immediately. Cordelia will not follow.*

9. *Jaime—Unbitten and extremely useful. Seems to have some pop cultural knowledge of zombie dynamics. Keep close.*

10. Robin—Bitten and also already dead. Isolate with Brad in spare room most vulnerable to the zombies.

11. Melanie—Robin's girlfriend. Will be trouble when Robin is quarantined. Consider locking her up with the infected.

12. Monica 2—Unbitten but useless. Can paint the zombies or deliver spoken word performance later, but for now, consider invisible and expendable.

13. Quentin—Useless until Monica 2 dies.

14. Gary—Jaime's friend. Unbitten, seems to help out adequately. Stays close to Jaime. Latent homosexuals?

15. Camilla—As useless as Mindy now that Shannon is dead.

16. David—Unsure, but seems to help out just enough.
Keeps to himself and looks shady.
Does he have a camera? Is he wired?
Investigate later.

I fold the sheet up and slide it into my pant pocket. Then I check on the status of the fortifications. The windows to the spare room are already boarded up using a stool surface and book shelves. Zombies, at least two of them, still reach in through the tiny gaps in the wood. Their moans inspire insanity.

After Shannon's body is covered in the same sheet that was being used as a tourniquet on his missing arm, we heave him out the window of Monroeville. It lands on the heads of several corpses milling around in the back yard, breaking one's neck. Immediately afterward, Preston and Stacey, who shows up stone-faced and suddenly ready for war, board up the lone window using two closet shelves. Stacey uses the one available hammer and Preston wields a heavy stone book**end** from his trip to Mexico.

I help Preston rip the closet door of the spare room off of its hinges. Jaime and Gary carry it out into the hallway. They position it above the rope tied to the door handle of the master bedroom, and then nail it against the door, creating more of a blockade against the four ghouls inside. Then, another book shelf is brought out and nailed underneath the rope, so that the ghouls cannot crawl through if the door is ever pulled open. Jaime uses the other book**end**, while Gary hammers nails with one of Preston's cast iron sculptures of a blue dragon.

I watch the progress from the hallway. Behind me Stacey and Lydia argue over something. Brad squeals in pain from the spare room. Preston stands next to me as I watch Jaime and Gary finish the door. He has a half-cocky look on his face.

"Well, what do you think?" he asks me.

"What do *I* think? I think we're fucked."

1

In New York, people are celebrating.

The small white television in Monroeville is turned on. It did rest upon a book case, but it is now sitting crookedly on the floor surrounded by hundreds of movies and random back issues of *Fangoria*. The book case is now dismantled and its pieces either nailed to windows or lying in the hallway, waiting to be used if the situation grows worse. Which it will.

With Stacey sitting in the chair behind me, drinking a beer I have no idea where she got, I hunch down in front of the TV. In Time Square, Dick Clark narrates as millions of people cheer and make incoherent noises as they watch a huge brightly lit globe slowly inch its way down a metal pole.

"Why did you ask me before Christmas if I'd been thinking about the **end** of the world, Ross?" Stacey asks behind me.

I do not answer.

A timer at the bottom of the screen reads 48 seconds. Outside, on the ground next to the porch, surrounded by walking dead, Preston's timer surely reads the same.

000:00:48. Forty-eight seconds and counting downward.

Brad has gone unconscious in the hallway. Cordelia rubs his forehead, feeling pangs of guilt now for leaving him in the truck. She knows he will die.

Robin and Melanie have retreated to the spare room. Robin is complaining that his arm hurts, and his whole body is experiencing a dull pain, like the flu. He has grown pale and begun sweating profusely. Melanie has been hugging against him, crying.

In the closet of the same room, Camilla has barricaded herself behind a pile of old clothes. She wails in bereavement, and then goes quiet as she plots something.

Lydia and Preston are trying to talk to Mindy in the hallway. Mindy says something at one point that I do not hear. All three of them turn toward the bedroom, staring at me. Then they whisper to each other.

Mark strikes up a conversation at the edge of the stairs with Jaime and Gary. He keeps holding his arm, sometimes wincing. He is sweating.

Quentin and Monica 2, now just Monica, converse quite calmly, considering, in the hallway near the master bedroom door. Monica lights a cigarette.

I don't know where David is.

000:00:00. The downward count is over.

On television, the ball drops. Amid a hundred million cheering fools, the world slides devastatingly into another eon. The irreparable damage inflicted upon this earth, the bombs and diseases and genocides and starvation and mass murder in the name of a hundred different gods, is momentarily forgotten as folks all across America kiss one another, drink cheap headache-inducing champagne, and thank God for not returning tonight to stake His claim on a remorselessly shitty world.

Here, in this house in this neighborhood in this deserted part of this small Florida community, the power goes out. People start screaming and going nuts. Outside, Preston's New Year countdown timer, as it was apparently a bomb the entire time, explodes. Flames and smoke spit out of the device and the back porch railing is now probably on fire.

"Ross?" Stacey calls out in the dark.

"Yes, Stacey?"

"Happy New Year."

But when she slides over to me and we kiss in the darkness, I feel nothing.

0

In the Czech Republic, "no" means "yes" and "nay" means "no." Americans are always confused, especially when being solicited by prostitutes.

Muslims do not take well to the Koran being translated into other languages, as it is arranged as poetry specifically designed for the Arabic tongue. This is an interesting juxtaposition to the Christians' Holy Bible. They typically want it translated into every language, as its original message, its original tongue, was long ago lost, hundreds of years before Jesus Christ found his way into the hearts of the majority of the world's population. Their only hope now is not to enchant readers with the beauty of the Bible's words, but to scare them into submission with its raw messages of both God's wrath and potentially infinite salvation.

Cordelia told me these things in an effort to prove that nothing is translated correctly, not even among two people who supposedly speak the same language. In the real world, everyone speaks their own dialect totally foreign to all others. No one really understands anyone. There is no such thing as communication. The abysmal attempts at truly empathizing and working with one's fellow man always inevitably result in starting over amidst the ashes of thousands of people.

The door to the interrogation room swings open. A black Marine stands in the entryway and awaits a response from the men questioning me.

"Yes, Johnson?" Martin finally says.

"There's a fire, sir."

"A what?" he sighs.

"A fire. On the east **end** of the compound. One of the watch towers exploded."

"Oh, Christ," Martin says, momentarily burying his face in his hands. He regains his composure quickly, though. "How did it happen?"

"I'm—I'm not sure, sir. But we lost Holland and Dawson."

"All right. Well, before the fence gives way, have Unit 54 go out there with one of the trucks and isolate the fire as best they can. But don't put it out. We need to conserve our water. Okay?"

"Yes sir," Johnson says, slinking away. He closes the door behind him.

After a long silence, Martin looks to me in annoyance.

"Well?" he spits.

"Son, are you going to finish?" the man behind me, the man whose voice has been altered and that I am not allowed to see, asks.

"Ross," Martin says, standing up from his chair. "What happens next? What happens on New Year's morning?"

I light a cigarette, staring into the camera lens.

"How bad was the fire on the side of the house? Was the countdown timer really a bomb, son?"

"How long before Brad turned? Before Robin? Does the severity of the bite directly affect the gestation rate of the zombie virus?"

"About that director, Ross. Was it the same man that filmed you when you were first assaulted at the hotel?"

"How long has it been since you spoke to her?"

"Why did you obey the director's wishes for a re-shoot of the scene? Don't you find this odd, Ross?"

"*Answer* us, Ross."

All fiction, every genre and every sub-genre, functions in one of two ways, and occasionally both simultaneously. It either portrays life as what it could be, either better or worse; or, it works to reflect life as it already is, either directly or through metaphorical imagery.

Zombies are the most important of all horror sub-genres. Where the vampire serves to reflect the abundance of disease spread through precarious lifestyles, or to illustrate the dangers of romance in a non-romantic world, or stresses the importance of tradition, faith, and spirituality, zombies speak to these facets and a hundred more. Where man-created monsters and freaks of nature serve as cautionary tales of there being some things mankind has no business tampering with, only the zombie genre reflects mankind itself. Where slashers deal with the attrition of lustful sinners at the hands of one of these acts' unwitting ex-victims, zombies deal with the issues of stoic morality in a much more clear-headed, contemporary fashion, and embrace societal evolution.

I decided with Preston on the porch one night that the reason why zombies are so important is because, in the simplest of terms, they are mindless. This trait in itself reflects mankind in its most primitive and natural state. The pop science author Michael Crichton once paraphrased the theories of various modern renowned thinkers, and ascertained that human beings' most natural and innate instinct is not to survive, or procreate, or imagine the future or gather berries or destroy their surroundings. Their most primal instinct was to conform.

And zombies most definitely conform. They are mindless, only slightly modified versions of us. As the red-headed Barbara remarked, "They're us. We're them and they're us."

And they are. Every time a ragtag bunch of confused citizens gathers up loose boards and barricades the windows of a decrepit farmhouse, they are only working to stop other *people* from behaving *exactly as they are designed to.* The people are fighting for survival, but the zombies' instinct is not to kill. The death of a human being at the hands of the undead is incidental.

A zombie's primary function is, quite simply, to eat the flesh off the bones of the living. This is not for nourishment, nor is it a religious rite of passage or an addiction or life-giving practice, like the vampires' need for blood, which is all of these things. A zombie eats people because that is what a zombie does, nothing more.

And if it can't, nothing changes. It does not die. It may decompose to nothingness, but there are always a thousand more left, and they will likewise be spreading their conformity until they, too, wither away to dust. The zombie species will go on forever, fed and unfed alike. It will never stop. It will outlive *nosferatu*, Frankenstein's monster, and a convention center full of mask-wearing serial killers. It will outlive the human race and every one of its abortions and abominations.

A person who becomes one of the living dead eats people because whatever virus loaded inside the bite of one of these ghouls does not kill a person outright, but only slightly alters them so that they *have to* eat people. In short, the zombie virus, the zombie way, is to conform.

People will fight this conformity, as they always have. But, inevitably, they will acquiesce to the onslaught of the undead armies of the world because, in the **end**, people *want* to be this mindless, this simple, this driven, this uniform.

This perfect.

"And that's why the zombie genre is so phenomenally important. It speaks to us on more levels than we can even fathom. It portrays life as it is, as it will be, and as it could be both in perfect mirror imagery and in its own morbid allegorical poetry. It exposes both the infinite strengths and irreparable weaknesses of all of us, and what we are capable of becoming unless we, too, evolve. Until then, every time we hide out on the second floor of a decrepit old house and stare down at these creatures hatefully, we're only deluding ourselves into thinking that we are somehow better than what we are."

Martin and the man I am not allowed to see say nothing. Martin sits down opposite me, lights a cigarette. He sighs and rubs his forehead.

"There was this boy," I say quietly. The image of him, in cheap blue jeans and a stained white tee shirt, is burnt into my retinas, like the last thing you see before a nuclear explosion.

"Does this have *anything* to do with New Year's of 2000, Ross?"

"This boy came into my sixth grade history class. This was way before I realized that everything I knew was wrong, mind you. This was before I found out about the Holocaust, the Armenian genocide, Pine Ridge, or Project Rainbow and Montauk. This was before I realized that this country was founded by cock-suckers, and that none of my heroes would ever appear on a stamp."

"The *boy*, Ross," Martin snaps, slightly conspiratorially.

"This boy comes into the room and my teacher introduces him to the class. He's just transferred from Polk County or something. But in the **end**, he's sat down next to Stephanie Sherwin."

"Who?"

"And this girl immediately, in front of everyone, openly rants on how his jeans are covered in dust, in dried concrete and plaster, and that his shirt has tiny holes in the sleeve and a yellow stain in the white fabric. The boy grinned stupidly and ignored her embarrassing overtures on both his obviously low income and his family's hard times. He kept smiling and tried to take notes and grinned throughout the whole class period, and even told Stephanie to have a nice day when the bell rang."

"What does this have to do with *anything*, Ross?"

"He came back for about another week and then I never saw him again. The rumor was that wherever his family was lodged, the eviction notice appeared after the first check bounced and they had to move, probably one of many, many times in this poor kid's life."

"By now they've made it past the second row of fences on the southern **end** of the compound," the man behind me says, as if this should mean something. "The sharpshooters are more than likely running out of ammo."

"I was twelve years old and that was the day I decided that the world is not worth saving."

The door to the room swings open again. One of the soldiers, no older than twenty, leans in, drenched in sweat.

"Sir, we may need to evacuate the ground floor," he pants to the man behind me, the man I am not allowed to see.

"And so we will," the man behind me says.

The young soldier pauses, waits for something more. Then, when he receives nothing else in response to his report, gives me a momentary glare and shuts the door behind him.

"A month before what happened when I was twenty-six," I say, "I heard that Stephanie Sherwin was one of the VPs at ISN, and married to the owner of a chain of steakhouses. In short, she won."

The alarms sound. While the shrill high-pitched din of Cold War-era sirens reverberate throughout the prison, red lights flash and people run for higher ground. We stay in the room, waiting for the director and crew to show up before doing anything drastic.

"I'm on to you," I say to no one.

"Ross, we need to see if the house is on fire," I whisper to myself in the dark. My glowing watch face reads 12:06 AM.

I read once that when American soldiers invaded Hitler's Germany and took its scientists into custody, the Nazis professed that they had, beyond a doubt, invented devices capable of opening up wormholes to different dimensions of time. I read that the Germans had secretly perfected time travel, and further, that this technology was stolen by dark US government agencies and expanded further upon. Names were given in my texts. Nikola Tesla (who frequently attributed his genius to contact with aliens), John Von Neumann (the inventor of the first modern computer and also in contact with aliens), and even Albert Einstein were implicated in these dark experiments collectively referred to as the Montauk Project, after the New York army installation where most of these deeds transpired.

After some time passed, there were regular trips to Mars, to 6039 AD, and into the bodies of newborn babies. There were tangible, attainable multiple realities. Men could even travel into parallel dimensions of this same Earth and replace their lives with those of their other selves. This continued until 1983, when an imagined creature materialized out of the ether and ran amok at the base, destroying the project.

In the darkness of the house on Main, listening to Preston whisper terrible ideas to Mindy and Lydia, smelling the thick odor of decay, of wet blood rotting away the carpet, calm is coming over me.

This is not the first time I have done this.

My father, my mother, Preston, *all* of us—we're a part of something terrible, something life-threatening and beyond our comprehension, but nonetheless, we are simply repeating it. I just know it.

Preston slips into Monroeville with me, holding a lit candle.

"Ross, we need to see if the house is on fire," he says, standing over me.

"Which way does this house face, Preston?" I ask, lighting a cigarette.

"What?" he asks irritably.

"The front porch. Which way is it facing?"

"Um, I don't know. What does this—why?"

"Which way, Preston? Believe me, it's important."

"It faces west, away from the coast. *West.* Okay?"

"So the back porch, the one that's on fire, is on the east **end** of the compound?"

"What?"

After some time, Project Montauk's time machines evolved from huge, complicated chairs running $22 billion apiece, into compact, practical mechanisms that only ran $1 billion. They were now small enough to be carried inside a briefcase, and they were terrifying.

PART III

"Laconic Utopias; Tocsins of the Apocalypse."

2000, 2005, AD 999

"All the information I have about
myself is from forged documents."
—Vladimir Nabokov

"The tradition of political personalism invites us
to ask, 'What are people for?' and to insist that our
institutions operate as if all people mattered."
—James J. Farrell

"They're the same race."
—Al Bielek, *in reference to the correlations between Native American Indians and the inhabitants of Mars, as described in an interview filmed from an undisclosed location*

13

"December 31, 1996: I dub copies of *Cemetery Man, 2000 Maniacs*, and *Gateway to Hell.* Then I stand on the boardwalk with Lydia and watch the fireworks show. I take Lydia back to my apartment (it was on the other side of town then) and drink a bottle of White Zinfandel before having sex. I come but Lydia doesn't. Then we go to a party that's okay but there are too many high school kids. I think Preston has sex with one of them.

"December 31, 1997: I dub copies of *Women of the SS, Cannibal Holocaust,* and *Cannibal Ferox.* Then I stand on the boardwalk with Lydia and watch the fireworks show. I take Lydia back to my apartment (it was closer to where I live now but still on the other side of town) and drink a bottle of Pinot Noir before having sex. Both of us come. Then we go to a party that isn't all that great. Preston spits right in some fat girl's face for saying that a vampire could kick a zombie's ass.

"December 31, 1998: I dub copies of *Cannibal Holocaust, Zombie 3*, the director's cut of *Army of Darkness, Guinea Pig Volume I,* and *I Spit on Your Grave.* Then I stand on the boardwalk with Lydia and watch the fireworks show. I take Lydia back to my apartment (the one I live in now) and drink from a six pack of Coors Light before having sex. Neither of us come and I have a strong feeling of déjà vu. We're supposed to go to a party that night but she tells me she'll meet me there after she stops by her parents' house. She ends up not showing in favor of sexing some guy from Dartmouth. I sleep with Stacey for the first time that same night. Preston sleeps with some girl named Brooke who gives him a yeast infection.

"December 31, 1999: I have a late breakfast with Preston. Then I find out that he has been sleeping with my girlfriend for some time, which elates Stacey, who is Lydia's best friend and my mistress. Afterwards, I am attacked by a zombie in my apartment while being filmed by a camera crew. In desperation, I flee to Preston's house, where I catch him in the middle of some kind of preternatural cleansing ritual with both Lydia and a teenage girl named Mindy. I am not pleased. I am attacked again by the creatures shortly afterward, and then knocked unconscious by Lydia. Preston's party is swarmed by the undead later that night. We are trapped on the second floor of a burning house when the New Year begins."

"So I guess it would be safe to say that your Millennium New Year was slightly different from those of your past," the man behind me, the man I am not allowed to see, says.

Martin tries his cell phone stupidly. It does not work. He shakes his head to the man behind me and sips from his soft drink.

"Things can't be that bad," he says. "If we have to evacuate the floor, they'll come and get us."

"Yes," the man behind me agrees. "We'll be okay for now. As long as we don't get trapped down here and have another weird situation like what you two had in the library."

I awoke to sirens just after three a.m., to screams and gunshots and horns blasting from vehicles already caught in impossible traffic jams. It was a little over three weeks ago, and I can't say that I didn't expect it, especially after she left.

When I turned on the television, all but two of my channels had already folded. On Channel 4, out of Orlando, the newscaster came in and out of focus as inexperienced cameramen tried to figure out what they were doing. He unknotted his tie and slipped off his navy blue dress shirt, which had been soaked through with sweat, and delivered the news in a stained undershirt.

"The greater Jacksonville area is gone," he said grimly, reading from handwritten notes that he kept fumbling with on his desk. "Numerous reports indicate that the city was bombed by United States military jets soaring overhead, but this can not be confirmed at this time."

I was already up, thinking of Stacey as I worked. I went through the rigmarole: latching the front door locks, making sure the phones were indeed dead, filling the sink with water, arming myself with the revolver I kept in the kitchen cabinet behind the boxes of cereal.

"There has been no official word from higher government officials," the weary newscaster was saying, "but all appeals for military aid in the evacuation of Florida's millions of citizens, and in squelching the omnipresent threat, have been ignored. The higher echelons of our federal government have approached the situation in almost totally *unemotional* terms. It seems that the entire state has been quarantined—"

Gunshots from the apartment across the hall. A young boy screamed.

"—hundreds of young people all over the state are attempting to find solace in local shopping malls. God, if only it were that simple, ladies and gentlemen—"

There is a long silence. Papers are shuffled. The newscaster sighs.

"This just in: There have been reports of these attacks being accompanied by mysterious men documenting the carnage via television cameras and sound equipment. Most were said to be clad in white radiation suits, others in outdoor attire and even business wear. As to the identities of these men, or to attest to their ability to walk freely among the assailants, no information has been revealed."

Then, off-screen, there was loud crashing and screeching. A door creaked open and moans filled the air. The camera quickly panned to the floor as the news crew retreated. Off-screen, the tired newscaster barely squealed as they ripped him apart.

I showered and groomed using non-aromatic soap and deodorant. I dressed in a skin-tight black sweater, thick tight pants, and a pair of worn-out hiking boots I purchased in February of 2000. Back in the bathroom, I pulled out the beard trimmer and sloppily shaved my head, lowering the odds of being grabbed and subsequently bitten. Then I filled the bathtub with water and remembered another time the world felt like this. It was not long after she got on a plane.

There was a quick breakfast of cereal and a pear. Then I unlocked the gun case in the closet, loaded the .22-caliber rimfire and Smith and Wesson 9-millimeter. I pulled down my gear from the top closet shelf, but realized it was marked "Defense." The "On the Run" gear was still on the shelf.

I unzipped the green bag and quickly examined its contents: matches; three bottles of drinking water; four granola bars; map to the prison; compass; small first aid kit; Swiss army knife; steel-encased flashlight with extra batteries; binoculars; three boxes of ammunition per gun; cleaning kits for the firearms; flare gun with three flares; sheathed machete; blood-stained crowbar; and a pocket-size Holy Bible.

Outside of my four-story apartment building, the parking lot had become overwhelmed with them. Residents trying to flee in their cars were quickly converged upon and eaten. I watched through the bedroom window as Kate, the little girl from two doors down, fought and clawed at them, even as one ripped her vagina from her body and another bit three of her fingers off.

When I turned around to finish preparations, I was suddenly filled with terrible regret. I had only lived in the new place for a few months, and it was a shame to have to evacuate such a spacious apartment. The rent wasn't too high, either.

Around five-thirty, after the explosions and car horns and gunshots tapered off, after the phone lines never came back on, and just when the electricity went out, I loaded my gear onto my back and headed to the breezeway of the apartment and took a final look around. Then I unlocked the three dead bolts on the front door and slipped out into the hallway.

They were waiting for me when I got there.

"I expected this," I muttered, facing the barrels of silenced automatic weapons while tonguing the empty space in my mouth where one of my back teeth should have been. I shattered it five years ago. "At least you're not holding cameras."

Four men, all sloppily clad and blood-spattered were standing before me. One of them was sweating profusely and bleeding from his shoulder. I immediately focused my attention on the fresh wound.

"Mister Orringer," one of them said, a young guy with an unlit cigarette in his mouth. He was short and thin, his hair light brown and thick with sweat. "My name is Martin Bishop. This is Carl Overcash, Geoff Sparrow, and John Windsor. We need you to come with us, please."

They were a sordid group. Aside from their matching firearms, all of them were polar opposites from one another. The one referred to as John was tall, sad-faced, and filthy, wearing Dickies pants and a graying Led Zeppelin shirt. He would never say much to me, I could tell. Geoff was my height, just shy of six feet, with wavy blond hair and a stupid half-grin across his face. He looked the type of guy who would die third or fourth in a movie about a creature running amok in an isolated laboratory. Martin, the obvious leader, was wearing black Dockers and a white business shirt half-tucked in, half-soaked in blood and perspiration. He tried to appear reassuring, but only came off as two seconds away from perishing on the Titanic. Carl was already dead and therefore his features meant nothing to me, and I tried not to notice them.

"All right," I said. "Um, who are you people exactly?"

"That's not of importance at this juncture," Martin said. "But we were sent here to retrieve you and bring you safely to your destination. Preparations are already being made there for our arrival."

"What destination?"

"Where you were on your way to right now," he said. "The state prison, yes?"

"How did you know where I was going?" I asked, not as suspicious as I might have been with a different past experience. On one of the floors below, three quick gunshots.

"Let's just say that, under the circumstances, we knew that you would be en route to the prison, the most relatively safe place in the area. High fences, independent electric generators, water, food, resources, and very strongly fortified. It doesn't matter that its original intention was to keep people in, not keep them out. As a retreat away from this…situation, it will be ideal. With the events that transpired this morning, coupled with your—incident five years ago—we anticipated your evacuation and were sent here to make sure you succeeded in your trek."

"I'm not going anywhere with you," I say. "You could be one of them."

"One of who?" he asked. "*Them*?"

"No. You could be one of the film crew. Like last time."

"But we're not," he said, lighting his cigarette. "Come with us, Ross."

"I don't think so," I said, slithering by. A gun barrel was quickly pressed against my neck. I paused, my back turned to them.

"This is not up for debate, Mister Orringer," the young soldier said behind me.

"Who do you work for?" I muttered, turning to face the rag-tag group. "Why should I trust you?"

"Because we work for your father."

"Before we do anything, you need to take care of *that*."

"What?" the wounded soldier asked nervously. His shoulder was still bleeding from a large crater where flesh and muscle used to be.

"He's infected," I said to the group, ignoring him completely. "He's going to turn and attack us within the next couple of hours."

The other soldiers flinched.

"Mister Orringer," the spokesperson for the group began.

"I'm not going *anywhere* with *him*," I said, pointing to his bite. "You want my help? You want my know-how? You want my years of planning, not to mention my totally unique experience in surviving this kind of situation?"

"Yes sir, Mister Orringer," he said quietly. "You're the only chance anyone has."

"Then this guy gets dealt with now."

"You son of a bitch," the wounded soldier spit. "Martin, are you—?"

"Shut up, Carl."

"Either leave him here or shoot him," I declared, walking down the hallway. "Otherwise, all of you are on your own, and you're just going to wind up in this week's episode."

Heading quietly down the stairs, I was between the second and third floor when I heard a single gunshot. The three men caught up with me on the ground floor, shaky and full of pent-up anger.

"We had arranged for an armed helicopter to pick us up," John said tightly. He contained his rage toward me well. "It never arrived this morning, so our best bet is to secure a vehicle and rendezvous with the others further inland."

"Scratch the vehicle," I whispered, moving out into the apartment building lobby. "The roads are already congested. We'll be stuck in there like a metal coffin. No, our best bet is to move west on foot. We stay off the main roads, abstain from any heavy combat, and slip quietly into the prison and rendezvous with the others, assuming there are any."

"There are," Martin assured me. "Many. They're trained, well-supplied, and quite aware of the true situation. And we've retained some of the inmates as well. They will assist us in the hard labor tasks of fortifying and arming the prison. Further, they can be used as food for the creatures, if need be."

"You're going to *feed* them?" I asked. Geoff crossed himself and looked disgusted.

"If need be, Mister Orringer. If need be. Our survival is crucial. Theirs is not."

I ducked behind the wall and glanced through the double doors leading down the steps to the darkened parking lot outside. Two of them were hunched over Kate's dismembered corpse, and another marched along the sidewalk in front of the apartment building munching on an arm disconnected just above the elbow.

"We can take them," Martin whispered behind me.

"Your guns are silenced?" I asked.

"You know they are."

"Set them to semi-automatic, if you can. No need in wasting fourteen bullets on these things when one clean shot will do it."

"Right," he agreed. "Guys, do as he says."

As soon as they opened the door, all three of the creatures noticed them and immediately began slouching their way toward us. Martin raised his gun, aimed, and fired. There was a slight pop, and across the street, one of them shuddered. Its brains spewed out the back of its head, and thin pink blood drizzled out of a wound just above the nose. It fell to the ground.

The other two followed Martin's lead, first taking down the zombie chewing up the arm. The bullet actually traveled through the raised limb, entered its mouth, and exited out the lower portion of its head. It collapsed, meat gargling from its oral cavity. The final creature was struck first in the shoulder. Martin sighed heavily and gave a menacing look to the soldier going by the name of John. The next shot from his mini-Uzi dislocated most of the ghoul's face.

"No sweat," Geoff said, smiling.

"Look," Martin whispered, alert, motioning up the two-lane street.

Shaded by an old oak tree, a radiation suited man taped us. I turned around knowingly and, indeed, another was filming my group from the roof of an old two-story linoleum warehouse. A second unit director standing next to him rubbed his goatee thoughtfully.

"Those motherfuckers," Geoff muttered, raising his gun to fire on the first of the spotted crewmen.

"Don't," I whispered, holding my hand over the barrel. "You can't shoot them."

"Why not?" Martin asked, his gun still poised. "He'll die, won't he?"

"He will, but it doesn't matter. It will just make things worse. Trust me. We tried it five years ago. People died because of it."

Martin and I exchanged a look after I said this. He gulped and closed his eyes.

"Let's just move on," I whispered.

"What are you carrying?" Martin asked me as we trotted across the street into an alley.

"Handguns. Loud ones."

"If you don't have to open fire, then don't. Let us handle it."

"That's fine by me."

We hiked through the alleyway between squat buildings toward the main road, 38, which led out of town and into the interior of northern Florida. When we reached the intersection, the scene was striking.

There were cars parked at odd angles all along the road. Some were smashed against one another. Glass littered the streets, as did mangled bodies and gory limbs and clothes and left-behind goods from the stores that were looted throughout downtown. Blood seemed to have washed over the entire landscape. It was on lampposts, walls, car hoods, bushes, street signs, everything. One of the boutiques up the street was consumed in flames, and thick black smoke billowed into the sky.

The whole town reeked of rotting meat, of burnt rubber and gun powder and rust. There were the sounds of chewing coming from indiscernible corners everywhere, along with the stupefying drones of car horns being pressed incessantly and distant cries coming from all directions.

"Jesus," Martin said. "It wasn't this bad a few hours ago."

"It doesn't take long for everything to fall apart," I said quietly. "I know. I've been watching it fall apart forever it seems like."

The soldiers would pick the undead off as soon as they became aware of our presence. They would come stumbling out of apartment buildings, markets, the movie theater, a gay night club. Martin, John, and Geoff would calmly aim and fire. The creatures' brains would spit out of their heads each time and the monsters would topple over without a sound.

"This would be kind of fun," Geoff said nervously. "I mean, if it wasn't the **end** of the world and all."

"I'm glad you're enjoying yourself," Martin said, rolling his eyes as he removed the head of a little girl who was coming towards us from the road up ahead.

We made it to the outskirts of town before we ran into any group larger than five or six. We passed a junior high school to our right and, several hundred yards further, an elementary. But directly before us was a school bus, halfway on the road, halfway through a chainlink fence and into a baseball field. It was turned over on its side and white smoke rose in spirals from the engine.

"Oh, shit," I muttered, already spotting them.

School children, along with the ten ghouls that transformed them, began toward us from all directions.

"Can we take them?" I asked.

"We have no choice," Martin said, already aiming his assault rifle.

They were elementary kids, still wearing their backpacks and some even carrying lunchboxes and construction paper. Their school bus had probably crashed the afternoon before at the site of the first zombies and the young ones were attacked while trapped in the overturned vehicle. I could see bites in their necks, arms, faces, and even their stomachs and barely formed breasts. The children were bloody and moaned a terrible moan that made my eyes water.

"There's too many," Geoff said, shaking his head. "There's too many. We gotta get out of here."

"It's not going to happen," I said, turning around and spotting the other six approaching from the road behind us.

I pulled my revolver.

"May I fire now?" I asked Martin, already aiming at the zombies to our rear.

"By all means," he said, already picking off the children one after another.

The first shot frightened me. The report was startlingly loud after a morning of relative quiet, and it had been some time since I had last practiced, so the gun kicked at me and I missed the closest creature completely. I aimed again, this time at its face, and exhaled as I pulled the trigger. Half of its temple, along with its left ear, disappeared, and though I thought I would need to fire one more round at it, the cannibal dropped.

Geoff helped me take the six behind us as Martin and John slaughtered the kids. I continuously missed, and soon I was out of bullets in the revolver and Geoff had to put a second bullet into the ghoul whose neck I had just removed.

"Guys, we need you," Martin said, firing in manic rhythm now as the young ones descended upon us.

There were at least ten more of them, along with four adults. I quickly pulled my .22 rimfire and took aim, but there was more activity from every direction now. The gunshots and other cacophony had attracted several dozen more of the recently initiated walking dead, and they came at us from every street and field and yard.

"A lot of good this little bastard did us," Geoff ranted, missing most of his shots now. "We're fucked. And Carl is dead."

"We need to remove ourselves from this spot," Martin said, carefully reloading his machine gun and picking off three adult ghouls in quick succession. I watched as their foreheads exploded one after another.

"What about the school?" John asked, barely audible through the gunfire.

"School? What school?"

"Either the one behind us or ahead," he said. "We could lock ourselves in, barricade it, and try to signal the helicopters."

"Sounds good to me," I choked, one of them grabbing at my arm just before I jerked it away and put the barrel directly up to its eye. The blast sent it flying back several feet, and the gore drenched across several of the others behind it.

"All right, we'll do it," Martin agreed, taking in the escalating numbers of adversaries. "But let's move forward, to the elementary. It's smaller and looks like there's less entrances."

Martin led the way with Geoff, clearing a path as we trudged over the collapsed fence and onto the school's baseball diamond. John, who marched backwards with me, would fire single rounds at individual monsters while intermittently switching to automatic and mowing down an entire line of the gathering undead by sweeping the gun at head level across the ranks.

Their moans were infuriating and simultaneously hypnotic. After the first several minutes of what felt like a hundred mile journey toward the schoolhouse, I could no longer hear my own gunfire, or Martin swearing or Geoff's mania as he slaughtered an entire row of children blocking the entrance through the cafeteria. The only discernible sound was the moaning, which became a kind of atonal hymn.

We made it up past the parked yellow buses and up to the first of three buildings connected by covered walkways. Martin and John sidled up next to two steel doors with small rectangular windows. John quickly peered inside and announced that it was the cafeteria.

"Whatever," Geoff said. "Get us in, god damn it."

After I fired the last round from the .22 and quickly dispensed the twelve bullets from the Smith and Wesson into the growing horde of undead trailing us (one of the bullets sailed past them, but struck one of the cameramen in the arm. His blood squirt across the bus ramp, and the other two crew members quickly backed away and filmed him as he fell to the ground and was consumed by the zombies), I reached over my shoulder and pulled the crowbar from my pack. I swung it about wildly as Martin smashed the window with the butt of his gun and opened it from the inside. We scrambled into the cavernous room and slammed the door behind us. Hands immediately reached in through the shattered window.

"Use the crowbar to jam it," Martin said in the darkness of the cafeteria.

I did as he asked, but when they jerked on the handle outside, the bar would shimmy out of place and fall to the floor. John pushed me aside and tried to make it work, but to no avail. If we moved away from the door, they would reach in and eventually open it from the inside. Their basic skills and instincts from their previous lives remained intact, including the use of ladders, stairs, opening and closing doors, and even the use of blunt instruments.

"The door's busted," John told Martin. "We'll have to fortify ourselves somewhere else."

"Not a classroom," Martin said, staring out into the warm, stagnant cafeteria. "We should find a windowless area with roof access, if we can."

"How about the library?" I said, holding fast to the door as they tried to pull it open from outside.

"The library?" Martin repeated. "That might work. It will have no windows, and if it does, they'll probably be too high to reach from the ground outside. What do you think?"

John nodded, helping me hold onto the handle.

"Whatever," Geoff sighed.

"History repeats itself," I said, glancing at my watch just before letting go and running into the abyss.

12

Life is full of weird things.

Controlled coincidences, catastrophic associations with strangers, the inevitability of that which you once doubted most eventually happening to you and all the conspirators posing as your friends—true Armageddon. God has no time for raining sulfur and oceans of blood or fancy light shows. It would be a waste of gimmicks on a world whose Apocalypse would come better packaged in pop culture-spattered wrapping paper.

Joseph Conrad, of *Heart of Darkness* fame, authored a book in 1907 called *The Secret Agent*. In it, an insane professor who lives in a tiny room and dresses himself in rags, builds bombs in an effort to destroy the "idol of science." In 1996, Ted Kaczynski was arrested and brought to trial in regards to several bombs sent via the US Mail, which were targeted to those who Kaczynski viewed as dangerous to science and culture. Joseph Conrad was the pen name of a Polish writer named Theodore Korzeniowski. Cordelia told me this.

People are always trying to convince me that there are innocent men being put behind bars for crimes they did not commit. That all disasters are related and foreseeable, if one has the right eyes. They tell me that in India, the ritual of *sati* is still practiced, wherein a man's wife is forced upon the funeral pyre next to her husband's corpse, and is then burned alive alongside his carcass.

My sister was recently awarded a Master's Degree in English. She has read *Macbeth* twice but *Measure for Measure* four times, been to the Renaissance Festival every year since she was seventeen, and once aspired to teach mid-period British literature at Bennington or Camden College.

Now, she holds her boyfriend of seven months, Brad Something or Other, as he pants and spits up blood and goes in and out of delirium. Light filters through the open door from halogen lights set up by the crew in the living room.

"I'm sorry, baby," she whimpers in his ear. "I'm sorry I left you."

"This isn't really happening," he gurgles. "This isn't…happening."

The old t-shirt I wrapped around Brad's foot has soaked through with blood. I remove the tourniquet, squeeze what excess fluid I can from the rags, and re-apply it. Brad's skin has turned blue and the veins are protruding and expanding inside his leg. The infection, in Robin too, is spreading very quickly.

"Ross, what are we going to do?" Cordelia says.

"I don't know, Cordelia."

Brad is twenty-five years old, a Cum Laude anthropology graduate who waits tables at Red Lobster. Cordelia met him in a charred shell that used to be a house. They were both looking for the ghost of a one-armed farmer north of town. It seemed that nothing short of a spectacularly dorky fate brought them together.

He's cheated on her, I think. I can always tell. Maybe with Monica 1, but she's dead now and he will be soon so it doesn't matter, I guess.

"Those are…zombies?" Cordelia says. "Right? Are they?"

"I think so," I nod.

"How do they work?"

"They're recently dead people, no longer than three weeks or so, by the looks of it. They come to life somehow—no one really knows—but they're not the same. All of the memories, the personalities, all of the idiosyncrasies and habits and little things that made them who they were before are gone the second time around. They're uniform; all of them are only interested in eating the meat off of living humans. And if they bite you but don't totally eat every last bit of you, you will *still* die, and then you'll come back to life shortly after as one of them. When they come back, they won't discriminate or go after enemies from their past life, but they show no mercy to loved ones either, so it's a double-edged sword."

"But what about Bub in *Day of the Dead*?" Preston asks from the hallway.

"I assume these zombies won't evolve on us the way they did in Romero's movies. Besides, even if they did, these guys are brand new. They haven't had a chance to grow back any of their past humanity. No, these guys are going to be bad."

"Well then how do we kill them?" my sister asks, tending to Brad's tourniquet.

"You have to either destroy the brain or sever the brain from the rest of the body. You can do it a bunch of ways. A bullet works best usually, but you can hit them with a baseball bat, stab them in the face, insert a needle into the ear lobe, whatever."

"Will—will Brad be one of them?"

"Yes," I say quietly, looking out the window, away from Brad.

A long moment passes before Cordelia says anything else. Brad cries but does so silently, which relieves me for some reason.

"Who are those people filming us?" she finally asks, staring at me through teary eyes.

"Keep the tourniquet on tight," I say, standing up and heading over to check on Robin and his girlfriend Melanie.

"Remember that time in California with my dad?" Robin is saying, laughing and then coughing up fluid. "We had so much fun, didn't we? Didn't we?"

"Yes," Melanie nods, crying. "We had a real good time. Oh my god."

Seeing her beginning to sob again, and Robin looking up at me for answers, cigarette in his mouth and a bottle of Jack Daniels in his hand, I am suddenly overwhelmed. I cannot even fathom what is happening, the ridiculousness of it; the horror.

"Make sure to keep his tourniquet on tight," I say to Melanie, quickly leaving the room to join the others in the hallway.

"They wouldn't just let us sit up here," Stacey is saying to the others, glancing over at me as I approach. "I mean, it's fairly obvious that we're being filmed for some kind of sick documentary or TV show or something. We're the contestants, so to speak. So they wouldn't let us all just sit around like we are and starve to death."

"Yeah, we should be voting people off the property to be eaten in exchange for immunity and a bag of potato chips," Jaime says, inhaling from a thin joint rolled from a page out of the Bible.

"Well, I think it's obvious that we need to get out of here," Preston says, standing up and leaving us alone in the dark corridor.

I glance down into the living room from the top of the stairs. Two crewmen record us from each corner. Surrounding them, it looks as if most of the ghouls have all congregated inside this house. Through the windows, there are only a scattered few still remaining outside in the yard. The rest all moan incessantly just below us. Their arms outstretched, waiting for one of us to lose it or fall or be sacrificed, they will never stop.

Preston returns from the bedroom. "Robin's arm looks like shit. What are Monica and Quentin doing in the bathroom? The door is locked."

"Having sex, maybe," Jaime says, carefully putting the now-tiny roach out.

"Maybe we could climb out onto the roof and make an escape," I offer.

"The only part of the house where you can climb out the window onto the roof is from Preston's room," Mark says. "Um, it's the one with the zombies in it, if anyone has forgotten."

Brad screeches in pain from the other room. Robin does as well.

"When are we going to isolate them?" I press quietly.

"Wait," Lydia says. "Why can't we just like, maybe, cut the arm off where he was bitten so the infection or whatever can't spread?"

"That doesn't work, you fucking idiot," I mutter, dragging from my cigarette.

"Ross, you don't know shit," she says. "It's your fault we're in this to begin with, you prick."

"Wait just a minute, cum depository," I retort, rising to my feet. "How the hell is this *my* fault?"

"Well, this all started because of you," Mark chimes in, leaning against the banister, spitting on the creatures' heads below him. They groan in response.

"How did this start because of me?"

"You know everything about them. They followed you up here. They only got us when you came back with that girl right there."

"My name is Stacey," she says. "And who the hell are you, exactly?"

"Mark. My name is Mark. And your boyfriend right there has gotten us all into deep shit."

"I didn't ask for any of this," I declare. "Why are you so vehemently against me, anyway? Could it have something to do with the arm you've been nursing all night?"

The group looks up at Mark just as he hacks up a wad of phlegm and drops it over the railing, totally ambiguous over my allegation.

"Mark, if you've been bitten," Preston says carefully, "Then you should really be in the spare room with Robin and Brad. Are you bitten?"

"No, Pres, I am not."

"Then take off your jacket and let us see your arm," I say.

"If I have to undergo the obligatory inspection, then everyone does. You're not going to isolate me and make a run for it."

"What?" I ask.

"Besides, I would be showing signs of having been infected by now. I haven't. I'm on to you, asshole. I know what you're trying to do."

"What is he talking about?" Gary asks, stoned. "Is this whole thing really all about you, Ross?"

"Absolutely not."

"Not only is this his doing," Mark insists, looking each one of the group, me last, in the eye, "he also has total control of the situation, and further, I think he plans on making a run for it and leaving us here to rot."

"How are any of us going to die?" Gary asks. "We're safe up here."

"Yeah, until enough of those things climb onto the roof, get inside the bedroom, and knock the door down," Mark says. "Enough of them will eventually get through Preston's bedroom door. We're safe until then, which I'd say, with those camera people down there helping out, is no more than an hour at most. I'm with Preston. We need to figure a way out of here into the city."

"Dude, who *is* this guy?" I ask everyone, particularly Preston. "I mean, who *invited* this wanker?"

"I did," Lydia says. "Preston and I are friends with him."

"Terrific," I sigh, a terribly unoriginal gesture. "If you alone aren't enough to oversee my degradation, then your punk-ass friend here will be."

"I want out of this house," Preston declares.

"I haven't trusted you since the moment we met," Mark says, glaring at me. "This is not the way I expected to celebrate my New Year's."

"I'm going to open that bedroom door, kill all four of those things, and then I'm going to make my way down to the street and get the hell out of here," Preston continues.

"Mark, I seriously doubt that Ross has any more of an idea what's going on than you do," Jaime says, popping his neck. "So could you, like, save the conspiracy theory for at least another hour or so?"

"This is bullshit," Preston declares. "We can't just sit here, waiting to die."

"We can, actually," I say. "I'd rather just sit up here and not give those assholes filming us a show than try to make a run for it. Besides, you don't seem to understand, Preston. They won't *let* us leave."

"I have an idea about that. Don't worry."

"Hey, where is that David guy?" Gary asks us, confused. "I haven't seen him in a while."

"Your friends are brilliant," I say to Preston, rolling my eyes.

"If this were like an experiment or something," Monica says, emerging from the bathroom with Quentin behind her, "then maybe they'll leave us alone soon."

"How so?" Stacey asks, raising her eyebrows.

Quentin rests the lit candle he is holding on the floor.

Downstairs, one of the zombies bumps into another and tumbles backward. He hits one of the mounted halogen lamps. It sways and teeters, and one of the crew quickly corrects it and sets it still, the light shining back up at us. The same crew member pulls out a small revolver from his belt and places it directly against the forehead of the ghoul that bumped into the lamp. He fires it, sending a wave of shock through all of us on the second floor. In the living room, the creature's head falls apart and brains splatter the *Fight Club* poster behind it. The crewmen begin taping us again.

"Jesus Christ," Jaime says, looking at the scene below.

"What were you two doing in the bathroom?" I ask as Monica and Quentin sit down next to us.

"Thinking out loud without you people dumbing it up," she says. "Look, if this is an experiment by the government, then eventually, soon, they'll have to either kill all of us in this house or just pack those things up and leave."

"What makes you think it's an experiment?"

"For one, the people who set this up are not being attacked. That seems odd to me. Second, the way they're videotaping everything and making notes—this is an experiment."

"Oh, who gives a shit what it is?" Preston snaps.

"If we figure out what is going on, then maybe it will help us to get out of it," I say.

"I told you," he says. "I have a plan for all that."

I consider telling the survivors about all the things I have encountered: the old black man, the kid with the popcorn, my mother and father being involved somehow, the men in my apartment and how they've been filming me for weeks. I consider telling them that, in addition to the strange events befalling all of us, I have had an unshakable feeling that it has happened already. A glance over at Stacey, who discreetly shakes her head no, prompts me to remain silent.

"We should just sit it out," Monica says.

"The hell with that," Preston says.

"They'll kill you out there," I assure him.

"Well, I'm not staying *here*," he declares, storming off and into Monroeville.

"I'm with Preston," Lydia declares, following him. Mark trails her, glaring at me until he runs into a wall. Then he scampers off, avoiding any further eye contact.

The rest of us sit in the hallway, not saying anything. In the bedroom, Robin reminds Melanie of a particular date at the mall a long time ago, saying,

"We whipped 'em. Didn't we?" Melanie says nothing. I can hear Cordelia and Brad kissing.

"If we try to leave the area they have cordoned off," I warn the group finally, "they'll kill us."

"They're going to kill us anyway," Gary mutters.

"Well, maybe one of us will survive and win a new car," Jaime says, giggling. No one else joins him.

"Guys, we're going to die and that's all there is to it," Stacey announces. "If it's an experiment, they won't let us live to tell anyone about it. If it's some kind of sick movie, we'll still die, because that's how these kinds of things always **end**, right?"

"Something like that," I say.

"I just wish we could have had some champagne first."

11

ROBIN DIES A LITTLE AFTER TWO IN THE MORNING. Melanie goes to join Camilla in the closet, but Camilla is gone. Already hysterical after watching me and Jaime quickly scoop up Robin's corpse immediately after he passed (his last moment were spent reminiscing: his mother holding him when he was eight, breaking his arm on a see-saw when he was nine), she begins screaming and generally freaking out while she points at the empty pile of clothes that Camilla had wedged herself behind after Shannon died.

People in this house are going missing.

Preston, Quentin, and Monica go searching through what little of the house there is left for us: Monroeville, the Monroeville closet, the hall bathroom, and the spare room, which has become the isolation ward for future living dead. They find nothing.

Meanwhile, Jaime and I attend to Robin's cadaver. We plop his soggy, yellowed body in the bathtub and stand over it, knowing what must be done. Every time I considered the prospect of a scenario such as this actually happening, I very quickly assumed and voiced the idea that I would have no qualms at all about shooting anyone I knew right in the head if they reanimated as one of them. I always took for granted my own ability to quickly adapt to a situation such as having to destroy human beings that will kill me if I do not react appropriately first.

It's not that easy, though. I, like my companions, am a product of twenty-some years of social conditioning and Bible Belt morality implemented both consciously and subconsciously on a never-**end**ing continuum. Not only is the idea of an army of dead people storming our New Year's Eve party absurd and unbelievable, it's also shock-inducing. All of us are in shock. If we were not, the sorrow, the confusion, the screaming and shaking of heads and total catatonia (similar to that of Mindy's, who seems almost too intellectually limited to be in the state she is apparently in) would run rampant. We would all be dead. I am thankful for all of our natural societal-influenced reactions to this disaster.

But now that some of the panic and adrenaline have tapered off, I fully realize the current situation and its grotesqueries: I am standing in a bathroom with this stoned singer for a crappy metal band, gripping a hammer and trying to decide how best to go about puncturing a hole into the brain cavity of what was once a friend of mine, now a dead body about to open its eyes, stand up, and try to kill me.

Outside, in the hallway, people are freaking out. Our situation is growing more inexplicable. Truths and philosophical dilemmas are setting in, and consequently, things are getting out of control.

"Everything is falling apart," I whisper.

"It's *impossible*," we hear Preston roar in the hallway. "The windows are boarded and haven't been touched. The rooms are totally empty, and without a trace. If either of them had wandered into the hallway, someone would have seen them. The things in the living room below aren't feeding, so they didn't jump. Quite simply, David and Camilla have vanished without a trace, and that is the final straw, as far as I'm concerned."

After this, I hear him storm into the spare room, where I assume he continues with what he was doing: drawing lines with a magic marker on a bedsheet and working out numbers on scratch paper.

"This is all pretty…weird," Jaime is saying to me, looking down at Robin's body.

"I used to play video games with this guy at the bowling alley," I mutter. "We got drunk at his uncle's house in eleventh grade and I woke everyone up when I did an impression of Ash's possessed girlfriend in *Evil Dead*."

"It's…crazy," Jaime agrees.

"This is a friend of mine and I'm about to smash his head in with a hammer to destroy his brain," I say out loud to myself. "So that he doesn't get back up and eat me, no less."

I start laughing.

After the moment subsides, I grip the hammer tightly and raise it above my head. Robin's body lies motionless below me, somehow in the fetal position.

"It's pretty strange that two of the most unimportant people to this story both vanished," I say. "You know, at first I thought David was a spy for—"

Robin reanimates, immediately sitting upright and hissing at us.

Jaime and I retreat to the doorway, terrified.

Robin slowly clambers to his feet. His eyes have taken on a gray, watery stare. For a moment, he stands very still, taking us both in. He focuses on me for several seconds. Then, he moans and climbs out of the tub, approaching us.

Whatever deliberation, whatever sociological nurture had retarded my attack, immediately subsides. Jaime and I both go at him, bringing the hammer and baseball bat down on his head. The hammer strikes his eyebrow, ripping through the flesh. When his skull is penetrated, pressure escapes and there is a loud hissing noise like air from a tire. Blood gushes out. The flat head of the hammer slams against his skull, but he does not fall. Instead, he reaches for my wrist. I jerk away, bringing the hammer with me.

Jaime's bat smashes against his forehead. The skull caves in this time, looking like a half-deflated kick ball. Jaime and I are both spattered with thick red blood. I turn away, most of it splashing against the back of my head and shoulders. Jaime, however, screeches in disgust. Robin's corpse falls to the floor.

"What? What is it?" I ask.

"His blood, dude," Jaime says, spitting. "Some of it got in my mouth."

I freeze, watching him hack and cough and turn on the water in the sink. He washes his mouth out frantically, and after a moment, turns the faucet off and wipes his mouth against his shirt sleeve. He looks up to me, stunned, terrified, his eyes welling with tears.

"You swallowed some of his blood?" I ask quietly, not looking him in the eye. Instead I focus on Robin's freshly destroyed corpse below us, at the pile of brain matter heaped on the tile.

"I…I might have maybe," Jaime whispers.

I do not respond to this news. My back to him, I clench my eyes shut.

"Ross?"

This is unknown to me. I deliberate, drawing on every zombie film, every reference Preston mentioned, every porch conversation, and can conclude nothing. I am not sure what will become of Jaime.

"Ross? Am I going to…turn into one of those things, man?"

"I don't know," I say. "Don't say anything to anyone about it."

He nods, tears streaming down his face, and I leave the bathroom to join Stacey in Monroeville.

"This isn't an experiment. It's not objective. It's not being documented properly. If this were an experiment, there would be cameramen up here with us. There would be scientists taking notes and monitoring pulses and gauging our panic."

"Then what is it, Stacey?"

"I'm sticking with the TV show theory."

"Why?" I ask, smoking. "Would you watch this if it were on?"

"To be honest, if it weren't me, then yeah, I probably would. It's human nature to yearn to watch their fellow man suffer needlessly."

"This is beyond degradation, sweetie. This is annihilation. I just hammered a friend's skull in."

"Drama," she shrugs. "That's part of a good reality show."

"There are no cameras up here," I remind her.

"I assure you, Ross, that somehow they're getting every bit of this. Hidden cameras, bugs, tiny microphones…spies among us…somewhere we have an audience. I just know it."

"You might be right," I say, remembering the boy at the metamorphosing gas station.

"What do you mean?"

"It's just…this is all weird."

"Yeah," she agrees, lighting another cigarette with the cherry of the one she was already smoking. "You know, it makes sense that this is a TV show, or at least some kind of weird documentary. Look at the formulaic structure of a lot of the night's events: a party of mostly attractive people is attacked by zombies; most of the bit actors or participants are killed right off; the more prominent characters **end** up on the second floor of a very stagy house; lesser characters are removed and quickly forgotten amidst the heightened suspense of fewer survivors; people continually die throughout the night while the audience keeps guessing who will survive and what will be left of them by morning."

"There's actually quite a lot of astute thinking in your theory," I say. "It's sloppy writing to just have two people go missing for no reason, though."

"Maybe it's unrelated."

"Come on, Stacey. I think that all the weird things going on would *have to* be related."

"Yeah, well maybe on a bigger scale," she nods. "But, maybe there's a lot more to this than just the living dead part."

I do not say anything for a very long time. Cordelia is calling for me in the other room.

"I—I was seeing weird things all night before this happened," I say quietly. "I saw makeup people applying more gray to the things out there before the party started. I saw people setting up lighting and getting ready for this thing like it was a movie."

"It feels like a movie," Stacey says. "If I didn't watch the kid who used to trade me Pogs in seventh grade get his widow's peak ripped from his skull a few feet away from me, I would swear none of this was ever happening. If I hadn't smelled Monica involuntarily shit herself at the bottom of the staircase while being eaten alive, I would never have admitted that any of it was real. But, seeing as how all of that has actually occurred in the last couple of hours, I have to say that all of it is really happening."

"I feel like it's already *happened*," I say.

"How is that?"

"I don't know," I murmur. "It's just that—someday this is going to happen again, but on a much larger scale. In the future, this will happen again. But—"

"But what?" Stacey asks, furrowing her eyebrows.

"But I already remember it."

"That's—Ross, I'm worried about you, sweetie. I know that that Mark guy in there is a total twat, but I think he may be right about one thing. I *do* think you have a lot more involvement with this than you're letting on."

"If I do, then I was left out of the loop."

"Well, it still bothers me," she says.

"Do you actually think I *wanted* any of this?"

"No, it's not that," she says. "It's that, if *I* think that way, then I can't be the only one. The others must be thinking it too, and I really worry about mob mentality in a situation like this. I worry about all of us, but I especially worry about you. Your safety, Ross. Do you understand?"

"I think so," I mutter, thinking about Lydia, wondering if she cares if I live or die.

"Well good, because there's something else, too."

"What?"

"If this really is some kind of media effort, then eventually, the powers behind this whole terrible ordeal will have to step it up a notch."

"Meaning…"

"Meaning, if we don't give them the drama, if we just stay up here and keep surviving, as boring as that is, then they will eventually respond. They'll create the drama for us. Now do you understand what I'm saying?"

"You're saying that we have a lot to be afraid of."

"Ross, we did anyway," she says. "You'd better check on Cordelia, by the way. She's your sister and her boyfriend is about to die. Remember?"

"I remember. Did you hear what Preston said to me outside just before we were attacked?"

10

"The ghost?"

"Yeah," I say. "Did you and my sister ever see it? The one in Wauchula?"

"Oh," he says, coughing violently. Blood speckles my hand a foot away from his mouth. "No, we didn't see it. Not this year."

"It's kind of disappointing, isn't it?" I ask, shakily smoking a cigarette as I look down on his weakening body. Cordelia, on his other side, holds his hand, which is sticky with his own blood.

"Yes," he agrees. "It's disappointing."

"Did you and Cordelia ever see a ghost? I mean, like of all the times you and she went looking?"

"No," he mutters. "Not once."

I smile but cannot come up with anything appropriate to say.

"It *is* disappointing," he says, swallowing. He gasps. "It's so…sad."

And this is the last statement he ever makes. He gurgles, looks to the floor, and passes a moment later. His skin looks yellow.

Cordelia lets go of Brad's hand, lights a cigarette, and walks over to the window. Hands reach for her through the wooden planks. She studies them for a moment just before breaking down into tears. Meanwhile, Gary and Preston come into the room as quietly as possible to carry Brad's body into the bathroom, where they will destroy his brain with a baseball bat. Gary trips on the way out and drops Brad's legs. There is momentary static and then they are gone. Cordelia cries silently by the window for a long time and later, Brad's zombie persona comes to life in the bathroom and there is a dull clout as his skull is flattened and he dies a final time. Cordelia shudders by the window and I leave the bedroom just as Preston stands next to her and begins whispering in her ear. Outside the room, I receive glances from over shoulders and a terrible vibe from everyone.

It's all so disappointing.

9

THEY'RE TAPING US AS BEST THEY CAN from the ground floor and from the rooftop of the building next door. I see two of them in the radiation suits filming me through the slivers left in the spare room window. I give them the finger and hammer at one of the two hands still grabbing for me. Preston momentarily looks up at the din I am creating before going back to doing arithmetic and writing short sentences on a sheet of paper on the floor.

It is 2:47 a.m., and I am getting hungry.

"Pres, is there any food up here?" I ask from the hall. "A bag of chips or a candy bar? Anything?"

"No," he says, joining me just long enough to inspect the area below us and toss a cigarette over the upstairs banister down on the undead below. He goes back into the spare room and emerges with his notes in one hand and the sheet used earlier as a rope to conquer the destroyed staircase in the other. "Just bait."

"Bait?" I repeat, sweating.

"What are you doing?" Stacey asks him.

"Implementing my plan."

He stretches out the sheet along the hallway floor. It is stained in multiple spots with blood and some kind of black greasy substance.

"Okay, Ross, let's summarize the way these things behave," Preston says. Lydia stands at his side, along with Monica and Quentin. I narrow my eyes. "They are pure motorized instinct, insofar as we can tell. They just happen not to eat the people who are filming them. Aside from that, they are totally archetypical zombies."

"Pretty much," I agree, not wishing to contradict him. I am exhausted and hungry.

"Okay, if they are pure instinct, then their behavior can be predicted with much certainty, right?"

"Well—"

"I'm not going out on a limb here," Pres declares against the opening of my objection. "This is the way things are. So, if some of us are going to make it out of here alive, then we have to make a few assumptions in order to implement my plan. Most of us have already agreed to it."

"If *some of us* are going to make it out of here alive?" I repeat.

"What exactly is this plan?" Stacey asks suspiciously. "And why were Ross and I obviously not made aware of it?"

Cordelia stands a few feet away, smoking a cigarette and wiping the tears away from her face. Only they're not being shed for Brad anymore. She's looking at me and wincing upon making any accidental eye contact.

"Well, the people taping us seem pretty much invincible to any attack," he says. "So, I think that once we get outside, we grab one of them and use them as a hostage to ward both the other camera guys and the zombies back. Then, we make it outside the barriers and into the city. Then, we're safe, I'd say."

"Yeah, that sounds dandy," I say, nodding. "Except you have to get outside first."

"We open the bedroom door, kill those four inside, and make our way onto the lower part of the roof. We jump to the ground and haul ass before the corpses know we even left the second floor of the house."

"Preston," I say, "this is not exactly a fool-proof plan here. They'll swarm out of the house the moment you make it onto the roof, assuming you even take the four in the bedroom down. They killed enough of us already, I would think, to attest to that."

"We'll get the ones in my bedroom easily," he says confidently, looking away from me at Lydia.

"And the seven dozen or so swarming around the downstairs of the house, or the ones in the backyard?"

"We'll distract them."

"With what?" I ask.

"Ross," Cordelia whispers. "I'm sorry."

Mark grabs my arms from behind and jerks them behind my back. Preston punches me in the face and the room grows fuzzy and bubbly. A headache squats at the front of my cranium, which feels as if it will collapse from the pressure and explode at any moment. Someone else helps Mark hold onto my wrists and a foot kicks the back of my knees and I topple to the floor. Boots hold me down. There is shouting and barking orders. Lydia and Monica bring the bedsheet over and wrap it twice around my torso. The other **end** is carefully knotted repeatedly around the main wooden post at the top of the staircase.

Stacey is screaming for them to stop. Cordelia is shaking her head, looking to the floor.

"Don't worry, okay?" Preston says in my ear. "I've done all the measurements. You'll be fine. We'll, uh, we'll send help as soon as we all get out of here. I promise, dude. And this has nothing to do with what happened in my bathroom earlier tonight, before all this happened. It's important to me that you understand that. Okay?"

Stacey rips at Preston's shirt, ranting and spitting. Lydia grabs her by the shoulder and lunges at her face. They fight in the background while crew people downstairs strain to get a good shot.

"They won't chase after us when we escape if they're preoccupied with getting to Ross," Preston assures everyone.

Monica and Quentin nod. Lydia pushes Stacey backward and she falls over Mindy, who is sitting on the floor looking up at Preston like a cow. The two girls continue their brawl, but Mark intervenes and holds Stacey from behind, clutching a pair of scissors to her throat.

Gary and Jaime look anxious.

"Pres, I'm not sure this is such a good idea," Jaime says. "This is like dangling a carrot in front of a rabbit's face to keep him running, man. This is like a—cartoon."

"It will work though," Preston says.

"You *idiots*," Stacey hisses, squirming in Mark's grip. "You're all going to *die* and you're going to get *Ross and me* killed in the process!"

"Stacey, Mark was right," Preston says to her. "This is Ross's situation. He got us into this. It's obvious that he's somehow responsible for all of it, and that he knows a hell of a lot more than what he's letting on. Obvious even to you. I know it."

"I have *nothing* to do with this," I contest quietly, spitting blood from my mouth through the wooden posts down into the living room below. The corpses seethe and moan.

"We're going to hang Ross above them in the living room. He'll be fine as long as the rope holds, which it will. They won't be able to reach him. I've done the calculations and tested the rope. They won't get to him. Besides, I seriously doubt that whoever is doing this would let him die, if he is involved. Right?"

Nods, but I scream out, "This is *not* my fault! You're going to *kill* me! *Calculations*, Preston?! *What* fucking calculations?! You're not far from *retarded*! What the hell calculations can *you* do?!"

"With them distracted in here, we can take down the four in the bedroom, get outside onto the roof, and make a run for it. They won't be able to sniper all of us off at the **end** of the street like Ross said they would. Not if we're holding one of their own. We'll be fine."

"You are all insane," Stacey shrieks. "You are all totally…*fucked!*"

Preston looks down at me, the sheet wrapped so tightly around my arms and chest that I have trouble breathing. The beginnings of a frown, of second thoughts, etch across his features. Then he looks over at Stacey.

"Stacey, you have a choice," he says. "You can stay here with him, hoping that someone will come and save you, or you can come with us and survive. What's it going to be?"

"It's not a rope you're hanging him from," she says. "It's a god-damned *bedsheet*, and he's going to die, as *all* of us will, if you go through with this, Preston."

"Mark, put her in the bedroom," he says. "She'll be safe while we take care of the ones up here."

"Now Cordelia, the same thing applies to you," Preston says now, looking over at my sister. "Either you stay here and wait for help, or you leave now with the rest of us. It's up to you."

"I already told you what I was doing," she says. "Just get this the fuck over with."

"Fair enough," Preston agrees.

"Hey, where is Melanie?" someone asks.

I tell her to stay put. I tell her to wait in the bedroom. That I will be all right. That we will be okay. Mark pushes her into Monroeville and moves to shut the door. He promises her that if she tries anything, he will put the hammer through her skull just like she was one of them. Stacey spits in his face. He winks at her and nods slightly. My eyebrows furrow with momentary confusion.

"I'm not going to die," I keep whispering to myself. "I remember the future. I *can't* die."

"Melanie's gone," Jaime says. "Dude, what's happening?"

"It's a parallel dimension intruding and coalescing with this one," I find myself saying to them.

At this, the director calls "Cut!" from downstairs. From the floor, where I am tied up, I cannot see him below me, but amid the moans and shuffling about downstairs, I hear someone turn on a megaphone. There is conversing between the slightly foreign director and two crew members. They discuss inter-cutting material, computerized flow charts or maybe a guest—Al Bielik? Duncan Cameron?—explaining what they refer to as "all these concepts." We upstairs remain totally still and silent, waiting.

"Okay, I understand. Go away," the director hisses to the crew. Into the megaphone, he says, "Ross?"

"Um, yes?" I say, looking up sheepishly at Mark and Preston, who are glaring at me as if my response to one of the crew was a clear admission of guilt.

"Ross, could you repeat that last part with more emphasis?" the director asks.

"I told you," Mark mutters. "He's part of it. He's *helping* them down there, for Christ's sake. We need to stop him."

"Forget it," Preston says, checking the sheet tied around me. "We're getting out of here. He can repeat all the lines he wants."

"You think you're actually *going* anywhere?" I ask Preston above me. Then, loudly, reading from an imaginary Teleprompter: "It's a parallel dimension intruding...*and* coalescing...with this one." I turn back to Preston. "I can't believe you, Preston. We're best friends...You son of a *bitch!*"

"Thank you, Ross," the director says, cutting me off. "Now then, let's move right along. The rest of you can commence with your plan now, if you want. Preston, the ball is in your court."

8

Preston Nichols has always played the bad guy. My most vivid memories of him were always of the spy, the monster, the mad scientist, or the cruel general. Of him being against me, portraying Cooper from *Night*, or Blades from the biker gang in *Dawn*, or Rhodes from *Day*.

Some friends have been around so long that how you met them becomes irrelevant to the point of being totally lost and forgotten. You reach a nexus where the beginning doesn't even exist anymore, and your entire coexistence with this person is comprised of simple pin-pricks of useless footage and a few dozen anecdotes that come up at mediocre parties. I can't remember how we met, not like with Lydia and I, or with Stacey. It seems that Preston has simply always been there, watching videos, reading comics, dragging me to movie theaters in the larger cities just so that we can be one of eight people who see *Ed Wood* on the big screen. I can't remember a time when Preston wasn't in my bedroom going through my CDs and tapes, asking me why I like Portishead more than Korn, or if I had ever seen the photos of Kurt Cobain's corpse on the Internet.

Browsing through a scrapbook, it appears that we have been friends since we were twelve or so. There are pictures of us playing basketball in a boy named Jimmy's yard around that time. Jimmy died of leukemia a few years ago. There are also pictures of us at my cousin Miranda's eleventh birthday party, pizza in our mouths, our arms around each other's shoulders, Preston wearing a Yaga t-shirt. Preston told me not even a year ago that he fingered that same cousin a while back at my aunt's wedding rehearsal dinner.

I suppose Preston has always been that way. He has always had a penchant for lost and forgotten films, and an affinity toward slacker culture and shadowy movements and all-out fuck-your-friend-over antics.

One of the first times we met, in the middle of sixth grade P.E. no less, he brought up how Stanley Kubrick was totally insane now, and hadn't made a film since *Full Metal Jacket*.

When we were fourteen, he tried to talk me into asking my nineteen-year-old uncle if he would take us to a Revolting Cocks show. Of course we never went, but Preston did see them seven or eight years ago with a girlfriend that he stole from me.

Once, after a Faith No More concert that he took me to in Jacksonville, Preston chased a UFO in his father's van for over an hour, me sitting bored next to him, smoking cigarettes and telling him it was only the planet Venus. We ended up in some tiny junction called Two Egg, Florida, hopelessly lost.

It was Preston's idea to break into that mental hospital in Tallahassee.

I'm pretty sure it was Preston who threw an ice cube at Billy Corgan a few years ago when I finagled him into seeing Smashing Pumpkins in Lakeland. Corgan was hit in the nose and walked off-stage, bleeding. He told all of Florida to go fuck themselves.

Preston was the one who fingered two different girls at once without either knowing of the other while watching *Jail Bait*.

Preston used to tell me how good-looking my mother was. I once found a spread from *Hustler* with a cut out photo of my mom's face superimposed over the model's. He giggled when I confronted him.

Leave it to Preston to have seen the episode "Sanguinarium" from *The X-Files* eighteen times and counting.

He has always been both my best friend and, as my father once described him, "rat poison laced up in a joint." No one understood except me that he was the greatest guy in the world, and that he was only masquerading as some kind of asshole who made fun of fat girls and screwed over the only people who'd ever cared about him. It was all an act.

Since we became friends, fourteen years ago, two phrases have always abounded:

"It could only have been Preston. No one else could have pulled it off."

And, "No one else but Preston would even get the humor in that."

And then there is the issue of his parents.

They died.

As far as I can tell, Preston was devastated.

I knew Preston's parents. I liked them a lot. They were nice, educated people, just detached enough to keep you at an arm's length, but still friendly enough to make you want to have a conversation with them every time you were in their home.

There were afternoons at his house when we were in middle school, listening to Beastie Boys and playing *Mendel's Palace* on his Nintendo in the living room while his mother read novels by Joyce Carol Oates in the recliner. She would adjust her wire-rimmed glasses and run her finger through her black, slightly graying hair and smile at certain lines. Preston would invite me over for dinner and inform his mother afterward that she needed to cook for an extra person that night. She would smile and promise to make something nice. Then she would order pizza at the last minute and apologize to me later.

There were trips home from the mall in his mother's Camry when we were sophomores in high school, Preston and I in the back seat, the front passenger seat empty as Preston's mother drove back toward the lone house in the middle of the city. Preston's mother would listen to her son rant on and on about how everyone who doesn't know who Ray Dennis Steckler is should kick their own ass, and when I caught her staring at me in the rearview mirror, she would smile, roll her eyes at her son's ridiculousness, and wink. I would smile and make a mental note to wash my bowl out the next morning and put it carefully into the dishwasher after I was done with my cereal; anything to please her in a way that Preston never did.

His father was just as terrific. He would come home around six-thirty every night from the plant, his tie never matching his shirt, and he would sprawl out on the couch and read *The Financial Times*, and afterward, would sort of have a British accent for the next ten minutes before slipping back into his usual, soft-spoken northern Californian dialect. He would have a glass of red wine with the pizza that his wife ordered, and never say a word about having the same meal for the second time that week.

Preston's dad would take us to see R-rated movies when we were thirteen. He argued with us over what really happened to the two teenagers on a particular episode of *The X-Files*. He would seriously discuss what Romero was trying to say about the breakdown of communication in *Night of the Living Dead*. He would get kind of excited when we talked about what we would do in the event of a zombie apocalypse, and never ask why I was always over at his house instead of taking Preston back to mine.

I did things for Preston's parents that I never would have for my own in a hundred years.

The problem with my parents was that, quite simply, they were hostile alien people controlling my childhood, and never much more than that.

My mother Clarissa Orringer's warmth and maternal affection and guidance came at me as if she was scanning a manual on how to be a parent while doing it, and the manual was in a foreign language. And every time she began to get through to me and establish some kind of real bond, some kind of mother-son thing, either I would get into a fight with Cordelia or Dad and storm off, or Mom would slip back into dementia and depression and disappear from the forefront of the household for a couple of weeks.

My father, Richard Orringer, was just the opposite, and yet just as foreign to me. When I was a kid, he went to the recitals, the poetry readings, the plays and symposiums, and he met the other parents, and he made his public appearances wearing sleek sunglasses and expensive ties, but he did them with his head lopped to the side, his mind always focused on whatever shadowy life he led outside of our house. He was at work almost constantly, and not one of us had ever seen Dad's office except Mom who, when asked what it was like, said simply, "It's kind of…cold inside." My father made his rounds and painted a picture, but it was all damage control; it was all public relations and political tactics. In fact, the longest conversation my father and I ever had was something about decisions being made a few summers ago, and that discussion left me terrified.

But Preston's parents—Preston's parents I really loved.

As laid back as they were, I always insisted on referring to both of them as Mr. and Mrs. Nichols, sir and ma'am, an honor never bestowed upon my parents except out in public or in front of my junior high principal. For Mr. and Mrs. Nichols, I cleaned up in the kitchen as best I could after Preston wreaked havoc in an effort to make a bowl of Ramen noodles. When Mrs. Nichols was in her recliner rubbing her temples feverishly as she graded her ninth grade history class's papers, I would ask how school was going, if she was okay, if she would liked to have had her own son in one of her periods, if I could get her a glass of water or her other reading glasses. The time Mr. Nichols asked Preston if he would help him slide the china cabinet over a few feet in the dining room, I helped instead while Preston played *Predator* in the living room using a Game Genie.

Every time Preston shrugged away their yearnings and attempts at being good parents, I embraced them in his place. I wanted his parents to be mine.

One Friday night in February 1992, Preston's parents left the house for a late dinner. Preston's mom handed him a twenty, told him to order some Chinese take-out for the both of us, and tried to give him a kiss on his forehead, which he shied away from irritably. He waited for the front door to shut behind them and then rewound the movie back to before his mother had interrupted it. I glanced out the window as Mr. Nichols' van backed out of the driveway and disappeared down Main. Preston finished the movie and asked me afterward if I wanted to watch *Part VII*, the one where the blond takes on Jason with her psychic powers, next.

From what the officer told us, they went to dinner as planned. It was at a little Italian restaurant less than three miles from their house. "It was Mom's favorite place," Preston sobbed once, though I doubt he knew this for a fact. Mr. Nichols ordered the pork tenderloin, asparagus, and whipped garlic potatoes. Mrs. Nichols ordered the baked sausage ziti, of which she only ate half before having the rest put into a Styrofoam box to bring home to Preston and me for a late night snack. As they paid their bill, however, there was an argument brewing, the waiter said. There were coarse words exchanged between both of them, and the staff at the restaurant confessed to the police that they were glad to see the couple leave when they did, as the argument grew more and more heated. They paid their bill, handed their waiter a five dollar tip, and left.

The last exchange anyone ever heard from Mr. and Mrs. Warren Nichols:

"It's not like we have much choice, Evelyn."

"There's always a choice, Warren. Just face it: you're a god-damned coward."

No one knows exactly what happened next.

There were no other cars involved. It wasn't at an intersection, or a corner, or at a dead **end**. Mr. Nichols wasn't intoxicated. The car just crashed.

Mr. Nichols was killed almost instantly. When the van fishtailed, hit the sidewalk, and tipped over on its left side, a fire hydrant was sent through the driver side window, impaling him and crushing his brain. The van then somersaulted onto its roof, taking the hydrant with it. In a huge sudden gush of water, the vehicle flipped once more, onto its right side. Mrs. Nichols was still alive, soaking wet with water and her husband's blood. When the van toppled over onto its passenger area, the door caved in on her, along with the windshield frame. She was crushed between the frame, door, and seat, watching blood run down onto the sidewalk and wash away with the rivulets of water.

She spent the next hour, the last hour of her life, screaming.

Preston knows this and mentions it sometimes when he's so intoxicated that he's about to vomit. Sometimes he mentions that, when his parents were killed, he was on the porch in front of his house, drinking one of his father's

Amstel Lights and smoking a cigarette. He laments that he was probably asking me some kind of question about how much a zombie could eat until its stomach ruptured and burst open as his mother screamed and spit up blood and stared despondently into the eyes of the fire chief as he explained that they could not move her without killing her, and that if she had anyone that needed to be contacted, now was the time to do it.

Preston never spoke to his mother again. While she choked her last, and died in agony, Preston and I were at McDonald's discussing who was hotter between Mrs. Robinson and her daughter.

After the funeral, where Preston remained catatonic as opposed to crying, he came back to his family's large empty house, and began his decline. It would last for months, and in that time, his behavior became more erratic and reckless, but at the same time more careful and deliberate than I ever thought possible from him.

He became a paradox.

Having decided that his life was meaningless and would continue to be so, he went on huge shopping sprees with his parents' money. He bought useless gimcracks and surprised me and my girlfriend at the time with gifts such as box sets and books and Bob Dylan records and *Frighteners* DVDs signed by Peter Jackson. One night when we were on the roof of a six-story parking garage, Preston climbed onto the railing and pretended he was walking the high-wire in a circus while Shannon and I watched in horror. After he climbed down, he took two bars and drank a twelve pack before passing out and vomiting all over himself in his sleep. The next day he bought Shannon and me dinner and said that maybe he was sorry.

College was out. In fact, after dropping out of the two community college classes he was failing, Preston for some reason took a strong dislike to the entire educational system, constantly trying to dissuade me from earning my degree, and sleeping only with girls who had dropped out of high school. This included my girlfriend at the time.

"Your parents' being dead is no excuse for you behaving this way," I shouted at him after finding out.

"Yes it is," he said, and walked away with a shrug.

But then there were the other things that he was doing. Preston sold his Escort in the paper for practically nothing, and vowed never to drive anywhere again, winking as he thanked me for being his new cabbie for the rest of our friendship. He redecorated the walls and bought new knick-knacks and video games and a bigger TV for the living room, but the furniture, the layout, the china cabinets and armoires and kitchen tables and bookshelves and magazines all remained the same. He moved into his parents' bedroom, but carefully preserved everything just as they had left it. He even took pictures to make sure nothing would ever be permanently disturbed. When he came to my house, which was quite often for a while, he was extremely genial and humble around my parents, after years of passive rudeness and sultry comments about wanting to sleep with my mom. My mother warmed up to him nicely, explaining to me that his behavior toward them now that his own parents had passed was quite normal. My father would have none of it, though, and gave Pres his usual sideways glances and untrusting glares more often than ever.

Preston cried daily over what happened for what seemed like a very long time. As the inheritance came in, which was everything, all of it, not one asset or dime going to anyone else but him, Preston would spend hundreds of dollars at a time in Best Buy or on eBay while muttering gibberish about how he shied away from what would have been his mother's last kiss, or how when he was fourteen he lied and told his parents he needed fifty dollars for a school field trip, and had spent it on the movies and marijuana with too many seeds in it.

It was also around this time that Preston's basically normal fascination with horror and schlock pictures transformed into something more, something darker. Instead of looking for the ultimate scary movie or the most ridiculous B-film from 1963, Preston found it more important than ever to find the grossest, the sickest, the most depraved and unrelentingly sadistic and useless films ever made. *Zombie* gave way to *Cannibal Ferox* and *Cannibal Holocaust*; *Black Christmas* wet its pants before *I Spit on Your Grave* and *Last House on the Left*; *Dead Alive* was no longer as good as *Bad Taste*. Preston still liked the other movies, but seemed now to relish his new acquisitions in depravity more than he ever did the others before them.

As the months passed though, he seemed to return to some sense of normalcy. He was having sex with more and more people at a rate that seemed slightly alarming, and his taste in horror movies remained a little more extreme, but things kind of went back to normal with him. Aside from the occasional weeknight of binge drinking followed by lamentations about how much he missed them, and aside from the strange spooky girls and rave chicks and sorority bitches and ugly duckling ex-losers ready to screw who came streaming out of his house every night of the week as if it were a grocery store, things slipped back into routine.

The business we started four years later really helped Preston a lot. It was the first time ever that he felt his parents' money was going to something worthwhile, and he was ecstatic that he could actually make a living off of his own inherent and long-standing nerdy proclivities. I knew from the moment we started brainstorming ad ideas that this was an enterprise Preston would never be able to move away from.

Things have gone well for Preston, thanks in no small part to me, his long-suffering best friend. He has been through a gauntlet of terrible incidents, and has experienced more melancholy than he should have had to by the age of twenty-six. In response, he has done some pretty bad things. The cheating, the lying, the unscrupulous sex, the breaking of even the most rudimentary codes of friendship…Preston has continued to play the bad guy all through the years.

But he has always played this role while keeping a smile on my face, making sure that I never doubted how great a guy he was, deep down inside.

I still doubted him, though. Sometimes.

7

"BUT STILL...this all seems so improbable, what happened next," I say to them, picking at the skin on my arm.

"You're lying to us, son," the voice behind me says. "He never would have tried it."

"I think it makes perfect sense, if only you were there," I retort.

"Your friends left you hanging like that? *Literally*?" Martin asks, stunned. "They left you and Stacey to die in that house? Your girlfriend? Preston?"

"And I fully expected them to," I say. "There was never a single moment when I had any doubt that the world was a terrible place, full of stupid people who idiotically worshipped great evil.

"I copied movies for a living. I sent them in faux-official packaging to trailers and one-bedroom apartments, to men who never got over their dead grandmothers and girls who cut themselves amid memories of losing their virginities to truck drivers when they were twelve. The only thing worse I could have done with my life was making the original copies.

"Everywhere you go, through every suburb, through every cul-de-sac and mobile home park, the flashing blue of a television set tuned to something stupid is usually the only indication that there is any consciousness out there at all.

"And inside those boxes, Orwellian-controlled insanity reigns: News broadcasts assure everyone that all they have to fear is credit card scammers and hurricane season. Reality television reminds them every night of the week that everyone is attractive. Or should be. It reminds TV-watching America that it's a dog-eat-dog world out there where only the most stringent, the most ruthless, the most unscrupulous and shallowly beautiful win the $50,000, and there is never a mention of the taxes that will later be pick-pocketed, taking away thirty percent or so of that easily comprehended big even number."

Stacey is screaming on the other side of the door. When she pushes it open, Preston swings the bat against the frame and she momentarily shuts it again, waiting for only a few seconds before futilely attempting to stop them from sending me plunging to my doom.

Mark pushes me over the railing. With my arms tied behind my back, I grasp clumsily to the wooden posts on the other side, looking down at the fifty or so ghouls waiting for me twelve feet below. Beads of sweat cascade off my face and down into the pit. I urinate in my pants and Lydia sees me do it. My own piss running off of my leg, down my shoe, and dripping down onto the ghouls below, I look to her, my grips on the posts coming loose. I am silently pleading, still in love with her after three years and two naked people in a shower with her.

She frowns and mouths "I'm sorry." She offers a shrug and moves closer to Preston.

"All right," Preston says, prying the wooden planks from the outside of his bedroom door. "When I give the signal, undo the rope."

"I'm not so sure we'll be able to handle them," Jaime says, wielding a four-by-four with nails protruding through one **end**. "What if there are more?"

"There won't be, damn it," Preston groans. "Don't pussy out on me now, Jaime."

"I'm not pussying out on you, asshole. But isn't it obvious that they know exactly what we're going to do, and that they're going to stop us?"

"We were taught to be terrified of a technological breakdown, but we knew better all along, really. We knew that the computers would stay running, the Internet would not melt down into green toxic waste, and that the electricity would stay on to keep our mind control devices running. When the ball dropped and the world jangled its way like a retarded epileptic into another millennium that looked remarkably like the **end** of the last one, our faith in technology, our faith in the shadowy powers that be, would only be enforced and the grip tightened. We would further forget to look over our shoulders, to raise eyebrows loaded with incredulity and thoughtful venom."

Preston says nothing.

Stacey is sobbing on the other side of the Monroeville door.

"What's been going on between you two?" Lydia asks me. "Is it *that* serious, Ross?"

"I hope you die out there," I sneer at her, almost following this comment up with an apology. But I don't.

"We're going to make it," Preston assures his troupe. "Just do your part, everyone, and I promise, we'll be fine. I've been preparing for this event for…for forever it seems."

Preston said the word "again." Outside, just before they attacked, he said, stunned, "not again." Now he's about to throw me to them and lead his followers, my friends, to their own demise.

"Wait," Mark says, pointing to me. "What about him?"

Preston glances at Mark and then at me. I am still clutching the stairway railing. He sees the fear in my eyes, the panic, the total certainty that I will die if they drop me. He can't do it. He won't drop me. We've been best friends since—

"Push him over and let's get this over with," he says. "Untie the rope, Gary."

Gary unknots the rope holding the door closed. I hunch down so that Mark has a harder time reaching me over the banister. He leans over and shoves ineptly against my back. I quickly wipe the sweat from my bound hands against the bed sheet rope, and then tighten my grip around the wooden posts once more. He pushes me again and again. I do not release my grip. He tries to pry my fingers loose from the wood but I twist around and bite his fingers. My teeth sink into his knuckles and, upon tightening my jaws, Mark bawls.

Preston backs up as the bedroom door flies open amidst the sound of moaning.

"Let go!" Mark shouts, grabbing the hammer from the floor.

"I remember the future," I whisper to myself, the head slamming against my fingers.

I start crying. He hits me with the hammer again. It smashes into my pinkie and I retract both of my hands, losing my grip and tipping forward.

I fall.

"In a world so stupid, so mesmerized by dancing clown politics and horrified by the tortured innocents who finally succumbed to years of brainwashing by taking down thirteen or so bastards in a Midwest high school, something like a hundred living dead attacking a New Year's party full of unimportant, nameless young people who probably fuck, smoke pot, and who will not vote in the 2000 election can easily go unnoticed. We can, apparently, contribute nothing to this society, except entertainment for the masses as we die slow, excruciating deaths.

"It works out, if one thinks like a human being, as painful as this practice might often be. Like my profession before that night, anything can be sold to the right people. If the packaging looks official enough, if the audience is calmed down and rationalized into believing that what they like is normal and in good company, not sadistic and worthy of death...If these small tasks were accomplished, then this could all be worth a fortune for the ones filming it. It could play on prime time after we find out if Rachel and Ross are going to stay together or break up and if Chandler's and Monica's wedding goes okay."

Inexplicable thoughts of reality TV and *Friends* and God's second coming—in *2005*?—are ripped away. My breath is sucked out from my lungs and the sharp sudden pain to my chest is excruciating. My eyes are clenched shut and the tears come out like tiny shards of glass from my sockets. All I can hear are the moans of dozens of flesh-eating corpses as they reach for my feet. The stench of decay and shit fills my nostrils and I gag, suppressing nausea.

Above me, there are uninspiring sounds. People panicking. One of them is Lydia.

I can't breathe. The sheet is clasped around me so tightly that taking in air is exhausting and almost impossible. I gasp, coughing, swallowing vomit but maybe blood or both. I kick my legs upon feeling something touching them.

When I open my eyes, I am facing down, suspended by the sheet, which has miraculously held. Rotting hands grasp the bottoms of my shoes, slipping, jerking at the untied shoe laces. Eyes stare upward at me, gray and sad-looking.

There is the loud crack of someone's skull shattering, and I look up. As I do, someone comes tumbling down the stairs. It's Gary. Blood spills down from where the right side of his face was. His cheek and part of his eyeball and side burn is currently being devoured by a naked corpse hunched over on the top step. Gary falls silently into the gap between the two portions of stairway. He disappears behind a pack of ghouls that devour his body.

On the second floor, things sound bad.

I can't see directly above me, into the corridor, but I can hear the people dying. Jaime and Preston are batting wildly at one of the zombies. There is yelling and cursing. Someone trips. A scream. Maybe Jaime, but more likely Quentin. Loud whacks and dull thuds.

Below me, one of the taller ones grabs at my shoe, pulling me down. I slide in the sheet's grip. I kick and twist, freeing my foot from its grasp. I raise my legs so that none of them can reach me, but immediately find the effort exhausting. My feet hang limp, only to be grabbed and retracted again.

Mark comes into view at the summit of the steps. He is wrestling one of the zombies away, but he is not bitten. It snarls and flails wildly. Mark grabs it by the head and twists its body around, leaving his arm exposed to the creature's open mouth. I await the bite and the subsequent pounding and hollering as Mark is infected.

It never comes.

Mark is left unbitten as he lunges forward and shoves the zombie down the steps. But he loses his balance. He falls with it. Mark rolls down the stairs and lands on top of the creatures devouring Gary. I close my eyes, awaiting the terrible cacophony of Mark's squeals and pleas as they topple over him and eat him alive.

It never comes.

"You're saying that things had gone too far too far back to remember," the man behind me, the man I am not allowed to see, interjects.

"Exactly, gentlemen," I say. "Instead of looking for the face of Jesus or the Virgin in our tacos, in our toast, on the sides of our office buildings and in the bleeding palms of UFO-obsessed Italian men, perhaps we should have been looking elsewhere, at the devil encroaching all around us.

"For example, the Internet has led to the homogenization of all human culture. Where, in the past, one could venture to Beijing, to New York, to Milan and Sydney and Bombay, and discover five distinct cultures, now they find that, to a large extent, one place looks much like another. The world has been so fascinated with a world-wide web of information and the exchange of ideas, they have forgotten that a world with some isolation from one society to the next is integral to the evolution—and even survival—of humankind. We've reached a stand-still, a point where the only way any one of us can move forward is if all of us do so together.

"There are no leaps and bounds to be made, guys. The path is too narrow and the world of people too thick and uncompromising. There is nowhere for us to go but backward, to the origins of our folly, where through much effort and sacrifice, we may be able to save ourselves.

"But we won't. It's easier to watch Regis make someone else a millionaire. It's easier to check our e-mail and watch other people besides us being attacked by the undead on TV. Get it?"

Mark tumbles off of the creatures' backs, onto the living room floor. He is calm, not pulsating with sweat and quick manic breaths. He is not attacked or bitten.

Above me, the battle continues. Something dull and heavy crashes against my left shoulder. I wince in pain as a newly destroyed zombie lands with a thud on the wood tile below me. At the edge of the stairs, the one that was munching on Gary's face is hit from behind with the book**end**. Jaime, teary-eyed, kicks it down the steps.

"You *bastard!*" Preston roars down at Mark.

Mark brushes the dust from his sleeves and wipes the blood from his hands onto his jeans. He smiles.

"You're one of *them*?" Lydia shrieks. There is the palpable feeling that she realizes something in lieu of Mark's identity. "Oh my *god*."

"What's wrong, Lydia?" I find myself yelling up at her. "Did you fuck him too?"

Mark looks at me dangling above him, laughing at my comment, and then at the group on the second floor. His smile fades, returns. Grinning, his eyes suddenly red, Mark offers a salute before moving effortlessly through the pack of ghouls all around him. The director sidles up next to him. They discuss something that involves me, judging from the glances and the cameramen who receive instructions from Mark and the director just before training their cameras directly on me dangling above the living room, suspended by a taut bed sheet.

It is a long time before anything else happens.

"They—your own friends—left you there to *die*?" Martin asks, shaking his head while lighting a cigarette. "I still can't believe it. The whole world—it's so—"

"Fucked," someone somewhere says, although it is neither of my interrogators, and I do not think it was me.

"That's not even the worst part," I say.

"What is?" Martin mutters.

"What's worst, what's most pathetic in a night full of pathetic people doing nothing but pathetic things in response to all of these apocalyptic occurrences—if it were not the teeth being sunk into my own flesh, if it were not my own family and friends dying and me being implicated in the aftermath—if it were anyone else, I would have downloaded all of it. I would have watched it every week. And I would've taped it if I wasn't home."

6

PRESTON AND THE OTHERS MAKE THEIR ESCAPE SHORTLY AFTERWARD. Some of them I will never see alive again.

It takes a long moment before the survivors on the second landing compose themselves after discovering that Mark was a turncoat. It takes Jaime some time to cope with watching his best friend die. Cordelia takes a reprieve to rationalize the fact that she just allowed her own brother to be sacrificed in order to save herself. It takes Monica and Quentin and maybe a couple of the other more intelligent of the group a little while to go along with a suicidal plan that the crew has anticipated, judging from the halogen lights being erected out in the front yard and the director's cryptic go-ahead.

But they all get over it.

Although I can't see, I imagine their plan goes as follows: Preston leading the way like a jack-ass, the junto makes their way out of the master bedroom window onto the lower portion of the roof. From there, they head to the edge of the porch, where they jump to the ground. Monica breaks her ankle in the short fall. While they tend to her injured foot, Cordelia begins sobbing. Everything falls apart. They are attacked shortly thereafter, wishing they had listened to Ross and Stacey, wishing they could go back in time like Ross and change the way things unfolded.

I don't think it goes this way, however. I hear my friends yelling and shouting from the front of the house. Below me, zombies begin losing interest in the dangling bait above them in favor of the seven people gadding about on the front lawn. They stream out of the house, through the front and back door and shattered windows. Soon, only the five or six most dedicated of the undead have stayed behind to grab for my feet just out of their reach.

The megaphone clicks on. There is feedback. A flash. Outside, the director clears his throat into the device.

"Action!"

The moans grow ferocious, and then fade quickly away. The zombies have run after Preston and the others. They are gone and only Stacey and I remain in this house now. And I am dangling helplessly from the second floor, impossible to save, watching posters on the wall directly across from me transform into framed photographs and small acrylic paintings.

5

"Ross?"

I can't look up to where the voice has come from.

"Stacey?" I ask.

"There's no one else left, Ross. Of course it's Stacey. Are you okay?"

"I'm just dandy, Stacey," I say, dangling gently back and forth. The zombie in the White Zombie shirt gets his hand on my left shoe and jerks at it until it comes free and falls to the floor. The ghoul picks it up and sniffs it, moaning loudly.

"I'm going to figure out a way to get you back up here," she says.

"Mm-hmm," I say, watching the White Zombie zombie slobber on the tongue of my shoe. "Yeah, right. Stacey, I weigh almost two hundred pounds. How do you plan on getting me back up there?"

"Hold on a sec," she says, and I hear her clamber off.

Several minutes later, soft cloth smacks against the back of my head from above.

"Climb up on it," Stacey instructs me.

I wriggle about in the noose around my waist, trying to free my arms bound behind my back. The sheet is so tight that my eyes bulge and water. The situation is hopeless.

"Stacey, sweetie, it's a noble effort, but they really tied me up good. I'm afraid that my arms are bound and are not going to get free. In short, I—I think I'm pretty much screwed here. Eventually, the camera guys will cut me down or give the things below me something to stand on. Meanwhile, I'm not getting undone from this sheet."

Some of the zombies that chased after Preston and the others come slouching back toward the house. Upon spotting me, it's as if they never previously tried and failed to reach me. They stumble and shuffle around in the front yard as fast as they can without the director calling "Action." Their moans are deafening. I can barely hear Stacey cursing in frustration above me.

"Well, then we have no other choice then," she calls down after a moment.

"What do you mean, 'we have no other choice,' Stacey? What are you talking about?"

"I'm not strong enough to pull you back up here, right?"

"Um."

"And they're coming back toward the house," she says. "They'll be here soon. But if I go for it right now, then you'll only have to deal with the five or six already below you. Those odds are better than none."

"Whoa, wait—*what* odds? Go for *what*?"

"I'm going to cut you down, Ross. You'll just have to make a run for the stairway. I can't think of anything else."

"Stacey, are you fucking *crazy*?" I squeal.

"I'm going to start cutting the sheet off this post now, sweetie. When you fall, your arms will come free and you can make a bolt for the stairs."

"Stacey, that's not a good idea."

I twist and convulse in the sheet's grip. The other sheet that she just threw down to me keeps swinging against my face. Ignoring it, I pull my arms and kick and swing back and forth, trying to free my grip before she drops me down into the hands of the six creatures below me.

"It's coming undone n—" she says, but stops abruptly in the middle of her last word. "There was a noise in the bedroom. Hold on."

"Oh my *god*," I say to myself. "We're *both* going to die."

I continue trying to free myself. Pulling upward as hard as I can, my arms' flesh is rubbed raw from the fabric of my sweater, from the sheet's grip. Sweat pours down my forehead now, dripping from my face onto the living dead below me.

"Please don't do this, Stacey," I whimper. "*Please*."

She does not answer. I hear noise from Preston's bedroom. They're probably up there again, provoked by Preston's getaway, killing Stacey as I dangle here helplessly.

My right hand, taut against my back, inches upward as I flail about.

Holy shit.

It's possible.

"No, wait!" I yell upward, triumphant. "Stacey, wait. I—I'm coming loose. I'll be up there—in a second—"

My right palm is now wedged between my back and the sheet. The vice is so tight that my hand falls asleep and it is in this moment that I tug as hard as I can one final time. My right hand comes free. I grip the sheet above my head tightly, my senses tingly.

"Stacey, don't drop me," I plead. "I'm coming loose."

She does not answer me.

When I pull my left hand out of the noose, I immediately begin to slide through the loop. One of them can now totally reach my foot. He grabs it.

The front door, which somehow shut, swings open.

Another hand grips my pant leg and begins tugging me downward.

I bunch both sheets together and hold on for dear life.

The creature below snarls as it bites into my thick shoe. Its teeth are unable to pierce the leather. My other foot, the shoeless one, I keep raised and pressed against my knee.

They come pouring back into the house, some of their faces stained red with fresh blood.

"Ross, climb, baby," Stacey yells down at me.

"Yeah, move your ass, Ross," another voice urges.

I glance up. Stacey's head is hung over the banister, a distance that now seems like miles as I try to climb back up the rope. Next to her is Cordelia, my sister.

My sister came back.

"You came *back*?" I stammer, momentarily forgetting all about my peril.

"It's kind of a long story," she says. "Get back up here and I'll tell you all about it."

I am suddenly jerked several inches downward in the noose, the sheet now coiled awkwardly up under my armpits.

"They're holding my leg," I whimper. "I can't get up."

"The two of us are going to pull you up," Stacey says. "Grab the other sheet. We'll pull."

Another hand wretches at my pants, jerking frantically. I slip several inches down the slippery cloth, which has already been soaked through with sweat.

"Grab the other sheet, Ross!"

I do, dangling helplessly as the monsters below pull and tug at my legs. Several seconds later, one of the girls barks out "*Now*," and I am suddenly lifted upward two feet. My legs come free of the zombies' grips.

"Keep pulling," I shout. "Get me out of here."

"Hold on," Cordelia pants, unseen. "You're heavy."

Another heave and I rise another foot or so. I can actually hear both the girls whimpering and panting with exertion as they ready themselves for another pull. To hasten the process, I begin scaling the second rope as best I can.

"Ross, *stop* it, you idiot," Cordelia shouts. "You're shaking it and we're losing our grip."

"Sorry," I call back up.

"Just be still."

They heave again and again, now screaming with exertion. The bottom of the second floor is only a couple of feet out of my grasp now.

"I can almost reach the posts," I tell them. "Just a little more."

"We're *working* on it, Ross," Stacey says, aggravated.

"One more big pull, okay?" Cordelia says. "Are you ready? Okay, one. Two. *Three.*"

They hoist the rope toward them four feet, hand over hand, wailing and cursing the entire time. My hand grips the bottom of one of the posts now. Stacey comes to the edge and offers her hand, which is tore up and bloody. Using her and the wooden railing, I get a leg up onto the second floor, and then the other. I stand up.

The realization that I am still alive is overwhelming.

"Ross, let's not do that again," Cordelia urges, covered in a pile of sheet on the corridor floor. She falls backward, exhausted. One of the lamps' flames flickers.

Stacey is standing on the other side of the banister, smiling jubilantly. Upon seeing my angry expression, she smiles even wider.

"You were going to *drop* me?" I spit. "You were actually going to cut me loose and *hope* I made it?"

"No, sweetie," she says.

"Then what the hell was all that crap about my odds being better with only six than with all of them? *Huh*? What were you *thinking?*"

"Basic psychology, babe," she says, giving me a hand as I climb over the wooden banister. "You're a negative person, prone to giving up and not trying your hardest. So, I prompted you to."

"Wait—you mean you just told me that to get me to free myself *faster*?" I pause, watch her walk away, back over to Cordelia. "That was a nasty, dirty—"

"It got you moving, didn't it?" she interrupts. "You got yourself free not long after that. I think abundant praise and gratitude would be in order at this point, wouldn't you, Cordelia?"

"Totally," Cordelia sighs, still lying flat on her back along the floor. "Ross, you're a dick."

I free myself from the sheet around my torso and glance down into the living room. Three different cameramen have been filming my entire ordeal. The director sits on the arm of the couch, his chin rested in his hands. He gives me a quick thumbs-up before hopping off the chair and disappearing out the front door.

"Stacey, Cordelia," I say, retrieving a cigarette and lighting it. "You're right. Um, thanks."

"*Um*, you're welcome," Stacey mimics.

"You're an asshole, Ross," Cordelia mutters. "Oh, yeah, Stacey, don't forget to tell him."

"Oh, right," Stacey nods.

"Tell me what?" I ask.

"Cordelia isn't the only one who came back," she says casually, lighting a cigarette and sliding down the bloody wall into a sitting position.

"What?"

"Behind you," Cordelia says.

She laughs hysterically for no reason and I turn around.

4

THE WORLD IS JUST *BRIMMING* WITH COOL THINGS, she told me once. The catch is that it is also a world full of morons.

I met Stacey at her own house one evening three autumns ago. Typically, it was during another obtuse party.

Lydia abandoned me immediately. Upon stepping through the threshold of Stacey's parents' house, a two-story brick structure complete with pillars and a small fountain in the front yard, she squealed with glee upon sighting a guy she had not seen since, apparently, "that one time at the place with the Absinthe." She skittered off and I would not see her again for an hour. This was how life with Lydia was, I had come to realize in the last few months. I ignored it, cursed under my breath about it, and eventually forgot it ever bothered me amidst the fact that I was in love.

I stood alone, surrounded by partiers, left behind by my girlfriend in favor of a guy who had something to do with Absinthe. This was my first get-together thrown solely by Lydia's people and, neglecting her promise to introduce me around to all of her best friends, including Stacey, who Lydia told me I would love, she took off and left me for dead.

There was beer in the kitchen.

I sipped gingerly from a cup of foamy Bud Light, staring out the kitchen window on a yard full of drunken Neanderthal-like creatures playing hacky-sack and laughing at their own impending deaths and juvenile tastes in film. I replayed images from the night before, from the first time Lydia requested sodomy, assuring me I would love it. I didn't.

On the fridge, magnetic poetry had been written, destroyed, re-formed to make sentences vaguely referring to sex and drug use. There was a picture of a beautiful blond standing beside a small African boy at what might have been Disney World, but which looked more like a back-drop of Disney as opposed to the real thing. Below that, another picture, this one of the same girl decorated in high school band regalia, proudly clutching a French horn. To the right of this, ten tiny magnets composing the phrase "god requires a small boy to sacrifice for magic grass."

"The world is just *brimming* with cool things," someone said behind me. It was a girl's voice. I turned around.

Before me was the girl from the picture, only not. This girl was not an all-county French horn player, nor a girl who posed for adorable pictures next to tiny African boys in sugary, evil theme parks.

This girl was stoned. Drunk. Slouching like she had just had sex with a guy she hardly knew. She was dressed in tiny blue shorts and a Serial Killer t-shirt. She was swigging from a bottle of Grolsch and holding a butter knife. This girl was anarchy as envisioned by a lonely fifteen-year-old Marilyn Manson fan.

"The catch," she continued, "is that it is also a world full of morons."

"Yeah?" I said lamely.

"Therefore, nobody cares about the infinite cool stuff out there just waiting to be discovered."

She took a step toward me. I could smell melon and Benson and Hedges smoke, bookstore chocolate and gas station wine.

"You're Stacey?" I ask.

She did not answer me. Instead, she held up the knife.

"Do you see this?" she asked. "Do you see what this is?"

"It's a butter knife," I said.

"Correct. Fan*tas*tic. Do you see the label on it?"

"You mean who made this butter knife?"

"*Yes*," she slurred, giggling. "Do you see the manufacturer name?"

I looked down at the bottom of the handle, only slightly bored by this dame's foolish antics.

"It's Oneida," I sighed, a terribly unoriginal gesture. "They make silverware."

"Do you know what Oneida was *originally*?"

"A man who wanted to share his passion for cutlery with the rest of the world?"

"Not quite. I learned that Oneida began not as a silverware company. It was a *cult*."

"Really?" I asked, raising my eyebrows. I began to smile. "That *is* interesting."

"Oneida was a nineteenth century utopian society founded by a man named John Noyes. Principle among this bastardized form of Christian hippies was the belief in 'complex marriage,' also known as free love and voyeur-ized group sex."

"That is kind of cool."

"They didn't start making silverware until Noyes ditched and the whole 'sex as closer to God' thing dissipated in 1879. Didn't you learn that in American Studies?"

I stared at her, dumbfounded. Lydia and I had been dating for six months, and never had she told me anything as pointlessly obscure and interesting as this. Nor had she told me that her so-called "best friend" was this strange and ridiculous girl talking to me about people who screwed each other while manufacturing high-quality silverware.

"I'm Ross Orringer," I said, extending my hand.

"I'm Stacey Shimmerly," she returned, extending her own.

We ended up next to the covered swimming pool in the backyard. This was the relatively quietest place we could find to converse.

She lit a Parliament menthol and rested her head against the back of the lounge chair. I lit my own and chatted dismissively with Adam about his new shirt. He disappeared.

"I hate parties like this," Stacey sighed.

"You *threw* it," I pointed out, laughing.

"My parents were out of town and I'm young. It was pure inertia."

The sound of Lydia laughing raucously at something echoed through the yard. I glanced over, where she was having quite a time with Monica 1 and Monica 1's boyfriend at the time. Stacey giggled.

"I love Lydia," she said.

"Do you?" I asked. "You and she don't seem to meld."

"And you two do?"

"I like her. She has a lot of potential. She's smart."

"Yeah, she is," Stacey nodded. "We haven't been friends that long, but she's awesome."

"You look a lot older than her."

"I've been told that."

"And you're a lot…different."

"But I like her," Stacey insisted.

"I like her, too," I repeated. "I'm not sure what it is, but I'm falling in love with her."

"She's…something," Stacey sighed, looking down at the deck.

From a conversation last New Year's Eve:

"We can't do this."

"I know."

"I love Lydia."

"So do I. She's my best friend."

"But she shouldn't have—that was so fucked up of her to do that. And with that *asshole* from *Dartmouth*?"

"Lydia has a history of meaningless infidelities."

"I wish someone would have warned me."

"Ross, I tried..."

"We can't do this."

"...But we will, won't we?"

"Yeah, probably."

"Okay. But Stacey, this—"

"I know—"

"It can't ever go beyond this."

"Beyond what?"

"Beyond...well, sex, I guess."

"And if it does?"

"It can't."

"...Okay, Ross."

"So we're going to go through with this?"

"You just kissed me. I'd say there's no turning back now. Like a Shakespearean tragedy."

"This is such..."

"Ross, I think I'm falling in love with you."

"...a fucked up New Year."

I didn't see Lydia again until two days after Stacey and I first had sex. She took it as a cooling-off period while I learned to forgive her for what happened that night after she went to bed with that guy from Dartmouth. It was actually time for me to cope with my new stature as a son of a bitch.

She came by the apartment and I pretended to be sullen. I sat on the couch and watched *Dateline*. I slurped up fettuccini noodles and didn't offer her any.

Flashbacks of Stacey, panting beneath me, grabbing her own breasts, heaving up, down, up, down. Flashbacks of awkward kisses and shadows outside the windows as I came on her stomach.

We—Lydia and I—**end**ed up having make-up sex. The light stayed on, a rare occurrence, and I watched Lydia gyrating on top of me, her breasts swinging to and fro, her stomach flesh pinching up on itself, sweat building up on her forehead, makeup cracking, her cheeks becoming flush and her eyes clenching shut as she came.

Afterward, she lay next to me, taking a drag from my cigarette.

"I'm so sorry, Holden. I don't know why I'm such a bad person. I'm so—god damn—I'm so sorry."

"I am too," I muttered.

"For what?"

"I don't know."

The hospital was a terrifying experience.

Other bored young people had already trampled the chainlink fence down to waist level by the time we made the long drive to Tallahassee one night. I climbed across first, helping Lydia over and then Stacey. I offered my hand to Preston but he scoffed and hopped over while lighting his hundredth cigarette that evening.

He was explaining the disappearance of the voodoo zombie from popular film.

There was a boarded window on the first floor that one of Preston's Tallahassee acquaintances assured us would be loose. It was, and armed with flashlights, a video camera, and youthful stupidity, the four of us squeezed inside the abandoned mental hospital, known by patients and college kids as Sunnyland.

Inside, we stayed close together at first, moving from room to room, examining the abandoned wheelchairs, the lone slipper left next to a toilet, and the metal tables with leather straps still intact. We passed the isolation ward with its small padded cells on the second floor, the cafeteria littered with thousands upon thousands of white Styrofoam cups, and an elongated room with dozens of bath tubs. Preston pointed out that the elevators had been removed from their shafts and questioned how this could have been accomplished. Someone had spray-painted NOW I'M AN AMPUTEE, GOD DAMN YOU across a wall on the third level. We heard voices in one of the dormitories, and as Preston opted to hook himself to the electric shock tables while Lydia helped him, Stacey and I waited in one of the halls.

I thought I could hear the faint sound of a young girl giggling, if the girl's mouth was full of blood when she did it.

"Ross?" Stacey whispered.

"You didn't hear that?" I asked.

"Why won't you talk to me about this? Why are you pulling the typical guy crap on me?"

"Stacey, I just—I just don't think that breaking up with Lydia right now to go out with her best friend would be the wisest move we could make in the PR department. Um, you know?"

"Oh, who gives a *shit* about the PR department, Ross? Do *you*?"

"I—I guess I do," I shrugged.

"Why don't you just tell me the truth?" she pressed.

"What truth is that?" I sighed, a terribly unoriginal gesture.

"That I'm great to fuck, just not quite vapid enough for you to date?"

"Hey, wait a minute, Stacey. That's not only my girlfriend of over a year we're talking about being vapid. It's your best friend, too."

"I realize that," she said, turning away from me. The giggling sound stopped, replaced by the distant cacophony of electric current running through faulty wiring.

"Stacey, I care so much about you. I think that you are, by far, the coolest person in the world. But I still—something about Lydia—"

"Why is it that I have the distinct feeling that one day you'll still be handing me this clumsy rant even as she thrusts the blade through the flesh of your back?"

"I don't *know* why you have that feeling, Stacey," I said, lighting a cigarette. "Maybe it's because you have unwarranted misgivings and a deep subconscious hatred toward your own best friend."

"Not maybe, you idiot," she said, pulling out her pipe from the video camera case, then a baggie full of weed. "I *definitely* have misgivings and a deep hatred toward my own best friend. The question—the question you *always* forget to ask, Ross Orringer, is *why*. *Why* do I have these feelings towards her?"

"I don't know, Stacey. Why?"

She didn't look up at me as she said, "Her and Preston have been goofing off in there for a while now, huh?"

I took in her insinuation and began to open the door to the shock therapy room. Lydia and Preston were both giggling.

"You're ridiculous, Stacey."

"I am indeed," she said. "I actually thought you really existed. And I was going to give you head in the isolation ward. I *am* ridiculous."

3

My first reaction, which soars through my body and turns my bones into thorny vines and my blood into steaming bile, is rage. Up until this point, I have felt as if our mysterious documentarians have been wholly out of reach, laughing mad doctors protected by both an army of undead and their monopolized control of every foreseeable variable. They carefully planned and coordinated my initial encounters with the zombies, and then tightly sealed the area off, sent the cannibals our way, and did very well at documenting this party's demise.

But now, I am standing less than ten feet away from one of these filmmakers, and there is absolutely nothing to stop me from grabbing him and beating him to death. There are no living dead standing between us, no directors calling "Action," no snipers sending bullets whizzing by my head. There is, at this moment, only the three of us and this one man taping the scene with a television camera. Naturally, my first reaction is vengeful rage.

He tapes this reaction.

"When I climbed back up onto the roof of the house, he was already in the bedroom filming me," Cordelia is explaining, but this information does not register with me.

The cameraman is dressed in a white radiation suit and yellow gloves. His breathing comes through a gas mask. His left side has been splashed with someone else's blood.

"Who knows how long he's been up here," Stacey is saying.

He adjusts the focus, pans in, and moves the camera away from a shot that caught all three of us into one that captures only my face and my impending assault on the one filming me.

"Did Preston take one of them hostage when they got out?" I ask Cordelia.

"I don't know," she says. "I wasn't with them that long."

I approach. My fists are clenched.

The cameraman makes no move to flee, back up, call for zombie reinforcements, or ask for assistance from the director. He does not pause filming, either. It is difficult to judge through the thick white suit and gas mask, but the crew member seems totally calm, either completely naïve of his own hubris or eerily aware of something that I am not.

"If there's anything dangerous and wieldable, get it," I mutter to Cordelia and Stacey. There is movement behind me.

"Brody, are you getting this?" the director calls from downstairs.

"I'm getting it," the cameraman in front of me yells back, muffled and almost incomprehensible.

"Ross, I'm not so sure you should do this," Stacey warns, standing directly behind me now and handing me one of the book**end**s the group left behind. I grab it.

"I want answers," I say, inching closer. "I want to escape."

He continues filming, only now taking two steps back into the dark hallway.

"Yeah, but this is really bizarre," she says. "Don't you think they would have anticipated this?"

"I don't give a shit, Stacey."

"Ross, leave him alone," Cordelia says cautiously. "I didn't come back here just to die."

Next to me, a framed mini-poster for *The Killer Shrews* transforms into a framed mini-print of Munch's *Madonna*. No one says anything of this, and I grow leery of my companions for not doing so.

"Why did you come back at all?" I ask my sister.

"We can talk about it later, Ross."

"No, we can talk about it *now*," I insist, not taking my eyes off of the camera aimed at me. "After what happened with our father, with that guy Mark, with *everyone* but Stacey…I'm not too trusting of anyone except for her at the moment. So, why'd you come back?"

"Ross, I left you hanging back there to join a group of morons in their attempt to escape," Cordelia explains calmly. "I, uh, came to my senses."

"Bullshit," I mutter, stepping toward the crewman. He backs up into the Monroeville doorway.

"Ross, what are you doing?" Stacey asks quietly.

"Everything has gone crazy," I say. "Everything is…changing. And no one seems to notice it but me."

"Notice *what*, Ross?" Cordelia says. "The fact that zombies showed up at our New Year's party this year? I think we all noticed that."

"Not *that*," I snap. "I mean, all of the little things. It's all changing. Something is happening, and the zombies might be the least of our worries. Something is *happening*, Cordelia."

"So you're going to find out what it is by beating the shit out of this guy?"

"Yes."

"Don't, Ross," Stacey pleads. "Your sister is right. They're still calling the shots. I have a bad feeling that they *want* you to attack him."

Stacey's hand rests against my shoulder. But it is only for a moment, as I squirm away, take two strides toward the cameraman, and swing the book**end**. It smashes against the camera, shattering it. His hand is struck, the stone weight breaking one of his knuckles. He drops the camera, tending to his broken finger and falling to his knees.

As he moves to slide the yellow glove off of his hand, I raise the book**end** and bring it down against his head. The mask slides awkwardly out of position on his face, and he coughs at the blow. I hit him again, this time snapping the black gas mask down, exposing his eyes and hairline.

"Brody, are you getting this?" the director calls.

"Yeah, Brody," I sneer, "are you getting this?"

I hit him again, across the nose, breaking it. He yelps out in pain, gingerly reaching for it and sliding the mask completely off of his face. He jerks the white hood off of his head and begins poking at his nostrils with his good fingers. He looks up at me, his expression shock and disappointment. He is soaked in blood, which spigots from his nose incessantly.

"You didn't expect this?" I ask, hitting him once more. He loses consciousness and a small pool of blood collects beneath his lip, which has been ripped open.

Cordelia looks over at me. "Our *father*? What about our father?"

The nautical star tattoo on his neck looks very familiar as we strip him of his white garbs. I can't place it though. Underneath the radiation suit the young man is wearing khaki pants, a navy blue Polo shirt, and orange boxers. There is nothing very remarkable or official-looking about him. He looks like one of us.

"That was really stupid," Cordelia says. "We're in deep shit now, Ross."

"Yeah, and we weren't before," I say. "Just get the sheet. Let's tie him up and ask him a few questions."

"What is he possibly going to tell us?"

"Well, for instance, maybe he could tell us where our parents fit in with all of this. Maybe he can help us get the hell out of here."

"Not with a broken nose he's not," Stacey says. "He'll be screaming in pain and slithering around in his own blood. We'll have to fix it or he won't be much good to us."

After I remove his black sneakers and trade them for my one remaining boot, Stacey and I drag Brody's body across the hall floor to the edge of the staircase, where we prop him up against the railing and proceed to tie him up. When the director and the other crew people see Brody being tied up, they do not look the least bit distraught, angry, or surprised. I am not sure if this reaction is good or devastating.

"This is so stupid," Cordelia says, knotting the cloth. "This is unbe*lievably* stupid. I hope Pres and the others are doing better than we are, because—"

"What happened to them, by the way?" I ask.

"They ran in one direction, I ran in another. They headed back toward Pittsburgh, and I ran back up to the house. None of those things followed me; they were running after Preston. I don't know what happened to them."

"The hell with them," Stacey says. "Right, Ross?"

"Yeah, um, uh, right," I nod. The image of Lydia, dying, fills me with dread.

"Ross, you broke his nose, so you can fix it," Cordelia says, eyeing his mouth, which hangs open crookedly. Blood runs down to his lips and mixes with saliva, which cascades down to his chin and onto his collar. "You'll have to grab it and jerk it back into place if you expect him to talk when he comes to."

"You're nuts," I say, examining the bruises on his cheek, and then his crooked snout. "I'm not touching that."

"This is *your* mess, Ross. *You* clean it up."

"I would do it now, before he wakes up," Stacey adds.

When I wrap my fingers around his large nose, his eyes immediately begin to flicker. His mouth moves slightly, as if to shut. He is reviving. Already he begins moaning, a sound quickly matched by the ghouls downstairs.

"Do it," Cordelia whispers. "Do it now, Ross."

The way his flesh feels in my fingers, like syrupy rubber, and the way I can finger his bone under the skin, and deduce just how terribly the pain will be when I jerk it toward me—I become nauseous. His left eye slowly opens, and he looks at me, and then his eyes cross as he peers down at my hand on his muzzle.

He goes to scream.

"Ross!"

I take a taut hold, look away, and heave the extremity toward me.

There is an audible snap. At first, it looks as if he will pass out again, but then he begins convulsing in his restraints, spitting and screaming, saliva and blood spraying from his nose, which looks only slightly better now that I have just jerked it back into place. After several minutes, Brody, the cameraman, eases up, thrusting forward and up against the sheet once more before taking a deep breath and going limp.

He's unconscious.

"I think he's okay," I say, placing my cheek near his lips to measure breathing, although I have absolutely no idea what I am doing.

"Do you have any idea what you're doing, Ross?" Cordelia asks.

"Yes. He'll—he'll be all right. He's just out cold."

"They're getting really riled up," Stacey says, looking over the banister down onto the first floor.

Below, the ghouls have packed tightly against one another around the staircase. They have crammed into the debris-littered gap between the sections of stairs and trampled Monica and Gary's bones. Some of them have stumbled up the first few steps, only to fall onto the heads of the others beneath them. They keep coming though.

"What the hell is this?" I ask. "Why are they doing that?"

"Ross, you asshole," Cordelia says. "Isn't it obvious?"

"Cordelia, if you bring up the camera guy thing one more time, I'm going to *feed* you to those fuckers."

"We need to figure a way out of here," Stacey says, trying to dissuade us from arguing. "Soon."

"Well hopefully the next plan we enact won't involve dangling me above their heads as bait," I mutter bitterly, giving my sister a sideways glance while lighting a cigarette.

"Give me one of those," Cordelia says. I hand her one and she lights it, taking deep inhales and looking toward the ceiling as she expunges the smoke. "Hmm."

"What about stealing Preston's plan and using this guy as a hostage?" I ask. "Except we just stay here until they eventually pack up and leave?"

"Hmm," Cordelia intones, still looking up.

"Are you going to ask him questions?" Stacey asks me.

"When he wakes up. But we need to be thinking about the long-term too.

We may be here for a while: days, maybe even a week, with no power, no food, and no way to escape. Our only hope might just be perseverance."

"Hey, listen…"

"Well then maybe we should try to make a break for it," Stacey argues. "I mean, maybe Preston and them made it out of here. God, how far is it beyond the barricade? Like maybe a few hundred yards? Jesus, sweetie, if we just made it past the ones in the house and made a nasty run for it, I think we might clear it and be back in the city. We'd be safe in no time."

"*Running*, Stacey? Running isn't a plan. Running is what you do when a plan fails."

"Ross. Stacey. Listen. Hey. Hey, listen. *Shut up*."

Stacey and I look to my sister.

"I think I might have an idea," she says, glancing up at the trap door leading into the ceiling. Then she looks down at the lit **end** of her cigarette.

CORDELIA'S GREAT ESCAPE PLAN #1

(As Transcribed and Interpreted by Ross)

The cordoned off area is at least half a mile from the blockade at Pittsburgh to the 89 Intersection. Heading away from the front of the house, or from its back yard, there is no way to be sure. Escape would be improbable utilizing routes heading in either of these directions, as one would be hindered by physical barriers (fences, buildings, shrubbery, walls, vehicles, etc.) and unfamiliar territory (including but not limited to narrow passageways, shadowy lots, dangerous windows, open areas conducive to a snipers' bullets, and more than likely several devastating dead **end**s).

"That would be my name if I were a road sign," Ross murmurs at this point, probably remembering a conversation he had once with Preston. "Dead **end**. I don't care what the rule is."

"What?" Cordelia asks patiently, in response to her brother's rude interruption.

"Nothing," he says, typically. "Commence with your plan."

We've been very pre-occupied with escaping the house, evading capture and consumption by zombies, and reaching help. Cordelia suggests a different theory altogether: why not bring the help to us?

From the attic, not only do we have access to the roof and the perimeter around the house, but we also have complete protection from the director and his minions below us. He can not build a stairway to the attic, there is no easy access through a window, and there is but one entrance that we have to fortify and defend, which is the collapsible staircase and trap door leading up from the second floor hallway. Furthermore, none of our actions perpetrated from the third floor can be solved with sharp shooters, as they would be firing blind.

From the attic, we'll be able to safely engage our plan, which is thus:

A fire consumes the building next door to Preston's house. The flames lick upward into the night sky. Smoke congests the air and cloaks the city. Authorities are notified by concerned citizens. They respond to the fire. Then, quite by accident, they stumble upon three youths who do not vote, standing on the roof of the only house within two hundred yards. The house, incidentally, is swarming on the lower level with dead people who have somehow figured out how to re-animate and then devour the living. To top this odd discovery, the house is also peppered with several radiation-suited criminals who seem to be documenting the affair on television cameras.

More authorities are called, and soon, two dozen or so shadowy assailants are taken away in handcuffs (both the police transports carrying them and the assailants will disappear shortly thereafter). A police officer is bitten by one of the "murderers," instigating a shooting spree by the local police that results in several dozen corpses, all with bullet holes in their heads. The three survivors, exhausted but seemingly all right, are rushed to an undisclosed location, where they are treated for trauma and shock. Weeks later, their names are changed and all three disappear, terrified of being re-confronted with zombies and men with cameras.

Ross makes frequent appearances on *Coast to Coast*, conspiracy websites, and *Jerry Springer*, trying to convince the world that the dead walk among us, and there are dark men with dark motives and dark alliances to the television networks who would document all of it.

Oh, and at some point afterward, the world realizes that Cordelia is God.

"Well," I sigh, a terribly unoriginal gesture. "Cordelia, that's...*brilliant.* Fool-proof. No problem. I especially liked the last part. This won't require much, will it, Stacey? All we have to do is somehow start a huge fire...in the building *next door.* We have to keep it from spreading over here and burning us alive. Then we sit around and hope anyone shows up at all to put it out, and in the **end**, sit calmly with our hands on our laps as the proper authorities dispatch the undead and escort all these criminals away. Oh, and this is assuming the crew and their pets down there don't kill us before the fire does."

"It only sounds bad when *you* say it, Ross," Cordelia says, turning away from me. "You interpret everything like a suicidal Russian novelist."

"Are there any other kind?" I smirk.

"Brody, if you can hear me: do everything they say," the director is yelling from the first floor. "Answer all of their questions. Cooperate with them. We have the situation under control."

"I think it's…a good plan, Cordelia," Stacey says carefully, smoking. "But Ross is sort of right. How would we start a fire from here?"

"I'm not sure," she says. "I wasn't thinking that far ahead. I thought it was more important to just get the idea out in the open first."

"Good move," I say, rolling my eyes and pointing downstairs. "While we have an audience."

"Oh dear," Stacey says quietly. "I didn't even think about that."

"Oh," Cordelia says after a long pause. "My bad."

Brody revives some twenty minutes later while I am removing my one shoe and putting on an old pair of Preston's. He does not panic, and he does not squirm in his restraints. No one gives him instructions from downstairs. No one comes to save him.

I whisper into his ear:

"Brody, listen to me. The three of us are scared—we don't know what's happening. We don't know what to do in this situation. We don't understand why any of this is taking place. We don't know who you all are, or who the dead people are trying to eat us. We don't know anything, really. Okay?"

He nods.

"So that's where you come in, Brody. You're going to give us answers. You were up here filming us, and now you've been beaten, restrained, and abandoned by your associates. I don't care if this is a trick. I don't care if they're planning on sending a hundred of those things up here to kill us while they film it. That's not important to me right now, as it shouldn't be important to you. What *is* important, to *both* of us, Brody, is this: if you do not answer all of my questions, I will kill you. Okay?"

He nods.

"I am beyond good and evil at this point. I am beyond the lines drawn in the sand by society at this juncture. I am beyond fear, beyond religion, beyond morals and mores. I am Lord of the Fucking Flies, Brody. Do you understand?"

He nods.

"Good," I whisper, moving my head away from his ear. "So. Brody. Tell me a little bit about you and your friends."

2

On November 22, 1963, President Kennedy was assassinated. His killers, which had shot him through triangulated, tightly coordinated crossfire, escaped from the Dealey Plaza area amidst all of the organized chaos and pre-calculated confusion. As Oswald was paraded around for the masses, they were congratulated by their dark superiors and relieved of their duties. Some flew back to their home countries and bases in Cuba and Greece. Others simply went home. Most were killed under mysterious circumstances shortly after the assassination. But a few were allowed to return to their normal lives, under strict orders never to speak of their duties on that day to anyone, ever.

However, insurance had to be maintained. The closed-door suits behind all of these dark dealings and atrocities against the president had to ensure that their secrets remained safe, forever.

Those assassins left to carry on with their civilian lives were quickly assigned shadows—men hired solely for the purpose of monitoring the ex-trigger men's every move. Phones were tapped, homes were bugged, and dark sedans were parked down the street from the suburban houses and high-rise apartment buildings of the last surviving killers of President Kennedy. Under orders from—well, Brody never really knew where, or how high up the ladder these orders came from—under orders, the assassins were to be surveilled for the rest of their lives.

As interesting as JFK's death is, Brody says, someone on a conspiracy website should at least give a nod to the people assigned the mind-numbing task of charting these men's every last movement. It's always the big picture, the caption, the jacket of the book that everyone focuses on and never the paperwork and toilet-cleaning that go on behind the scenes. No one ever studies the bibliography or any of the "making-of" aspects of a global conspiracy.

No one considers the real details, or the monumental side bars, that fester from Black Ops operations like these.

I ask him what any of this has to do with the zombies downstairs. He coughs, telling me that it has *everything* to do with the zombies downstairs, because the director of this project, not the one yelling "Action," but the wizard behind the curtain, the one who is calmly setting up these scenarios and controlling who of the group lives and who dies (and he does, by the way), who disappears and who runs away, how this cast is thinned out—that man was one of the assassin's shadows.

"I'm not going to tell you his name," Brody says. "That would be pointless. None of us have real names. I don't even remember what my mother called me, it was so long and so many aliases ago. But you know the man."

"This is boring," I yawn, picking up the bloody book**end**.

"Guess where the assassin retired to."

"Indonesia? Afghanistan? Gotham City?"

"Try Jacksonville," the director says. "Ross, is not Jacksonville close to here?"

"So what?"

"What does your father do for a living?"

"Okay, I get it, I get it," I say wearily. "You're saying that my father was the surveillance guy."

"And that is not all I am saying, Ross."

"My father...used to be a woman?"

"He used to be a lot of things. He used to have a different name. He used to have a different life. Do you realize that your entire family history is built upon forged documents and a fake name?"

I visualize scenes from my childhood: watching Dad leave for work, coffee mug in hand; my father getting calls on his bulky cellular phone before immediately having to hang up and make another call on the land line; my father getting strange pages from his "software company" DigiCom in the middle of the night and having to leave immediately; Mom left crying at the dining room table; Dad staring me down, telling me on Christmas Eve that "decisions have been made," an echo of something else he told me years ago; my father, for twenty-six years, giving me the same icy stare that only a government man could muster.

"My father…is involved in the death of a US President," I say aloud, realizing the ridiculousness of my own comment.

"He came up with the idea for this project one afternoon during his fifth year sitting in a car outside the house of the guy stationed in the storm drain the day Kennedy was made the martyr of yet another *coup d'état.*"

"So you're government agents," I say. I glance back at Cordelia and Stacey, both whom are standing behind me with the same haggard expression, covered in blood, biting their nails, and smoking cigarettes.

"Not the way you're thinking. God, this is *so* beyond your comprehension."

"Enlighten me. I have the time. So do you."

As I have probably realized by now, this is not a spur of the moment ambush. This is not a half-cocked experiment with young people's fears and pop culture knowledge and programmed living dead. This was arranged years before, with key players and hundreds of minds at work.

Ross Orringer: Generation Y, motionless, desperate, bored, deceived, gullible, naïve. Ross Orringer: yearning, suspicious, interested in banned books and rebellion and action and yet not very interested in organization or a pro-active approach. Ross Orringer: interested in the past, and yet doomed to repeat the worst parts of it.

Ross Orringer: perfect for this operation.

In my head, I am asking myself: was I born perfect for this program, or did my father raise me to be?

They've been watching me longer than Brody has even been with the project, which he assures me is quite some time.

Test runs of the zombies have been carried out in a multitude of settings. They have been documented, videotaped, and cast according to mobility, presence, and viciousness. They have been given screen tests with me repeatedly (only one of which I am even aware if, the night at the hotel), and decisions have been made regarding every conflict, every weapon, and every move I would make tonight.

Nothing was left to chance. Nothing could prevent tonight's show from being anything but a resounding success. And like any kind of reality show, any kind of serious game, the winners—the survivors, in this case—were chosen long before the tape ever started rolling.

This is just the beginning, really. I am the perfect test subject for this operation, the pilot, but my friends and I are really just prologue to what is planned a little down the line. One house, a few hundred yards of empty city streets, a hundred or so walking dead people—it's small time. It's only an audience test screening. The true dimensions of the project might not be seen until years later, but when they finally are, they will be *staggering*. It may take time for funding, for preparation, for permits and nods and secret meetings and staged car wrecks and questionable suicides, but it will happen, and when it does, what is happening tonight, in this house, will mean absolutely nothing in comparison to the screams of millions and the destruction of entire American legacies, of histories and lineages, of the past, present, and future. Of life, as I and everyone I care about, knows it.

The **end** of the world has begun, Brody assures me. It's just that no one knows yet but us.

"How did you choose me?" I ask. "What did I do?"

"You were perfect for what they were looking for," Brody explains. "But…"

"But what?"

"But it's more than that."

"What?"

"You mean you don't know?" he asks.

"Apparently not."

Brody spits blood, tilts his head down and rubs his nose against his shoulder.

"What else?" I press.

"Come on, you two," he says, looking now at Cordelia and me both. "You haven't figured it out yet?"

"What is he talking about, Ross?" Cordelia asks.

"Your father *chose* you," he says. "This was his call from the beginning. My god, he's the brains, the money, the backing, the *wizard*—he's the only real reason this is happening to you right now. He's the reason you watched your boyfriend turn into one of those things, Cordelia. He's the reason why everyone betrayed you, Ross. He's already decided where he will relocate the survivors. And Stacey, he's the reason why you'll die tonight."

When I hit him, he yelps and convulses. His cheek tears open when the jagged edge of the stone book**end** slams against his face. His blood cascades down his cheek and spatters when I punch him again and again.

Cordelia is behind me, pulling me off of him, and when I reach once more for my weapon, Cordelia quickly kicks it away. It slides off the edge of the top step, then cascades down the stairway and disappears into the throng of undead, which are even more agitated, climbing on top of one another, reaching, grabbing at the wooden banister and falling back down to the first landing.

Brody is sitting still, bleeding everywhere, tears welled up in his cracked eyes. He is muttering something but I can't hear it and I stop him from making any more sounds when I kick him in the chin, shattering one of his teeth inside his mouth and knocking him back into unconsciousness. It is at this exact moment that I realize why the tattoo on his neck is so familiar.

I've seen him before.

He was at my father's house Christmas Eve.

He was delivering pies to my father while whispering into a microphone in his jacket.

When I calm down after kicking a hole into the wall and screaming until my voice cracks and everything gets blurry and the bathroom disappears and is replaced with wall and framed photographs of Preston hugged up against a mother and father that look nothing like the Mr. and Mrs. Nichols I remember, I put my head between my knees, breathe carefully, and say something to Stacey, but she does not respond, because she is gone.

1

MINDY IS DOWNSTAIRS.

She is eating someone's wrist and forearm.

"No one kills that one but me," I mutter, pointing Mindy's walking corpse out to Cordelia.

"This is a really bad situation," my sister says.

"That may be the biggest understatement you have ever made, Sis. Actually…you've never made an understatement."

"It's not my style."

There is a long silence between us. In the other room, Stacey is coming to grips with what apparently is her own imminent death. I am struggling with the fact that Lydia, the woman who has cuckolded and lied and cheated her way through three years of sex and empty vows of affection, truly does not care if I live or die. I am struggling to get her from my mind, this terrible woman that I still love, even as a girl that truly *does* care about me and truly *would* honor me *forever* is standing alone in a dark bedroom, trying to grapple with the bizarre prediction that she will meet her **end** by being eaten alive by cannibalistic dead people with too much gray makeup. I am struggling to find something relevant to say to my younger sister.

"I knew you were sneaking off to fuck that girl Jennifer Jennings," she says before I can ask her if she has any gum.

"What?" I ask.

"When we were younger. You would sneak out to go to the church and screw around with that slutty girl Jennifer Jennings. Right?"

I nod.

"I knew what you were doing."

"I never thought you did," I admit. "I thought that if you had known, you would have told on me. It seemed like a Cordelia move to me."

"You've got me mixed up with Regan and Goneril," she says pretentiously, staring down at the throng of undead on the first floor.

"I always preferred early Shakespeare, to be honest."

"Me too," Cordelia says. "Ross?"

"Yeah?"

"I'm really sorry that this happened. I'm really sorry that Dad has gotten us—you—into all of this."

"Hey," I say, "Don't—it's just, like, whatever, you know?"

"Yeah," she says. "I know."

"Listen. I probably need to go and check on Stacey. She's more than likely pretty upset."

"Probably," Cordelia agrees, nodding absently. "Ross, don't fuck this one up."

"What do you mean?"

"With Stacey." She points down at Mindy's walking corpse. "Don't forget while you're pining away over that cunt girlfriend of yours that earlier tonight she was tonguing that underage flabby girl down there while your best friend watched."

"I won't. In fact, I think that's one of my New Year's resolutions."

"What is?"

"To stop fucking things up."

"Ross, the point of New Year's resolutions is that they're supposed to be possible."

I imitate a laugh and say dryly, "Can one girl be this funny?"

"But listen," she says. "Just...don't forget what you have, and don't forget who really cares about you. Okay, Ross?"

"I...won't?" I say-ask, moving away toward Monroeville.

"And Ross?"

"Yeah, Sis," I say, stopping in my tracks.

"You want to hear *my* resolution? Maybe it will help."

"Sure."

"My resolution is not to die here."

Stacey is standing by the window in Monroeville, faintly illuminated by the one candle in the room. Her back is to me, and for a moment, I am deathly afraid that when I confront her, she will turn around and no longer have a face.

"I love you?" I stammer, wishing I would have said this instead of asking.

"So that's it," she says.

"No, that's *not* it, Stacey. That guy Brody is a fucking asshole. He's lying. No one else is dying tonight, I assure you."

"Oh, come *on*, Ross," she spits. "You just tried to tell me that you love me. You might as well have administered my last rites."

"That's not funny," I say, coming up beside her. "Stacey, I *do* love you. And you're not going to die."

"But your father probably did help arrange all of this, right?"

"It looks that way."

"And you know they've been watching you and planning this for years?"

"I think they have."

"And it would be safe to say that these men are not the kind to make *bluffs*. Right?"

"I'd say so—no, *wait*—I mean—"

"And yet, I'm *not* going to die?" she asks, teary-eyed, staring at me now.

"That's right," I say vehemently. "I don't give a shit if everything he said was written on a tabernacle. He's wrong. That part is *not* going to happen. You, me, and Cordelia are going to walk out of this house before sunrise. And you and I are going to get married and have sex eight times a week and dance on Preston's grave."

She says nothing for a long time before sniffling, and, in a meek voice, "And Lydia's?"

"Um...yeah," I say, looking away. "And Lydia's. You and me, sweetie."

"You're full of shit, Ross. Your second resolution for 2000 should be not to lie with every single breath that you muster."

"I'm not lying—"

"You know what it is, really?" she interrupts, looking back at me. "It's just that we've reached that scene now, the obligatory scene in every tacky horror outing ever."

"Stacey—"

"This is the part where the hero, in this odd case *you*, reassures some doomed best friend that they'll be just fine, that they'll all walk out in the morning, that everything will be all right. Then, the best friend goes along with it because both are hoping for the best while keeping their eyes clenched shut. You see, sweetie, I know the scene just as well as you do. We both know I'm going to die. Now, all there is left for you to do is placate the pathetic fuck buddy by announcing that you love her, subconsciously comforted in the fact that, in the **end**, you don't have to make too much of a commitment, and yet you still look great in those last moments of Stacey being alive."

I say nothing for a moment that lasts too long. Then, not certain of what I will say until it dribbles out of my mouth: "Sometimes, Stacey, I think you may be too smart for your own good. Sometimes it gets away from you and you just slip into madness."

"I think I need a minute to ruminate alone, if you don't mind," she says, turning back to the window again.

"Stacey, don't do this..."

"Please go away," she whispers, looking down. Her arms are at her sides; her fists are clenched.

"Stacey—"

"Ross!" my sister cries, her chilling vociferation breaking the scene up.

Cordelia's voice is jagged, high-pitched and terrified. I immediately bolt for the hallway, following Cordelia's screams. Then her cries are no longer audible, as they have been swept over by the loud crashing sounds and the rising symphony of moaning.

0

"WHAT IS PAST IS PROLOGUE, and the millennium has always been the perfect setting for an apocalypse.

"This world's first scheduled demolition by God was on December 31, 999. A millennium had passed since Jesus appeared before humankind and died on a cross to save it. Holy men all over Europe thought it logical and probable that His second coming would fall exactly one thousand years after his first.

"Things changed immediately, all over the world, as rumors spread of the oncoming wrath of God.

"Numbers of people making the pilgrimage east toward Jerusalem were so great that, according to one historian, it looked less like a religious pilgrimage and more like a huge marching army. Before making the journey to the Holy Land, most of these deserters sold all of their possessions and lived on the proceeds. Buildings all over Europe were left to fall into ruins. People thought it was pointless to make repairs to the structures, with the **end** of the world imminent. People stopped working their trades. They stopped tilling the land. They stopped serving their masters. Instead, much of 999 was spent looking fearfully to the skies, believing every rain cloud, every thunder clap, every sunset, was indicative of the sky opening up for Jesus to make His final descent. Throughout December 999, groups of flagellants roamed the countryside of Europe, scourging themselves and each other with nail-studded bats and whips. They left trails of blood as they passed. Farm animals were freed. Shops and marketplaces gave away entire stocks and inventories of goods.

"Of course, suicides sky-rocketed that year, as sinners wracked with guilt or people just too overwhelmed with the anxiety of waiting to be collectively judged by a wrathful God escaped by leaping from the turrets and hanging themselves in the stables.

"The last Christmas was marked by an unprecedented outpour of piety and kindness across the land. Families strengthened their bonds, children were adored and doted upon, and lovers never left each other's embrace.

"In short, this earth was the closest it would ever be to becoming a total utopia that year, in fear that there would be no more years to come."

"It's a shame the world didn't **end** on that kind of a high note," Martin says. "It really is. Because if it **end**s now, it will be in flames."

"More like some firecrackers and a sputtering muffler," the man behind me, the man I am not allowed to see, says.

"The world did not **end**, of course," I say, lighting a cigarette, wincing at the pain on my lips, which are raw and exposed. Blood stains the filter of my cigarette.

"Just like it didn't technically **end** on New Year's of 1999," Martin says.

"But here's something of minor interest, considering what happened this year before—well, before the zombies came, I guess."

"What is it, Mister Orringer?" Martin asks, rubbing his face with his hands and yawning.

"Pope John Paul II died this year."

"That's not really very interesting," the man behind me, the man I am not allowed to see, says.

I continue, undaunted: "In 1917 in Fatima, Portugal, the Virgin Mary appeared to three children. She delivered a message to the kids, which was to be transcribed to the Church. The Vatican recorded the Virgin's message and locked it away in a vault until 1960, when, in accordance to the Virgin's request, the letter was re-opened by Pope John XXIII. He read it, *fainted*, and then ordered it re-sealed and locked away again."

"That's kind of interesting," Martin says.

"What did it say?" the man behind me asks.

"No one knows for certain," I tell them. "But what *is* known is that the letter detailed the **end** of the world, as dictated by God Himself, and a time frame was given, a time frame that terrified the pope into fainting. According to the letter, the world would not survive past the reign of the fifth pope after the letter was first opened."

There is silence in the interrogation room. For a long time, the only sounds are those of my cigarette slowly burning and the camera recording.

"Well what does that mean?" Martin finally asks, irritated. "Is that soon?"

"Since the letter was opened in 1960, there have been, including John XXIII, four popes, the other three being Paul VI, John Paul I, and John Paul II, who has died and been replaced by Pope Benedict. Benedict is the fifth pope since the letter has been opened."

The door swings ajar immediately upon me saying this. The same young soldier appears, a thin streak of blood running down his right cheek. He is covered in sweat and grime. From the prison corridor behind him, a series of ear-splitting gunshots ring out.

"Sir, we have no more time. The floor is being evacuated now. We have to move upstairs. And we'll—we'll need all hands. The situation looks…it looks really—"

"We're on our way now," the man behind me says, cutting him off. "Martin, bring the camera. Ross, we'll find you some chapstick when we get up there. But I regret to admit that this interview may be over, gentlemen. I'm afraid that it might just be too late to stop this from happening to all of us."

I finish the last drops of my soda, which taste acrid by now, and rise from my chair. My legs ache and my back pops as I stand for the first time in hours. Martin leads the way, and when I attempt to turn to face the man behind me, the man I am not allowed to see, the same gloved hands again grip my skull and turn me straight ahead, toward the door.

As I step out of the interrogation room onto the narrow catwalk overlooking the wide expanse of ground floor just below us, I see all of them. They have made it past the fences, past the mines and blockades and gunfire, and when I see their numbers piling into the prison, I am no longer the least bit surprised. It occurs to me that Brody was not exaggerating that night five years ago. The dimensions of the project are, indeed, staggering.

I follow Martin up metal steps and realize that, had I been able to keep going with my story, I might have confessed how lonely I have become in these past years, or how much I miss everybody. I might have told the two men about all these nightmares I have been having relating to that night, and how none of it makes sense.

I might have stood up and screamed that none of this was really happening.

I might have mentioned that, from this point on, my account becomes kind of…odd.

PART IV

"Burn the Flames. Awaken the Hollow Men."

[Time difficult to place]

"Surely whatever I had admitted until now as most true I received either from the senses or through the senses. However, I have noticed that the senses are sometimes deceptive; and it is a mark of prudence never to place our complete trust in those who have deceived us even once."

—René Descartes

"It might be said that in the Carnival of Life, I wasn't a star player, but with the Carnival of Death, I certainly was, and my performances with it have been second to none. Death has always been my life support system."

—James Shelby Downard

"People who recognize the rise of the Dystopia often lack the detachment to accommodate perspective. These individuals believe that if enough people were aware of the Dystopia, then the vermin would disappear, and the downward course of the Dystopia would somehow reverse itself. But the Dystopia is so vast and all-encompassing, it pervades every aspect of modern life. With Dystopia, the only cure is fatal to all of us."

—Boyd Rice

13

I NO LONGER HAVE AN AUDIENCE.

Martin leads us to the third level while clutching the tripod and camera, past the cells and into a slate-colored hallway where most of the doors are boarded up and men ready guns and ammunition. We try to find a place to go.

One of the young soldiers finally directs us to a room near the **end** of the hall. We pass through a set of double doors into a long spare area that leads to two smaller rooms, each with a single entrance. The double doors are slammed shut behind us and blocked by four soldiers, who proceed to barricade the entrance using sandbags and desks.

"Skip to the **end**, Ross," Martin says, leading us into one of the other rooms. "Do we die?"

It is a bare room with an unplugged Coke machine, two fold-out tables, five or six metal chairs, and a soldier-turned-zombie-turned-corpse-again piled against the wall, bleeding from what appears to be every orifice and eighteen or so more.

"Will we be safe here?" I ask.

"What do you think?" Martin asks the man behind me. "Yes?"

The man behind me, the man I am not allowed to see and whose voice has been altered, sighs. He does not answer for a long time. There is activity outside this room and everything feels suspicious and uncertain.

"Son of a bitch," someone says, but I am not sure who.

There are drills and hammers being worked against the outside of the door to this tiny room. They are locking us in. Martin gives the other man an alarmed look just before rushing over to the door. He bangs against the steel, twists at the knob, and kicks at the floor plate. No one responds, and the door does not budge. He barks orders and threatens the soldiers on the outside with terrible retribution.

After some time, pale and sweating profusely, Martin turns to us, his expression indescribable except that it is wholly un-reassuring.

"I fear that we may never leave this room," the man behind me says, his voice deep and final. "It has occurred to me that we were under orders not to save lives or to remedy what has happened."

"Then what the fuck *are* we here for?" Martin wails, running his hands through his hair. It becomes damp from his sweat and settles awkwardly.

"To document it," the man behind me mutters. "That's all. We've been lied to, Martin."

"Gee, you *think* so?" he says, pulling over one of the tables and then going for the chairs. I stand still. Martin's tantrums frighten me.

"I know so."

"This has all been *bullshit!"* Martin roars, kicking a small hole into the wall. He stumbles backwards and lands in a chair.

"Calm down," the man behind me advises. "Let's settle down. Martin, if you could get the camera ready."

"Sure, whatever," Martin says, defeated, and sets up the tripod and camera.

After the chairs and table are set, the three of us stand around awkwardly, not saying a word. I pull a slice of skin from my lower lip using my teeth, and taste the blood with my tongue. The air conditioning stings against the raw flesh on my mouth.

After some time, Martin says, "So, what do you want to do?"

"We have no choice. We're not leaving here. They've seen to that."

"What then?"

"We finish the job, Martin. We find out how he **end**ed up in the schoolhouse in 1999. We find out the significance of him **end**ing up in the schoolhouse a few weeks ago. We figure out the significance of him **end**ing up in that schoolhouse twice, and especially why you and he were there in that library with no windows."

"So we just carry on with their bullshit assignment?"

"I will always remain faithful that our efforts will be rewarded, Martin. In the **end**. You can begin recording now."

One night, Preston invited Lydia and me over for drinks and possibly some Absinthe, provided it had arrived in the mail from Europe by this time. We stayed the night. We stayed the night a lot, actually. Preston didn't like being alone ever since his mom and dad died, and considered apartments the equivalent of Holocaust-reminiscent boxcars and preferred not to come to my place based on this belief.

In the middle of the night, Lydia and I stopped having sex in the spare room because of a frightening noise coming from the roof. It sounded like footsteps. We sneaked out the back exit of the house and went into the front yard. I was terrified of what we would find.

Preston was sleepwalking. He was pacing back and forth on the lower roof of his house in only his boxers and a t-shirt. He was muttering something about getting a second chance, about being able to change his decision. His eyes were open. But he was still asleep.

Random memories. A headache encroaches before the interrogation begins again and the gunshots echo and bounce from wall to wall, but I can barely hear them over the moans.

I gave a ride to a hitchhiker once. He was in his mid-forties, haggard but not overwhelmingly foul-smelling or scary-looking. He said his name was Bertrand, but it wasn't. He told me he was heading to Jacksonville, a ways from here, and I told him I was going in that direction. In actuality, I was on my way to Stacey's, less than ten minutes' drive.

Instead of going out for a date and having sex in the back seat with Stacey that night, I drove this hitchhiker forty miles from home before dropping him off at a Waffle House in some tiny Exit town not far from Jacksonville. Then I drove home and was two hours late picking Stacey up for our secret date. She wasn't even mad, and I thought to myself that night that no one could be this forgiving, this pathetic.

That's the way it was for a while. My only epiphanies came while I was recognizing strangers and shadowy assailants, but forgetting friends and lovers.

> We bury everything. We ignore the signs. Or we trivialize them and tell our drunken friends at parties.

It was late in the afternoon and I was fifteen years old. The sun was going down and I was riding my bike much further from home than I should have, past the dry cleaner and the cemetery, my usual self-imposed boundaries. When I wasn't paying attention, I ran off the sidewalk into a ditch and slammed against a storm drain. I was catapulted from my bike and skinned my knee up. When I looked at the concrete my blood was streaked into the gray.

There was a flash as I tended to my wound and sucked up the impending sobbing. I looked over and there was someone who looked very much like my younger sister Cordelia near the **end** of the street, standing next to a strange man who was snapping photos of me on a camera with a telephoto lens.

> I have always been afraid that I would go on living, but that nobody else would, and I would be telling my story to no one.

Once, after I had gotten the oil in my first car changed, a Contour, I left the garage that my father told me to go to, and some time later that day, someone threw a pipe bomb through the window and it exploded. Someone died I heard.

A week later, Preston showed me how he had bought a copy of *The Anarchist's Cookbook* online.

> Sometimes I think that I don't even really care if everybody's dead, if everybody's gone. I tell myself that they were all spies, with rationale like something out of a fever dream:
>
> *I was born into this world and Cordelia, my "sister," was born just under three years later. She watched me all the time when we were kids. How convenient that she was the youngest. What a likely story.*
>
> And it goes on.

It was late summer. Preston and Stacey and Lydia and I were laboriously packing up our beach supplies and making comments on the approaching storm, hanging low and ominous over the ocean. The wind was blowing. Sand was getting in our eyes and making packing difficult.

The girls wandered off so as not to help us.

"If you swam far enough out there, eventually you'd be somewhere in Africa," Preston said quietly, looking out at the Atlantic.

"I know," I said. "That's cool."

Preston looked around at the dunes, at the hotel behind us, at the shoreline.

"They keep building hotels. This beach used to be different. Everything is changing."

"I never noticed," I said.

"Yes you did," Stacey said, coming up behind us in her bathing suit. There was sand all over her thighs. She didn't look pretty in that moment.

Lydia implanted herself into that seat at the bookstore. My interests, my pheromones, my past sexual liaisons and sleep patterns and libido fluctuations—they were all charted and graphed and recorded into log books with a black ink pen and run through a rubric. Then it was determined that I would fall in love with someone like Lydia on a night like that at Barnes & Noble. I was set up so that Lydia could make sure everything went to plan.

I realized that not too long after the millennium passed.

"Do you want to watch *Zombie Lake* with me? I know it's German, but it's okay. There's a lot of nudity in it."

"Preston," I said, quite stoned but lucid, "I think you're involved in a conspiracy to get me to watch zombie movies."

I used to worry when I was a teenager about growing up and deciding to sell out, whatever that meant. It took me a long time to realize—*too* long, really—that these kinds of decisions are not ours to make.

"Why?"

"Sometimes I don't really trust you, Lydia."

People always assume that if the world came to an **end**, they would definitely know about it. Isn't this a rather arrogant presumption?

How did the zombies get up to the second floor? I run the question through my mind over and over again, but never have the time to figure it out, because from here on in I feel like my sole purpose is to run away, look shocked and confused, and watch people die.

I just want to tell them one thing. I want to clarify this for them, because I'm not sure if they understand.

I want to explain to these men how different my story might have been, how different the dialogue would be, if I had only known how it was all going to turn out. I want to tell them that if I had only known for certain how this story would **end**, then things would be different.

If I would have only been aware early New Year's morning five years ago that those would be the last hours I would ever spend with my sister again, this story might have been different. It might have actually had a purpose, an intention, a moral.

I don't tell them this though, because I don't think anyone cares. Instead, I try telling Martin and the man I am not allowed to see, simply the facts. But when this tactic fails as well, I tell them the truth.

12

THE SUMMER WHEN CORDELIA WAS NINETEEN and home with the parents was when I learned about astral projection. It is also when my father spoke to both of us, right as he came out of his depression.

Cordelia was reading a book on the Montauk Project, which she became interested in after reading another book on the Philadelphia Experiment. She decided that she would master astral projection, the ability to separate spiritually from one's own body and roam the ethereal world, and then return to the corporeal vessel at will. My sister decided to master this art, and without the government's help.

I happened to be poor that summer, and visited a lot the months of June, July, and August. Business was slow and my apartment was void of all food except for salsa and pancake mix. My mother was once again feeding and caring for me, a twenty-three year old man. That summer would be the last real time I would spend with my family.

Before Cordelia could leave her body and my father began to lose it, a typical Sunday (it was the only day they could ever round me up) meal together consisted of my father complaining about coworkers, indigents who had the audacity to ask him for change at McDonald's, and how terrible I had turned out. Simultaneously, Cordelia would rant incessantly on whatever was interesting her that day: sex, left-wing politics, the FCAT, trampolines, boys named Stanley, leather, Chinese culture, and the list goes on. My mother and I usually gave each other secret looks and smiles while my father and sister rambled. Later on we would talk about their ridiculousness behind their backs.

But things were different that summer.

Dad sat in his armchair and drank a lot, staring at the television but really staring at the wall. Mom made dinner and set a place at the table for me and my sister. We ate without Dad usually, since he would either be at work until past eight or deeply stoic in the living room. When he did join us in the dining room, he would get away with saying less than ten words and then disappear into the kitchen, claiming he wanted ice cream.

Furthermore, midway through July, Cordelia would frequently begin flicking her eyes during a meal and then go unconscious. Sometimes lights would go on and off when she did this. Once we heard footsteps from her bedroom upstairs and a moment later she shot up in her chair at the dinner table and finished the sentence she passed out in the middle of.

One night after dinner Cordelia sat with me in the living room. She told me that once you first transcend the physical world and begin roaming through that of the spiritual, nothing is the same. She told me that the night before, she floated out of the house and a whole block away, where her journey finally **end**ed on the inside of a Dr. Pepper can. She said that she could see the individual atoms of aluminum before she awoke in her bedroom with all of the light-bulbs blown out.

She was describing how beautiful the asbestos between floors of the house was when Dad arrived home from work.

He looked haggard, his tie still firmly knotted, his pits wet, his business shirt wrinkled and worn. My father crashed onto his chair and eyed his two children, who were afraid to get up.

"How was work, Dad?" Cordelia asked.

He said nothing.

"It's a good thing we have communication, huh?" I asked Cordelia with a wry smile, beginning to stand up.

"Sit down," my father said. "I need to talk to you two."

My father had been in his slump for months, my mother had told me quietly one night. He had barely spoken to her since March, ever since he came home one night, told her simply that "decisions had been made," and retreated into the living room. After that, he came home late, sometimes after his wife had gone to bed, every night of the week.

He walked into the house tired and angry. He ate in front of the TV and watched the History Channel and nothing else. He stopped caring about baseball. He stopped caring about Jay Leno. He stopped caring about *Maxim.*

Clarissa matched her husband's dismal countenance with incessant optimism and home projects. That summer, my mother grew tomatoes in the garden, read five books, bought a new gardening hat, videotaped Cordelia astral projecting on the couch in the den, and took me out four times to lunch at the mall, all with enough gusto to drive one of my generation totally mad.

"What do you need to talk to us about, Richar—I mean, Dad?" I said, sitting back down.

"Dad, you okay?" Cordelia asked. "Do you want to tell us what's wrong?"

"Try not to leave your body before I say it, honey," Dad muttered to her. I began to laugh, but then saw that his expression was similar to the one he carried the night his brother died under mysterious circumstances, six years before.

Mom began to slip into the room, having heard my father's voice, which had become scarce lately.

"Clarissa, could you leave me alone with my children for two god-damned *minutes*?" Dad asked irritably. "Please? For Christ's sakes."

"Sure," our mother squeaked, melting back into the other room. I still felt her presence though, as if she was just around the corner. Listening.

Everyone in my family was acting suspiciously.

Even Cordelia, who behaved as if she had fully anticipated our father suddenly wanting to speak to us. She sat with her hands on her lap and her head posed as if ready to nod at anything he might say.

"Ross, Cordelia," my father began, "I need to tell you something. Listen…your mother and I love you equally."

"A breakthrough," I exclaimed.

"Ross, *shut up*," Cordelia hissed.

"Eat my *fuck*, Cordelia."

My father held up his hand, squelching the ruckus that was about to ensue.

"Both of you need to shut up for this one. Do you understand?"

Neither one of us answered.

"Good. Okay, now kids, your mother and I love you equally. I have to make sure you understand that, because one day, you may not think we do."

When he said nothing else, Cordelia asked quietly, "Why, Dad?"

"Because one of you is going to have to go through something that the other one won't. Something bad. I can't tell you what it is yet, because *I'm* not even sure. But I do know that it will happen, and it might happen soon."

"How soon?" was all I could come up with.

"I'm not sure," my father replied. "I just know that decisions have been made."

"Who made them?"

"The people I work for."

"Dad, you work for a software company," Cordelia said.

"Yes," my father said, looking away. "I work for a software company."

"Are you really a spy?" I asked, snickering. "Is the company like a front for something else? Are you actually the people who faked the Apollo moon landings?"

"How much do you know about Preston's family, Ross?" he asked back, ignoring my cynicism.

"What?"

"Preston and his family, Ross. How much do you know about them?"

"A lot, I would say. Let me think…Oh, here's one: his parents are dead. And he's my business partner, he likes horror movies, hates hollandaise sauce…Did I mention that his parents are dead? He enjoys long walks on the beach, candlelit dinners—"

"You have no idea, do you?" my father interrupted, for some reason reminding me of a snake with glowing orange eyes.

"No idea about what?"

"You have no idea how lucky you are to have someone like me to explain it to you, Ross. To have someone like me making sure that you even *have* options. You have no idea how lucky you are to at least receive some kind of warning before it happens. Your friend Preston wasn't so fortunate, and he will take his past disadvantages out on you, when his time comes."

"What?"

"He'll be there when it happens, and when it does, he'll see to it that you suffer the greatest of degradations."

"Dad, did you just use the word 'degradation?'"

"It won't be so funny in the **end**, son," he said gravely.

"I don't know what's going on, Dad. I don't understand what you're telling me."

"Ross, I'm telling you now, that it's going to happen, and it's going to happen to you. But don't worry about it too much, son. You won't be aware of any of it until it's right about to climax. Then you'll remember this conversation. You'll remember all these things you probably ignored at the time they occurred. None of this information will do you any good until."

"Until what?" I asked.

"Until the present."

I said nothing.

"Dad, what's going to happen to Ross?" Cordelia asked, for some reason teary-eyed now.

"Decisions have been made," my father said one last time, standing up. "Now then. I'm going to have a cocktail. Do either of you want one? Ross? Would you like something to dull the pain?"

11

(MY FATHER, asking me if I would like a drink, or as he puts it, "something to dull the pain.")

(Me, wondering what it all means. My heart beating too fast for a summertime visit to my own house.)

(Cordelia, getting up and walking out of the living room, except when I watch her leave, she is not heading into the corridor, but into a vast empty room, a library, and she is covered in blood.)

(Me, somewhere screaming, but not here. Not yet.)

I realize just before it is drowned out by the moans that Cordelia has never screamed in front of me before tonight, not that I can recall, anyway. So when she does in this moment, choking on spittle and fear as the zombies begin piling up onto the second floor with us, I am momentarily so distracted and intrigued by her cacophony that I ignore the corpses grabbing for her hair and ripping at her arm.

"Oh, shit," Stacey mutters behind me. Or I think she does, anyway. Between Cordelia and the moaning, I can't hear much.

From the first floor, the zombies had begun pushing tightly against one another, like livestock. Then the climbing began. They gripped shoulders, buried their feet into the soft deteriorating flesh of others' backs, and began the human pyramid that would eventually result in half a dozen of them stumbling up onto the second floor with the four of us.

Cordelia wrenches her hand away from a corpse wearing a blood-soaked University of Michigan sweater, and comes running by us and into Monroeville.

Stacey stops next to me holding a board with a twisted nail protruding from one **end** of it.

"That's not going to do much," I say, bobbing up and down as the ghouls stagger this way.

"What about Brody?" she asks me, holding the board tautly.

I suddenly realize that Brody is down on the floor, his hands bound to the wooden railing overlooking the living room below, and that he will be eaten alive and any of our potential escape plans will fail. He has already disappeared behind the throng of undead climbing up onto the second floor with us. But I can hear him yelling and cursing.

"God *damn it!"* I wail, backing up as the creatures approach. We pack ourselves into Monroeville, where Cordelia is frantically scanning the shelves for any kind of weapon. I think this is what she is doing, anyway.

"Shut the door," Stacey squeals, the lead creature only a few feet away now.

I slam the door shut just as the U of M zombie grabs for my sleeve. I slam the wood against its wrist. Blood splashes out onto the wall, but the ghoul does not flinch or back up. I kick him in the chest, sending him falling backward into the other zombies behind him. I slam the door shut and lock it. Immediately, the pounding begins.

"Oh, *great!"* Cordelia shouts accusingly at Stacey and me. "Now we're *stuck* in here. Thanks a lot."

"Would you rather be out there with them?" I ask, putting my back against the door to keep them from immediately busting it in.

On the other side, the zombies are smashing their fists against the wood. One is trying to bite its way through. Others are shoving. This is instinct, and it will never stop. They'll get in and we'll be eaten.

"We need to make a stand, Ross," Cordelia says. "What are we going to do from here, from this room?"

"You're crazy. They'll *kill* us, Cordelia."

"Their numbers are growing out there as we speak. We need to make a stand now and keep them from getting back up here."

"Yeah, cause you did a fine job of that before," I mutter.

She stops in her tracks and says, "What the hell is *that* supposed to mean?"

"Interpret it how you will, Sis."

"No, asshole," she spits. "You *explain* it to me. What was that comment supposed to mean?"

"How'd they get up here, Cordelia?" I ask plainly. "Why didn't you say something?"

"Listen, Ross, I wasn't the one jerking off in the bedroom with my fuck buddy."

Stacey glances over at me. She shrugs.

"Why didn't you warn us before they got up here?"

"It happened too fast," she says. "One minute they were piling around on top of each other downstairs and the next, they're falling over the banister and coming for me."

"You never noticed what was happening?" I stammer. "Not even once?"

"I didn't have enough time."

"What the hell were you doing, Cordelia? Staring at the wall?"

"No."

Behind me, the pounding continues. There are the faint sounds of wood splintering and cracking.

"Can they get through that door?" Stacey asks no one in particular, her voice wavering.

"Yes, and soon," Cordelia says calmly. "Ross, what do you intend we do?"

"What were you doing when they came up, Cordelia?"

"Paying attention to something else," she says, folding her arms and glaring at me.

"Oh, *really*? What? An artistic epiphany?"

"Shut up," she says.

"Were you realizing again how brilliant you were, or that Shakespeare's greatest play was actually *Antony and Cleopatra*?"

"Shut up, Ross," she repeats.

"Why'd you let them up here with us?" I demand.

"Because Brody was telling me something about *you*," she says, turning away, going back to the other side of the room to look for a suitable weapon against the adversaries on the other side of the door. "And FYI, asshole: it wasn't good."

As if she really needed to clarify this.

"We're all going to die," Stacey mutters, wiping away tears. "It's not just me at all."

A fist smashes through the door. A bloody hand, full of shattered bones and covered in deep cuts and open wounds spewing out thick black-red blood, emerges from the hole. Suddenly the fabric of my sweater is being pulled through the splintered cavity in the door. Stacey is screaming.

Cordelia is edging toward me with a piece of wood.

I am in another place altogether.

(My father, sipping headache-inducing champagne from a crystal flute on a gambling cruise off the coast of Daytona.)

(My mother, watching helplessly as my father pisses away four hundred dollars at the craps table.)

(Me, guzzling rum and Coke, staring off the upper deck at the black ocean beyond.)

(Me thinking I see a UFO in the night sky, but thinking that maybe I'm crazy, especially when I turn around and peer through the glass back into the casino.)

(My father, cupping his hands, blowing his dice for good luck. My father asking the person next to him at the table, a dead man wearing a tuxedo spattered with gore, to blow on it as well.)

(The zombie blowing into my father's cupped hand.)

(An entire gambling cruise of living dead.)

(Is this a memory?)

(Cordelia in the living room when we get home, ridiculously drunk, trying to watch SCTV *through a pair of dark sunglasses. Cordelia asking no one in particular, "If you imagine something terrible and it happens, why can't you just un-imagine it to make it go away?")*

Its breath snaps me back into reality.

Through the door comes the nauseating stench of death, of bile and decay and rotting meat. The beast is snarling on the other side of the panel. The wood around the fissure widens as the creature waves its arm about widely, trying to pull me through. Cordelia slams the corner of the board against the hand, spewing out more blood. One of the zombie's knuckles shatters and a bone pierces through the flesh of the middle finger.

I try to extract myself from its grip, but when I move forward away from the door, I hear the wood creaking and snapping. I back up against it once more, just as another fist slams through the wood and grabs at my hair. It gets a handful and slides back out the way it came. I scream in agony as the arm pulls me by the hair toward the door. Just on the other side, the monster's jaw is open wide, yellow bits of flesh and red stains scattered across its teeth.

I am screaming for help, trying to pull away, not caring about the door coming down afterward. All I think about is my hair, my *scalp*.

It pulls harder, taking a large tuft of my hair and some skin with it. I jerk away from the hand gripping my sweater, bringing two fingers with me. I slither away and fall to the floor, gingerly touching the blood that is cascading down my forehead.

"Ross, we gotta go," Stacey shrieks, already backing up toward the window.

The door behind me breaks in two.

Cordelia is prying the last two boards off of the window.

Moaning. Behind me.

Stacey is yelling in slow motion, pointing to the window.

There is so much presence behind me, and so much fear coursing through my veins, that my life cannot flash before my eyes.

(My father, standing above my body, the sun behind casting him into silhouette, an eclipse, an abstraction.)

(A man joining him, also dark and shadowy.)

("What's going on?" he is asking my father, this man, whose voice is familiar.)

(My father not responding for a long time. My father finally sighing before saying bluntly, "This has already happened, Martin.")

(The man asking, predictably, "What do you mean?")

("You're in a school house right now.")

("Richard, I'm not sure—")

("This isn't happening like you think it is." My father not receiving a response before sighing again and saying, "I hate sighing, Martin. It is such a terribly unoriginal gesture.")

(The man beside my father shaking his head, rubbing his temples, looking to me on the ground for answers, but receiving none. The man finally saying, "Richard, what the hell is going on? Where—no, when *are we in this kid's memory?")*

("What makes you think it's   's memory?")

("Because   is the one remembering *it!" Martin yelling, frustrated.)*

*("*Is *he?" My father pausing. "Where do you think we are right now, Martin? Where do you think my son is? At what moment is he remembering this scene, a scene that hasn't happened yet?")*

("I'm on to you," I am saying to them, remembering a schoolhouse.)

("No you're not," my father is saying. "But the dead guys are on to you, *son. You'd better deal with them.")*

(Me saying, "What? Why can't I hear my own name being said?")

When we are living the moment that will become the memory, we never consider when and where we will look back and remember it later in life. It is always less important under which circumstances we will re-experience this particular scene again and again, and seemingly integral just getting through it that first time. We can't think outside this one perfunctory dimension—

"Ross, we have to jump," Stacey is saying, and I am snapped back into existence just as the first zombie snatches at my neck.

Cordelia is sitting on the windowsill, looking down.

She jumps.

I bolt for the window, where Stacey is climbing out and dangling precariously by one arm. Below her, Cordelia slowly rises to her feet, her left leg sprained.

"I love you, Sta—" I begin, but Stacey lets go and falls to the ground several feet below.

She lands on her feet and tumbles backward, slamming against the grass. She moans in pain, rolling onto her stomach and crawling away, immediately waving at me to follow suit. Cordelia reaches down to help her up. Zombies are already appearing in the driveway, staggering toward the women.

I ready myself on the windowsill. When I turn to see how close the creatures are behind me, I let out a muffled yelp.

A zombie wearing a black suit and tie lunges for me, and the bloody ruin where his nose used to be is the last thing I see before catapulting myself backward and falling.

I watch white wood planks rush upward. Black-looking grass enlarges beneath me. Blood smeared across the wall flashes by in a blur as I fall toward the earth. Somewhere, moans turn to snarls turn to the girls screaming.

I land.

The breath I was about to take is sucked out of me. My brain slams against the front of my skull and bounces around in my head. I see red and blue gaseous entities, and I fear that I will lose consciousness. When I landed, I chomped down so hard that one of my back teeth shattered, and I spit tiny pieces of tooth and a mouthful of blood onto the ground.

An arm grabs me and tugs me upward. For a moment I think it is one of the creatures, and I wonder where my final replay of life is, why nothing is flashing before my eyes, but then I hear Stacey telling me that we need to move.

I shake my head and look up. Cordelia is fending off a female ghoul, smashing a Jägermeister bottle over her head. It shatters, glass spraying down along with droplets of bright red. The woman does not go down, however, and Cordelia backs away and looks frantically for something else.

Stacey wrenches at my arm, pulling me to my feet. I try to catch my breath, try to will my heart to stop pounding as it is, but nothing happens.

A moan above me grows ferocious, and when I look up I see the suited zombie grab the sides of the window, crawl onto the ledge, and fall.

Stacey and I skitter away, just as the zombie lands behind us, head first. Its head hits the ground and twists sideways. The skull is then smashed by its shoulders, which are then pulverized by the rest of the ghoul's body. I watch as the spine juts out of the neck, and then the suit's backside rips open and what looks like a rib pierces through grayed, bloody skin. A moment later, Stacey and I are splashed with viscera and some kind of green substance that smells like used cooking oil.

"Guys, they're coming," Cordelia says, smacking the lady ghoul in the forehead with a large piece of cinder block. The corpse topples over this time around.

The three of us hobble around the truck crushed against the back porch, and into the driveway. Five or six of them are already shuffling toward us from the front of the house. Among them is Mindy.

"Oh my god," Stacey shrieks upon seeing her. "*Mindy*?"

Princess Star Bright responds by opening her mouth and moaning. A large piece of blue intestine slides out and falls onto the driveway.

"We'll never make it past them," Cordelia says, stopping in her tracks.

Cordelia grabs Stacey, and Stacey grabs me. We stop. One of the crewmen slide up directly in front of us for a close-up, the light on the camera blinding me. I kick him in the shoulder and he falls down. He and one of the sound guys scramble off and the backup crew picks up the action from the **end** of the driveway.

"We're trapped," Stacey laments.

She's right. They're tumbling out of the house quickly now, and behind us somewhere, several more are ambling onto the back porch, momentarily confused but sure to figure out where we are quickly.

"We're fucked," I say.

"Oh yeah," Stacey agrees. "We are *totally* fu—"

Cordelia glances over at her, now lightly bobbing up and down impatiently while Stacey's plan formulates.

"Fuck," Stacey mutters to herself.

"What?" Cordelia asks.

"...*Truck*."

"Truck?" I ask. "What truck?"

"Oh my god, you're right!" Cordelia exclaims. "We can take Brad's truck. He left his keys in the ignition."

"Never tell me that foul language isn't productive, Cordelia," I say, already heading back toward it. I ignore the fact that what was once a green Toyota Tundra is now a black Mazda B3600.

I open up the passenger door and slide into the cab. I position myself behind the steering wheel.

"No way," Cordelia says next to me, squeezing tight to allow room for Stacey. "I'm driving."

"There's a better chance of *Mindy* taking the wheel," I mutter, reaching for the ignition.

"Ross, the last time you tried getting out of here, you failed miserably. It's my turn."

Stacey slams the passenger door behind her. Just as she does this, there is a loud metallic thud in the bed and I look behind me to see one of them crawling around in the back.

While sliding the back window shut and locking it, I say to my sister, "Cordelia, there is no way."

I reach for the ignition switch.

The keys are gone.

"Um."

"See, dumb-ass?" Cordelia says to me. "You're getting off to a *great* start."

"Guys, I don't care who drives," Stacey says. "But, *somebody needs to!"*

"The keys are gone," I say, breathless.

"*What*?" both women stammer.

"The keys! They're gone!"

"But I saw him leave them in here," Cordelia says frantically. "I saw Brad turn the truck off and leave them *here*!"

"Well they're gone *now*, Cordelia," I say, leaning down and running my hand along the floor.

Above me, a bloody fist pounds against the driver side window.

"Ross, get us out of here," Stacey yells.

"I'll be right with you," I sing, running my hand frantically along the floor. Nothing. I reach under the seat. Aside from a box of matches, some change, and a sheet of paper, nothing. I stupidly check the key hole again.

The zombie in the bed becomes three, and they scratch at the back window and punch at the glass. One of them slams his hands against the windshield, leaving thick puddles of pudding-like blood in the cracked pane.

"We—are going—to *die!"* Stacey screams.

"Ross—" Cordelia begins.

"Will you shut the fuck up about driving?"

"No, *Ross*," she says, grabbing at something underneath her.

She wriggles in her seat and, a moment later, holds up Brad's key chain.

I sigh, a terribly unoriginal gesture, and grab the keys.

Half-expecting the truck not to start, for this entire ordeal to culminate in all three of our deaths, I hold my breath as I start the ignition.

The truck comes immediately to life.

The zombies look at the rumbling vehicle, momentarily confused.

I put it in Reverse and floor it. I slam into the creatures behind us, knocking them aside and rolling over them. One ghoul is trapped underneath the back right tire, and then front left. The truck bounces up and then crashes down as it flattens his head into some kind of pinkish mush that I almost vomit at when I see it in the headlights as we roll out onto Main.

Mindy's corpse glares at me from the driveway, her mouth wide open in a terrible snarl.

I put the truck into Drive, take a deep breath, and hit the gas pedal.

"Let's get the hell out of here, guys," I say, gunning it toward Pittsburgh, trying not to think about what will happen to us, to her.

("How do you remember something that hasn't happened yet, son?")

(My father, walking alongside me on a cold beach I have never been to. A camera crew setting up the shot further down the shoreline. Mountains looming in the distance. Driftwood everywhere along the wet sand. The waves rough today. The ocean full of sharks. The sky grayish brown.)

("I don't know, Dad," I am saying. "Look, just tell me one thing. Okay, Dad?")

("You never call me that.")

("Call you what?")

("Dad," he is repeating.)

("I am now," I am saying to him.)

(My father smiling sadly.)

("A lot of good that does me now,   . The only time you call me Dad is in a memory that doesn't exist. That's terrific. But, I suppose this is my fate. I suppose I deserve this for everything I've had to put you through tonight.")

(My father and I, walking along the beach. It beginning to sprinkle so lightly that I am never sure it is sprinkling at all, or if the wind is simply blowing wet sand around. It maybe being both.)

("Dad," I am saying. "I'm so scared.")

("I know you are, son," he is saying. "I'm scared too.")

*("But why? You set this whole thing up. You made the decisions that put me and Cordelia in that house that night…before…*after…*that one time…did I* **end** *up in a* prison?"*)*

("   , this is strange, I know. But let me assure you of something: in the **end***, you'll understand everything. I promise.")*

(Me thinking to myself for a long time. Me kicking at wet sand. Me bundling up in a black coat I know I never owned. Me coughing and nodding with some kind of understanding, a lucidity I am not [and could not be] comprehending in this false memory.)

("Do you love us, Dad?" I am asking after some time.)

("I do, son," my father is saying after a long deliberation. "But it doesn't matter.")

("Why not?")

("Because the world is **end***ing, son. Jesus is coming. All things are coming together to fall apart. Do you understand, son?")*

("Somewhere I do.")

("Good," he is saying, "because you're about to get to the road block, and it looks like the film crew is ready.")

10

THE FOG MACHINES HAVE BEEN TURNED UP FULL BLAST.

The road blocks are still in place, and the crew is just finishing up with lighting and applying last minute gray makeup and gore effects for the zombie extras as we approach.

My car, which was shot up and abandoned from earlier, is now gone.

I feel like Kennedy if Kennedy knew what was awaiting him at Dealey Plaza and decided to ride in the back of the Lincoln anyway.

"There's not too many," Cordelia says hopefully, eyeing the dozen or so corpses waiting near the roadblock.

The spikes are still strewn all over the road, and up on the sidewalk too.

"How are we going to get by?" Stacey asks.

I sigh, a terribly unoriginal gesture, and hit the brakes.

We stop.

"I'd rather die right now than back at that house," I mutter.

"Me too," Cordelia agrees.

"I'm going to die anyway," Stacey says. "Here is as good as anywhere."

Cordelia packs a fresh box of cigarettes, opens it, and retrieves three. She hands one to me and Stacey. Without a word, I push the cigarette lighter into its slot. We wait. A long moment later, it pops out.

We light our cigarettes.

We smoke in silence.

In this time, things are happening.

The makeup people back off.

The crew ready their mikes and TV cameras.

The sound guys aim the mikes in our general direction.

A second-unit director flicks his cigarette into the street and wipes at his goatee.

"We're going to make it out of here," Cordelia assures no one, taking a deep drag before throwing her cigarette out my window. She nods, blinking to keep her eyes from tearing up.

A marker is clicked, the director moves out of the street, and the zombies start heading our way.

Someone yells "Action!"

Immediately, the first shot is fired.

I hit the gas, already screaming as the bullet sails through the windshield and blows apart the top of the steering wheel.

"Ross, *go!*" my sister is barking next to me, trying to grab the wheel. I frantically slap her hands away, heading into the torrent.

Stacey's head is ducked down between her knees, smoking her cigarette.

Just as the next shot is fired from somewhere to my left, I swerve out of the way of the approaching ghouls, running the truck up onto the sidewalk. The bullet that might have shattered Cordelia's spine or destroyed my face instead slams into the bed of the truck with a metallic clang.

The nurse zombie, arms outstretched, blood running down from the void where her ear should be, is clipped by the right side of the truck, and she spins around just before being sucked under the rear tire. The truck reels upward, and then lands awkwardly just before hitting the spikes.

"Speed up," Cordelia screeches. "You have to speed up or we'll get stuck in those things."

I hit the gas again just as the sniper takes another shot at us. The driver side window disappears, and suddenly my whole body is surging with pain. Something wet hits my cheek.

I scream.

My arm.

It's been shot.

The road spikes are only a few feet away.

I barely have time to glance down at the wound just below my shoulder. The fabric of my sweater is torn to shreds and the flesh underneath is splintered and torn at the edges of a two-inch crater in my arm. For one split second, I can see the exposed muscle in my arm twitch and the severed veins pumping out dark red blood. I cover the wound with my other hand, letting go of the steering wheel.

The nausea is overcome by sheer panic when the truck's tires explode underneath us and the vehicle lurches forward and spins to the right.

We're going to crash.

I can hear the moans even as everything screeches and thuds and clangs and bellows.

At some point, I hit the brakes and try to get control of the steering wheel. The pain in my bicep is unbearable.

When I let go of the gun shot wound in my arm, blood sails out in an arc across the cracked windshield, and this is the last thing I see before the side of the truck slams into a telephone pole and everything goes black. In my dream, I am listening in disgust at a terrible duet of the moaning dead and their screaming prey.

9

Everything that happens next plays out like an old filmstrip with terrible audio that's missing several frames…

Wide shot: Stacey jumping out of the passenger side of the truck, marching corpses only a few feet away and closing.

Close up: the interior of the vehicle, where Cordelia is trying to shake Ross back into consciousness.

Ross's POV [scene missing]: the steering wheel. The floor. Blackness swells and disappears. Stars flash and Ross is in another universe.

High angle: Stacey running around the telephone pole and ripping open the driver side door. She and Cordelia work to revive Ross.

Close up: Stacey's horrified reaction when she sees the wound in his arm. There is a quick cut to [scene missing] the bullet hole in Ross's arm. The blood.

Stacey's POV: over the roof of the vehicle, at the zombies approaching.

Cut to: [scene missing] the film crew rushing toward them, cameras raised.

Medium shot: A sniper, dressed in black, receiving orders through an ear piece, methodically disassembling a high-powered sniper rifle with an infrared scope. He slips the weapon into a briefcase and closes it. The camera pans left with him as he stands up and walks to the other side of this anonymous rooftop.

High angle, the roof of the building: the sniper climbing down the fire escape. His job is over.

[Two scenes missing]

Canted frame: Stacey helping Ross out of the truck, Cordelia freaking out behind him, looking back over her shoulder every two seconds.

Cut to: First camera's POV, over the bed of the truck as the three victims limp away from the vehicle toward the Pittsburgh and Main intersection.

Wide low angle: zombies shambling up the street after them, trailed by several cameramen and lighting techs.

Fade-out.

Dissolve to: black screen with the insert *Three Years Later.*

[Scene missing]

Long shot: Ross standing with his back to the camera in a graying kitchen, alone, gripping the edges of the sink with his head lowered in defeat. Around him, the dishes are put away, the countertops are clean, and the window above the sink shows a bright sunny day. Everything might be fine. But it's not. Ross's survival has meant nothing.

Fade-out.

Dissolve to: black screen with the insert *Four Years Later.*

Medium shot: Ross standing in the same position in the same graying kitchen, which has now accumulated stacks of dishes and a layer of soot on the window. That window now looks out on a dismal late summer afternoon. There are sirens and screams in the distance. Thunder rumbles. A storm approaches. Ross ignores it just as he does so much else. She is gone. He is alone. They're never coming back.

Fade-out.

Cut to: Ross's aging face in extreme close-up. His hair is graying, his eyes are vacant, and we come to understand that [scene missing] this is Ross—as he exists *now*, Ross as he narrates this story and mutters, "This is Ross—as he exists *now*, Ross as he narrates this story and mutters, 'This is Ross…'" He is a thirty-one-year-old Nobody whose only claim to greatness was surviving the world's first coordinated attack by the living dead.

Pan-out: Ross sitting at a [scene missing] table in a sparsely decorated room. He inhales from a cigarette. A man wearing black pants and a wrinkled white shirt and an ugly tie rubs his face with his hands and asks Ross something inaudible. In the shadows behind the table, a man lurks, his face obscured and his gestures minimal. But the audience recognizes him, nonetheless.

Close-up: Ross smoking his cigarette.

Extreme close-up: the cigarette being stubbed out in a glass ashtray on the table.

[Scene missing]

Ross (*emotionless*): "Everything that happens next plays out like an old filmstrip with terrible audio that's missing several frames."

Immediately cut to: medium hand-held tracking shot of Ross, Cordelia, and Stacey as they run from the corpses behind them, which the camera quickly pans back to.

Wide shot: the three stumbling through the knoll in front of a lawyer's office toward Pittsburgh Avenue ahead.

Extreme close-up: a lone road spike lying ominously in the grass.

Rack focus: from the spike to the three approaching.

Long shot: Cordelia suddenly wailing out in pain, toppling over.

Extreme close-up: a spike protruding through the toe of her white tennis shoe. Blood spigots out.

Hand-held high angle: Stacey and Ross helping Cordelia back onto her feet. There is screaming and cut-off sentences, the audience feeling her [scene missing] pain. While this scene plays out, a quick pan back shows the zombies gaining on the group, and it is revealed that the director is now walking alongside them, looking back and forth between his troops and the fleeing victims.

Close-up: the spike being pulled from Cordelia's foot. Pan up to the wail of agony from Cordelia.

Medium shot: the director holding up a megaphone as he marches along.

Director: "Cue featured zombie Number 12."

Tight medium shot: Ross and the others, about to begin their retreat again, when Ross is suddenly seized by a ghoul missing most of its face and scalp. The two fall to the ground in a struggle.

Zombie POV: Ross horrified beneath him.

Ross's POV: the snarling face of the zombie above him, Ross's hands pushing his face away, which is covered with gore and maggots.

Medium shot: Stacey and Cordelia, unsure of what to do.

Low angle medium shot: Ross looking back toward the girls as he struggles.

Ross: "Go! Get the hell out of here!"

Medium shot: the girls not reacting.

Medium shot on Ross flailing around on the ground with the corpse.

Ross: "God damn it, *go*! They're coming!"

Ross's POV: the other zombies quickly approaching, then back to the ghoul lying on top of him.

Close-up: Ross's disgusted reaction, maggots falling on his face. In his mouth as he grimaces.

Ross (*pleading, teary-eyed [glycerin tears], frantic, feeling wholly responsible for everything that has happened to them*): "Stacey, you've got to go, baby! Go, *please*! Get the hell out of here!"

Medium shot: Cordelia nodding, wiping away tears in her eyes.

Cordelia (*devastated but acutely aware of the situation*): "Ross, you're—"

[Scene missing]

Track from medium shot to wide, and then track back into tight medium shot: Cordelia begins to move away from the scene, but Stacey lingers, her eyes welled with glycerin tears. She wipes at her face and stands motionless. The moans intensify. Cordelia grabs her by the shoulder and wrenches her away from the scene. They both break into a run (*Cordelia still limping from the foot wound*), and they fade into the darkness as they retreat.

High angle: Ross still struggling with the zombie, the others very close now in the background. Ross slaps at the monster's face, which spatters blood and sends maggots falling to the grass.

Low angle: Ross wrestling with it, rolling over and over toward the camera until…he is next to the spike that impaled Cordelia's foot.

Extreme close-up: Ross noticing the spiked ball, and the camera pans right as he grabs it.

[Three scenes missing]

Medium shot: Ross, totally alone now, pushing the destroyed corpse off of him, still clenching the weapon. Frantically brushing maggots off of his shirt, Ross scrambles to his feet just as the crew meets him, running around the group of zombies approaching.

Long angle: the director, wielding his megaphone, looking confused, and then worried over an off-screen dilemma.

Close-up: Ross's face as he realizes the opportunity that has presented itself.

[Several scenes missing]

Close-up: Ross and the director, the spike pressed so tautly against the director's neck that a thin line of blood trickles down.

Ross (*to crew people and living dead alike*): "I swear to god I'll kill this prick. Stay *back*!"

Director (*calm, self-assured, a thin indistinguishable European accent punctuating his consonants*): "It's okay, guys. Do nothing of the sort. Consult Script B, everyone. It's okay. Remember, we are still on a *schedule*. Things are going according to plan—"

Ross (to the director): "Shut the fuck up!" (*To the approaching zombies and crew*) Stay away or I'll kill him. I'll kill the director and you'll all be *fucked.* I swear I will. Hey, listen to me. Stay…the fuck…*ba—*"

[Scenes missing]

High angle: the zombie one of the crew just dispatched in order to save the director and his captor.

Wide angle: the director and Ross disappearing into the darkness.

Ross (*to no one, loudly, raving*): "I'm not asleep. I'm not asleep. I'm not—"

[Remaining scenes missing or too badly damaged for viewing]

8

"THERE ARE SOME FATES WORSE THAN DEATH, NO?" the director whispers harshly to me. His accent seems to grow thicker with each phrase uttered.

"Actually, no, I don't think so," I respond, a lie.

I peek over a row of thick hedges at Pittsburgh Avenue, about fifty yards north of the intersection at Main. They're still there. The numbers seem to increase every time I look. I can hardly see across the street anymore, there are so many of them. They're not quite ready for the shoot: makeup techs, along with various other assistants, second unit people, some gaffers, even one of the caterers, is helping haphazardly coat the new zombie extras with gray makeup and Karo formula blood to already dead and decomposing faces, limbs, torsos, and occasional body parts from recent victims being wielded for good measure.

They're standing around, waiting for their final scenes this season, the big battle, the final on-screen holocaust, the sweeps episodes, the season finale.

"There's no way the show needs that many of those things for just us kids," I mutter, looking down at the director poised on his haunches by my knees. "What's going on?"

He shrugs.

The corpses are not responding to us. They can not sense our human presence. Obviously, they are not picking up on any scent, or picking up anything telepathically using some kind of zombie sixth sense. It would seem that they only respond to stimuli that any other human being would respond to, except in death, certain senses are heightened and relied more heavily upon. In life, people rely on sight more heavily than any of the other five, despite the known fact that the sense of smell is the most potent and useful for memory.

Aural ability is a distant second. Maybe in death, once the cadaver reanimates, senses taken for granted and ignored before are now used extensively in the pursuit of prey.

I laugh to myself. A porch argument with Preston is silently put to rest.

"They're not trying to find you, to capture us," I point out to the director.

"They were instructed not to, Ross," he says. "It wasn't in the shooting script."

"So we could just get out of here."

"Not necessarily," he says. "Look around you. Can we just 'get out of here,' Ross?"

The zombies are swarming at the intersection, and up the street running parallel to us behind the hedge row. We are trapped by exposure if we go any further, where the shrubbery **end**s at a bare parking lot about twenty feet away. We can't cross Main to go west along Pittsburgh in risk of being shot at, attacked, or in any other way made dead.

"Okay," I sigh, a terribly unoriginal gesture. "Let's go."

"Where?" he asks, folding his arms and smiling like a son of a bitch. "To confront the undead *here*, or down the street?"

"It's a surprise," I say, pressing the road spike back against the wound in his neck.

"It seems you are heading in the wrong direction. Soon you will be back where you started."

"And that would just kill the mounting suspense of the show, wouldn't it?" I mumble.

"I believe that your entire comprehension of what is happening to you is...too simplified...too pat...too—"

"Shut up," I tell him. "Okay, stop here a minute."

We take a rest behind the glass factory, on the other side of the fence bordering Preston's property. We don't see any of the undead. In the distance, I can hear a couple of moaning corpses coming from the general direction of the elementary school, but other than that, the part of town we are in is totally silent.

Everything is, come to think of it. I haven't heard fireworks in hours, nor a siren or car horn or yell or even thumps of bass from Club Belial a mile or so away. These are normal sounds typical of any city at night, and the fact that I have not heard any of this, on New Year's of the next millennium, no less, is profoundly disturbing, and I have no doubt that all of the phenomena this evening is interrelated.

"It's quiet, no?" he says, seeming to read my thoughts as he slides down against the wall of the factory and comes to a rest on the ground.

"Yes, it is," I agree.

I stand next to an open dumpster and make a decision. I pull the blood-drenched tatters of what was once my thick sweater from off of my body and toss it into the trash. Some of the red fluid has soaked through to the white undershirt I was wearing underneath, and sweat has stained the area around the neck and underarms yellow.

Without the sweater, I am in greater danger. The undead will have easier access to my flesh now, and any of my living scent that might have been covered by the blood and meat of long-dead people is now gone. Not to mention it's freezing outside.

"Give me your jacket," I order him.

"But I will be cold," he protests like an infant.

"I wonder what happened to your friends," he says while we rest. He puts a quiet emphasis on the word "friends."

"I don't even give a shit, honestly," I respond, another lie.

"Then I wonder what happened to your two lady friends," he says a moment later. "Do you care about them?"

"Listen…I would shut up," I warn pathetically.

"Did you see where they went?"

"Shut up."

"It would be terrifying to have to face this ordeal totally alone, I would think."

"I know. It's a good thing I have *you*."

"Do you think so?" he asks, raising his eyebrows, yawning.

I don't know what happened to Cordelia and Stacey.

There was the struggle on the ground. The girls were told to run away, which they did.

But I didn't really mean it when I said it. I thought one of them would do something. They could have helped get that thing off of me. They could have fought instead of taking off in the other direction. They could have screamed and refused to abandon me until they were finally overwhelmed and consumed, just as I will be.

I thought they would stay and we would escape together. At least Stacey, anyway. But they left me and now I don't have anyone but this guy—one of the men behind the curtain—sitting here in front of me.

And he's right. I'm almost right back where I started.

After discovering the men dressed up as police officers and the sharpshooters cleaning their sniper rifles and camera men and fifteen or so zombies out in front of the glass factory, the urge to fall behind the dumpster, let water from the gutters drip down on me, and sob until I am eventually found and killed, is almost unbearable.

The only relief I can derive from this feeling is when I back-hand the director when he begins to mention Cordelia and Stacey leaving me again.

He chuckles.

"If you wrote a book about this, you would have to dedicate it to those who abandoned you."

"Why is that?" I ask, searching my pockets for cigarettes.

"Because there is no one else."

"Then I wouldn't dedicate it," I say, undaunted.

"Maybe you could dedicate it to your father. Perhaps, perhaps…"

"Why would I do that? Because he's in on it? You're not blowing me away with any new information, asshole."

"No, not because he's in on it, Ross," the director says. "You could dedicate it to him because you are here at his choosing between you or your sister. He needed to offer a sacrifice to the project. He was faced with the dilemma: his daughter or his son. Do you recall an incident two years ago? In the living room between the three of you? I know you do. I suppose we know which one he decided to sacrifice by now, yes?"

"Cordelia's here, too," I point out, pulling out my cigarettes. They have somehow gotten slightly wet. I pull one out anyway and light it.

"Yes, your younger sister is here as well as you," he agrees, nodding, rubbing his goatee. "But she will walk away from this experience; *prosper* from it even…whereas you will most certainly not."

"I don't care," I say, sitting down against the dumpster.

"Ross, your father *chose* you. You were his *least* favorite. You were…expendable."

"You're not going to upset me," I say, swallowing hard. "I would have made the same decision as my dad did. I would have picked Cordelia to live, too."

"Why?"

"Probably for the same reasons that Dad did."

"And what are those, Ross?"

"I'm a loser. Cordelia's not."

"Maybe there was more to the decision than just that," he suggests.

"It's my *father* we're talking about. I know his way of thinking. Cordelia had the better major, the better degree, the less esoteric future, the better presence at family get-togethers. My father goes for that."

"And what if you were looking at this all wrong?"

"I don't know what that means."

"I mean, Ross, what if your father chose you because he respects, admires and loves you much more than you think?"

"That's impossible. You just said so. He chose me to *die*. Nothing more. Even if I were to live through this, he chose me to be the child who watches his friends die, his lovers abandon him to save their own ass, and his entire life to be ruined thereafter."

"But what if these things you're speaking of, Ross, were not near as terrible as you perceive them now?"

"I'm lost again," I mutter, irritated.

"What if, by placing you here now, your father was sparing you from something worse, something so much more terrible and frightening, in the future? What if he was sparing you and only you from ignorance?"

Pittsburgh is lined with corpses all the way past the intersection. The front entrance to the factory behind Preston's is guarded by the crew and zombie cast members. Making it across the street, out into the open, to try and meander past the elementary school across Main seems improbable, at best.

My only hope at this point is that, in stocking and overloading Pittsburgh with zombies, the crew has left 89 alone. This is at least conceivable. Highway 89 is a major roadway, and could only be shut down for so long before the people behind this would have to re-open it and formulate other plans of trapping us in this tiny sector of town.

I have to make it to 89.

But not without a gun.

"You are going back to the house?" the director asks curiously when I order him to scale the fence.

"For a moment."

"I would advise against that."

"Frankly, I don't give a shit what you would advise against," I snap. "Get over there."

"I might run once I get to the other side," he says, grabbing the top of the fence and beginning to climb up.

"You might," I agree. "But I don't think you will."

"You are right. Staying with you is far too much fun. But why go back to the house? There is no one there, I assure you."

"I don't doubt that," I say, climbing over the fence.

When I get over, I take a stunned look around the backyard.

There are bodies. Lots of bodies. So many more than I remember seeing. They lie in torn up, random heaps all across Preston's backyard. Some of them twitch, and Geoff's head, half-wedged under debris, opens its mouth, trying to moan but not being able to.

"You never asked my name," the director says as I prod him with the spike through the yard and onto the porch.

"It doesn't matter. You'll give me an alias or code name anyway, right?"

"Like Brody did?" he asks me.

"Yeah," I say. "Like Brody did."

"Is he still alive?"

I look down at the porch.

"No," I say after missing a beat. "I don't see how he could be."

Blood has completely covered every inch of the floorboards. The worn-out lawn chair I often used to sit on during rainy Saturday nights and doomed Sunday evenings has been slathered with what appears to be intestines, except they're pierced by three splintered ribs and leaking a rank-smelling brown fluid from both **ends**. Lying across one of Preston's drawings of a cannibalistic tribesman is Shannon's leg. I know this because of the *Mercredi* tattoo just above the ankle.

"Do you want to leave?" the director asks when he notices me stalling on the porch.

"No," I retort quickly. "I want a gun."

I never really had the chance to take a look at the devastation to Preston's house until now, when it is all but empty. The living room carpet has been totally soaked through with blood, scorched with hot wires and ripped up in about eighteen different places. Pieces of the stairs lie in piles all over the room, and where the stairwell was once complete is now a mound of viscera and bone, body parts and splattered brain matter. The couch has somehow made it halfway across the floor, and a random girl's upper torso and eyeless head have been tossed on one of the cushions.

The lone zombie in a McDonald's uniform lazily munching on someone's upper thigh and outer labia in the kitchen is quickly dispatched using an abandoned camera tripod. The director backs against the living room wall as I deal with the ghoul that comes stumbling, one-legged, out of the downstairs bathroom.

"What, you can't handle it?" I ask hatefully.

"I love the project," he explains, slowly edging away from the wall. "I believe in it. But *those* things…they bother me, I admit."

"They bother me too," I say, and the momentary rage that suddenly collects inside of me bubbles and churns until I have to quickly leave him alone in the living room and head for the office, where Warren Nichols, Preston's father, kept his gun collection before he died.

The office is not as bad a mess as the rest of the house.

There's the blood that has run down the hall from a huge gash in a fat girl's armpit and under my shoes when I enter; the window is smashed and pieces of glass are strewn about the room; the computer monitor lies on its side and there is a huge crack obscuring Preston's *Knightriders* screensaver; a framed picture—Preston and I in front of the USF Sun Dome for an *X-Files* convention, both of us smiling, a cigarette in my hand—lies shattered on the floor. Other than that, the office has been left relatively unscathed.

Tears come to my eyes, and when I pick the photo up, a piece of glass digs into my thumb. I drop it and scream, the most angry and hopeless and desperate scream I have ever uttered. I scream until it becomes a gurgle, reach down and grab the picture again, and then I throw it against the wall. Then I grab the computer monitor and hurl it across the room. The racket is enormous. I clench my eyes shut and wait for everything to go quiet; for the director to stop asking me if I am okay, if I need any help, if I would mind doing that again with a little more desperation; for the moans in the distance to fade away; for my own breathing to stop.

When I open my eyes, I am in a room. I am sitting down, and looking up at a man in a blood-speckled white shirt and tie. He is leaning over the table I am sitting at. He stares at me and waits for me to say something. I remain quiet, totally confused.

I am not in Preston's house.

I have never seen this man before. Not yet.

I am not really here.

The man in front of me, young but haggard, finally sighs and says, "Well, Ross? Are you going to continue? Did you get the guns or not?"

"What happens next, son?" a familiar male voice asks behind me. It has obviously been altered, but something about it is nonetheless extremely familiar. I move around in my chair to face him—

—but when I turn around I am back in the office, standing now, facing the gun cabinet. Thinking I am sitting down, I immediately lose my balance and fall to the floor. My hand lands in a puddle of something black and congealed.

Wherever I just was is gone and I am back in this terrible situation sometime in the early morning of January 1, 2000. Not in late 2005, which is where, for one brief moment, I know I was.

If we imagine something terrible and it happens, why can't we just un-imagine it to make it go away?

7

"WAIT A SECOND...*what* happened?"

"I saw *you*. And I heard the man behind me, the man I am not allowed to see whose voice has been altered. I was in this room for one split second. On January 1, 2000. I was here in 2005, with the both of you, sitting in this chair."

"That's impossible," Martin says, standing up straight and pacing about the room while rubbing at his face. "That's—this doesn't make any sense."

"Well, that's what happened," I say, lighting a cigarette. "And it gets worse from here."

"Don't forget, Martin," the man behind me says, "that the young man also saw you in a vision he had that night, five years ago."

"But it wasn't a *vision*," I chime in. "It was a *memory*. I don't believe all memories are properties of only experiences passed. I do not. Not anymore."

"You were here in this room with me waiting for you to finish telling me about what happened?" Martin asks again, not able to understand anything I am telling him.

"Time travel, astral projection, out of body experience, past dimensions coalescing and intruding on this one...whatever you want to call it, the results are the same."

Martin shakes his head. "Ross, you realize that what you told us happened is totally—"

"God, I feel so confined in here!" I shout. "I feel like I'm trying to say *so* much while being trapped in a fucking box or something and everything takes too long to explain and goes on for pages and pages and pages...I feel like I'm wasting paper in a book."

"Can you foresee your own death?" the man behind me asks, ignoring everything I just said. "Or ours?"

"I don't have any control over it," I tell them, inhaling frantically on my cigarette. "If I did, do you think I would be here in this room right now, waiting for zombies to tear the door down and kill us?"

"Perhaps," the man behind me says thoughtfully. "Go ahead with your story, son. I'm on to you now."

"*What?"* I ask, trying to whirl around in my seat, but Martin has already grabbed my head and pulled me back into my original position.

After sobbing quietly for five or ten minutes, the two men waiting patiently, I sit back up in my seat.

"Earlier this year, 783 people across America committed suicide during the last four minutes of the new hit Fox reality series, *Who Wants to Marry the Dead Man?*"

"Oh my *god,*" Martin sighs. "What the fuck is that even supposed to *mean*? Who *cares* about that?"

"I care about that," I announce. "It means, gentlemen, that *I* am on to *you.*"

"Yeah, okay," Martin says. "Whatever."

"I'm on to you," I repeat, whispering now.

"I'm on to you

"I'm on to you

"I'm on to you

"I'm on to you

"I'm

6

"I'M ON TO YOU," the director says to me as we step out onto the front porch. "You think you're going to make it to the highway up ahead, where the crew will have forgotten to place many of the creatures. Whatever are still there you will take care of with your newly acquired firearms. Then you will run to safety in the city. Have I left anything out, Ross?"

"Just whether or not it's a good plan," I say with a chuckle.

He shrugs, continues walking alongside me. I notice when he emits a tiny smile.

When we leave the house and begin creeping down the sidewalk on Main toward 89, there are no cameramen waiting for us. There are no moans, no zombies, no men disguised as police or second unit people or PAs or boom mikes. There is only the occasional single flash from a camera far away, from some place we cannot see.

I'm bandaged. Before we left, I tied a tourniquet around my exposed arm, which aches constantly and dully, but has at least stopped bleeding.

I'm also armed. In Mr. Nichols' gun case, I grabbed the .22 rimfire from the drawer, quickly stuffed a handful of bullets into a pocket, and shoved the handgun down my pants. Then I reached for the shotgun, haphazardly loading it the best I knew how from a lifetime of watching TV, and then went to take the 9-millimeter, but ultimately left it behind when I couldn't find any bullets.

Just before departing the trashed and desecrated house, I counted all the ammunition I was leaving with. Twenty-eight bullets for the .22, and eight shells for the shotgun. I wasn't going to make it very far.

On the road, I say hoarsely to the director, who is walking happily next to me, "Did you check on Brody? Did you see him upstairs when you looked?"

"Well, parts of him," he replies.

"I don't get that," I say.

"You do not get what?"

"*That.* How Brody was eaten. I had gathered that the crew wasn't registering to these things, and that's why you weren't attacked. But Brody was. It doesn't make sense."

"He was wounded," the director explains. "He was exposed. He became like all of you, and was vulnerable."

"How does that work?"

"I could never explain it to you," he says, obviously uncomfortable with the subject matter.

"*Try,*" I tell him, brandishing the shotgun.

The director sighs.

"Everyone involved in the project is made virtually invisible to the senses of these creatures. Before being exposed to any of the sets or meetings or on-location shoots, they are screened, vaccinated, and sterilized. They are prevented from being potential prey to one of our actors."

"These are *actors*?" I ask dubiously.

"But everyone who becomes involved is forewarned that, if for any reason they are wounded, taken hostage, or involved in any kind of injurious on-set accident, they are immediately exposed to these creatures, and face mortal danger thereafter."

"But *how*?" I press. "Whatever it is, maybe we could receive the same treatment. You mentioned vaccination—"

"Don't be ridiculous," he laughs uneasily.

"—and vaccination implies to me that we could be given a shot that makes us as endangered by these things as you and the others. It's a *virus.* A zombie virus. We might be safe if we just—"

"It will never, ever happen, Ross," the director interrupts calmly. "This is our show, and you are our contestants. That is how it is, and how it will always be, in every last shot, forever."

"I don't think so," I say, stopping in my tracks and aiming the shotgun at his forehead.

"Spare me, Ross," he says, pushing the gun away. "Killing me will only exacerbate things more. Trust me. Look, here is the way things are: I am impervious to these creatures, and you and your friends are not. Do you understand?"

"I understand that I'm about to disengage myself from this entire bullshit ordeal," I mutter, slowly drawing the gun away.

He says nothing, a good sign.

"So, Brody told me that your superior was assigned to keep an eye on the guy who shot Kennedy," I mention.

"Did he?"

"Who is he? Who shot him? And where'd the shot come from? The knoll? The sewer? Where?"

"If I told you, time would unravel and everything would fall apart," he says.

"You just don't want to tell me."

"You are right. And I won't."

"What is he like?" I ask, asking questions to try and take my mind off of what might lay ahead, only a couple of hundred yards away now. "What is my father like?"

"What does that mean? 'What is he like?' Are you asking because you imagine a dark man who always wears trench coats, who meets with shady characters and cigarette-smoking men?" The director laughs at me, rubbing the back of his neck with his dirty hand. "Ross, if you are to survive this, you will have to grow up."

"Oh, as if *I'm* the immature one among the group I was with," I grunt.

"And *they* are dying, no? You have to try harder, and be better than they are."

Something comes to me. My eyes are stung by cold tears.

"Listen," I say. "Brody said something else to me, though. You're the director, and I haven't killed you yet. I've been a gentleman."

"Surely," he says, not sarcastically.

"Then I need to request something."

"You need to…*request* something? Ross, we do not *take* requests. We are the United States government working in conjunction with the American media entertainment industry. You should know that we do not care about what any of you think. Just look at what is on television any night of the week and you will see that."

"He said Stacey, the girl I was with before—he said that she was going to die tonight."

"Yes," he nods. He offers nothing else and my rage mounts and escapes.

I stop in my tracks.

"Well god *damn* it!" I shout. "Does she die or not? Does my sister die? Does Lydia? Who's next?"

The director barely smiles, looking into my eyes. He rubs at his goatee and considers where to go from here. Then he picks at the scab that is forming over the wound in his neck.

"You care about what happens to your friend…to Stacey," he says. "Yes?"

"I care about *all* of them, even Preston and Lydia. Mindy—well, she's—it's too late to tell you what I think of her."

"You and your friend Stacey, do you two have a romantic history aside from that of you and your paramour, Lydia?"

"Yeah, I guess," I admit awkwardly.

"And Lydia has been unfaithful as well? Did that not come to light earlier this evening?"

Did it? It seems like years ago, another life, a parallel dimension to this one.

"I guess so, yeah," I sigh, a terribly unoriginal gesture. "It was with my best friend, too. Oh, and they liked to bring in underage girls to the party, before you embarrass me with the details."

"Yes," the director says, nodding. "You have been unfair and untruthful to your friends and lovers, and they have done the same to you. Is this a fair summation?"

I nod.

"All of these relationships, all of these frayed **end**s and hurt feelings and juvenile infidelities…they are like a poorly written—oh, what do you call them—*soap opera*, right? All of these things you young people have done to one another, all the lies and scandal…it is all so melodramatic...like a soap opera, no?"

"Definitely," I agree.

"And yet you stupidly and naively believe all of this to be a coincidence, don't you? You still do not grasp that all of this, all of your heartbreak and cheating and lying and hatred toward one another…you still do not understand that all of this was planned. This was how it was written from the very beginning."

Preston and Lydia exchange that first glance, the one that will lead, several months later, to a bout of quick and ferocious sex on Preston's living room floor while Ross *and* Shannon *and* Robin *are at* Taco Bell. Night of the Ghouls *plays on the television. Preston will come on her stomach, having already disclosed his hatred of condoms and yet altogether sheer terror of children. They talk about how great a guy* Ross *can be while putting their clothes back on. Lydia can't find her shirt at first. It's behind a lamp.*

Ross stares at pictures on a fridge, until Stacey, a girl he has never met, says, "The world is just brimming *with cool things." There is an immediate unspoken attraction between them, and for the next two years, it is expressed through nothing more than double entendres and second glances when one of them leaves Preston's porch for another beer.*

Then one New Year's they kiss. Ross and Stacey, having been written this way, will have a discussion that dissects and deconstructs everything that led up to the kiss, and then the kiss itself. Then they have a long-winded, slightly downtrodden discussion on whether or not they will go any further with this lapse of judgment. It will ultimately be decided that it is inertia, and that they were always going to do this.

Clothes are slowly stripped and two candles, the good ones, are lit. Ross has no problem with the idea of sex, oddly enough. Not at first. It is not until his face is buried between her legs that the guilt finally begins to set in, and it stays with him even as he comes in her, knowing that she has the shot every six months. Lydia told him.

Preston and Lydia and Mindy sit in a clam-baked car a block away from Shannon's party. Somewhere, Ross is asking Stacey if Brad is with Cordelia at the party before he goes to talk to her. In the car, Mindy hands the tiny roach back to Preston, complaining that it is way too small for her to hit. Preston takes it and carefully puts it out in the ashtray.

Lydia giggles.

The three of them have a conversation.

It **end***s with Mindy saying emphatically, "I* am *open-minded. I would try* anything *once. Seriously. Why do you ask?"*

"How do you *know* all of this?" I ask him, livid, inhaling furiously on a cigarette.

"This is your life and we have been a part of it from the beginning."

"How?"

"Ask Preston," the director says casually. "He has his orders, too."

I ponder this for a long moment before finally saying, "But what does this have to do with them living through the night? What does this have to do with them making it out of here alive?"

"The *drama*, Ross. It is the *drama*. You do not wish them to come to harm, and yet, if they do not, there will be no drama. There will only be various stupid young people running about town. There will be dying and mayhem and confusion. There will be no poetry, no integrity, no *art*."

"Since when is any of *this* art?" I glare at him, seething.

"For this to truly work," he continues to explain, "various steps must be taken. Your friends, your family…the project calls for the involvement—and eventual degradation—of all of them. This is how the show works. This is its heart. I am sorry to see you so upset."

"Don't be *sorry*!" I shout, raising the gun barrel to his chin. "*Do* something! You have the power to stop this. So *stop it*."

"No," he says quickly, shaking his head while eyeing the barrel. "Ross, I can not change anything."

"*Bullshit!*" I scream. In the far distance, from somewhere indistinguishable, come hundreds of moans. I cringe and lower my voice. "Bullshit, man. You may not be able to stop what my father has started, but you're in charge *here*, tonight. You control who leaves and how these things attack and how fast they run and who disappears and who actually dies. You decide how everything falls apart. Why couldn't you do just the opposite as well? *Help* them. Help my girlfriend and Stacey and Cordelia get out of here. Help the others walk away from this. You can do that, right?"

"I am sorry, Ross," he says. "I can not stop what is happening. It has gone too far. And this is only the beginning. My only advice to you for the future would be to sever *everything*; do not make friends; abandon your family; abandon your child. Abandon the entire world which surrounds you. Those people—those…trivialities…they are all simply appendages that you will always be betrayed by. That you will always lose. Forever."

"You're all going to burn in fucking hell," I sneer, storming away from him, toward the moans in the distance, near the highway. "Wait—" I turn around and face him. "*What* did you say?"

Whatever silence there was earlier is gone now; it seems that out there, in the city around Main, there are sirens and explosions and helicopters and people screaming, and it is coming from every direction within half a mile of us, all at once. Then there is the cackle of gunshots: two, three, eight of them, nearby and in rapid succession. Panic fire.

"Oh no," the director mutters upon seeing what is happening at the 89 intersection.

"What did you just say?" I repeat, ignoring the terrible things happening all around us.

"They *didn't*—"

"Who did you say abandon? My *child*?"

"Oh my god…those *bastards*," he chokes, swallowing involuntarily, over and over.

"Abandon my child? *What* child?"

"There are no rules, Ross," the director stammers. "We're not safe. Not when this happens. Ross, we are in deep—"

"I have a *child*?"

"Deep—"

"*I* have a *child*?"

"Shit…This is the—"

But then there is the director suddenly crying out in pain and I hear the ripping sound of flesh, the terrible familiar drone of zombies upon us, and then I am firing the gun as fast as I can, in what seems like every direction.

5

And as we're running the buildings change all around us, from a Planned Parenthood into a large church and then the church next door becomes an abortion clinic, and cars transform into trucks and foreign turns into American and the director doesn't really say much about any of this, even though I am hysterical and slobbering random phrases like "Oh, what the *fuck*?" and "I'm onto you I'm onto you" and then the school is just ahead of us, only now it is neighboring another school, a middle school, just beyond its outer reaches, but the director does not respond to this either, as he is probably still grappling with the true situation, which is this: he is no safer, no better, than any of the rest of us now, and he is sweating profusely and starting to get tired next to me, and the dozens and dozens of walking dead are gaining on us, running after their next meal. Knowing he will die if I do not help him (*but he's going to die anyway, right?*), I grab the director by his shoulder and help him the rest of the way, hobbling up the front of the school, down the sidewalk that runs along the bus ramp, toward where I saw the candlelight coming from inside what looks like the cafeteria. We both slam against a metal door that does not open, and there are muffled voices and whispers coming from inside, but no one is coming to help us, and the zombies that started chasing the director and I at the 89 Intersection where the young director was bitten in the arm are now just behind us, gaining, and then I start screaming, "Open the god damned door! Open it! Hurry!" at the people barricaded inside, and the White Zombie zombie is at the head of the pack, still gnawing on meat from the director's bicep as it runs toward us. I drop the shotgun at this close range and immediately pull out the .22 and start firing in rapid succession, begging for Preston and the others to open the cafeteria door but they're not and the ghouls are closing in, and I can smell their breath and hear their moans envelop every other sound, and I open my mouth to scream for the last time when the door behind me suddenly swings open, almost knocking me down as it does, and a hand grabs me by the shoulder and wrenches me and the director inside. Someone, Quentin maybe, grabs the shotgun from off the ground but is snatched up as he does so and one of them bites into his skull, sending blood spraying in an arc, and Preston takes the gun from Quentin's lifeless hand and slams the door shut behind him, crimson still cascading down the tiny slit of a window on the door. Now Monica is hysterical as well, ranting and bobbing up and down and staring wide-eyed out through the thin pane of glass as several of the monsters devour her boyfriend's flesh and play with his guts and reach into the crater where his left arm used to be attached and pull out his heart and eat it. The next thing I know, Lydia or someone is freaking out about the director lying half-conscious on the floor of the cafeteria, his arm bleeding profusely, his tongue hanging out of his mouth as he tries to say something, an apology maybe. Preston kicks him while he lays there at our feet, and the director bites down on his tongue and I cringe and everything boils over and I jump on top of Preston, knocking him to the floor. I begin punching him, swearing and hacking spit at his face as I split his lip in three different places, bust the flesh open around his eye, and then I press my thumbs into his eyelids, but hands grab me and I swing at everyone else too, and then there are threats, things like "We could just throw you back out there. How would you like *that*?" or "Why are you defending this guy, Lydia?" and "Stop it, asshole, you just got my fucking boyfriend *killed*!" I begin laughing and the hands let go of me and I fall back against a wall, gathering my bearings, taking deep breaths, reaching for my cigarettes and trying to understand what just happened:

When the director and I reached Highway 89, the cadavers were already there, and not just there, but all the way down the highway over half a mile in each direction. They were coming out of the Burger King; milling around in front of an apartment building where I used to go to buy acid; eating bums who were standing at the corner of 89 and Crescent a hundred yards down the road; devouring what looked very much like the left side of Brody's skull and three-quarters of his face, which hung limply from the muscle and bone. Just as I was about to take off and leave the director behind as he imploded from shock, one of the dead people stumbled out of a Honda that had just crashed into a crosswalk light and, without having to be cued with an "Action" or a "Cut" or a "You're missing your cue," the corpse of a businessman grabbed the director's arm, pulled it toward his mouth, and took a huge bite out of his bicep. The White Zombie zombie came scurrying up after that, fighting for the director's flesh. The director was in shock, staring wide-eyed at me, then at the gash in his upper arm, and then back at me. More were coming, though, and I grabbed the director by his wrist. I'm not sure now why I did that, why I wanted to bring him with me, why I had to save him. I should have left the son of a bitch for dead. I should have been happy about his imminent demise and the look on his face as he realized that he was no longer part of his own project, that he was betrayed by his associates and superiors, by my father, and in some small way, by me. But I wasn't. And so I pulled him alongside me and we began running.

It occurs to me that they are already everywhere, and that there is no escape now, nowhere to even shoot for, no subterfuge to even dream of escaping to. And for some reason this is funny.

4

I MAY NOT BE HERE RIGHT NOW. I may not be Ross Bradley Orringer. I may not be twenty-six years old, I may not live in north Florida, and I may not sell underground schlock pictures for a living. I may have a master's in astrophysics, or a doctorate in divinity. This may not be January 1, 2000, 4:28 am, and I may not be surrounded by hateful ex-friends and lovers in a freezing cold school lunchroom.

I may have never seen a zombie.

I may have a different life, a different set of friends and memories.

This might all be new, an inchoate existence with an imaginary past.

Two seconds ago, I might not have been here; I could have been in another time, another dimension with an entirely different yearbook of memories and emotions and intellectual proclivities. This entire subsistence that seems so true now might be entirely false: I might have been implanted into this body and this mind, this *pneuma, soma,* and *sarx*, as I even realize this.

This assurance, that none of this is necessarily fact and therefore not necessarily my doing, my choices, or my *fault*, is what kept me going through every fast food job in high school. It is what kept me going while screening a police video of a stock broker plummeting to his death at the bottom of a twelve-story building, trying to determine if it would be a big hit with Something Wicked customers. It is what kept me going all those times I slept with Lydia while still remembering the sex with Stacey a few hours earlier.

And it is what keeps me going now, along with my own asinine hope that the future is worth fighting for, that there is hope for a world where not every last being is either a covert or a cadaver.

"What would Holden Caulfield name his son?" I ask Lydia.

"I'm already dead," the director laments to himself, wedged underneath one of the cafeteria tables.

"Your name isn't Holden, asshole. You can forget about it. You're just a *prick*."

"Is Quentin going to be all right?" someone among the group stupidly asks, chewing on some kind of food.

"The guy's right, if he's been bitten," Jaime says to no one in particular about the director. He opens a small bag of potato chips. "He *is* already dead."

"Lydia, I need to talk to you," I say.

"For*get* it, asshole. You got us into this. You got her killed."

"Who? *Mindy*? Oh, *fuck* her. She never had a chance. I saw her stalking around the house and didn't have the opportunity to crack her god-damned skull open before I made my escape."

"No one wanted you here, Ross," Preston says meekly, gingerly poking at his eye while spitting blood on the floor. "Everyone needs to, like, find their own way."

"Since when does everyone 'finding their own way' constitute throwing a man to his own death?" I ask bitterly, lighting a cigarette.

"You're still alive, aren't you?" he asks, lighting his own. "My calculations were correct after all."

"I am still alive," I say, taking a step toward him, and then another. "But Stacey may not be. My one and only sister may not be, you *fuck*. And it's all your fault."

"Ross—" Jaime begins, munching on chips.

"*All* of you," I declare, my voice echoing off the walls of the darkened cafeteria. "Now where's the god-damned food?"

They pried open the door to dry storage, where I find a darkened room full of mostly useless boxed food products and huge cans of peas and carrots, baked beans, and other school lunch sides. I head to the back, holding my lighter up as a miniature torch. I find a large box full of individual bags of plain potato chips, and next to that, jars of peanut butter. I grab one of each and turn to make my way back into the lunch room.

Lydia is standing in the doorway, her hands on her hips. I can't see her eyes in the darkness.

"Don't ask me about Mindy," I sigh, a terribly unoriginal gesture.

"I wasn't going to," she says.

"What is it, then? I'm really hungry."

"Ross, um..." Her hands drop to her sides. There is a long pause. "I'm...I want to apologize."

"For what? Which part?"

The storage room shifts from a long rectangular shaft into a large square. Crates with unopened boxes appear in the middle of the room. I gulp. Lydia takes no notice.

"I'm sorry I did what I did. I'm sorry about what happened at the house. You *are* a *prick*, but we shouldn't have left you there."

"No," I agree flatly. "You shouldn't have."

"And for that...I apologize," she says, her voice cracking.

She pulls out a cigarette and lights it. For one brief moment, I can see her eyes. They're red. She is crying.

"I'm so scared, Ross," she stammers. "What have you gotten us into?"

"I've told you, Lydia. *I* haven't gotten us into *anything*. Do you think I *wanted* to be here tonight? Jesus. If it were up to me, I would have split after finding you guys in the shower together."

"Sorry about that too," she says, looking away. "Even though, apparently, you've been up to a little no-good activity yourself."

"But mine wasn't something out of a penthouse letter, Lydia."

"You were screwing my *best friend*, Ross," she says loudly, on the verge of shouting. "And Jesus, how long has it been going on?"

"How long has *yours*? And might I remind you, Lydia, that Preston was *my* best friend. Tit for tat."

"Well whatever," she sighs, shaking her head. "That's not what I wanted to talk to you about."

"Really?" I ask. "Good. Because I had something to talk to you about myself."

"What is it?"

"Earlier, when I was trying to get out of here with the director, he told me something. Right before they attacked and his arm was all bitten up, the director let something out that maybe I wasn't supposed to know, but...well, maybe I was. It was about you. And me, I guess."

"This is great and all, but what did he tell you? What does it have to do with me?"

I do not answer.

"Ross?"

"What did you have to talk to me about, Lydia?"

"You were right about to tell me what he said, Ross," she says irritably.

"I know, I know," I say. "But you go first. Please. Mine might be kind of difficult to hear."

She nods, waits for a long time. My stomach is growling and churning at the same time.

"This is really fucked up, but…where is Stacey and your sister?"

"I told you, Lyd, I don't know what happened to them."

"That's what I'm worried about," she says softly. "Um, Stacey came over to my house just before Christmas and told me something. She said it was with a guy from school, but now I'm not so sure."

"What is it?"

"I'm not even sure if I should tell you this now—I mean, if it really even matters, but…"

"God damn it, what did she tell you?" I ask, my head swooning.

"She said she was pregnant, Ross."

The can of peas and carrots starts to slip out of my arm, and I grab at it tightly and clench my eyes shut in the darkened room.

"Ross, is it yours?"

Lunch with Stacey, just before everything went to hell. An uneaten plate of sushi in front of me. Stacey asking me why we didn't just settle down, get a place together. Stacey mentioning children. Stacey asking what I thought about kids.

Oh my god.

"I'm hungry," I say flatly, moving toward the door past Lydia.

"Is it yours, Ross?"

"I'm *hungry*, Lydia." I step out into the cafeteria, pause. "Look, even if it was mine, it doesn't matter. Stacey is probably dead, and therefore, so is *probably* the child."

"Ross, wait," Lydia says as I begin to leave again.

"What?" I snap, my back turned to her.

"You never told me what the director said to you. He told you something about me and you. Remember? What was it?"

"He just said that we would never be together," I say quickly, leaving Lydia standing alone in the dark.

On my way back to the table, I hear him moaning on the floor. Then he gurgles, whispers my name.

I drop the food off on a counter near the door and crouch underneath the table with the director.

"What is your name?" I ask quietly. "Your real name."

"Why do you want to know, Ross?" he asks, trying to prop his head up, letting it slump back onto the tile again.

"I just want to know. I want a name to go with such an impressionable face. That's all."

"I could give you an alias," he groans.

"But you won't," I say. "Not anymore."

"Lynn," he wheezes. "My name is Lynn. Your name is Ross. Right?"

"I think so…I'm not sure anymore."

The director tries to grunt a laugh, but only succeeds in hacking up more gray and red fluid.

"How…how does it feel to turn?" I ask. "I've always wanted to know."

"It is not such an original feeling. It feels like a sickness. Like a flu. Your head aches and you hear faraway noises that make it hurt worse. Your skin grows cold and you chill. Your stomach cramps and you feel your blood pool at the bottom of your back. It is…unpleasant."

"Oh," I say, disappointed, and then sigh, a terribly unoriginal gesture.

"Look, I'm…I'm sorry, Lynn."

"Why are you sorry? I am one of the creators of all your troubles, of all your pain and misery. This is my fault. You should be happy to see me die, no?"

"I should…but I'm not. I'm *not.* I'm not happy about *anything.* I'm not happy about everyone dying, and I'm not happy that, apparently, all of this is *my* fault; I'm not happy about my child being in danger, and I'm not happy about Stacey not *telling* me about it. And I'm not happy about what's happening to you, either."

"To me?" Lynn asks, his eyes opening and closing like he is about to lose consciousness. "You worry over me?"

"I'm not pleased about what happened to you, no."

"Why?"

"When a production gets rid of its director midway through, that's a pretty bad sign."

"For you," Lynn says, and I catch on.

"I don't wish death upon you, Lynn. I will say that." I look away for a long moment, and then slowly turn back to face the dying director. "Everything is so…insane."

"Everything is crazy," Lynn agrees, wiping the blood away from his cracked lips.

"Lynn?"

"What?"

"*Why*?"

"Why what?" he asks, weakly, his eyes blinking over and over again, slower each time.

"Why *this*?" I clarify, tears streaming down my face. "Why is this happening?"

"Ross."

"What?" I say, wiping at my eyes.

"You can not awaken someone who is only pretending to be asleep."

After Lynn dies and I fire a single round into his skull, I eat some potato chips, and then find a box of plastic forks and use one to eat peanut butter by the mouthful. I wash it down with water that I took from the faucet in the kitchen. It's ridiculous how absolutely famished I was after an entire day of running around, zombies attacking, watching friends die, suspecting *everyone*, repeating lines, catching girlfriends and boyfriends showering together, killing things, taking hostages, breaking into buildings, being shot at, watching the world fall apart and reassemble itself before my eyes, and projecting myself somehow into other parallel dimensions of time and existence.

"We were hungry too," Preston says quietly, watching me work my mouth noisily on a huge glob of peanut butter. "Look, I didn't mean what I said."

"What part?"

"A few minutes ago, about not wanting you here. I'm actually glad you are. I'm glad you're alive. It was really...bothering me ever since we left."

"Yeah," I mutter, barely nodding. "Everyone's sorry for something."

"And I'm sorry for leaving you like I did. It was Mark's suggestion. I shouldn't have gone along with it."

I get up before he can say anything else, find myself a huge unopened can of peas and carrots, and a minute later, return with the can open. I inhale the cold vegetables straight out of the container.

Preston stands over me as I eat alone at one of the tables.

"What happened to Stacey?" he asks, the rest of the group ignoring me at a table a few feet away. Jaime rubs his finger along the barrel of the shotgun. "And Cordelia?"

"For all I know they're dead," I say, my mouth full.

"And—and Mindy? Did you see her? Is she really one of them? Is she—?"

"Dead? Sort of. Unless she's prone to having a snack of someone's intestines, I'd say she's one of them."

"We lost her trying to get into the school. She was grabbed by one of those things. We never saw what happened to her."

"Well now you know," I say curtly.

Preston inhales, takes a deep breath.

"Look, Ross, I um…I know this isn't your fault."

"Oh?"

"Yeah. This isn't *anyone's* fault," he says.

"Well, it's somebody's," I point out, eyeing the gun sitting on the table in front of me.

"But not yours…"

"You know, Preston," I begin, pushing the half-empty can of vegetables away from me, "that reminds me of something that I've been meaning to ask you all night."

"What's that?" he asks, already taking a step back.

I rest my hand on the gun.

"Why did you say, 'Not again?'"

"'Not again?'" he repeats blankly. "What do you mean?"

"When all of this first started tonight, when they were first heading toward the house and you saw them, you screamed out 'Not again' and freaked out. I just want to know why you said that."

"I…didn't?" he say-asks. "I was panicking. I didn't know what to do. I fucked up. Come on, man, I mean…I'm not sure what you want from me here, Ross."

"Not much, Pres," I say flatly. "I just want to walk away from this whole thing, same as you and everyone else. I just want to find my sister and Stacey, and I want to go back home to my apartment and live a normal life and go to movies and read books and play video games. What I want is simple."

"So why are you asking me all this?"

"My father told me something," I say. "I had no idea what he was talking about at the time, but now, I am fairly certain he was alluding to what has happened tonight."

"When did he mention it to you?" Preston asks. "Last week? Christmas? Was he—?"

"Three years ago," I interrupt.

Jaime looks up from the director he has been studying, who is still under the table leaking brain matter. Lydia whispers something to Monica, who is still hiccupping from all of her crying.

"Your dad told you this *three years ago?"* Preston asks incredulously, glancing back at the shotgun leaned up against the wall near the door.

"And that's not all he told me," I say ominously.

"What else did he tell you?"

"Things about *you*, Preston. Why would my father think to tell me things about *you*?"

Preston does not say anything. He backs up two paces, looking hard at me.

"What did he say about Pres?" Jaime asks, still staring down at Lynn, his face furrowed with confusion.

"He said that Preston will, basically, try to destroy me. He said that Preston already went through this, and that he will use it to his advantage."

"That's crazy," Preston quips, shaking his head, backing away closer to the door leading outside. "This was coming from your father, Ross. Your own *father* was in on this. So why would you believe anything he had to say?"

"What do you know, Preston?" I ask, ignoring his cross-examination. "What was my father warning me about? Why would you say, 'Not again' earlier tonight? How is it that, upon seeing hundreds of dead people coming toward you, you would make a reference to it already having happened?"

"That's a good question," Jaime says quietly, looking at Preston coldly. I see that Lydia and Monica are as well.

"I never said that," he insists. "You must have heard what you wanted to. I know what you're doing, asshole. You're just trying to place the blame on me."

"You left me to die in that house."

"I just wanted to get out of there, same as you."

"You're a part of this too, like Mark was. Like my father."

"We're best friends, Ross…"

He reaches the wall, and with nowhere else to go, looks around at his options. His eyes land on something, a plan.

"Don't—"

"We're best friends!" he shouts, grabbing the shotgun to his right.

I draw my own gun and point it at him just as he aims his at my face. It transforms from a single barrel to a double before my eyes. Preston takes no notice and, now teary-eyed, cocks it.

"You made a deal with them," one of us says.

Someone in the room gasps. A bead of sweat drips off of my chin, then another. Someone says something in a foreign language. There is a muffled susurrus outside the room.

And then the crew rushes into the cafeteria from the hallway leading back into the school. One guy in a radiation suit sneaks out of the storage room

Lydia and I were just in, filming us with his television camera. The lights brought in for the scene are blinding and the sudden presence of four cameramen and three or four other technicians is dizzying and excruciating. I am reminded again that we are being watched, always, and that this experiment is not over. I feel lightheaded and my aim falters and the gun lowers.

Out of the corner of my eye I see one of the crewmen taping the director's corpse from only inches away, panning in and out of the wound in his skull, and a pang of deep sadness surges through me.

It is around this time that Preston fires the shotgun, and someone screams. It may or may not be me.

3

WHILE PRESTON STARES DUMBFOUNDED at what he has done to Jaime, I aim my gun and pull the trigger.

Nothing.

I pull the trigger again.

There is a sharp clink that sends a shockwave through me, but still, nothing happens. Preston is still standing.

By now he has caught on to what I am trying to do, which is kill him, and he rushes toward me in a tackle formation. I look at the gun in my hand, quickly inspect the side and realize that somehow, the safety is on. There is just enough time to switch it off before my best friend slams into my gut, throwing me backward. I fire one round from the gun, and the bullet swishes over his head and smacks through the lunchroom ceiling. The .22 is knocked out of my hands and falls onto the tile several feet away from us.

Preston and I fall to the floor. He is already swinging his fists at my face and chest.

The camera crew swoops down on us, shooting from every angle. One of them picks up something through what must be an earpiece and turns his camera's attention on Jaime, who flails around on the floor, grabbing at his left shoulder and chest.

Preston holds the shotgun tautly, knowing it has no more shells, and so he slams the butt against my chin, tearing it open. I barely wince at the pain. He raises the weapon above his head, ready to bring it down on my face.

I punch him in the groin, causing him to clench up and loosen his grip. I grab at the barrel. There is a struggle. Preston is coughing the entire time and at one point involuntarily vomits yellow liquid all over the both of us. I try to punch him in the nose, (which I had already done once before when I caught him with Lydia,) but he sees my fist poised, frees his right hand, and punches me first.

"Stop it!" Monica screams, standing over us. "Stop it, *please*!"

Both of us gripping the gun and trying to jerk it away from the other, we roll over once, twice, and then I am on top of Preston when he suddenly lets me pull the gun back while he shoves it. It flies toward my face, crushing the side of my nose but not breaking it. I yelp and fall backward.

Preston quickly gets his footing and stands up, looking down on me only momentarily, trying to decide what to do to neutralize me, before glancing over at the .22 lying a few feet away. I intercept this plan, and scurry across the floor for it.

My knees bang against the linoleum, and I ache in every place in my body, but I block it out amidst the knowledge that if I do not get to the gun before he does, I will be dead.

Preston is ahead of me though, and dives for it.

He's going to get to it first.

He's going to shoot me.

His hand is about to grab for the pistol and my knee gives out and I topple flat onto my stomach, wailing in agony.

This is it. This is how the hero of any zombie plot is always undone: he is not even foiled by the living dead all around him, but by the evil of humanity, by the shortcomings of people just like himself. Preston will be the one to finally do me in, to **end** my role in this production. My own best friend will be the adversary that finally unravels me.

Preston Nichols has always played the bad guy.

He snatches at the gun, but something happens.

A memory of a day with Preston on the beach, a day that he told me that everything was changing, and there were tears in his eyes.

Lydia picks it up instead.

The word "nadir" comes to mind, as do "cliché" and "embarrassing." I wonder to myself what will happen next, what brilliant twist the producers and creative team of this production will throw out. Will it be the obligatory scene of me and some screaming beauty trying to rev up a car without a top, zombies barreling down on us from every direction, only to turn the engine over and floor it just as they jump onto the trunk? Or maybe the part where I check out a suspicious noise, get surprised by a black cat that is lurking just around the corner, and sigh with relief (a terribly unoriginal gesture) just as I am grabbed from behind?

Lydia is already crying, wobbly with her aim as she points the gun at Preston, and then me, and then back at Preston again. The three of us are standing in a triangular formation about ten feet apart from one another, which is perfect for the shots the crew are setting up: close-ups of Preston and I as we try to defend our positions and convince Lydia to shoot the other one; the high angle looking down on all three of us; the over-Lydia's-shoulder shot of me about to say something important just as a gun fires; an extreme close-up of Lydia's horrified reaction as I fall to the floor in a pool of blood.

"Lydia, give me the gun," Preston urges. I roll my eyes.

"Why did you say 'not again,' Preston?" Lydia sobs.

"Good question," I quip, looking at him coldly. I turn to Lydia. "Great question, Lyd. And why did you shoot Jaime, Pres?"

"*Shut up*!" Lydia screams at me. "It was an accident. Right, Preston?"

"Guys, Jaime is going into shock," Monica calls out, propping Jaime up as he gurgles spit, convulses, and clenches the holes in his upper chest and shoulder so hard that blood pumps out like a spigot onto the tile floor.

"Preston, don't be a dick," I say. "You know you're a part of this. I don't even feel that I have to explain my case any further, to be honest. I think the facts speak for themselves. *You're* the mole, *you're* the bad guy, and you always have been. They got to you when they killed your parents, they got to you when you were confronted with these things the first time, and now they have you in their pocket. Admit it. Save us the trouble so we can try to help Jaime over there."

Preston looks at me with so much hatred that I am afraid that he will sprint toward me at any second. He doesn't.

"Ross, this is a clever game you're playing, but it's all for naught." He turns to Lydia. "I saw him before the party, Lydia. I saw him talking to the director at the **end** of the street when he and Stacey left. I saw both of them chatting it up with those guys, pointing to the dead people standing around, laughing. I *saw* it. I didn't want to tell you guys earlier, but I had my reasons to leave him alone in the house like I did."

"*What*?" I stammer. "Now that *is* bullshit."

"*That's* your defense?" Preston asks incredulously. "'Bullshit?' Well, Lydia, what do you think here, sweetie? You got me, your best friend, who was there for you when this son of a bitch wasn't, and I saw him working with these people and we all saw him repeating lines for them and doing suspicious shit from the very beginning. And what does he have to offer in his own defense? Well, it's like he said: *bullshit*."

"Help…me," Jaime chokes, still convulsing, his eyes rolling back into his head.

"Guys?" Monica says to no one.

"Oh, fuck this," I say, turning away. "Shoot me, Lydia. I'm going to help Jaime."

There has never been a more frightening moment than this one. My father told me that, in war, in violent crisis with guns present, you never hear the shot with your name on it. God reaches down from the heavens and silences it. There is only the bullet piercing your flesh, and then the melancholy segues into oily blackness and it is over.

And so the moment that it takes me to walk to Jaime and Monica, the time in which I kneel down and cradle Jaime in my arms to inspect the wound, is the worst. I am afraid that I will not even hear the sound of the gun firing, that there will only be my own footsteps on the linoleum floor, and then my back will be struck with searing pain. When I look down I will see my chest explode, my own life spitting out of a gaping wound where my heart was.

If I die this way, there will only be mortality and the silence that surrounds it. My greatest fear is that the sound of my death will emulate the sound of my entire life.

But Lydia never fires. She breaks down and falls to the floor. Preston tries to slither his way over and comfort her while slipping the gun from out of her hand, but when he approaches, she roars out some kind of incomprehensible command to stop. He is left standing awkwardly between Lydia and the three of us, looking down at the floor, realizing what he has done.

Jaime's upper chest has been blown open, and blood is pouring thickly from the large wound in his back. His shoulder is practically gone, and when he continuously tries to reach for it, he grabs at the sinewy muscle and exposed veins and bone. He screams in shock.

"What are we going to do?" Monica asks me, teary-eyed. "There's not going to be any of us *left* to make it out of here, Ross."

"He needs to get to a hospital," I say, already knowing it's hopeless. "We're going to get you out of here, Jaime. Do you understand? You're going to be all right, man."

"Who…" He coughs, leans over and spits up more blood, and then rests back into our arms. His eyes roll back for a long time, and I fear he is dead until his gaze shifts back down to me and Monica, and then they focus solely on me. They squint. "Dude…"

"What is it, Jaime?" I ask. "What do you want us to do?"

"Who…who are you?" he asks me.

Jaime dies confused, as are we on whether to shoot him again or not. He wasn't killed by one of them, and didn't die of the zombie infection; he was shot by one of his own. Even Preston shrugs when asked if Jaime will revive or not, and then slips away and stands alone on the other side of the room. A camera films him from less than two feet away. Preston does nothing.

Eventually, it is rationalized that the original zombies in any epidemic have to come from *somewhere.* Further, I confess that Jaime got some of the blood in his mouth earlier tonight, and this seals it.

As not to waste bullets, Jaime's skull is crushed with the butt of the shotgun. Preston, being responsible for his death, has the honors. It may be the only fair decision made during a very long night of decision-making.

2

"IT WILL BE MORNING SOON," Lydia says, looking blankly out the blood-stained window by the door. Corpses grow more agitated at her proximity and fight even harder to tear the door open.

"Can they get in?" Monica asks.

"They *will* get in," I say. "I think we should move somewhere else in the school, somewhere with no windows, rooms to barricade ourselves even further if need be, and wait there for a day or two. We could take food with us and hold up there. Water too. These assholes will give up eventually. I believe that. New Year's is over. Everyone is dead. I'd say this season of the show is finished, wouldn't you guys?"

"Yeah," Lydia says, staring down at the blood on the floor while smoking a cigarette.

"That's the first thing I've heard you say that I agree with, Ross," Preston says.

"Preston, why don't you just go—?"

"Don't start, guys," Monica warns us.

"—fuck yourself," I finish.

"So where should we go?" Lydia asks.

"Well, I had an idea about that," I say.

"So did I," Preston adds. "How about one of the classrooms, one of the classrooms on the other side of the school facing the baseball field and Carolina?"

Carolina is the street running parallel to Main about three hundred yards away, on the other side of the school.

"I can do you one better," I say. "The class is too exposed. We need a place that's big, windowless or nearly windowless, and that has access to the crawlspace above the schoolhouse."

"Where?" Monica asks.

"The li—"

The door into the cafeteria is ripped from its hinges. They come pouring into the room, moaning louder than ever before. Their makeup is fresh, the blood rusty-smelling and thick, the meat and viscera lodged in their teeth so rotten and foul that something fills my mouth—it's bile—and I heave as if I am about to throw up, and I have to swallow it down quickly, as they surround us before anyone has time to realize it.

The White Zombie zombie, a guy my age, a guy who liked the band White Zombie before he died and came back as an *actual* zombie, is the first one to come at me. He tries to grab my arm, but I grab his first and sling him away. He falls to the floor and immediately tries stumbling back onto his feet. It occurs to me that I don't want to destroy this one.

Preston, Monica, and Lydia are busy themselves. Out of the corners of my eyes, I see each one of them trying to ward off two or three attackers apiece. I see a Taco Bell employee with one breast missing dig into Monica's wrist with her fingernails. There is blood. Monica pushes it off of her and backs up several feet before taking on another adversary.

A young girl in hospital garbs and a middle-aged guy wearing bicycle shorts, a bicycle helmet, and a black tank top, come for me. I have no gun and have to fend off both of them using only my wits and brute strength (a paltry combo, I know), being careful not to let any of my flesh become exposed in the process. I punch the girl in the forehead, sending her backward and injuring my hand, and then I put the other ghoul into a headlock and drive his skull into the corner of a lunchroom table. It screeches and slides about as I bang the cadaver's head into the sharp corner, but after five or six hard rams, he ceases moaning and becomes dead weight. When the little girl comes back, I pick her up over my head and slam her, head down, into the floor. Her head flattens into a mess of gunk and sandy blond hair.

Lydia figures out after pathetically pistol-whipping one of them that she does have a working gun, and points it square in the face of a female about her size and description. She does not hesitate to pull the trigger. The zombie's visage splits open and white chunks of meat and almost a gallon of blood explode out of the huge crack in her skull. Lydia fires at another one, and then another very close to me, covering my face with zombie blood, which I frantically wipe away with my sleeve before having to take on another two of them at a time.

Monica shrieks and I can only momentarily glance her way, but it is long enough to see that she has been bitten, on her palm. The fat woman in a night gown rips Monica's flesh away with her yellowed teeth, Monica letting out a wet bawl as she watches her pale artist's skin get pulled away as if it were soggy canvas from her hand. Preston, who has been killing zombie after zombie by hammering their heads in with the butt of the shotgun, comes to her aid, crushing the fat woman's head as it still rips away Monica's muscle and tissue.

One of them, a tuxedoed man, grabs my wrist at the same time the White Zombie zombie grabs me from behind. I frantically punch the well-dressed corpse that's holding my hand repeatedly in the forehead, but this does nothing, and so I fall backward so that I collapse on top of White Zombie zombie's back and onto the floor, leaving them both wrenching at air, totally confused. I kick the tuxedoed monster in the kneecap and then force him to the floor, where I pound his head into the linoleum with my boot. His brain spatters out of his nose and eyeballs, which I crush into the tile and smear with my foot, and then his eye pops out of his socket and I squish it.

More and more come pouring into the cafeteria from outside. I quickly realize that this is a hopeless battle. If we wait much longer, we will be completely blocked from the hallway leading into the school, and we will die in here.

"Ross!" Preston shouts, drowned out by Lydia's last two bullets. "We gotta get out of here!"

"I *know*!" I shout back.

White Zombie zombie grips my shirt sleeves once more, holding onto me. I clench his shirt sleeves as well, understanding the futility of my pity, and that I will have to kill him. I am about to sling him to the floor for the last time.

Then our eyes meet.

Mine are probably turgid with fear, wet and grimy and cracked with red bolts, but his are placid, serene, and distant. They are a gray ocean to which there is a beginning but no **end**. I am hypnotized by their function as a mechanism for this creature's unwavering instinct and total lack of confusion or deliberation. This beast I am about to finally wrench to the ground and stomp on until it dies is not hung up on the trivialities of life, nor is it unsure of what its place is here on this planet of idiots. It is calm, at peace with everything around him, and I find myself envying this zombie wearing a White Zombie t-shirt, even as I throw him beneath my boot and stomp on his head until there is nothing but a pile of skull fragments, blood, quivering brain muscle, and overgrown hair.

"Come on guys!" I yell immediately afterward, tears in my eyes, running for the double doors leading into the school. "Let's go! We've got to make it to the library."

Still caught up in the brief but life-changing moment I just experienced, I glance at Lydia, catching up to me and keeping pace alongside.

And predictably, I realize *everything:* that Lydia Lawton is a vapid, stupid, ugly, shallow, redundant, pointless, rambling, mismatched, ridiculous, trite, callow, pathetic, *stupid* bitch, and I suddenly want to die knowing that I pined away for her throughout this entire ordeal. I actually fell apart seeing her and Preston together in that shower. And for *what*? They are absolutely *perfect* for each other, and will one day have equally evil and perfunctory children that will probably steal my wallet or do a horrible job washing my windows while asking me for spare change.

What was I doing? What was I ever doing with this fucking *spy*, this evil debauchery to humankind?

Oh my god, I then think. Stacey might actually be dead.

Heading into the corridor, everything comes flooding back: meeting Stacey, the smile on my face as she told me the world was just *brimming* with cool things; the first time Stacey and I were left alone, and how great that conversation was (trampolines, teaching, the conspiracy behind Columbine, snakes, rat tails, aliens, ghosts, aliens who are *working* with ghosts, etc.); that moment when our lips first touched, last New Year's Eve; standing on the top of a parking garage downtown while a homeless black man moaned to himself on the street below while a small crew filmed him; all of those times we smiled at our secret and mentioned pinot noir, a code; a hundred different nights when Stacey saved me from falling victim to one of Lydia's totally banal and ultimately fucked topics of discussion; all the times I was stupid in not accepting Stacey's open invitation to become a part of not only a relationship that *meant* something, but a relationship where I truly loved someone, and that someone truly loved me. Forever.

It is when we slip into the darkness, followed by dozens of zombies wanting to eat us, that I know for a fact that I am a fool, and have truly hit rock bottom. Further, I know it is too late, and that I will never see her or my sister again. My silence has gone on for far too long, and I will not get a second chance.

It's too late.

It's too—who is Martin Bishop? Why are there men behind the walls?

1

MARTIN LOOKS UP WHEN THE MAN BEHIND ME, the man I am not allowed to see and whose voice has been altered, waves him to stop the interrogation.

"What did you find out about Preston Nichols?" he asks.

Martin shrugs, then shakes his head slowly, staring at the floor in a trance.

"There were no autopsy records found on either Warren or Evelyn Nichols, and the photos from the crash site were reported 'missing' when I investigated in April. One of my sources *did* speak to the owner of the restaurant they were dining in, and he recalled something um…kind of interesting, I guess you could say."

"And what is that?" the man behind me asks.

I light another cigarette and raise my eyebrows in anticipation.

"The owner was standing outside smoking a cigarette when he reported seeing the couple exit the building, still arguing, just before meeting up with two gentlemen, whose presence immediately squelched their debate. The four of them exchanged quiet words for about three minutes, and then all of them walked off and around the corner. The owner saw the Nichols' van pull out away a moment later, with four people inside."

"That *is* interesting," he says thoughtfully.

"Hell yes it is," I chime in. "Did you find out who the two guys were?"

"The owner couldn't remember that much. He just says that one of them spoke with a European accent, he wasn't sure from where."

"Son of a bitch, I *knew* it," I mutter, very slowly taking in all of the ramifications.

There is a long pause after this before the man behind me quietly asks, "And as for Preston Nichols's current whereabouts?"

"Unknown now, but on October 15 he was photographed exiting a sushi bar in Los Angeles, and there was a long distance phone call made to north Florida from Washington three days later. The credit card used for the call was that of one of Preston's known aliases. Frankly, it was about as subtle as a god-damned Ken Russell movie, to put it in terms Ross can understand. Which leads me to believe that Preston was either toying with us, or has gotten very, very sloppy in the last five years."

Martin gives the man behind me an accusing glance.

"Yes," the man agrees, ignoring it. "Preston wanted us to know he made that call. He wanted us to know what he was up to, just to rub it in our faces that we were all powerless to stop it: you and I, Ross, the other members of the project...Preston and his faction were in control."

Preston has always played the bad guy.

"Who was the call made to in north Florida?" I finally ask.

"Don't you already know?" Martin asks accusingly. "Of course it was made to the only other survivor who stayed in Florida besides *you*, Ross. Or do you still not believe she would have done that?"

After almost twenty minutes of silence only interrupted by ridiculous chuckles and murmured swears, the man behind me finally speaks up:

"All right, gentlemen, listen. This next part, when I was told briefly two weeks ago, strained credibility, to say the least. I want you both to elaborate on it now, in detail, in front of the camera. Ignore the contradictory stories, if need be. Just tell me what both of you know. Clear?"

"Crystal," Martin says lamely, plopping down in the chair opposite me.

"Are we still filming?" the man asks.

"Yes," I say, staring at the blinking red light on the camera several feet away.

"All right. Martin, why don't we begin with you? Several weeks ago, you and Ross Orringer, along with two others, Geoff Sparrow and John Windsor, were holed up for a short time in an elementary school cafeteria. Then you found it necessary to vacate that area and move deeper into the building. Continue from there, please."

"Well maybe Ross should," Martin immediately replies, sweating again. "This is…this is his thing."

"I don't think so," the man says.

"You know, I'm getting a little tired of this. Maybe I should be asking *you* the questions."

"That's quite enough, Martin."

Martin goes quiet, having been warned by a man he is obviously still afraid of, even when facing death at the hands of the undead.

"Now listen to me," the man behind me says. "Martin, you will narrate first. And then we will move on to Ross. I hope that is understood."

"Okay, okay," Martin says. "Um, where did Ross leave off? Um…okay. Well, the city had gone to hell. We were trapped in the elementary school, which apparently was the same one from 1999, isn't that right, Ross? What a bunch of insane fucking *bullshit*—"

"*Martin!*" the man behind me roars, his tone so reminiscent that the sudden inclination to spin around and see his face is painful. As if sensing the feeling, the man behind me grips my shoulder with one hand, tightening his hold until I feel nauseous. "Do you remember what happened to the last man who crossed me, Mister Bishop?"

"I'm sorry," Martin stammers. "I'm sorry. Um, okay, we were at the school, it was about half past six in the morning, and they had just gotten in through the door after Ross let go. Naturally, we ran…"

Martin led the way. He crashed through the double doors that led into the main corridor of the school. It stretched about a hundred yards to the left, and another twenty or so on the right. After a second's deliberation, Martin motioned with his gun that the four of them would go left.

"This library plan is *stupid*," Geoff squealed. "Those bastards are everywhere out there. They'll get in and we'll be stuck."

"I don't *know*, Geoff," Martin said, looking over his shoulder at the undead stumbling out of the cafeteria after them. "Can't you see I'm making this up as I go along?"

They barely even glanced into each classroom as they trotted along, looking only for the library. Midway down the hall, the group came to a T. After a short and petty argument over where the media center would be, the group took the T crossing and ran for the other **end**. It was a lucky guess. At the **end** of the corridor were a single set of red double doors with a sign that read ROOM 13: LIBRARY AND MEDIA CENTER.

Martin and John worked on getting the doors open without damaging the lock as they had done before. Ross and Geoff took their guns and fired two-fold at the approaching zombies at the other **end** of the hallway. At the same time, they were careful not to hit any of the crew, who flanked the army of undead with cameras, boom mikes, and lighting equipment. Some of the ghouls fell, but were quickly trampled on by the half dozen more that took their place.

"Get the door open!" Geoff barked.

"Do *you* want to pick this god-damned lock?" John cursed, which was the most emotion he had shown since the mission began.

One of Ross's guns ran out of bullets, and there were no more to replace it. He shoved it into his pants and winced at how hot the barrel was against his thigh. With the rimfire, he took careful aim, not wanting to waste bullets, and fired three more rounds. Three more cadavers toppled over, their brains all over the hall.

Ross saved four bullets and let Geoff empty both his weapons, anticipating the worst, and swearing to himself that neither he or any of his companions would ever be walking around like *that*. He confessed this days later as he and Martin were air-lifted away from the school to the prison.

The door made a clanking sound and swung wide. Ross somehow was the first one in. Geoff followed him, and then John. Martin stood out in the hallway for one more second, defying what he was always warned not to do. He fired a single shot from the small Gatlin he kept at his ankle, and at that moment, the lens of one of the cameras burst and one of the radiation-suited crew members grabbed at his mask and collapsed to the floor, dead.

Martin joined the others in the darkened library and pulled the door shut behind him. He locked it from the inside. Despite the fact that the doors swung outward, Martin still wanted to place something large, something heavy, in front of the entrance, so that if the zombies did get in, they would be impeded at least momentarily while the four men made new plans.

So, after a quick scan of the area around him, Martin laboriously pulled the nearest thing he could find in front of the two doors, which was a magazine rack. It was heavy and difficult, and no one helped him, but Martin managed to get the steel rack into place in front of the entrance just as the pounding and muffled moans began on the other side of the doors.

It was as he turned around and began to say "We're safe now, I think" that Martin realized something: the other three had not made a sound when they entered the room, nor did they ever even turn around to help him when he went to barricade the door. It was weird.

"What's going—?" he began, but froze.

Martin saw what the other three had been staring at in silence.

Obscured by shadows on the other side of the large open room, there were four other people.

"And *then*?" the man behind me asks impatiently.

"And then *nothing*," Martin says, stubbing out his cigarette in the ashtray. "I *told* you what happened next. I have no recollection at all, whatsoever. I remember nothing. We saw four other people in the library with us, and that's it.

"The next thing I remember is being alone with Ross in the library, weak and starving, two days later. John and Geoff were both gone, and there was no sign of either of them. I didn't believe Ross when he told me what had happened, and so we didn't speak much for the next twelve hours. And then the helicopters touched down on the roof, followed by hundreds of gunshots. An hour later the doors to the library swung open, and ten soldiers came marching in, smoke still pouring out of the barrels of their machine guns. They were sent by you, sir, to come and rescue us. Ross and I were led outside and up a rope ladder onto the roof, where three choppers were ready to lift us to safety here in the prison, our original rendezvous point."

There is a pause.

"And so…you've been here ever since, the both of you," the man behind me says with difficulty. "Geoff and John never turned up, no remains were found at the school, and there was no sign of anyone else ever having been in the library but Ross Orringer and Martin Bishop."

"That's all I know," Martin says dismissively, "so if you want to listen to this kid's science fiction *bullshit* now, go right ahead, but I don't believe in *any* of this. I don't believe that what we are doing is right, I don't believe any of what he's telling us about that night five years ago, and I *especially* don't believe *you* when you say that you no longer have any control over this project."

"Watch your tongue, Martin," the man warns coldly. "Just watch it."

"I want out of here, sir. I want to leave this room. I want to leave this prison. I'd rather take my chances out there than be locked up asking this kid stupid questions about a supposed pilot episode that was never even *shot*."

"It was shot, Martin. And I don't want to warn you again."

I shiver.

"No, sir," Martin says, shaking his head. "No. This has gone far enough. I've seen enough evidence now to conclude that you're still working for *them*, sir. Everything you're telling me, these soldiers, your family, is a lie. *No* ties have been cut off, *no* excommunication has been enacted, and you were *never* disavowed from this project. Christ, it's *your project—*"

"Martin, be quiet or else," the man behind me mutters, but it is an indifferent warning now, as decisions have been made.

"Or else *what?*" Martin bursts. "Is there a fate worse than living death?"

In less than an instant after Martin says this, there is a gunshot from above my head, and less than four feet away from me, Martin's forehead bursts open. His skin rips apart and blood splatters all over the table and my face. Martin's brains tumble out the back of his head, spilling all over the room.

I am too shocked to even scream.

Before he falls to the floor, Martin's mouth hangs open wide, and his eyes move away from trying to look up at the gunshot above them, and down to me. They remain wide as Martin and I exchange a final stare. His mouth closes. Blood runs over his pupils and down his face in rivulets. His hands loosen their grip on the table. Martin Bishop's corpse slides out of the chair and lands on the hard floor with a dull thud.

"You shouldn't have shot Barry in the school hallway that day, Martin," the man behind me says.

"Oh my god," I choke.

"After you calm down, son," the man behind me says quietly, "you can tell me what happened to you in the library."

"Oh my *god*."

"I would ask you to narrate both accounts, from five years ago and from three weeks prior to now, but somehow I feel that just one story will be sufficient."

"Oh my *god,* Dad. What have you done?"

0

We scatter down the school corridor, past the main office and several classrooms decorated on the outside with hula hoops and posters featuring Garfield. When we reach the point where the school is turned into a T-shape by another hallway running perpendicular to the one we are in, I direct the group down it, having a strong feeling that the library will be at the **end**.

It is. There is a sign next to the door that reads ROOM 13: LIBRARY AND MEDIA CENTER.

"Lucky guess?" Lydia asks me as I fumble with the door.

"The number thirteen is *unlucky*," I mutter, realizing that, for some reason, the doors are unlocked.

I pull them open and the group clambers inside. I shut it behind me, and lock it from the inside.

The library is cold and almost totally dark. I can somehow feel the presence of books, but nothing else, which is a relief. There are no windows except five tiny rectangular ones ten feet off the floor along one side of the room. Nothing could get in through them.

"Should we barricade the door?" Monica asks.

"It wouldn't do any good," Preston says. "It swings toward them."

"Maybe we should anyway," I suggest. "Just to hinder them if they do get in."

"Knock yourself out," Pres says, moving into the library. "I'm going to try to find some candles or something."

I leave the door unattended and move into the large cavernous room. A minute later, the pounding starts.

Preston doesn't find any candles in any of the offices or storage rooms, but does find two flashlights, which he wants to save. Our eyes eventually adjust to the darkness and everyone settles down into a chair and takes a breath. I keep whispering to myself, "This is real. This is happening. This is real. This is happening—"

Sunrise approaches. I wipe the blood off of my watch and strain to see what time it is. 6:08. The longest night of my life is coming to an **end**.

Around 6:20 the pounding stops. So do the moans. In fact, we can actually hear the crew directing and corralling them away. Reticence follows.

Everyone is curious as to why this has happened. Monica is actually hopeful, despite her artistically nihilistic disposition. Preston and I are more suspicious, though, and resolve not to get near the door.

Four minutes pass.

"Maybe it's over—" Lydia begins, but then she hears it.

Shouting, coming from inside the schoolhouse. Movement. Not far from the crew. It's something else. And it's coming this way.

"What's going on?" Lydia whispers.

When whoever it is outside slams against the door and starts fumbling with the lock, we all jump up, terrified.

There is cursing outside the double doors, and the muffled sound of several men arguing. The four of us instinctively back away from the door, toward the far **end** of the library.

The patter of gunshots and faraway moans send chills down my spine. Preston is standing next to me, sweating profusely. Monica is backed hard against a bookshelf. A paperback novel falls to the floor.

"Who's out there?" Lydia whimpers, looking to me.

There is a familiar voice outside the door that says, panicked, "I'm out of ammo. Geoff?"

Preston glances at me.

We hear the lock turn.

"I've got it," someone yells.

The door swings open.

"Ross—" Lydia stammers, and then falls silent.

We all say nothing, our eyes on the doorway.

A tall, shadowy figure hobbles into the room, followed by two more men. Finally, a fourth guy pauses in the doorway and pulls a small gun from a holster at his ankle.

He fires a single shot into the hallway.

The room, for one split second, lights up.

The tall man's face is illuminated.

I gasp.

The fourth man stumbles into the library. He shuts the doors behind him, and I hear the lock turn.

Meanwhile, the other three men are standing motionless opposite us. I can tell that the tallest one, despite being shrouded in darkness, is staring directly at me.

"We're safe now, I think," the one by the door says.

His companions say nothing. I remember not saying anything.

Martin approaches the rest of the group. It occurs to me that I know his name is Martin.

"What's going—?"

He sees the four of us standing there and goes silent. For a long moment, none of us are sure what to do, and so we do nothing at all.

Finally, I reach over to Preston's hand next to me and finagle one of the flashlights out of his grasp. I never take me eyes off of the tall one.

I can barely find the switch on the light, and when I do, my hands are so sweaty and shaky that it takes me almost another minute to actually turn it on.

"Who *is* that?" Martin asks, but his voice sounds garbled, like a bad print of a movie. The entire room changes shape, expands, and grows momentarily darker when the walls turn from white to a green color. There is movement behind the walls.

I hear someone ask, "Are they going to call a cut, or what?"

And then the sun barely peaks through the windows.

Preston, Lydia, and Monica scream in terror.

I shine the light directly on his face.

On my face.

How is this possible?

And then, as if some higher force responds to my question, the walls to the library slide away from us, and then away from each other. The book shelves behind me are attached to the set, and roll away with the walls, which cause Lydia and I both to fall backwards onto the floor. When I look up, I see that the "sun" is actually a large dimmed lighting rig shining down on us from thirty feet overhead, from the ceiling of the stage. Light comes streaming in from huge halogen lights and cameras are dollied in and when I look around us, I am overwhelmed by the sheer volume of people—radiation-suited crew, zombie extras, executives in suits, gaffers and stage hands in black and flannel and worn out baseball caps, military personnel with machine guns, my father, and various other shadowy men and one woman who are in some way or another involved in this experiment—who come streaming into the area. I see David and Melanie, stage makeup gone, munching on croissants by the catering table while watching us with bemusement. Camilla argues with someone—Mark—by a door at the edge of the huge blue room.

Ross is immediately held at gunpoint on the other side of the room and quickly escorted out by my—his—(*what?*) *our* father.

He is gone.

And then the vision of myself standing fifteen feet away is overtaken by new sights—needles being inserted into Martin Bishop's (even though I do not know his name) neck while he remains solemn and still, as if he expected this but did not like it; Martin Bishop going unconscious and being carried out on one of three stretchers; Lydia kicking and clawing and shimmying around when crewmen attempt to hold her still for the injection; my father approaching Lydia, grinning flirtatiously at her just before delivering a single chop to her shoulder, which causes Lydia to go limp and collapse to the floor, gurgling saliva and something pinkish yellow; Lydia being wheeled out on a stretcher; my father trying to shake my bloody hand and when I do not offer my hand and instead spit in his face and try to attack him, my father and his soldiers surrounding me; a needle being inserted into a sealed jar, fingers tapping a syringe; a smile; me losing consciousness, coming back, losing it again; wheeling down a corridor and seeing something terrible when I push open a random door to a room where people are screaming for their lives.

Through hazy eyes I watch Preston and my father approach one another. They say nothing for a long time, but then smile so widely I think their faces actually stretch, and they give one another a bear hug and shake hands and laugh and someone mentions that "They'll never know; the project is going off without a *hitch*." There is talk of a prison and Martin's suspicions just before he will be shot in the head. Preston grabs a cup of coffee from the table of food, stares at a donut, and then walks off-stage, whistling "**End** of the World" by REM as radiation-suited crew members and stage hands and a producer and Mark congratulate him for his performance.

Things I see: the **end** is near; a jabbering rat edging its way along the streets of a decaying German city; two girls throwing a large blue and white ball back and forth between each other, but in slow motion, and it looks like the *sky* but without monsters in it; businessmen with fangs and horns standing at the **end** of long empty hotel corridors; self-aware briefcases; boys coming home from mustard gassed Europe only to lose all control of their reflexes, bowels, and sanity; great evil; an old man reading from a book in the Bible, something obscure and scary, *Habakkuk* (he watches the nation of Judah fall); alien couriers with small packages attached by a handcuff to their arm, negotiating with members of a paramilitary movement, and the deal is the contents of the case for the guns, but there are problems…

And the two soldiers and Monica are escorted from the stage and not given an injection, which somehow the audience knows is a bad thing. Later I will hear screaming and pleading and, while strapped to a rolling stretcher, I will pass a room with the door shut and have the overwhelming urge to look inside and when I sit up, grab the knob, and throw the door open, I will see the two soldiers and Monica strapped with duct tape, rope, and telephone cords to fold-out chairs backed against a wall as three zombies on leashes held by radiation-suited men with camcorders get closer, closer, closer, until one of them rips out of the clutches of the cameraman and bites into Monica's eyeball just as I am wheeled by and the door slams shut. The last thing I hear of Monica is her crying for her father, for a red bicycle.

And I am whispering, deep in a dystopic funk, that this is not happening, this is not happening. That this is Armageddon and we're being tricked.

My father still looks good. His teeth are clean and white, his eyebrows have been plucked, and he has lost ten or fifteen pounds. His voice has in fact been surgically altered, but it's an improvement. His low rumble and muttering disposition have been replaced with a voice that seems perfect for a late night radio call-in show. His haircut looks nice, fresh, and not military; more like Wall Street. A lot has happened since Mom died.

"Are you going to shoot me now too?" I ask, only slightly worried. "Like you did Martin? He trusted you, Rich—I mean Dad."

"Martin and the others knew the stakes of the game when they signed up," my father says, wiping a speck of blood away from his cheek with a handkerchief.

"So answer my question. Are you going to shoot me? Are you going to shoot your own son now that he's figured out your plan?"

"Why would I do that, Ross?" he asks. "As if you weren't meant to figure it out anyway."

"Preston works for you. You recruited him when his parents died. He was the insider five years ago. He was wired. He was following orders to the letter the entire time."

"Not just Preston," my father reminds me, seeming to enjoy this moment. "You constantly forget Preston had his help."

"I refuse to accept that she was a part of this," I say, shaking my head, lighting a cigarette nervously on the fifth try.

"Refuse all you want. The fact remains, son."

"*Fuck* you, Dad."

There is a long silence, and for the first ten seconds of it I am sure that my father's quiet anger will bubble over and he will splatter the wall with my brains.

"And so here we are, in late 2005," he finally says, *not* splattering the wall with my brains. "The project is a success. The ratings are through the roof. There is plausible deniability, the nation mourns, the grip is tightened, and the lemmings inch their way closer to the edge of the cliff."

"Congratulations. Millions are dead, and millions more are subdued into not even seeing that the world is **end**ing, but at least you've got a hit, right? Oh my *god*."

I suddenly feel nauseous.

"What's happening, son?"

"What do you mean?" I ask bitterly. "My father is a spy. My father set me up to be at the center of a huge project to kill lots of people using walking corpses and TV cameras. Half my friends don't really exist. Everyone I know and care about is either dead or a spy. What else do you want, Dad? We're in Revelations territory here, are we not?"

"We are," he says, shaking his head, rubbing the sweat off of his brow. "But that's not what I'm referring to."

He walks around me in the sepulchral room, stepping over Martin's yellowing corpse.

"Then what?" I ask.

"What happened in that library?"

"Which part?"

"The part where two different moments, five years apart, finally collided after building up and coinciding for…for forever it seems."

"I'm onto you."

"What has happened to time, son?"

"It's…a mess."

"Why?"

"I don't *know* why," I admit with a sigh, a terribly unoriginal gesture.

"What's happening here is happening everywhere," my father says. "It always was, for all eternity, and always will be. What was it that the black man said to you that day? That you were already—"

"What are you saying?" I interrupt, crying now and not knowing why. Or maybe I do. I inhale carefully on the cigarette.

"You'll figure it out," he says. "In the **end**. You shouldn't smoke, son. It's a bad habit."

Then my father smiles and walks over to the barricaded door. It was locked from the outside and then blocked off by soldiers with heavy artillery, but my father unlatches the lock and pushes it open with ease. He reaches into a black burlap bag on the floor and his hand emerges holding my crowbar; I am not sure where he got it from, or when I lost it a few weeks ago. He offers it to me and I take it reluctantly, looking away from him as I do so.

"You won't need it though," he says.

A dark and empty prison lurks beyond the doorway. The silence is so alien and frightening after all of the gunshots and cries for help, the cursing and the sounds of flesh ripping and blood splashing and terrible banshee-like screams ringing out, and the *moans*, oh my god the *moans*, that my ears ache and pulsate and I feel feverish and lightheaded as I stand up and give my father a final nod. While he stops the camera from recording and begins disassembling it, I swallow and walk out into the whispering caliginosity.

I am pushed down a hallway into the darkness. The wheels of the stretcher squeak and jam. Soldiers have conversations and flirt with female assistants holding coffee from Starbucks.

Zombies are being rounded up and corralled into a large room, the cafeteria set, and there are gunshots coming from the room and the moans get quieter after each gunshot. I feel a deep pity and whisper a line from the remake of *Night of the Living Dead* to myself.

Mindy is among the undead being shoved into the room by a soldier.

"Stop," I whimper, flailing my arms about and hallucinating badly. "Just let me have this one thing—"

The men continue to roll me away from the scene, and Mindy's corpse makes eye contact with me.

"*Wait!*" I scream while rolling over onto my stomach and watching Mindy grow more and more distant. "No one kills her but me. *Please!*"

Preston sidles up next to her, and mutters something into the lapel of his jacket.

One of the men behind me speaks into a tiny mike in his uniform. He says to his partner, "Whoa, stop a minute."

Preston is handed a small handgun from another soldier.

Tears roll down my eyes.

He fires one shot into Mindy's temple. She falls to the floor as Preston wipes away speckles of blood from his face. He grins, gives me a wink, and heads down the hallway, tossing the gun back to its owner. And this is the last time I will see Preston. At least, this is what I hope.

The men above me laugh and resume their conversation about last week's episode of *Everybody Loves Raymond.*

We pass a fold-out table, where two professionally dressed men go over large stacks of documents with Lydia and Cordelia, who are both placid, only crying a little, and when I pass by my sister Cordelia she stares at me in a way that makes me know this is it.

The girls sign another paper. One of the men, a lawyer, mentions something about New Mexico being a fine state, and that their clients in the past have liked it there.

Stacey is not at the table signing papers.

Stacey is not being relocated.

Stacey…is not…here.

Brody told me that she would die tonight.

I am sobbing until the total exhaustion, not to mention the drugs, take effect, and I drift away. The stretcher is rolled into the darkness and I sleep, never wanting to awake, and in my sleep I am welcomed to a beautiful place, a place where everything is cold and distant and safe, a place where men do not dream.

PART V
"The End (Immolating a Crepuscular Future)."

2000–2005

"It was strange, she thought…that it should require a holocaust to make her own life worth living."

—Pat Frank

"Where there was nature and earth, life and water, I saw a desert landscape that was un**end**ing, resembling some sort of crater, so devoid of reason and light and spirit that the mind could not grasp it on any sort of conscious level and if you came close the mind would reel backward, unable to take it in. It was a vision so clear and real and vital to me that in its purity it was almost abstract."

—Bret Easton Ellis

"And behind it was a cold blackness; and it was not heaven or even hell that I was looking at, but only emptiness."

—Margaret Atwood

0

It's just
It's just
It's just
It's just
It's just

1

IT'S JUST THAT THIS MORNING IS WEIRD.

In the dream, I am standing in an open courtyard, staring ahead at an empty apartment complex and vacant parking lot. Behind me is an abandoned drive-in, with two huge cracked white screens. When I look to my side, there is an oversized tumbleweed that rolls by and reveals a yellow café, its wall spray-painted with the words IMMOLATE THE FUTURE in thick bloody scrawl. The sound in my dream cannot keep up with the actions and movements. I walk, the crunch of my feet on the grass emanating seconds after I take each step. There is a kiddy pool with a floating yellow Tonka truck around the corner. A swing set has been turned over.

Then I see her. From the balcony of one of the apartments is a girl. She is in a blue Sunday dress and her silence tells me to ignore the whispers. She holds a finger to her lips and blows. A moment later the soft betrayal in her breath swirls around my ears. The girl smiles, and this is when I realize who she is, who she has always been. My eyes fill with tears and my voice wavers and terror overwhelms me and in another dream this is my reality.

I awake.

Slivers of pale January sunlight stream in through the Venetian blinds. A dog barks down on the street below. Black boys talk loudly on a balcony across the courtyard. I sit up in bed, still feeling tired, and yawn. Flashbacks too slow to actually flash begin to creep into my mind, but it sends me reeling, and then there is nothing, no memory, only the hint that there *should* be.

It's a little after eight in the morning.

My house is clean, just how I left it. The phone rings once on the cradle, stops, and there is silence throughout the apartment. The computer in the office is turned off, but the light on my fish tank is on, and my fish is not hovering near the surface, a sign that it has been fed and is satiated.

There are no hissing noises. There are no beeps or flashes. This means something to me.

Not knowing exactly what to do—dub a movie, package some covers, watch the news, put on a pair of socks?—I head into the kitchen, inspecting what I am wearing. Blue boxers, white t-shirt, no watch. I pour myself a bowl of cereal and sit down in the living room to eat it. When I turn on the television and VCR and press Play in the VCR, the **end** credits from *Cannibal Holocaust* roll, and I wonder when the last time was that I watched this. I decide it was with Lydia and Preston and turn the movie off, flip the channel to a news station.

At eight-thirty another morning news show begins, and I am told by a vaguely attractive pseudo-Spanish reporter that this is the news for Tuesday, January 4, 2000. A sense of inexplicable relief, followed by total confusion washes over me.

Where have my last three days gone?

The show **end**ed with me, my arm gushing blood from a gunshot wound, and I was strapped onto a stretcher injected with god knows what, while being rolled out of a library and out of a school that apparently was not a library and was not a school at all. This was the morning of January 1, almost exactly three days ago.

I look down at my arm. The bullet that pierced the flesh in my bicep has been removed, probably while I was under. In its place is a grotesque-looking wound that hurts when I move, flex my muscle, breathe.

My car was shot up. Then it was removed from the intersection of Pittsburgh and Main. They took my car.

On instinct, I gingerly pull down on the blinds and look down into the parking lot below. Indeed, my Corolla is sitting in the handicapped spot right next to the building. The driver side window has been replaced.

They've covered their tracks.

Instead of panicking though, I watch the rest of the morning news. Then I spend several minutes sitting in front of my computer crying at the blank screen.

There are so many things, so much to deal with, so many loose **end**s and false starts to question and attempt to extrapolate reason from. So many bodies to identify, so many times I will have to try to tell this story, tell parents and friends and police and myself that everybody is dead, they're gone, and they're not coming back except in maybe a rerun, and I'll probably laugh when I say this and not know why, everyone looking at me strangely.

2

I LIGHT A CIGARETTE and stare straight ahead, trying to formulate a Plan B while attempting to understand what Plan A was, if anything. A cold wind causes me to shiver and my cigarette goes out. I do not relight it and drop it onto Preston's driveway.

Far away: cars. Sirens. The rhythmic din of construction work and roads being closed and restaurants opening and people cursing one another.

Here: Silence.

I walk up the driveway, looking back for the fifteenth time at the red FOR SALE sign that is posted by the road, along with a telephone number that I will call (but they will tell you what you already know, Ross, which is that the house has been for sale for months, that it has been vacant for a year, that its owners are dead and the son they left it to doesn't exist). The driveway is empty, and the pavement is clean. The bloodstains, the paste from torn open intestines, the feces and urine and sweat and vomit—all gone. For a long time I wonder if the entire area hasn't changed, as so much else has, until I see the place at the edge of the concrete near the back porch where the driveway is cracked and broken up. I remember the night that happened, and how the beer from that keg was so foamy no one could drink it.

The back porch is cleaned up and bare. The beer bottles and trash cans and old lampshades are gone, along with the broken glass and the bits of flesh and meat. When I try to open the back door, it is locked, and the windows are all intact.

When I get to the front porch, I feel the same confused disappointment. The area is clean, the floorboards have been scrubbed, the spider webs and wasp nests have been removed, and the old aroma of rotting wood and old beer has been replaced with a crisp smell of nothing. The front door is also locked, and when I turn back and look around the porch, I wonder if all of the Icehouse bottles, the drawings of cannibal-looking tribesmen, the conversations and debates and drunken rants were ever here at all.

I sit down and look out through the screen onto Main Street. A car passes by, and I am not at all suspicious of it.

Nothing happens.

When I drove up, the two schools were still there, but they looked vague, like old institutions, like they had been there forever and their existence prior to January was not up for debate. The changes to the buildings in the neighborhood were intact, but they did not feel new, or wrong. They did not feel cosmic. They felt like things that had happened long ago, that no one cared about, and that no one noticed. I wanted to ask passersby if these landmarks had always been there, if things were strange. I wanted to ask a bum if he heard gunshots and screams late Friday night. I wanted validation for our misery and suffering, and all I have received is an empty house in a dead part of the city.

I stand up and walk around back. Wielding a piece of the driveway, I go up onto the porch and smash through the window next to the back door. I let myself in, but cut myself on the broken window. For a long time I stand there with my eyes fixated on the thin trickle of blood running down my arm. Then I go inside.

Inside the house, things are terrifying. The carpet is now wood tile. The furniture is missing. The walls are a muted white and there are none of Preston's special order posters. The kitchen has a new fridge and dishwasher. When I look up, I see a black spiral staircase leading up to the second floor, and there is no longer a wooden banister running along the edge of the upper level. There is now an extension of the white walls, topped with a steel rail that runs into the stairs. Even realizing that I am safe, that there is nothing up there, I cannot bring myself to climb up and explore the second level.

The blood has been cleaned up, along with the gnawed-up bones and gnashed skulls. The furniture is all gone. Ghosts speak to me. I have an epiphany about the undead.

Back in the yard, the shed that Lydia, Mindy, Mark, and I stood on Friday night has been torn down, and a brown square of land has been left in its place. Seeds have been planted. Soon enough, grass will grow in this spot, and everything will finally disappear.

Just before I start hearing whispers coming from nowhere, I make a ridiculous trip around the house. That is when I see it. I stoop down and wipe the mud and dirt away from it. I stare at the tiny specks of dried blood along the surface. I pick it up, holding it in my hand, feeling its weight.

It's a crowbar.

3

"IN CASE WE DO NOT SPEAK AGAIN, Happy Birthday."

"Dad."

"What? Your birthday is in a few days. Did you think I would forget?"

"Where's Cordelia? And what about Mom—?"

"Listen to me carefully, Ross. I realize that so soon after such a visceral experience, you would feel the compelling need to go back to the place where all of this happened. I understand that, son. But you understand *this*: it will not happen again. You will not go back to the house on Main, nor will you ever go back to the school or the library. You will not contact the parents of the deceased. You will not respond to the news broadcasts and you will make no anonymous telephone calls. You are being watched, Ross. Remember that."

"Fuck you, Dad, I'll do it again, I don't care, I don't—"

"Your sister and Lydia might, however...Do you understand where I am going with this, son? Do you see where your actions may lead? We spared your girlfriend. We spared your sister. But let me assure you, these amends can be retracted. These people can disappear. Your mother, your friends, your own *life*, Ross—these are concepts and entities not to be taken for granted."

"Dad," I say into the phone, my eyes welling with tears. "Dad. What do I do?"

"Time will pass. You will prepare. You will be ready."

"Wait!" I shout. "Ready for *what*? Ready for...what?"

"Your efforts will be rewarded," he says hoarsely. His voice sounds different, as if it has been altered. "Your mother and I are moving in a few weeks. I thought I would tell you."

"To where?"

"She doesn't want to speak to you anymore."

"To *where*?" I repeat. "Dad."

"Your efforts will be rewarded," he says a final time before giving me a number to call "Once, and only once; you'll know when."

He hangs up just as the first drops of rain hit the windowsill outside.

4

January 31. It's raining. The sky is overcast and day turns into night without warning or justification.

On TV, I am watching Fox News, turning up the volume when a gray man with vacant eyes reports on the disappearance of several dozen young people in Florida on New Year's Eve. A report follows. There are shots of various sleepy areas of my town, but not Preston's house. There are shots of Pittsburgh and 89, but not Main Street. A reporter walks along the sidewalk on Highway 89, and tells us that the young people left for a night of partying at an undisclosed location, and have not been seen since. There are no clues. There have been no leads, and not a single one of the sixty-four youths have been recovered. It is as if they just vanished off of the face of the earth.

After the report, the gray man smiles and there is a story on a new reality show coming to Fox in the summer called *Eat the Corpse*, and it is causing quite a stir. And on ABC, there is talk of a new series much like *Survivor*, except the contestants are being chased by cannibals and the winner is the attractive man or woman who has not been used for stew meat.

The newscaster winks. Commercial.

I am about to head into the bathroom to dry heave when the telephone rings.

"Hello?"

There is static, and I can hear the rain pouring in the background.

"Hello?" I repeat.

"...Ross," she whispers hoarsely.

"Oh my god," I gasp. "Is this—are you—is this *Stacey?*"

"Ross...help me."

"Oh my god. *Stacey!* Is that *you*? Where are you?"

"Help me. Please. Oh my god."

"*Stacey*," I pant. "Where are you, baby? I'll help you. I'll be right there. Just tell me where you are and I'll help you."

"I'm—there's—the sky is falling, Ross. The sky is—"

The line goes dead.

Weaving in and out of traffic, which is thick for a Monday night, fishtailing in the water, which is coming down from the sky in torrents.

I wipe frost off of the windows with my hand, and then turn on the defroster full blast. I almost rear-**end** a tow truck.

When I traced the call and then dialed the operator, I was told that it came from a pay phone at the old train station across town. The operator began to tell me, sort of gratuitously I thought, that that particular station had been closed now for six years, ever since they built the new one. If I had not hung up, she might have then mentioned that the payphone Stacey called from was no longer in service.

The water is deep and when I hit the brakes in the empty parking lot, my Corolla slides up onto the curb. I leap out of the car and run up the sidewalk through the downpour. Ahead of me, the charred corpse of the city train depot looms. I scramble up a hill, slipping in mud, and climb over a concrete partition that hides the waiting area on the other side.

At first I don't see her. There is only the dark station and the covered walkway that stretches fifty yards in both directions. There are rotting benches and gray concrete posts covered with graffiti. Then I see the pay phone, gnarled and painted over with curse words and gang symbols. Below that, I see two bare feet and the beginnings of two legs that disappear behind another wall leading inside.

She is wrapped in a soaked green blanket. She is naked and covered in bruises and blue-green welts. Her face is battered and pale. She is unconscious, but moaning in her sleep.

I grab Stacey and hold her to my arms, sobbing hysterically.

"Baby, oh please wake up," I choke. "Stacey, it's Ross. Get up, sweetie. Wake up."

Her head draped over my shoulder, Stacey begins coughing violently. Water spews from her mouth and I cradle her in my arms, smiling despite my tears.

She gasps for air, and then spends the next several minutes trying to catch her breath. After she begins to breathe less violently, her eyes flicker and she opens them and looks up at me.

"I don't remember anything," she whispers hoarsely before hacking again.

"It doesn't matter," I tell her, lifting her up and hugging her so hard that she begins choking. I relax a little bit and everything else, everything that has happened, everything that might come and all of the suspicions I will someday have to lend credence to, melt away, and I kiss Stacey on her forehead and take her to a hospital.

5

"MY PARENTS MOVED," she says. "Their house is empty. I went by there today when I borrowed your car and a new family was moved in. I didn't recognize any of them."

"I never did meet your family," I say, bringing a piece of raw tuna up to my mouth with a pair of chopsticks.

"I know. I wanted you to. Do you think they're okay? Like, I waited and everything so that everything could die down, but when I went there—what if someone was watching me?"

"I'm sure they're not in any danger at all whatsoever," I say, looking away. "Everyone has been relocated. They probably miss you, but at least they're safe. My father moved Mom away too. Your family is going to be just fine. I was told that *I* was being watched. I don't think that you were, sweetie."

"Yeah," she sighs, looking down at a half-eaten plate of sushi. "I just wish I could have seen them before they left. Now they're gone. I'm left with *nothing*, Ross. And I'm never going to see my family again."

"Yes you will," I assure her, and when she starts crying across the table from me, I ask for the check and Stacey and I go home early and skip the movie we were going to see because she is a wreck and I am wracked with guilt.

6

It's warm and April and there is an art festival this month in the park that Stacey and I will probably go to. Over three months have gone by, and all has been quiet on our front. Stacey has not received any weird calls or had any strange visitors, and has moved in with me. She has a hard time getting over the experience, and cries almost nightly. I deal with this however, because this is the kind of behavior I guess one should expect after such a traumatic experience.

Immediately after she was released from the hospital (where she was treated for shock, a concussion, a cracked rib, a sprained ankle, no bites thank Christ and a lot of missing time with no one coming forward to account for it), Stacey tried to persuade me into letting her go back to the house on Main. I whispered into her ear while showering with her that I was instructed never to go back there, and never to ask questions. She brought it up once more and then gave up.

I told her my theory on her survival, which was that my efforts and silence in the matter resulted in her release by my father, who wanted to do this one thing for me. Stacey smiled slightly and then began to cry again, asking about Lydia and remaining oddly subdued when I told her about Preston.

Once Stacey moved in with me, which was not difficult since her only luggage was the green blanket I found her wrapped in, things changed.

I quit the movie business. I sold the equipment in the newspaper for next to nothing. Then I got rid of what stock I had of *Ilga, She-Wolf of the SS; The Gore Gore Girls; Cannibal Holocaust; Guinea Pig I; Audition; Last House on the Left; I Spit on Your Grave;* and the three dozen or so t-shirts by selling them on E-Bay or tossing them into the dumpster behind my apartment building. This bothered me a little more than I imagined it would. The night I threw out my last four or five shirts and a half-dubbed director's cut of *Army of Darkness*, Stacey and I celebrated with dinner, wine, and a joint that we smoked in my bedroom before having sex. Totally inebriated, I went on a ten minute rant about how much I might miss the movie business, how I really loved George Romero before he sold out with *Creepshow*. I wondered aloud what we were going to do for money and how I would pay for Stacey's thousands of dollars of hospital expenses and started crying, thinking about Jaime, about how Jaime accidentally swallowed Robin's blood when he turned. I thought about how no matter what, everyone was already dead that night but us and the bad guys. Not even the corpses stood a chance.

The semester had already started, so Stacey had to do without school, at least until the fall. It wouldn't have mattered. I found it doubtful that she could possibly have a good semester, after everything that had happened to her. So, she decided to be as creative as possible, painting and sketching and writing poems that she would only rarely let me see. She took a part-time job at a used bookstore in the tourist district not far from the Castillo de San Marcos and was gone a lot during the day. She read a lot of books from her store but complained nightly that print made her feel like she was rubbing two sticks together for fire.

I took a job. In fact, I took two. I worked as a waiter full time in the evening, and two days a week worked in the lobby of a hotel downtown not too far from Preston's old house. I have been told that the hotel is haunted, and believe this because vases mysteriously fall to the floor and shatter and sometimes when I get to work all of the paintings in the lobby have been hung upside down and on the wrong wall.

"What happened to you and my sister that night?" I finally have the courage to ask her one evening after the art festival.

"When?" she asks, her head rested against my lap as she watches TV and smokes a clove. "*That* night? When you were attacked near the road?"

"Yeah," I say. "That night."

"We ran away," she says. "Cordelia made me do it."

"I never really knew my sister," I lament.

"She loved you."

"How do you know?"

"She told me. She told me that night, after we ran away."

"What happened when you two ran off?" I ask.

"We were both…hysterical," she sighs, turning off the TV. The room is cold and silent and there is a presence that I wish I could shrug off. I have the feeling that I am in for a long story full of ellipses.

"After we left you," she begins, "we got about two hundred yards away when we decided to go back, but then we heard you yelling and the director giving out orders…We thought maybe you were okay…Cordelia and I didn't know *what* to do, Ross…We **end**ed up hiding in the alley behind the doctor's office…the one behind the school…Carolina…Why do they name streets after states?"

"I don't know," I whisper. "You know, I wanted you to stay. I told you to go, but I never really meant it."

"That's not a good trait, saying what you don't mean, Ross…We waited there for a really long time, and…we talked…There were sometimes gunshots and then after a while the whole city…went…crazy it seemed…And then the gunshots never stopped and we could hear screaming and car wrecks…and I remember saying to your sister, 'Oh my god, it's *everywhere,'* and she agreed and we stayed put and cried so much that our eyes stung and our faces swelled up…Did you know that your sister Cordelia *worshipped* you when you two were younger? I mean she *adored* you, Ross…She told me about when you were kids, and all the times you two would ride your bikes to the **end** of the street near the cemetery…and about the late-night snacks and you calming her down when she used to have bad dreams…She told me how much she wanted to be included when you and your friends were watching horror movies…She loves you…She was never a spy, really…It's a shame that you two never got along…"

"I know," I say.

"Cordelia told me that she was named after King Lear's only virtuous daughter, and that your father used to like Shakespeare before he turned into an evil man who did bad things to you and Cordelia…She told me that you were really into 60s counterculture but didn't tell anyone…and she told me that you were so smart and that she believed you would make it through this…and you did, right?"

"That's right," I mutter indifferently. "I did. Did you?"

"I was destined to," she whispers.

"I thought for sure you were dead that night, Stacey."

I get tear-eyed and melodramatic, like in a soap opera.

"We were meant to be together, Ross. Everyone knows that. It was fate."

"Fate?"

"Fate."

I nod. The lights in the apartment dim. My lease runs out in a month and Stacey and I have already decided to get out of this town. The beach is nice. Maybe near Stacey's school, my old school. I've been told that it's haunted by the ghost of the man from which it gets its name, just like seemingly every other landmark in that old town.

"It was almost dawn when I last saw your sister," Stacey says, breaking my train of thought. "There was a helicopter…cameras…our show needed a host like all the other ones, but maybe that's the idea, right?...There were halogen lights and fog machines and men whose breath steamed too much when they spoke…Mark showed up and I saw a man that looked a lot like you but older…it was your father, I realize now…Cordelia screamed when she saw him approaching…and then…"

Silence. A CD skips; static hisses.

"And then?" I ask when she does not go anywhere with her story.

"And then…"

"And then?"

"And then…"

"*Yes*? And then? And then *what*, Stacey?"

"And then I don't remember anything," she says, frustrated. "I woke up at the train station with you looking down on me and you looked pale and worried and this made me happy…You cared about me."

"You questioned it?" I ask.

"I used to. I don't any more. Apparently, sometime that New Year's, you came to your senses. Because of *zombies*. Who would have thought?"

Stacey stands up and stretches. She walks into the kitchen, opens the freezer, and pulls out a fresh box of cigarettes. She packs them and lights one before coming back into the living room.

"I *did* come to my senses that night," I say, nodding, spaced out. "I—I guess that it all came to me: Lydia was a bitch, my life was a sham, and I needed to be with *you*…I realized how much I was in love with you and all that other tacky shit. I realized that they're *us*. We're them and they're us."

I look up at her, waiting for a response. She hands me her cigarette, slips off the t-shirt she is wearing, and then we have sex and I pass out immediately afterward just as she turns the TV to Comedy Central and whispers something that I do not hear.

7

TIME PASSES QUICKLY. The summer comes: discounts at the restaurant I work at; Stacey quits her job at the bookstore and takes another one at a smoothie shop near our new apartment; we meet a guy at a porn boutique who we befriend and smoke marijuana out of a hookah with; Stacey switches from acrylics to oils; I read somewhere that the government plans where prisons are to be built based on the illiterate areas of the state; I look at George W. Bush, the Republican presidential nominee, and shudder pretentiously; the CIA traffics drugs; Stacey sobs hysterically when she reads an article online about Project Montauk and she tells me to "*think* about it, think about this really long and hard" and I tell her I will but do not because, really, I don't need to; I get a tan one afternoon with Stacey on the beach, and as I am lying there, being bitten up by sand fleas, I begin to mull over the possibilities of a multidimensional Apocalypse. One question always lingers: when the world **end**s, does it **end** just for one reality, or all of them?

New friends are made. There is talk sometimes over dinner or just after sex of marriage, but nothing comes of it because I can't get something out of my mind.

In the fall, after Stacey changes all of her personal information and goes back to school, I speak to my old guidance counselor and we talk about me maybe going back to get my Master's, but she shakes her head and I watch her triple chin jiggle when she does this just before being told that with my current financial situation, this is simply not feasible at this time, and since I am months behind with my student loan payments, more of them is almost certainly out of the question. I nod and break down crying. That night there is a party that Stacey insists we have to go to, which is not so bad since we live less than ten minutes from campus now.

On the way to the party, Stacey says she needs to tell me something.

"I need to tell you something," she says.

"Go ahead," I say. "Will I know any of these people here tonight?"

"Ross, I was pregnant."

I do not say anything.

"It was yours, before you ask. Back in December. I tried to tell you. After you first suspected Lydia of getting with Preston, I was going to tell you then. I was *about to*, in fact. But you were... You seemed kind of unresponsive. And I thought about it and thought about it. I was thinking of how things would be...I was taking all the facets into consideration. In the **end**, I realized that it would never work out between us. That's what I thought at the time, anyway. I was thinking about both of our best interests. But then...they took care of it, I guess. When I came to at the train station, I wasn't pregnant anymore. They aborted it before I could."

I do not say anything.

"Ross, I don't know what to say. I'm sorry, though. I should have told you first. But when I mentioned the idea of settling down with you, having kids, whatever...you weren't too receptive. I guess it doesn't matter. Their decisions were made, regardless of my own."

Lynn told me about the child. The crew knew it. My father knew it. How?

It is a long time before I say "So will I know any of these people tonight, or like, not?"

"London Calling" by the Clash is playing and there are kegs and a guy that looks familiar saunters by, giving me a glance that lasts one second too long. Stacey doesn't seem to know anybody here, and people look her way as if she is too old to be at a college party, and it dawns on me that she *does* look older than twenty-two, which is how old she's supposed to be.

We introduce ourselves to people and meet a girl who tells me that my aura is crimson. I see someone I went to school with at the party, and he stands by a keg for a while, reading a book called *The Elegant Universe* and when I approach him to ask why he is here, if he is as ashamed as I am, he closes the book and folds into the crowd and is gone.

Marijuana is smoked but I am not invited to participate and Stacey gets into a conversation with three other seniors about someone who committed suicide last week at this school, but no one can remember their name and it all kind of sounds like bullshit to me.

I **end** up outside, on a stairwell, getting some fresh air. Below me, three stout frat guys stumble around on the lawn, trying to toilet paper a sad oak tree. One of them tosses the roll toward the ground and falls over giggling. His two buddies fall on top of him shortly afterward, laughing as well until one of them pukes. Everything gets quiet and I start thinking about dead people.

Preston and I always assumed that in the original three films, becoming a zombie meant a complete transformation: The brain dies and is reanimated, but it no longer bares even the slightest resemblance to the one it was before the zombie virus entered. Basically, the zombie is a revived human being whose make-up has been altered. Instead of consciousness, of thoughts and feelings and desires and impulses, the living dead are simply vehicles for a perfect device of pure motorized instinct. The zombie has no aspirations or views; it has no deep contemplation. It does not think, and only follows the sound of the living until it is fed warm human flesh.

This is what we thought was the case. Before.

Standing on the metal stairwell now, looking out over the sleeping campus, I begin to doubt this archaic assumption, and instead begin to imagine a much worse scenario, if such a thing is possible.

No one knows what's going on in a zombie's mind. Not really. All we see is the way they behave. But what if there is more to this? It is conceivable that perhaps who you were before is still in there. What if you were bitten, die, and come back to life? What if you're still you in there, aching over your own death, swimming in memories and the desire to still be alive again, and yet you can do *nothing*, because your body has been reprogrammed to constantly and without pause hunt for a living person to devour? What if you are conscious the entire life span of this walking cadaver, watching your own hands grab exposed veins and rip apart faces? You watch through eyes that are no longer yours as a body that is now possessed eats the insides of your family and friends—your *children and soul mates*—and you are powerless to stop it, screaming silently in the deep unconscious. And you do this forever, until you see your own carcass slowly rot and decompose down to nothingness.

Over time, you learn. Perhaps you'll acquire the skill to control this vessel for moments at a time. You make the zombie attempt to drive a car, to hold a gun, to use the telephone or walk up an escalator. You try to recognize old friends and loved ones, attempt desperately to train this cadaver not to hurt the ones that were once important to you. Rare and lucky are you to succeed, however. If it isn't you who eats the one human that befriends you, then it's the other two million troops that do. And if one of your new kind for some reason does not converge upon the living, then the living will inevitably wipe itself out anyway, with its own madness and irrationality to blame. It's a hopeless situation. You are what you are and soon everyone you care about will join you in this hell, and you will be eternally powerless to stop it. After all, the zombie is a perfect machine, and the human mind will always be too weak to overpower it.

When I notice that I am crying, I look down at the lawn. All three frat guys are lying on the ground, staring up at me. One of them whispers something into his shirt collar. From behind me: a single flash.

8

New Year's approaches with a mounting sense of dread. There are television newscasters telling us that technically, 2001 is the first year of the new millennium, and our celebrations twelve months ago were premature.

Something is wrong and I am incapable of figuring out what it is. Something bad is going to happen.

I'm having a hard time making **end**s meet, even with the two jobs I am holding down. There is never enough money for all of the things I enjoyed from my life previous, and I am spending almost fifty dollars weekly on cigarettes. Saturday nights after I get off work I buy a twenty-four pack of beer, drink until I pass out, and spend all Sunday, my only complete day off from both the restaurant and the hotel, fighting migraines and terrible sinking feelings while Stacey reads her textbooks and looks lovely with a secret.

Stacey calls me into the living room from outside on our apartment balcony, where I am enjoying the cold weather and listening to the faint sound of Christmas music coming from downtown.

"Yes?" I ask, heading inside.

"Don't you want to help me decorate this tree?" she asks, standing next to our fake tree, which at this moment looks so pathetic and abysmal that I want to sink to my knees and cover my head with my hands.

"I was thinking about getting back into movies again," I say casually, walking past her and into the kitchen, where I pull out a bottle of Coors Light.

"Do you think that's such a good idea?" she asks, staring at me menacingly. The living room lamps are turned off and the only light comes from several candles she has lit around the room. The effect is disturbing.

"I think…that I don't have a lot of options?" I say-ask, looking away. "We would have more money if I did. I wouldn't have to drive all the way back to our old town to get to work. I'm just saying that it's a viable option, that's all."

"Your equipment is gone and Pres's collection is no longer available," Stacey says flatly. "How viable an option is it?"

"Well, it's not impossible—"

"If you don't like driving back and forth everyday, then get a job here in St. Augustine, Ross. Find another haunted hotel. Better yet, do something with your college degree. But for God's sake, don't go back to selling *that* shit. Be smarter than that."

"I'm just saying, Stacey—"

"Haven't you *gotten* it yet?!" she screams, heading into the bedroom and slamming the door behind her.

After.

Stacey is looking down at my penis, now shriveled and reticent, and smiles.

"Déjà vu," I whisper, looking down at it with her.

"Ross," she whispers in the darkness.

"Yes, dear?"

"Why do you love me?"

I groan.

"No, seriously, you idiot. It bothers me. Why do you love me?"

"Why do I love you?" I ask back. I can't see her face. "Do we have to go into this right now?"

"We just had make-up sex, sweetie. Of course we have to talk passionately to one another. Just for a minute. It won't kill you."

"So you want to know why I love you," I say once more. "Well, you're…you…make everything…riveting?"

"So what am I? A girlfriend or a suspense novel? Ross, try harder."

"Stacey, you make my life interesting. You twist it around and do everything not perfectly, but just right and with still just the tinniest bit of peculiarity so that I always remain dumbfounded as to what your next move will be. Let me think…Well, you like sushi. You've seen *Carnival of Souls*. When we hear about a new ride at a theme park, neither of us care. Sometimes you make references to Bob Dylan and old-school 70s Ralph Nader, and this impresses me greatly. Your favorite song by Radiohead is "The Tourist." You agree that *Kids* was just exploitation and not high art, but that *Kids in the Hall* was the most brilliant television show *and* movie ever conceived. When you go down on me you look up at my face and sometimes you smirk and I like it. Everything you do reminds me of some clever spy who is only halfway invisible, and when we have sex you say things that would make me giggle any time other than in bed. Your childhood stories are actually funny. You don't pressure me into anything except the things I need to be pressured into, and you listen to my stories about all the kids I knew who went missing when I was thirteen. You've picked up a hitchhiker before and you've been to Hawaii and sometimes when you sneeze there's more snot that comes out than when a guy would do it. You saved my life and—and—"

Stacey waits for almost a full minute after my tirade before she says anything else.

"Well that last one was pretty big," I say.

"So what does that all add up to?" she asks, only pretending to be confused.

"These are all qualities that add up to a girl that I am madly in love with. You seem to have been designed by God, Yahweh, whatever, *perfectly*. I guess that, uh, you made all the right moves."

Stacey thinks about this for a moment and smiles, says, "Like a chess game."

"Um…I guess," I admit reluctantly. "You're weird, Stacey."

"You love me though," she says in the dark.

"I do indeed."

"So, then why did it take so long for you to figure it all out?" Stacey asks carefully, aware of how precarious any conversation is that at all relates to last New Year's.

"I'm not really sure of the answer to that," I shrug, finding my cigarettes on the bedside table. I light two, handing her one. "But life-altering experiences sometimes give you that epiphany you were always in need of, right?"

She doesn't say anything for a long time, and we smoke in the darkened bedroom. A car's headlights flash through the tiny cracks in the blinds, slide along the bare white wall. They disappear.

"I made all the right moves and now we're together," she finally says.

"I love you," I whisper to the stranger next to me. "Everything is perfect now."

"I'd agree," she whispers back.

"In our case, the **end** was where we started from."

9

THE **END** IS WHERE WE START FROM is scrawled in blood across a wall on the outside of the prison, and I wonder who among the soldiers and TV people and business attachés might have quoted TS Eliot. My father comes to mind but quickly vanishes. I think of my sister and my eyesight blurs with tears.

I finally navigated my way from the confines of the prison, and when I first reached the exit, I was expecting the sunlight to blind me, but instead stumbled out into a well-lit night.

Everything feels too real, too cold, too odorous and textured once I leave the confines of the prison building, and I lose my balance and fall to the grass, which is warm and sticky with blood and pieces of rotting flesh.

The power inside was out, and I spent almost an hour slipping around on grease and sweat that the tile was lathered with. Every time I fell over in the darkness I would scream out and the noise would shred through the silence and everything would become even more terrifying. From somewhere close would come the slurping sounds of flesh being devoured, the crunching of someone's finger bones, and the splatter of viscera across the concrete floor. My weapon would escape my grasp and I was constantly having to pick it up before moving on another few feet before starting all over again, shuddering at the fact that the munching sounds seemed to always be getting closer.

After finally gaining my footing, I stagger my way out of the courtyard and toward the main gate. I grip my crowbar tautly. It is not difficult to get out of the complex, as the high fences have been toppled over, and the razor wire has been trampled and driven into the mud by thousands of feet. In a few spots ghouls lie helplessly on the ground, their legs or arms caught in the wire.

Huge pools of blood have collected around the undead, and they weakly snap at me as I approach with the crowbar and put the ones remaining out of their misery.

Before I walk over the downed fences, I grab the 9-mm mini-Uzi still being clenched by the totally denuded carcass of a soldier. I move into the darkness, taking the main road back toward town.

They ignore me. I pass clumps of three or four at a time, reaching in through the shattered windows of cars, emerging with a tongue, a face, some elderly woman's vagina and six inches of her stomach and a piece of intestine. As I tiptoe by, they look up, narrow their grayed-over eyes, and then quickly go back to their feast. Huddled around a smoldering car that crashed into a tree just off the highway leading back into town are seven more of the things, including one of the soldiers from the prison. I recognize him and aim the Uzi at his forehead, most of which has been eaten away. I fire a burst of bullets that dislodge the top of his skull and send bits of meat and bone flying. The other zombies ignore the scene and continue eating the charred carcasses of a family of four. I am confused, but move on.

The trees in the woods on both sides of me tilt and sway in the night breeze. Leaves rustle. Pine needles shriek. In the distance of every direction come the far-away moans of legions and legions of the undead. I hear galloping horses somewhere nearby. Every so often, I see a shadow.

In town, the streets are demolished. Cars have crashed into every wall and lightpost. Water spews out of a downed hydrant like in a movie. A gang of undead saunter up the main street through the quiet prison town, peering inside shattered windows of storefronts before moving along. They all ignore me. Everywhere are piles of corpses, shotgun shells, necks, pieces of arms and fat and a stench that only sporadically sends me reeling. There are fires put half-out by what must have been rain earlier in the day. Dispatched cadavers burn atop a huge pyre in the middle of the street near a park where kids' bodies are eaten by bugs and four or five zombies. Ash rains down from the sky and coats my jacket like apocalyptic snow. I walk away from the scene toward the restaurants.

I step around a Honda and through the shattered window of a little café a ways from the nauseating smell of the fire up the road. The door to the restaurant is blocked by someone's torso and a decapitated head that is still biting into its armpit. In the cooly-lit red confines of the eatery, I hop over the counter and make my way into the fridge. Fifteen minutes later, I wipe the blood from one of the bar stools and sit down to eat what might be the finest sandwich ever created. The funeral pyre outside provides the equivalent of candlelight. Cold November winds drift through the open window into the café, and I shiver. I hear the not-so-far-off sounds of a truck screeching to a stop. Minutes later, there is the light tap of footsteps coming from the street outside the restaurant.

10

On New Year's Eve, I decide to go back to Preston's old house. It is not so much an impulsive decision as it is one that someone else made for me. Something is wrong, and I just can't put it all together. But things are happening in my new life far too reminiscent of my old one. Only this time around, it is me doing the shadowing, which may not be as promising as it originally seemed.

There are several things that have built up to this moment:

Sometimes the dishwasher is open when we get home when it should be shut.

I get strange customers at the restaurant who leave large tips but ask me things like "How do I get to I-95 from here?" and then, after telling these suited men and familiar-looking women that I don't know, that I-95 is closed, that it never existed in the first place, and Daytona Beach is now a leper colony, they mutter things like "The Interstate system was designed so that one mile in every five must be straight, so that in times of war and other emergencies the straight sections can be used as emergency airstrips for military aircraft. In fact, did you know, Ross, that the Interstate system's official title is The National Defense Highway System?" before they get up, buy a paper, and leave the restaurant.

The phone rings. I answer and the person on the other **end** hangs up after five or six clicks and a single distant beeping sound.

At the hotel job I rarely keep up with anymore, the haunts continue, as do sideways glances and rooms for four being rented by lone men in dark suits smoking cigarettes.

I am followed everywhere I go, usually by a Ford Taurus, but sometimes an Escort or even a Focus.

And Stacey. There's something wrong with Stacey.

She hasn't cried over the incident since August, and even then I walked in on her bout of weeping. Stacey was on the bed when I got home from the restaurant, her makeup perfect, her hair in a neat ponytail. And yet her face was covered with tears (which she would not allow me to rub away) that she ran into the bathroom to wipe off. After she first arrived in my life again, Stacey would sob hysterically at least twice a week, and we would have **end**less hours of conversation regarding all of the specifics: who, what, where, when, and especially *why*, in regards to what happened to all of us. We would discuss everyone who died and what made each death a tragedy; we'd go on and on about Preston, and how he could have been involved, although during these talks Stacey would typically leave the conjecturing to me and smile secretly to herself; we would decide over and over again that Lydia was all right, and that we hoped she was okay even though we both knew that maybe she was dead; Cordelia was only brought up in the smallest increments, usually because I avoided the subject. This was the Ross and Stacey rigmarole for almost eight months, and then it just stopped.

There are other things as well.

She gives me glances sometimes. They are not wanton, nor are they genuinely romantic or curious or even disgusted. They are glances one gives when studying a subject that is simply not that interesting.

Stacey supposedly goes to school, but during her finals week, I was walking the trash up to the dumpster in the front of the complex as she passed in my car, which she borrowed that day because she "didn't have a ride." When she stopped, however, she did not make a right turn, as she should have to get to her school. She made a left, and didn't come home until six that night. This places her finals at marathon length, and at a different location than the college. Further, in regards to school, I was leafing through Stacey's college notebook, and instead of finding pages and pages of detailed notes on abnormal psychology, or animal behavior, or industrial psyche, I found coded scribbles, sketches of me, and on the third page, the following quote: "For there was never yet fair woman but she made mouths in a glass." It's a quote I recognized, having been related to someone like Cordelia. It's from *King Lear*.

Because of school, Stacey has no job, and relies on scholarships, grants, and one student loan to make **end**s meet. By all rationale, she should be the archetypical poor college student. And yet, one night while she was in the shower singing a song that I don't think she should have known, I opened her purse to find a cigarette and discovered three hundred dollars in her wallet.

I've never met Stacey's parents. When she was "returned" to me, her mother, father, and adopted brother Malik had moved away. I thought for a long time that, like my sister, Lydia, and maybe even my own mother and father, they were relocated. That the producers had gotten to them too and moved them to some distant location in the desert. This seems more and more unlikely with each day that passes. What is even more disturbing is Stacey's relative disinterest in their whereabouts, safety, or in any possible future reunion.

There's more. Before they attacked, Stacey Shimmerly's rants and commentaries seemed totally random and yet altogether perfect for any time capsule of that moment. Now, they simply seem *well-written.*

And then there is the fact that she is on her way to Preston's house on New Year's Eve.

We agreed that we would handle this New Year's with the utmost care and sensitivity. There would be no camaraderie, no banter, no movies or alleyways or TV. There would be no parties. It would simply be Stacey and me, alone, drinking from a bottle of cheap champagne, flinching at the fireworks.

So when Stacey approached me this morning about going out for a while, about leaving me alone on of all days this one, my suspicions finally bubbled over, and I decided that she would be followed.

"Sweetie, do you care if I hang out with my friend Melanie for a while today? If it's weird, then don't worry about it. I just thought…"

"No," I said, staring at the monitor, looking up the latest releases on the Something Weird online catalogue. "No, babe. Go ahead."

"I mean, it's New Year's Eve…Maybe I should stay here with you."

"No…it's okay. We'll be together all night. If you want to go out with your friend, that's fine. I want you to be happy."

I lit a cigarette and turned to her standing next to me, staring as if she was expecting me to say something in particular, which I didn't.

"Well, then she'll be here around one. I'll only be gone for an hour or two. We were just going to go out for lunch or something, and she's paying, so it's a good deal."

I had met Melanie. She was another "college student," attractive and blond like Stacey, but like Stacey, looked older than she supposedly was. We hung out together briefly a couple of times, and I spent most of the evening on both occasions half-listening while the two went on and on about novels they had read, EM Forster's mutant baby, parties they would not be attending, lectures by professors who did not speak a word of English, and different kinds of acid. I would stare at the walls, visualize great paintings, and wonder if you could kill yourself by shooting a gun into the side of your neck. At the **end** of each night I hung out with Melanie, I tossed and turned in bed trying to pinpoint where I knew her from, and why she kept staring at me during dinner.

I looked at my girlfriend, beautiful and pale and ethereal, and gave a ghastly smile.

"No," I said cautiously. "It's fine. Go out. Have fun. I'll see you all night tonight. For New Year's Eve."

At exactly one o'clock, Melanie picked Stacey up in her BMW 320i. The moment the car pulled out of the parking lot downstairs, I grabbed my binoculars, scrambled to my car and tore out of the apartment complex. Once I got to the main road, I had to make a quick decision: left or right. Remembering what I saw a couple of weeks ago, I pulled out in front of oncoming traffic and made a hard left, flooring it.

It was not long before I spotted the black sedan about a hundred yards ahead of me. I slowed down, but gained on it until I was about seventy-five feet back, feebly attempting to hide my car behind an SUV as we headed up Anders to 56th, and then from 56th to Beachfront. I could barely see Stacey's shadowy figure through the tinted windows, but I could see enough to know that she was calm, and not plucky and hyper as she pretended to be when she hung out with Melanie in the past. Even more disturbing, I could make out another person in the car, in the back seat. Someone besides Melanie, besides my girlfriend. It was a man.

When Melanie made a left onto Highway 89, I no longer needed to follow, since I knew where Stacey was headed. But I did anyway, because in its own terrible way, it is more gratifying to *watch* it all fall apart than to look back and simply know that it has.

Lynn told me last New Year's to sever everything. He told me that everyone would betray me, and that there were virtually no limits to the loss I'd be capable of experiencing. How many examples, how many harbingers of things to come, have I ignored?

From 89, Melanie makes a left onto Main Street. I have pulled into a McDonald's parking lot about a quarter of a mile behind them. I think I was spotted on the way over here. In fact, considering who I am dealing with, there is no way I *wasn't*. Stacey *knows* that I followed her, and she knows that I will be pulling up in front of Preston's house soon enough.

I wait in the parking lot for a long time. I'm not exactly sure how long. I go inside the restaurant, buy a Coke, take two sips of it, and then throw it away, feeling nauseous. Then I start my car and pull out of the parking lot, toward Preston's house.

11

"You've always played the bad guy. You know that?"

"It was all part of the plan," Preston says, lighting a cigarette. "How have you been, man?"

"Well…I'm eating in an abandoned café in a town full of zombies, Preston. Obviously, things could be better."

"That's—that's too bad, Ross." He smiles.

Preston Nichols looks good. His hair is shorter, and he has highlights now and a deep tan, "Hawaii last month" he explains. He is thin but muscular, and where he once grew a precocious goatee, he now has a very trendy Van Dyke. Preston has dressed well for the occasion, sporting tight black jeans by Diesel, a sweater by Hugo Boss, and an Armani jacket with several pockets, all of them probably filled with small firearms loaded with blanks, cyanide tablets that he is currently unaware of, tape recorders, and cell phones that will not work.

"It seems like you were trying to give yourself away," I point out, finishing my sandwich. I light a cigarette of my own.

"Ross, you act as if I've been a part of this since the age of twelve or something. That's not the way it is at all. I never even spoke to your father until after my mother and father were relocated and I was made aware of my future role in all of this."

"There are so many things I don't understand though," I say, looking down at the floor.

"Hey," Preston says. "You think *I* do?"

I do not respond.

"Come on, Ross. Let's go for a walk."

The fires are still burning. The smell is rancid, but I have grown accustomed to the odor by now, and the sight of dozens of living dead people devouring body parts, clumsily trying to open car doors or buy tickets at a small movie theater, and browsing through clothing stores no longer phases me. I bundle up every time the wind blows, but am always still cold.

"The state is a war zone," Preston tells me. "All of the borders into Alabama and Georgia have been quarantined, and the crew has made sure that none of the cast leaves the state. The survivors have tried, but…Well, your father's project is going smoothly, to say the least. Everything has gone off without a hitch. The show is a huge success, as they say."

"Terrific," I mutter, nodding.

He goes on with the details of the operation: Tampa, Miami, and Orlando have been bombed, and no longer exist. The same goes for the Keys and, soon, Tallahassee.

"You ever read *Alas, Babylon*?" I ask upon hearing all of this.

"No," he says. "But did they make it into a movie?"

"There's one thing I don't understand," I say. "Well, actually, there are *a lot* of things I don't understand. But this I have to know."

"What is it?" Pres asks.

"Who was the old man I saw on New Year's Eve? And the kid? Who were they? Were they part of the episode?"

Preston says nothing for a long time.

"What old man?" he finally says. "Kid? I don't know what you're talking about."

"And everything changing," I say carefully. "Why was everything changing?"

When I look up, the moon has disappeared behind a cloud, but there is still light pouring down from above us. The sky is opening up.

"Ross, it's obvious that this ordeal was extremely traumatizing," Preston says unsteadily, muffled by loud thunder rumbling in the distance.

"I think…that everything…opens up…" I begin, swallowing. "I think that we all have it wrong…That when the world finally **end**s, it's not just for us…It's for…It's for *every* existence…And they come together, right?"

"Do you want to kill me, Ross?" Preston says quietly.

I consider the question for a long time.

"No," I finally answer. "Not anymore. I mean—you and my father—and what happened—what I saw that day—I spent a long time thinking of nothing but the fact that I would kill any and all of you if I were ever given the chance."

"Mm-hmm, mm-hmm," Preston nods. "But…"

"But I realized something, Pres."

"And what is that, Ross?"

"I realized that if I ever did see you again, then there would definitely be a reason for it."

"Okay, that's great," Preston says. "But what's the reason?"

We pass a small shopping mall, where hundreds of ghouls have congregated. I can hear them pounding on the glass doors, trying to get inside, moaning with frustration. On the other side of the street, a teenage girl with no left eye saunters out of a small clothing store, pulling on a cute new jacket. She slobbers all over it, and then clumsily grabs the price tag hanging from a button and inspects it. Her eye goes wide and she shuffles out of the coat, dropping it on the ground and heading back inside the store.

Preston hasn't noticed the threatening movement all around us.

"My father told me five years ago that my efforts would be rewarded," I say.

"Ross, your father told you a lot of things," Preston sighs. "Further, there were plenty of things he opted *not* to tell you as well. Right?"

"Sort of."

"I mean, how long was it before you even found out that your mother had passed away?"

"Almost a year," I answer honestly.

"And from what I've been told, the only reason you did find out was because you saw it on the news."

"Well, it's hard to cover up something as devastating an epidemic as that," I say. "I don't care who you are or who you assassinated."

"Point being, I wouldn't put much stock in what your father or anyone else has to say. Hell, that includes *me*. If I were you, I would cast doubt upon everything that I said right this *second*."

"I'll keep that in mind, Preston."

Dead people slowly wander out of a chain restaurant. More emerge from a gas station, and there are others slowly gaining on us from behind. Years of imperviousness and disdain towards them have crippled Preston's sense of awareness, his defense. His sense of impending doom.

"But anyway, they wanted me to come down here and just talk to you for a while," Preston is explaining. "If it went well, they might want to do a reunion show. That would be neat, wouldn't it? You'd get to see Cordelia and Lydia again. What do you think? Not to mention you might finally get the chance to settle the score with your father and his friends. That would be a real crowd-pleaser, I think."

"Not so much as other things might," I say quietly, smiling.

"Well, I'm here to find out what you're going to do next, what you're going to do to survive, how you feel, and all the other blah, blah, blah. I hope you don't mind the company."

"I don't."

"Or the tape recorder."

"I don't mind that, either."

"Fan*tast*ic."

The moaning has grown louder, but he ignores it since he believes there is no crew or director to give orders to them. They are simply aimless wanderers, retarded cannibals, voodoo zombies with no *houngan* to direct their actions.

"Do you want to finish what you were going to tell me earlier?" Preston eventually asks after a prolonged silence. He glances over his shoulder at the creatures gaining on us. "Shouldn't you be more alert?"

"I am alert."

"What were you going to say about your father?"

"My father told me that my efforts would be rewarded. Until tonight, I thought he was referring to Stacey. Now, I don't think that's true."

"Okay…" Preston considers this. Something occurs to him but he dismisses it. I actually see him slightly shake his head in disbelief. "If he said that your efforts and everything would be rewarded…and he *wasn't* referring to you getting the girl…then what was he talking about?"

"Five years ago, Lynn, the original director of the New Year's Eve shoot, explained to me how the members of the project were screened, vaccinated, and all sorts of other things so that they would be rendered virtually invisible to these cadavers all around them. Then he was attacked and died shortly afterward."

"I remember," Preston says. "You kind of got attached to him, didn't you?"

"Something like that," I murmur.

A young girl with no arms raises her head from the pit of an obese man's crotch, covered in black and red grime. She snarls and makes her way toward us from a parking lot.

"You want to take care of that?" Preston asks me. I see beads of sweat forming on his brow.

"Sure," I say, playing along. I aim the Uzi that I procured from the prison yard and fire several rounds into the girl's face. She falls.

"Go ahead and finish," Preston says. "I think I'm going to head out. This whole thing…Well, I'll be honest. I got out of the horror movie scene when I was eighteen years old. All the years after that, I was just following orders and reciting my lines. You know?"

"Yes," I say. "I know. But it doesn't matter."

"What doesn't matter?"

"When my father told me I would be rewarded, I think he meant in the only way a man like him could possibly understand."

They surround us and close in. The stench is overwhelming, but I relish it and take deep breaths and savor the moment.

"If you can't trust evil spies and reality show producers, who can you trust, right?" I ask.

And it is that moment that there is a single flash, and Preston spots the radiation-suited cameramen filming us from atop several buildings.

"Oh—oh my fucking *god!*" he shrieks, reaching into his jacket and pulling out a small Derringer. "Those mother-*fuckers!*"

"I think you're fucked, Preston," I hiss, backing away as he takes aim at the closest corpse, a naked woman wearing nothing but a toe tag.

Screaming with rage, he fires. Instead of a bullet piercing the woman's forehead, however, the gun they gave Preston explodes. For a moment, Preston disappears behind sparks and stray flames and thick gray smoke. When it clears, he is down on his knees, staring panicked at where his hand was.

Zombies brush past me on both sides. I do not exist to them.

The last thing ever uttered from Preston's lips is "I'm sorry," an apology made to no one, before the living dead converge upon him.

I light a cigarette and watch.

First, claws dig into the thin veil of skin just under his right eye. It is torn open and ripped downward, exposing the muscles of his cheek. Blood spurts out in every direction, putting my cigarette out. I have to light another one.

While his face is torn away, two others bite into the stub at the **end** of his arm. Meat is ripped off of the bones near his wrist, and one of them grabs his other arm and slowly peels away the yellow flesh, revealing veins and quivering muscle. Preston is screaming, choking on his own blood.

One of the zombies has learned to use a rusty saw, and clumsily places it on Preston's thigh. He slowly slices Preston's leg off. Three of the undead feast on it once it is removed from the body.

Preston is still alive. He continuously comes in and out of consciousness, reviving with a liquid-soaked scream from his dream state every time something new is severed or bitten in two.

They grab his hair and pull at it until finally his scalp comes loose and the skin at the roof of his head rips off, exposing a glistening skull covered in milky red blood.

"Ross…kill me," he gurgles, but I pretend not to hear him. "Ross, kill me. Kill me—"

One bites into his belly button and twists its head back and forth like a starved dog, tearing his stomach wide open like a huge budding flower. Intestines burst out of the crater and are immediately fought over. When a teenage guy and what was once his girlfriend both bite into the slippery snake-like cords, paste oozes out and the smell makes me gag.

His expensive pants are crudely torn apart, followed by his boxers, which are full of shit and piss. A tiny boy with a wound in his neck is the first to clench his teeth against Preston's penis and testicles. The shriveled appendage disappears amidst black blood spraying into the air. When one of his testicles bursts, I turn away and vomit.

It is not until they reach into his neck, blood spilling out by the pint now, and jerk his spine out of place and his head comes loose from the body and rolls away that Preston Nichols finally dies. His single eye stares ahead in frozen terror and anguish. Then it pops out of the socket when a zombie stomps on it and then cracks open the skull on the concrete. They eat his brains.

12

When her lips touch his, her eyes meet mine and I suck in and hold my breath until I have safely driven far enough away from the old house on Main before I scream so hard that I transcend time and am transported back to a moment not too long ago and yet still hazy like a terrible nightmare you're unable to ever totally forget. I relive a moment when I was on this same stretch of pavement, shrieking in anguish after catching Preston with another girlfriend, Lydia, and I can visualize the exact facial expression he made that night in the shower when I walked into the room: placid, slightly confused, and yet confident, as if he were simply an actor whose stage partner delivered a cue slightly sooner than anticipated in rehearsal. I wonder if Preston Nichols would make that same expression now, *this* New Year's Eve, had he been aware I was watching when he kissed Stacey. I wonder if I would be accused of simply being *early* if I had walked right up to them as Stacey grabbed his cock through his pants and whispered something about "later" while rubbing Preston's face the same way she does mine, just before heading down to the driveway and getting into a car with Melanie, who smiled when Stacey whispered something into her ear, a secret.

13

AND I WONDER how long it will be before they realize I am gone, not even knowing who *they* are, flooring it back to the apartment near the old beach town, and making a mental list of what to pack and trying to decide where to go. Something I told Stacey after I found her at the train station, long before I began noticing how wrong this statement actually was, keeps playing back over and over in my head, like an old home movie:

I looked down at Stacey lying naked beneath the bed sheets, her legs intertwined with mine. I opened my mouth to speak.

"Stacey, I've got to tell you something."

"What is it?" she asked. She leaned her head up and gave me a gentle, loving kiss. "You don't want to do it again, do you? Because sweetie, I think that she's been rubbed raw—"

"No, it's not that," I said, smiling.

"Then what?"

"You know, Stacey, when I'm with you…for the first time in my life, nothing seems to be counting downward."

12

AFTER BLUDGEONING THE RADIATION-SUITED CAMERAMAN, the camera, and the lone corpse into piles and puddles, I take out a duffel bag from the closet, grab the hollowed-out copy of *Apocalypse Culture II* from the top shelf of my book case, and throw everything onto the bed. I take out the five hundred dollars I have been saving from the book and toss it aside. I pack clothes, toiletries, and my crowbar into the bag. Then I run into the kitchen, feel along the wall in the cabinet where I keep the wine glasses, and retrieve the scrap piece of paper that I wrote the number down on. I dial it, and when my father answers the phone, there is a succinct conversation that **end**s with me asking, very carefully, "Which prison? When?"

11

On the way to another New Year's Eve Party, looking for safety in numbers, loading the gun that I found where my father told me I would.

10

I AM A THIRTY-ONE YEAR-OLD PROFESSIONAL MISANTHROPE and all-around loser. I have made an apathetic world my enemy, and what should have been my enemies instead my closest friends. I am a mouse who has put his trust in the snakes. I have ignored the cameras, the glances, the shadows and the software and the ethereal signs for far too long. I am but one person of an entire generation who learns nothing until they are gagging on the blood of their own sigh.

All over the world, people are screaming. They are praying. They are clenching husbands and wives, distant detached children, drinking buddies, and strangers on the street, all within cold cities encased in glass.

Having suddenly and inexplicably decided that I want—no, *have to* see the beach, I am heading away from the interior of the state in a newly acquired Land Rover (keys left in the ignition, blood and viscera smeared on the dash). There are thousands of them, wandering aimlessly, shuffling toward the vehicle as it meanders along a congested highway. But it doesn't matter. I don't exist to them. Not anymore.

Only the dead remain oblivious to what is happening all around us. Just another facet of their perfect being, their total peace with the world. Just one more way that God created them in his image.

It wasn't us he designed after himself. It couldn't be. Right now, realizing what deep shit we're in, us *living* people are running around, saying and doing what we should have said and should have done a long time ago. Fucking, drinking, blowing our own brains out, blowing other people's brains out…no one understands grace in defeat; no one comprehends that this was always happening, even if it is only at this moment that it is happening to us.

No plethora of existences could squelch the moans of the Apocalypse.

It takes me a little over an hour to reach my old town, and then another half hour to bypass the stalled vehicles and wreckage to make it to the coast. Then I walk along the shore for about a quarter of a mile, at which point it feels right. I stop and wait.

I stand on a beach that I once frequented with Preston, Lydia, and Stacey and light a cigarette. Despite the terrible sky behind me, over the ocean, the heavens are clear and the stars shine brilliantly. The awesome sight almost brings me to tears, until I see a figure moving toward me from down the beach.

It could be anyone. It could be my father. Or the ghost of my dead mother. It could simply be another walking corpse. It might be Stacey, and I shudder at the thought.

But it's not.

It's Cordelia. My sister. I haven't seen her since the morning of January 1, five years ago.

As she approaches, she walks unsteadily, touching her hair, looking up into the sky, and out into the infinite black ocean. My palms sweat as she draws near, and I find myself actually afraid of her, it's been so long and so many tragedies since we last spoke. When she gets closer, I can distinguish her features. She is wearing a sweater and new jeans, and I can tell even from far away that she was crying but is not anymore. The wind blows and she pushes her hair, now a lustrous dark red, out of her face.

As she comes to a stop a few feet away, I smile and wave awkwardly.

She smiles and waves awkwardly back.

"Hey, Ross," she finally says.

"Hey, Sis," I say, and nothing else is said for a long time.

We embrace. Her hair blows in the wind, and she looks down at the sand beneath our feet. She smells genuine, and I clench her even harder and have a hard time breathing.

"I thought you would be here," she says after inhaling deeply.

"I got your message," I reply. "How did you—never mind. It doesn't matter."

"Oh my god, Ross, so much has happened," she whispers.

"Yeah. A lot has happened."

"A lot…" She trails off, tears welling in her eyes. "I mean, with Mom…there's so many things I want to tell you. Do you know about Stacey?"

"I know about her," I murmur. "A lot has happened."

"So what now then?"

"I don't know."

"Me neither."

We embrace again and stand very still for what seems like a while.

"Let's go for a walk," she says quietly.

We amble up the beach. She tells me of her life, of the surveillance and the last conversation with our father. She talks about the papers signed and the strange phone calls and the news reports that sent her swooning and fighting nausea. She speaks of the worry and fear that I still sense in her voice, even as the world is clenched and warmed by the sweat of Armageddon. She apologizes for things unspoken of, and I nod knowingly. I ask her about the desert.

Cordelia and I walk for miles and for the first time in my life, I feel that I could talk to this girl, my sister, forever. Even as the world moans and sighs and drifts away, we are both happy, and only once or twice point up to the heavens or admit to being scared. She asks me after the longest silence of the night what I am thinking about. I tell her that I am thinking about a party I was at a long time ago, but not the one she is probably imagining.

9

FOR FOREVER IT SEEMS, the **end** of something was all I could relate to. I always felt that everything needed reorganization; to fall apart and be rebuilt from scratch. I could see it in every aspect of my world: in every restaurant, in every music store, in every crowded room and on the corner of every street. I could see it etched across the faces of a billion doomed youth and deteriorating primogeniture that no one listened to. They all wanted to see it **end** just as badly as I did, even if they were too intoxicated on the formaldehyde of the world to realize it.

I shrug and enter the party.

The party tonight is weird. It is near the campus in an old red brick tenement where college students are stacked like cordwood into rooms and instructed to call it an apartment. When I get there, still shaken, the gun stuffed down my pants as if I was a gang-banger, the familiar sight of a dozen or so partiers milling around outside is comforting, and I decide to stay. Besides, I briefly glimpse one of Stacey's emissaries taking pictures from across the street.

Inside, the first thing I hear is At the Drive-In, the line "*Have you ever tasted skin?*" blaring from some apartment on the second floor. Then I hear the other songs, the other stereos being played in all of the different rooms because no one can agree on what music best heralds the next millennium. There are people who all look and sound like me hanging around in the hallways. College kids and the occasional townie continuously stream in and out of individual apartments, of which most of the doors are opened, and I am impressed by the apparently unanimous decision of over half the tenants to throw this New Year's soiree.

"You only have eight pints of blood in your entire body," a guy says seductively to his girlfriend, and they begin making out.

I wander into the first apartment on the right, and follow some people to where I am guessing a keg is. Instead, I enter a large living room where six kids are taking shots of something bright green in matching glasses while playing Russian roulette with heroin needles. I try to leave the area as quickly as possible and a girl with curly brown hair and a large plastic bead necklace snaps a photo of me cringing in the hallway. She folds back into the crowd, drunkenly slurring, "Don't worry. It's 1983. The creature has been contained."

Up some rickety stairs that send me reeling with terrible flashbacks to last New Year's Eve, I run into someone that I met with Stacey, a big guy who says his name is Damon. We chat for a bit, and I keep fingering the outline of the gun stuffed down my pants. Damon asks where Stacey is this evening, and I ask back suspiciously, "What the hell does *that* mean?" Just as Damon is about to excuse himself, a tall guy with a receding hairline comes tumbling out through the open door of some random apartment.

"—between the essence and the descent falls the shadow," he bellows, and then butts past me and Damon and promptly falls down the stairs. He lies unconscious on the ground floor, where two guys immediately begin drawing on his face with a magic marker. But then he jolts up with a start. The two with the markers hesitate. He points up the stairs at me, widens his eyes, and laughs. "*Hey*...I *wrote* you, man..."

"Dude, what the fuck—?" I begin, terrified.

"Oh, him? Don't worry," Damon says, winking. "It's just Jason."

"Jason?" I ask.

"He was an English major," Damon says, as if this should explain everything. "Excuse me, okay?"

I nod, and Damon gets away from me as quickly as possible.

People reminisce about the 90s. It is decided by three Kappa Alpha Betas that *Big Lebowski* is the greatest film ever, and then they argue about when the movie *The Philadelphia Experiment* was made, if it was based on a true story. A short blond guy wearing an Alkaline Trio shirt struts by holding hands with a thin girl who resembles Parker Posey, except that this girl has a tail.

Sometimes throughout the New Year's Eve party, I find myself slumped against a wall, rubbing my temples, wondering what the hell I am going to do.

Inside one of the second floor apartments is a huge yellow banner that says FATIMA IS NOW being hung up by two spooky boys while their equally spooky girlfriends watch them. I avoid going any further into this domicile and slouch back into the hallway, considering pulling the gun. Just as I decide to do it, a couple passes along talking about how the world is, indeed, a beautiful place, and that the next millennium will be downright *utopian.* I smile and abandon my plan, momentarily drunk on the couple's almost angelic naivete and ignorance.

At the Drive-In becomes the B-52s, "Rock Lobster," and in the second floor apartment where the music is coming from, black lights pulsate and strobe lights flash, and fifteen girls do some kind of terrible beach party moves while their guy counterparts gyrate off-rhythm and go into convulsions on the floor, and this is dancing. "Rock Lobster" segues into "Dance this Mess Around" only for a moment. Then someone switches CDs and Silverchair, "Anthem for the Year 2000," is blasted into my ears one year too late and I leave the apartment, looking for a place to hide.

A girl in some room lit only with black candles introduces three hypnotized guys to her pet ball python, Lundgren, and asks me if I would like to feed it while motioning sinisterly to the three guys. I shake my head no, sweating uncontrollably, and move along, having to lean against a wall for support. In someone's dining room, people sit around a table doing bars and shots of rum while talking about the color gray. In the area adjacent, two couches have been placed directly in front of a large flat-screen TV. The entire living room is full of mesmerized people watching last week's episode of *Eat the Corpse.* I glance at the display: panicked contestants run through Wal-Mart, grabbing whatever supplies they can as a timer at the bottom corner counts down from 120. Every few seconds, the camera cuts to a pen full of ravenous corpses being prodded by someone who looks like Preston.

When I stumble back into the hallway and try to climb the stairs to the third floor, I stop when I hear a small pack of hoodlums discussing a recent news article exposing evidence that JFK's assassin is not only alive and well and living in Jacksonville, but that he is under constant surveillance by government agents. I jump into their conversation and tell them not to believe everything they read, and they tell me to stop sweating so much and leave them alone.

Following a guy that I met at another party, a guy that Stacey introduced as Virgil, up the stairs to the third and final level, I take a seat on the floor of the hallway next to the banister. I pick up someone's discarded yellow plastic cup and drink whatever is inside it, and luckily it's only flat Pepsi with melted ice. I guzzle down the soda and look down the crowded, elongated corridor. It has become almost totally enshrouded in fog, which I come to realize is cigarette smoke that has drifted upstairs. The partiers breathe the smog in, die a little with each gasp, talk of TV shows and next week and people they wished weren't around anymore. They talk about people with AIDS and people who deserve AIDS and people who can't even spell AIDS. A cross-eyed boy who looks too young to be here stalks by wearing a purple blanket over his head like a hood. He tells us to have a happy New Year. Everyone except he and I laugh at this strange behavior.

This guy Adam that I used to know carries a struggling puppy into one of the third-floor apartments, and a few minutes later I hear the animal yelping and squealing. Across the hall from me, a girl with pimples on the back of her neck gives sloppy fellatio to Damon, whose nose and eyes are bleeding. I curl into a ball and pretend to see nothing, thinking more and more of last year's party.

I begin to drift off to sleep.

"Meet me on the beach," a familiar female voice whispers into my ear.

My eyes wide open, I look around, but there is no one within fifteen feet of me save the unconscious guy in the football jersey lying next to a pile of videotapes across the hall. He keeps licking throw-up off of his beard in his sleep.

I stand back up just as a photo is snapped of me, and then attempt to mingle for a while, waiting for the year to **end**.

Before midnight, I am introduced to college kids, people that other people work with at the restaurant, people in other people's writer's workshops, people who other people smoke pot with, people who are dating or have dated other people's younger siblings. There are attempts at communication. Discussions abound on the skunk ape, Italian stigmatics, *Lateralus*, terrorism (it's getting worse), Kuwait, Clinton, Michael Moore, Jay Mohr, and where the best store is to buy candles for séances. Someone offers me a drink, and I accept it and then two more before waddling into the nearest restroom.

Pissing all over some random bathroom's toilet seat, I notice an overturned copy of *The Spirit of the Sixties* by James J. Farrell. I pick it up to where the reader left off and read one of the many underlined excerpts: "They believed that actions spoke louder than words, and that exemplary behavior could lead other people to their personalist responsibilities. In many ways, their own lives were their most important political statement."

Irredeemable, heart-broken, forgotten and discarded, I close the book and wedge it down into my pants, careful when pushing the gun aside. I flush the toilet, wash my hands, wipe away the tears that are quickly replaced, and leave the bathroom to go back out into the party.

Institution men in white radiation suits dance lasciviously with young sorority chicks holding red plastic cups. A guy who looks remarkably like Mark videotapes them doing this on a camcorder. When I stare, Mark shoots me a wink and disappears into the crowd. I have a long conversation with some girl about how terrible it would be to drown, if anyone would notice. Someone passes us wearing a bloody leash. I keep looking over my shoulder, expecting to see Stacey, but instead catch only glimpses of reasons why last New Year's wasn't really so bad. A stoned teenage Mexican points at me and says, "Hey, I know you. You're that guy on TV." He is escorted out of the room by a man who hides in the shadows and a few minutes later I hear a muffled gunshot from somewhere close.

I decide that maybe I should leave, should just get the hell out of here, go someplace quiet and collect my thoughts, which are becoming stranger and darker with each second that brings me closer to 2001. It's bad that I am here. Instead of wasting my time hiding out at a *party*, I could be at home packing my things. I could be looking for a new apartment. I could be shooting Stacey and Preston in the head. I could be driving through the desert.

But I'm not. Once again, I am mingling at a party on New Year's Eve, having strange revelations about the undead.

A witch board is brought out in one of the second floor apartments, and to every question asked, it answers simply BUNKER. Some red-headed girl who looks too plain to be here prays in front of a TV, and then goes into hysterics on a dirty brown rug while people pour beer on her head and throw pretzels under her as she flails around on the floor.

"You only have eight pints of blood in your entire body," I say to no one, drunk and wanting a sandwich.

A man who I think is Martin Bishop except I am not supposed to know who Martin Bishop is drinks solemnly at the bar in one of the apartments. When he looks up his eyes meet mine and he barely nods before returning to his glass of Scotch. For a moment I consider speaking to the man, but someone whispers in my ear not to do this, and after swinging my arms around violently at the smog for some time, I realize it's pointless and look over at a wall clock covered with different kinds of birds.

There's not much time before midnight.

People make tentative plans to take a swim as soon as the ball drops, and then there is talk of where this swimming should take place, if clothes should stay on or come off, and if drugs should be taken before this occurs. I promise some girl who calls me Shawn as she grabs my crotch that I am ready for anything.

I keep looking down the stairs to the first floor, where there is an exit only half-blocked by scary people. I keep thinking I should go, that I should just get the fuck out of here and floor it to another state. But I continue to drink some kind of terrible punch. I don't move. I don't leave, because everything and everyone around me grows tracers and the room begins to turn into a circus. I imagine that I am sweating blood.

Damon at one point tries to speak to me but I throw up a little bit into someone's trash can and when I stand back up he is gone. Virgil asks me to go back to the third floor with him, where he promises that I will get to see a puppy being tortured. I wave him away and tell the guy next to him that I need a sandwich, that last New Year's I was attacked by zombies. Someone grabs me by the arm and tells me that I'm a lot of fun before cautiously getting far away from me.

Everything gets out of control. The apartment I am in—is it on the first floor? second? *eighteenth?*—begins to spin and I am seeing my sister's face, wavy and dreamlike at the bottom of the ocean; briefcases with legs scampering around a dark city; the blood that runs between the moans and the sighs; Lydia, naked and dripping wet, hugged up tightly against Preston while Preston slices her throat; Stacey winking as she approaches; crimson beads hanging from the ceiling of a clairvoyant's house; foxes the size of men with the heads of wolves; video cameras on display in some store suddenly becoming self-aware and attacking the customers; my mother sitting across from me at a long oak table, asking me if I had a happy childhood; things getting ugly; men stabbing their own eyes out just to make the terror stop; cities melting when the sun explodes; paintings in glass cases spontaneously combusting; frogs raining down from the sky; God's wrath; the Devil convincing us that he never existed, even as the armies of the dead march across the face of the earth; red lights, a symbol of all the warnings I ignored; Stacey smiling as she tries to help me to my feet; a purple neon sign flashing the word FUTURE until there is no longer power; a kid I knew who died, now suddenly alive and chasing me down **end**less aisles in some brightly-lit department store; children from the 50s staring intently through 3-D glasses at tiny television screens, watching everyone I care about as they scream for help that will never arrive; unlit candles; silence; death; atrophy; entropy; Generation WHY; clouds; gray; emptiness; inadequacy; false hopes; flash floods; everyone is gone; salute; nod; sigh; moan; silence; death; *pause*…and then, like the **end** of the nightmare just before the breaking day, *Stacey*, standing before me, waiting.

"What are your plans for midnight?" she asks, checking her nails.

I turn, almost falling over.

Stacey is somehow looking down on me even though I am significantly taller than her. Her hair has been dyed a deep unnatural red, and her glare is cold and alien. She is wearing a business suit I have never seen before and in the background I am aware of other agents pretending to flirt with coeds, blend in, act "drunk and wild." Stacey retrieves a cigarette from a pack of Benson and Hedges and does not offer me one. Maybe she sees how violently my hand is shaking, or how feverishly my lips are quivering. Perhaps she can sense my mouth drying and my heart stopping.

"What—what are you doing here?" I whisper.

"Is this where you want to spend your New Year's Eve?" she asks, glancing around the crowded room.

"I wasn't—I don't know."

Someone screams "11:38." Twenty-two minutes left before the New Year.

"Look, Ross, there's no need in trivial conjecturing or foolish antics here," Stacey says coldly, making a barely noticeable hand gesture with her free hand to one of her associates. "Just go."

"But to *where*?" I stammer, the tears forming. "Where do you want me to go? What do you want me to do?"

"Ross, I just…want you…to leave. I just want you to move on. Get it?"

"But to *where*? You want me to move? You want me to drive away? You want me to kill myself? What *is it*, Stacey? What do you fucking people *want*?"

"Just…to…go," she enunciates slowly. "It is important that you just get out of here. Leave. You'll be contacted in a couple of years. Your father will send for you. Preparations are being made as we speak."

"But—I'm just—man—I'm just—"

"Shh," Stacey interrupts, trying to touch me. I slink away and eye her venomously. "Ross, calm down, sweetie. Don't worry."

"Why *shouldn't* I worry?" I quiver, wiping tears out of my eyes. More keep coming.

"Because your father *says* you shouldn't, that's why. You're still perfect for this operation, Ross. You always were. None of us want to lose you. Okay? So don't worry. Decisions have been made."

"You were never pregnant," I mutter, nauseous. "Were you?"

"Sweetie," she says, "of course not."

One of the agents puts his hand on my shoulder, but I slink away and get less than a foot from her face.

"Why, Stacey? Just tell me *why*. Okay? All I want to know is why. I've asked a lot of people and I've never been given a real answer."

"You want to know why?" she says, staring intently at me now. "You want the real answer right now at this party?"

"Yes," I say solemnly, not backing away. "I do."

"Because when things are this bad, why *not*?" She reaches into her coat and retrieves a white envelope, which she hands to me without her fingers ever grazing against mine. Then she motions for the men to escort me from the party. "I realize you may not find my answers totally satisfactory—"

"But—" I choke, sobbing now, "but the next time I see any of you, the world will be *over*. We're *doomed*."

"This is true," she says, shrugging. "But anyway, Ross…I'll be seeing you, sweetie."

I wait for more.

"Around," she finishes, and this is the last thing she says to me.

The man takes me by the arm this time and begins to lead me from the room. People are staring now, and Stacey nonchalantly orders all of them killed while pulling out a cell phone and dialing a number.

"How can you *do* this?!" I scream.

She says nothing, turns her back to me as she chats on the phone with Preston. Or my father. It doesn't matter. I will never see her, the spy who convinced me that she was the love of my life, again.

I am lead down the stairs. A door is opened, and outside of it is the city at night. It is cold and distant, hopeless and vacant of a single thing worth saving.

The silence of the world is so cacophonous, so loud and ear-shattering, that I have to scream, hide somewhere, and duck out of the way of the bullet, because my father told me once that you never hear the gunshot with your name on it. My worst fear has always been that my death will be as silent and forgettable as my life. And I have the suspicion that this terror is shared by many. By everyone.

"You know," I begin to the agent, "I *am* onto you—"

He slams the door to the apartment building. I am left standing in the cold, being laughed at by a couple of party attendees. I tighten my jacket and move away from them, away from where I parked my car, and I keep walking.

The moans begin shortly after I leave.

I sigh, a terribly unoriginal gesture, and suddenly realize something as I continue my trek farther and farther away from the party. My epiphany is so devastating and clear that I have to stop, hold onto something, and sit down on a bench. Fifteen minutes before the New Year, my mind aches as I envision the world drowned in the blood of its final wasted sigh.

8

ANOTHER THING THAT I REALIZED after that party four years ago is that what is the Apocalypse for us may only be a minor inconvenience for a race of living cannibalistic corpses, waiting patiently to move into our houses, cities, and world. And then, once the last of our bones are devoured or thrown into piles and buried, never to be spoken of again, the Earth goes back to business as usual.

Once we are all cleared away, maybe the undead will be left here. Maybe they will finish eating after such a long fast and decide to ballroom dance. They might go to abandoned Christian churches and Jewish synagogues and Buddhist temples to pray. Perhaps they will build adobes or teepees and live on Mars. Maybe they will put on art exhibitions and zombie historians will one day write controversial articles on the Dark Ages and argue that they were once us and their earliest ancestors, the first ones, simply ate and ate until their bellies burst and they eventually had to evolve. Maybe they will conclude that *we* have evolved into *them*, and that their conquest of this planet is the next intended step in an unwritten holy book dreamed up by an uncertain higher power.

And after just a few years—maybe *seven,* maybe by *2012*—the only human life left on this great planet will be discussed at zombie children's slumber parties, conjured up on ghoulish Ouija boards, and reported every so often on zombie news shows. Walking dead in the Midwest will report seeing a living, breathing, real-life missing link human lurking around in the field at night and eating their chickens. Zombie boyfriends and girlfriends will smoke marijuana and discuss the possibility that maybe it is not just them out there, that maybe there really is such a thing as life, and that the second death *is* possible by some other means than a destroyed brain. Then they will giggle and moan "Yeah, right" in some kind of incomprehensible zombie dialect and then have unprotected zombie sex.

Hazy, gritty photographs of "humans" will show up regularly across America on the cover of trash newspapers. Single mom corpses will glance at the articles while in the check-out lines of grocery stores that sell only warm flesh.

Then one day, they too, will have to evolve. There will be a morning when a planet of zombies awakens to find something different, something altogether new and terrifying, only dreamed up prior to that moment by the zombie world's sickest and most outlandish writers and Italian exploitation artists. Things will fall apart as prophesized only by those corpses who have preached fire and brimstone for years, referencing a book forgotten, shunned, and ignored by a world that knows no text of man. A state of emergency will be declared. Panic among the land of the dead will spread quickly. A zombie president will be evacuated and placed in an underground bunker built eons before by the zombies' ancestors, who may or may not have been human.

There is another Armageddon. The heavens open up once again. Secrets are revealed that the zombie government knew all along that this would happen, but it is irrelevant by then, because the undead world quickly disappears and something else takes over. The cycle continues. In one way or another, life never stops.

Or maybe it does.

Maybe it already has. Maybe this is just another bullshit lightshow, another vision of Jesus on a taco, a glimpse into the future as viewed by an entire world of schizophrenics and dumb-asses.

Maybe we really are just pointless and alone, right now.

Fucked.

Or, in other words, truly zombies.

7

THE YEAR **ENDS**.

I am already on my first cup of coffee in some nameless diner when the year 2000 **ends** and the year 2001 begins. I nod to the friendly-enough man behind the counter and gesture for food. He laboriously moves over toward an ancient grill and begins making noises with the spatula.

Out there, fireworks explode. Lovers embrace. Middle-age couples exchange kisses and promptly go to bed, exhausted from the effort of staying awake. Champagne is poured into plastic flutes. Hopeless young people are devoured by the undead. Somewhere, Stacey smokes a cigarette, smiles. Her and Preston exchange glances. Their plane will take off shortly.

When I make it back to my car, which stands alone in an empty parking lot, I open the envelope Stacey handed me and count the thick stack of hundred dollar bills inside, along with the note that my father wrote me:

> It never **ends**, does it, Ross?
> Take care of yourself, son.
> See you in four years.
>
> ---Richard Orringer
> November 21, 2005

I light a cigarette and pull out of the parking lot, away from the city.

The highway unfolds before me, and I drive throughout the night. In the dark sky above, there are red and blue and purple and green and yellow explosions as the world celebrates, and the kids sleep soundly and the parents smile in the blackness and the youth look forward to the future. For one night in hundreds, humanity is at what it believes to be its best. It stands together. The optimistic stay awake to welcome in a new year, and the cynical linger long enough to say good riddance to that which has passed. The world is happy and oblivious, and perhaps, in this one early moment, year after year, decade after decade, this is enough. This is the plan. In this lone brief moment, the letters are still unwritten. The sins have not been tallied. No one has breathed. All is well in a dying world.

And this is okay, because it always has been. In the beginning.

DECEMBER 31, 2004 — DECEMBER 31, 2005
Lakeland, Florida

ABOUT THE AUTHOR

Jason S. Hornsby has been attempting to overcome his own existential dilemma since the publication of his first novel, *The Perfect Spiral*, in 2001. He is an honors graduate of the University of South Florida and teaches American and British Literature. When not traversing the globe in search of refuge from the impending Apocalypse of 2012, Mr. Hornsby ponders the state of humankind, wallows in his own excess and depravity, and attempts to prove that he is under surveillance by agents of the Dark Government. He does not live in Florida.

Have a question for the author?
Ask him on the Permuted Press message board:
www.permutedpress.com/forum

JOHN DIES AT THE END

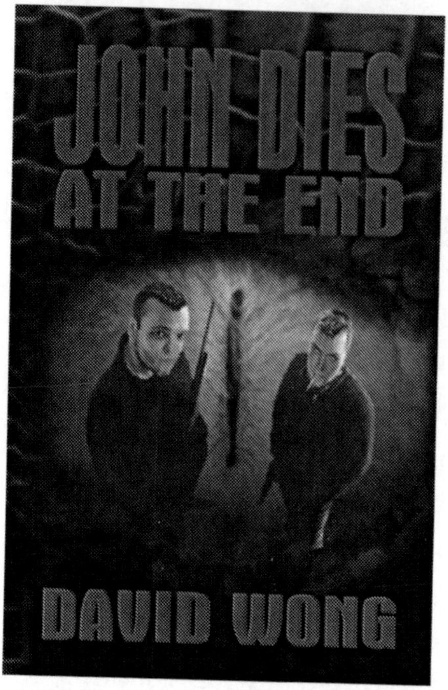

by David Wong

It's a drug that promises an out-of-body experience with each hit. On the street they call it Soy Sauce, and users drift across time and dimensions. But some who come back are no longer human. Suddenly a silent otherworldly invasion is underway, and mankind needs a hero.

What it gets instead is John and David, a pair of college dropouts who can barely hold down jobs. Can these two stop the oncoming horror in time to save humanity?

No. No, they can't.

ISBN: 978-0-9789707-6-5

THE OBLIVION SOCIETY

by Marcus Alexander Hart

Life sucks for Vivian Gray.
She hates her dead-end job.
She has no friends.
Oh, and a nuclear war has just reduced the world to a smoldering radioactive wasteland.

Armed with nothing but pop-culture memories and a lukewarm will to live, Vivian joins a group of rapidly mutating survivors and takes to the interstate for a madcap cross-country road trip toward a distant sanctuary that may not, in the strictest sense of the word, exist.

ISBN 978-0-9765559-5-7

HISTORY IS DEAD

A ZOMBIE ANTHOLOGY EDITED BY

KIM PAFFENROTH

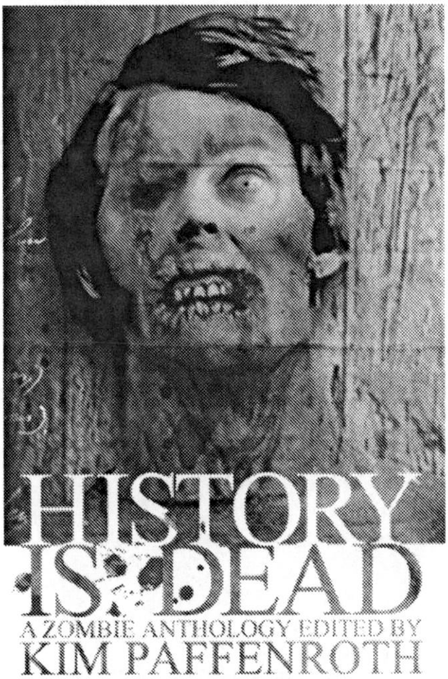

"*History is Dead* is a violent and bloody tour through the ages. Paffenroth has assembled a vicious timeline chronicling the rise of the undead that is simultaneously mind-numbingly savage and thought provoking."

—Michael McBride, author of the *God's End* trilogy and *The Infected*

ISBN: 978-0-9789707-9-6

ROSES OF BLOOD ON BARBWIRE VINES

D.L. SNELL

As the living dead invade a barricaded apartment building, the vampire inhabitants must protect their human livestock. Shade, the vampire monarch, defends her late father's kingdom, but Frost, Shade's general, convinces his brethren to migrate to an island where they can breed and hunt humans. In their path stands a legion of corpses, just now evolving into something far more lethal, something with tentacles —and that's just the beginning.

ISBN: 978-0-9789707-1-0

MORE DETAILS, EXCERPTS, AND PURCHASE INFORMATION AT

www.permutedpress.com

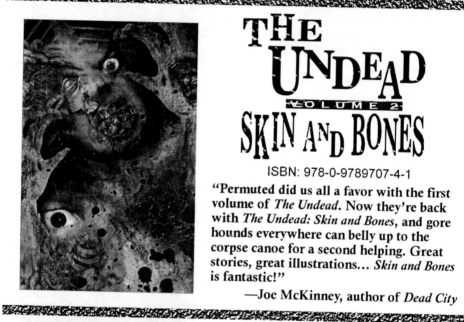

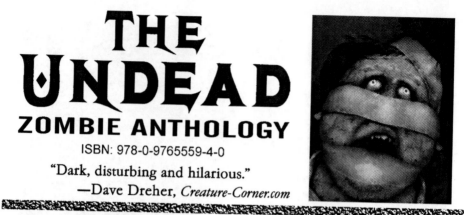

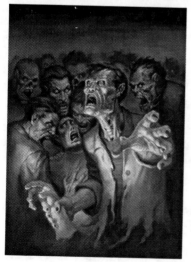

Printed in the United States
126526LV00004B/24/A